The Cardinal

Part 2

STEPHANIE HUESLER

Howdy! Hola! Bonjour! Guten Tag!
I'm a *very special book*. You see, I'm traveling around the world making new friends. I hope I've met another friend in you. Please go to **www.BookCrossing.com** and enter my BCID number (shown below). You'll discover where I've been and who has read me, and can let them know I'm safe here in your hands. Then... *READ and RELEASE me!*

BCID: 928 - 14728345

The Cardinal, Part 2
Copyright ©2014 Stephanie Huesler

First Edition

The moral right of the author has been asserted.

No part of this publication may be reproduced, stored in a retrieval system, or transmitted in any form by any means, electronic, mechanical, recording or otherwise, without prior written permission from the author, except in the case of brief quotations embodied in critical reviews and articles related to the book itself. This book is sold subject to the condition that it shall not, by way of trade or otherwise, be lent, re-sold, hired out, or otherwise circulated without the author's prior consent in any form of binding or cover other than that in which it is published and without a similar condition including this condition being imposed on the subsequent purchaser.
This is a work of fiction. All characters appearing in this novel are fictitious. Any resemblance to persons living or dead is purely coincidental.

1 3 5 7 9 8 6 4 2

Kindle: ASIN:
Paperback: ISBN-13: **978-1503183346**

Graphics and Cover Design: © Stephanie Huesler
Cover Image: © Inara Prusakova, Dreamstime.com

Printed by CreateSpace.
Available in Paperback and Kindle from Amazon worldwide, CreateSpace.com and other retail outlets.

Also by Stephanie Huesler

The Price of Freedom

Redemption

The Cardinal, Part 1

"The function of the imagination is not to make strange things settled,
so much as to make settled things strange."
G.K. Chesterton

1: Nordaländ

"There you are!" Aradan heard Gjurd call as he came running up the path. Gjurd's beard had already grown thick, of which he was immensely proud; he would always be the impetuous boy in Aradan's mind, though he had become a man of twenty-two to be reckoned with. His confidence outweighed his skills at times, but that never dampened his enthusiasm; he would make a charismatic leader. "We've been looking for you! We want to go a horn's blast away for hunting. You can finish chopping wood later."

Behind Gjurd followed his sisters, Hedda and Runa, both now young women of twenty winters. They each carried their bows and a quiver slung over their shoulders; Aradan had taught them to use the weapons, and they often took opportunity on sunny days of going hunting in the nearby forest.

"Will you join us?" Runa asked Aradan. "Mother has asked us to bring home hares or a boar," she twirled her thick blonde braid around her hand as she spoke, smiling at Gjurd, now a handsome man. She was bolder than her stepsister Hedda, and had already determined to make Gjurd her husband as they were in fact only distantly related. Gjurd no longer seemed to mind that notion, and gave her an infectious smile.

"Very well," Aradan smiled. He laid aside his axe and slipped on his over-tunic. "Lead on!" He tied the belt about his waist as he followed the young hunters into the forest.

They headed southwest from Oyarike following the coast. Gjurd was always rushing ahead, and the older he got the stealthier he became; he would usually herd the prey back toward the others. Gjurd had been gone much longer than usual, and his sisters had become bored waiting for him to flush out their prey, so they wandered off in search of him or prey, whichever came first. Not long after they had disappeared into the trees, Aradan heard cries for help and ran toward the sounds swifter than an owl on the swoop. He caught Hedda as she ran toward him, Runa following hard on her heels.

"What is it?" he looked into her wide, fearful eyes, a feeling of dread creeping upon him.

"There was a stranger!" Hedda panted, pointing down the path they'd just run.

"He told us to take this to Father," Runa held out a roll of leather, her lips pale and trembling. "They've taken Gjurd!"

"What?" cried Aradan. "Where did they go?"

"No! He told us that if he was followed he would kill Gjurd before caught!" the sisters cried hysterically, and all Aradan could do was try to calm them as they made their way back to the fortress.

Torsten was furious when he heard the news. The leather strip contained a runic message. People had begun to gather at the sound of the commotion and awaited the news.

Torsten looked from face to face. "Kjell," he said coldly. "His men have taken my son," he read through the note, "to be sacrificed at the Leirvik Nines." Anger erupted in a confusion of shouts through the crowd: Attack was obvious; but there had to be a more permanent solution to the hostilities as revenge killings were wearing their numbers dangerously low.

"What is the *Leirvik Nines*?" Moriel whispered to Ragnar, who was always standing close to her.

"It is a sacrifice to Thor, Odin and Frey... arranged by the ruler at Leirvik to vie in importance with that of Uppsala – though he'll never accomplish *that*! The festival usually lasts nine days, with nine male sacrifices each day, one each of nine kinds: Roosters, stallions, rams, bulls, boars, stags, he-goats, dogs... and men."

"But why?" she gasped. "Why would they offer the life of mortal creatures to these beings? It is not right."

"Right?" he repeated. "What is right or wrong when the gods demand blood? But this is not out of religious devotion," he lowered his voice. "There is another motive I think," he glanced from Torsten to Aradan.

"What do you mean?" she followed his gaze.

"See the way the jarl keeps looking at him?" Torsten was eyeing Aradan at that very moment. "There's more than he's said in that note."

Before she could ask further Torsten bellowed, "Leave us!"

People left quickly, whispering together in small clusters; they would await the decision of the jarl, but they knew there would be action very soon; the men went away to prepare their weapons for battle. Moriel had no choice but to leave, though she would hear everything that took place within. She lingered outside the mead hall door to listen:

"Do you know who took my son?" Torsten asked.

"No. The girls could not tell me, nor would they let me pursue."

"Girls!" he scoffed. "Only a fool would be dictated to by mere girls!"

Aradan made no reply as he saw that Torsten had immediately regretted the outburst.

"What are you, truly?" Torsten studied Aradan's face.

"I am loyal," came the reply.

It was not the answer he sought and it caught him unprepared. He relented. "That, I do not doubt. I meant, *what* are you? Are you truly from Alfheim? Answer me directly."

"We do not call it thus, but it is what your people call it, yes; though it is not as you think."

"Are you truly immortal? Or were you merely weaving a good tale when you told me of your king?"

Aradan hesitated. Would Torsten respond as wisely as he seemed? He chose an honest reply: "We are immortal. But we can be killed."

Torsten looked at him in surprise at both replies. "How?"

"In defence of a mortal life," was all he would say. "But I've made a vow that I must fulfil; I cannot – *will* not – defend a mortal."

"And if you have no choice?"

Aradan looked at him steadily. "I will always have that choice."

Torsten held up the leather scrap, scratched with runes. "I have a choice, too. My son... or you." As Aradan listened, Torsten reminded him of his dealings with the captives that were *volunteered* to take a message of warning to Kjell; the one most antagonistic, Vidarr, had instigated this revenge. "It is not revenge against my people that he seeks this time," he paused. "It is revenge against you. Either I hand you over to be hung in the sacrifice, or they will hang my son in your stead." Torsten sat back in his chair, wearied at the thoughts hounding him for the safety of his son and revenge against Kjell.

Aradan thought about it a moment. "It is clear what you must do," he said. "I will not be defending your son directly; therefore I will not die... but it will hurt."

Torsten laughed slightly at the understatement. Hanging was excruciating; he'd witnessed many a victim's death by such means. Being run through with a sword was far more preferable – and more honourable. Hangings were reserved for slaves or those deemed unworthy of an honourable death; his son was being treated as if a slave, and it was humiliating. That was Kjell's personal goad, and it would not go unanswered.

"What else *can* I do?" Torsten rubbed his forehead in weariness. "Kjell has made it clear that any attack on Kjellsfjorden would mean the instant death of my son."

"We will negotiate the exchange; I will go willingly. I will allow them to hang me... I only ask to be taken down as soon as possible by trusted men."

"I will tell my men to take you down as soon as it is safe," he promised. "The sacrifices usually begin on Midsummer's day," he thought a moment; "it will mean a journey for my men to Leirvik, which is twice as far beyond Kjellsfjorden... our families will be vulnerable. I'll send a message to my cousin, Wulf. Aid will be welcome in whatever form he sends, I think."

Aradan left the jarl's hall pondering the test before him. The jarl's men watched Aradan's countenance as he walked away from the mead hall and rushed back to the hall to find out what action would be taken.

Moriel found Aradan by the well washing his face in the cool water.

"Must you go?" she touched his shoulder. "Why do we not flee now?"

Aradan should have realized she'd heard. "I'll not go back on my word. And I cannot leave Gjurd to such a fate."

"How can you be so calm? We, who are gods compared to these mortals! Why should we submit to their primitive ways?"

"Fear will not improve my lot," he replied. "What comes will come. But take heed with your words; we are not gods! Only the Creator of all deserves that title... he who made our world, and this, and every other world far more advanced than our own. Never forget that our Kind has travelled to places where *we* are primitive by comparison... remember the tales, and be humbled!"

She relented. "You are right, of course." She took his hand in hers. "I am only distraught for your sake. What you shall face... I cannot bear to think of the pain!"

"I have little choice. But I have the jarl's word that someone will take me down as soon as possible."

"A man's word," she scoffed. "Will he leave his own family vulnerable, for a man he barely knows and less understands? A former slave?" Her words were scornful, but a touch of tenderness caught his attention, and he looked at her. She genuinely cared for him. "Do you not realize that I will suffer with you?" she wept at the thought.

He touched her cheek, and she looked into his eyes. Such compassion she saw there as she had never seen in another. He felt himself comforted by her presence. She rested her hands on his chest, and he could feel her warmth pulsating against his body.

"I will do what I can to ease your suffering while you hang," she whispered. "You know my gifting," she would not speak it out as she knew he did not approve of the way she used her powers. She only said, "I will be able to ease your pain if you keep your gaze upon me! I can help you forget the suffering! Please – let me help you in the only way I can!"

"Thank you, Moriel," he replied. "I will want your help before the sun sets on that day, I think."

"Then you must speak to the jarl – ensure that I am part of the group that travels to the festival!"

Three days later, Torsten and his best warriors led Aradan, bound with his hands behind his back, to the gates of Kjell's fortress on the island in Kjellsfjorden. The gates opened. Vidarr led Gjurd, also bound, between himself and Kjell, meeting the intruders half-way.

"A peaceful exchange," called Torsten.

"Do you question my honour?" shouted Kjell.

"Never," replied Torsten. He would have added that he considered him a man without honour, but that would have ended the exchange in bloodshed. Instead he said, "My son, for this man. And peace between us from this time on."

"Why should I leave in peace those who sit on my lands?" challenged Kjell. "My father conquered that land, and you usurp his authority there!" It was a point they would never agree upon.

"Peace until the harvest is over, then," Torsten tried to sound reasonable. "Your men are needed for your harvest just as much as mine," he added.

Kjell stalled, but eventually it was agreed upon. The prisoners were exchanged, meeting half-way between the two parties.

Aradan stopped and asked Gjurd, "Have they treated you well?"

He shrugged. "I have not been let outside, and had to be attended by a young girl for everything," he groaned. "A *girl* for company for three days! She was more talkative than my sisters *ever* were at her age!"

Aradan smiled. If that was his greatest complaint then he had fared well. "Go on, now, to your father. Runa eagerly awaits your return," he winked.

"But that girl told me what they are planning!" he growled. "I'll never see you again, and it is all my fault! I will avenge you!"

"There will be no need for that. You will see me again, I promise," he whispered. "But go!" Aradan walked forward toward his captors, looking over his shoulder to ensure that Gjurd was released to his kin.

Vidarr stepped forward and jabbed Aradan toward the fortress at the sharp end of a sword; he wasn't taking any chances. The gate shut, but not before Torsten caught Aradan's eye one last time, and nodded a goodbye and reminder of their agreement.

Inside the fortress was much the same as that of Oyarike. Aradan was led to the longhouse next to the mead hall where Vidarr and another man, who would stand guard, tied him to a pole, giving enough rope length to sit down but no more.

"You won't be so bold at the end of a rope or sword, I think!" Vidarr hissed, breathing Mead and fish into his face.

"Neither will you," Aradan said calmly.

Vidarr lifted his sword to strike when the other man grabbed his arm. "Don't! You know what will happen if he is killed before he hangs!"

At that Vidarr immediately backed off, shaken by whatever it was that the other man referred to.

Guard him well, Nils," Vidarr growled as he walked away. "And don't let him touch you!"

Nils shook his head slowly as he watched Vidarr leave. He turned to look at Aradan, who was watching him. "Don't get any ideas!" he snapped, as he stomped out and stood before the door.

Aradan was apparently to be treated well enough, like a calf fattened for the slaughter. Not long after Vidarr left, the door opened again and in came a young woman. She looked at Aradan in curious fear as she approached with a bowl of food.

"I won't hurt you," he said gently.

She swallowed as she stepped closer. She knelt down on the ground before him and stirred the stew with a wooden spoon, holding a mouthful to his lips. She said nothing as he ate, but their eyes spoke.

When he was done eating he asked, "Can you tell me what's going on?"

She looked toward the door. "Kjell—" she breathed, "I dare not speak of it!"

"Not even to a dead man?" he replied, at which she relented.

"Kjell is angry with the invasion of Christianity. He has forced the settlement to take part in the Leirvik festivities to prove their allegiance to Aasgard. He agreed to give one each for the sacrifices... lots were drawn for the man's sacrifice," she lowered her voice. "Vidarr's family was chosen... his eldest son, Olaf, if he could not provide an alternative before the festivities."

"I see," Aradan replied, to which she nodded, regret in her eyes. As she began to leave he said, "Please ask Nils to come in a moment."

She left, and Nils stuck his head through the door. "What do you want?" he barked.

"I have a message for Kjell that I must deliver to him personally."

Aradan was dragged, hands bound behind his back and a rope about his neck, to the mead hall. Men kept their distance, having been warned by the tales of the *volunteers*. The compliant one, Sigmund, stood beside Kjell who was seated in a large wooden chair covered with bear skins.

"That's far enough," Kjell said, eyeing Aradan suspiciously but with enough curiosity to have agreed to see him. "I've heard about you," he stood, pacing around Aradan at a safe distance, examining him. "How did you do it?"

"Do what?" Aradan asked.

"Fell my men like lightning fells a tree."

"What do you know of Alfheim?"

Murmurs rippled throughout the room at that question.

"Silence!" Kjell shouted. "Do you let this man mock our intelligence? He is no god!"

"I never claimed to be," agreed Aradan. "I am merely trying to use your terms to explain. In truth, there are no gods in Aasgard, or Alfheim."

At that Kjell strode over to Aradan and struck him across the face with the back of his hand, reeling him over backwards. He was dragged back up to his knees by the rope.

Aradan looked at Kjell steadily. "I will not allow that again," he said quietly.

Sigmund stepped up to Kjell and whispered something in his ear. Kjell sat down, grumbling.

"Your anger does not change what I said; but I am willing to make a wager with you."

Kjell laughed. "A wager? With a man who will be hanged in three days' time?"

"My wager is this: If I die at the rope, you win."

Kjell thought about that. "If I win, what will I have besides a corpse?"

"You will have defeated Alfheim... what other warrior of Midgard could claim that?"

"And if I lose?"

"You will make peace with Oyarike, on their terms, and no discussion."

Murmurs erupted, growing louder by the moment.

Kjell said smugly, "That's if you don't die."

Aradan nodded.

"Take him away!" Kjell shouted.

Two men stepped up, but respectfully motioned for Aradan to stand and follow willingly. He did so; the challenge had been voiced; it could not but draw Kjell in. Pride would not let the challenge go unanswered, and Northmen could never resist a wager they were sure to win.

2: The Clan

When the chariot crowned the hill looking down upon Maldor at last, Caitrin knew she had come home: Green life had reclaimed the burnt landscape, and there was a sense of freedom here like no other place she'd been. Niallan directed the horses toward the old citadel and let them roam, still harnessed, within the palace area which still formed a partial enclosure. By the time the others arrived, Caitrin had spread out the food on a flat stone that served well for a table. As they drank cold stream water and ate cold slices of smoked meat, they looked over the plan once more.

"This," pointed Angus, " 'tis a leather cord?" It was that part of the drawing that seemed to lash two beams together.

"Stronger," said Erlina. "It's ship's rope."

"And where are we to get that? We've no such amount tae spare, and it'll take weeks tae make that much!"

"Leave that to me. It will have to dry a few days before it's of any use, but we can prepare the wood in that time."

He looked at her. "Ye're not thinkin' what I think ye're thinkin' are ye?"

"Yes," smiled Erlina. The other two looked at her curiously. She smiled at Caitrin, "You'll soon have proof of my immortality."

They all followed her down to the loch shore; Niallan hadn't been with Hafgan's foolhardy raiding party that fateful night – truth be told, he'd been with Caitrin.

But Angus knew very well what she had in mind. "I canna even see it from here! It's far too deep tae reach!" he exclaimed.

"What is?" demanded Niallan.

"Oh, she's got a daft idea! There's a sunken ship – she sank it," he waved his hand toward the loch dismissively, "down there with riggin'!"

"And a mast!" she added as she stripped off her outer tunic and waded into the water with only her under-tunic. "Await the mast first – it shall emerge long before I do." She looked at Angus adding, "You needn't worry... remember that I cannot drown." She dived under the water; not a splash, barely a ripple, so perfect and smooth was her dive.

Time passed. Angus paced. Caitrin took Niallan's hand; Angus looked the other way.

"She's been down too long," whispered Caitrin. "There're no bubbles!"

Angus wrung his hands. "She's drowned, I'm sure of it! We should ne'er ha'e let her go!"

"She told ye not tae fret," Niallan reminded him. "If she says she canna drown, ye've got tae trust her in that."

"I'm goin' in after her," Angus decided, and began to undress to dive in after her.

"Ye canna swim, *eejit*!" Just then Niallan pointed. "Look!"

They saw a tree begin to emerge at a rather steep angle, and then begin to drop to the surface. Soon Erlina followed, swimming the mast to the surface. They all rushed into the shallows to take up the weight of the waterlogged mast, long and straight, dragging the log ashore.

Erlina accepted her cloak, wrapped around her by Angus, as she emerged; she wasn't at all breathless. She squeezed the water from her plait. "I took longer, to take a look around the ship," she explained. "I did not see all of it as I didn't want you to worry, but they had made profitable raids."

"How did ye—" Angus pointed at the water.

"I learned from an early age the art of...suspension."

"Sus– what?" Angus said.

"Holding my breath," she laughed.

"No one can hold it that long!" he exclaimed.

"Obviously one can," she smiled. "I'll go back for the ropes; I've coiled them already. The sail is a good quantity of cloth to use as well. I'll look around beneath the deck a bit more while I'm down there; if we can use something wooden, I must bring it up before it rots. They build superb ships and have treated the wood well, so most of it looks in excellent condition still."

This time as she disappeared beneath the dark surface, only Angus remained anxious at the shoreline. When Niallan began to drag the mast up toward the cart, Angus called after him: "How can ye just leave yer bride down there?"

Niallan turned toward him, the obvious accusation in his brother's tone irritating him. "I trust her. And I decided some time ago that I'd stop bein' shocked by every wee thing they can do that we canna. They're *Other*. It's that simple."

"And what are yer feelin's on it?" Angus asked Caitrin.

She was still somewhat in shock, but when she heard Niallan's perspective it helped her make sense of it (as much as any of it made sense). "If she's *Other*... well, then she is, and what I feel or think makes no difference."

Angus shrugged in defeat of reason. "Ach, off wi' ye! I'll be along to help when she comes up."

Niallan levered and balanced the log across the flat bed of the cart, wedging in into place with stones, and Caitrin walked along beside as he drove the horse up the hill toward the beginnings of a broch.

When they arrived at the broch, Niallan rolled the mast to the ground. "Come," he took Caitrin's hand, "I want tae show ye somethin'."

He took her in through the opening of the broch, and she immediately felt that this was Erlina's true home; it held in its heart the peaceful rhythm of enchantment. Entering was to bring time to a standstill, as if stepping over the threshold took you into the arms of rest and peace. The walls, several stones high already, were arranged in two semi-circles creating an entrance gap at one side and another gap opposite. The back gap led to a short flight of stairs leading down into a cave, on the floor of which was scattered fresh hay with a blanket spread atop, light streaming in overhead through a smoke-hole that had been made through the ground overhead. "She comes down here at times tae rest... tae be alone."

"Alone?"

"She's got many memories o' this place. Who knows how many. But her heart and mind find more rest here than in the toil o' the clan."

He took her outside again and pointed down to where the citadel had once stood, at a dark frame of fresh earth, covered with the green whisper of new growth, and told her about the occupants.

"But I thought they'd *all* be immortal."

"They are – except' they defend a human life, sacrificin' their own instead. Aradan explained it once. That's why some of them lie here... and Angus lives."

"Then 'tis clear – she canna e'er defend us! The cost'd be too great."

He only nodded.

Erlina and Angus soon joined them; Angus and Niallan retrieved the rope with the wagon, and they all helped to stretch out the coils to dry upon the grassy hill slope.

"What else is down there?" asked Niallan, pleased with the rope.

She held up a fist full of Maldorian arrows. "I got back what was mine," she smiled. "And we shall never want for gold or silver... we can purchase anything we'll need; and only I can reach it... not often does the sea surrender its spoil so meekly." It was an intoxicating feeling, the finding of lost treasures. "Next I shall bring up part of the top deck; the boards can be used for doors, and a table. There are well-built sea chests, mounted as seats for the rowers."

"Oars will do fer table legs," suggested Caitrin.

"Yes!" Erlina rolled out the vellum scroll and brought a small box from the back of the cave. Inside were a small glass bottle and a feather. Caitrin watched fascinated as Erlina took out the wooden stopper, dipped the feather tip into the bottle and began scratching odd symbols on the scroll.

"What's that?" she whispered to Niallan, close by.

"Written words," he whispered back. "The Irish monks told us about it, but Erlina's Kind have a different way. And much older."

"Perhaps they taught it to the monks," she whispered in reply, her eyes wide in wonder at the thought.

Erlina put the stopper back in the bottle. "There! I've started a list of what we'll make of the material I can retrieve."

Every day thereafter until autumn had passed they worked with a will in Maldor. The broch rose until it was two levels high and solid, and was then capped with a wooden conical frame covered in bundles of heather thatch. Erlina knew it was not yet the height she desired, but any higher would have made it rise above the horizon as seen from the loch, and therefore more prone to attack. As it stood now it was at one with its landscape, and would remain so until safer ages. The cave was accessible only through the broch, and the ground level had a flat stone floor rather than the usual compact dirt floor, stones having been hauled up from the citadel's ruins. Beside the broch Niallan and Angus had tilled the land and planted with a rich harvest for their efforts, while Erlina and Caitrin caught and preserved fish from the loch, adding meat to their stores.

When winter came and snow fell heavily across the Highlands, their work in Maldor rested and they retired to their roundhouse for the long, dark days. They had food to spare for the widows of the clan and Erlina and Niallan were generous with all. Erlina's smoked fish and meat were more delicate than any the clan had ever had. They enjoyed pleasant companionship, the women spinning, weaving or sewing, Niallan carving wooden bowls, spoons, plates, horn cups or toys. Erlina made a quern stone for the broch, the most finely constructed and smoothly working that Caitrin had ever used; Erlina also repaired their own daily quern to run smoother, using the same coaxing with which she'd once moved earth and stone for the tunnel (which was never far from her mind; it was her place of refuge, a place hidden for her alone within the heart of the Highlands).

Angus was a regular visitor during that long and harsh winter, lingering longer with each passing week until it was nearly assumed he'd moved. Sometimes he was safer staying than attempting to find his way home through the blinding snow storms; he would sleep upon sheepskins near the fire as Niallan had once done. When he would stay the night, Erlina and Caitrin would exchange beds, giving the appearance that Erlina and Niallan slept together; there was a trust and bond between the women now, as mother to daughter. Angus and Niallan would play Nine Men's Morris upon a scrap of leather, or plan a new patch of forest to clear for crops the following spring. Erlina took it upon herself to teach them writing in the Latin alphabet as brought to Britannia by the Romans, and she also taught them to read her own script so that the building plans would be clear for them. She expanded her ambitions for her home whilst knowing that most of it must wait to be realized in a safer age. On the plan drawn to exquisite detail, a tree was drawn near the broch. Erlina would transplant Darachi's sapling to the safety of her own home when the time was right.

Before the *calends* of April, sunshine at last began to thaw the frozen north. Green began to appear, and soon it was time for lambing to begin.

One afternoon Niallan and Angus had just returned from hunting, and they'd noticed a significant lack of men in the settlement; the flocks were in their pens, and no one was out of doors; it was as if the settlement were empty. They ran to their father's roundhouse to find their father pacing near the fire. When they entered he looked up, relieved to see their faces.

"Ach, I'm pleased to see yous – yous dinna follow the fool!" he spat at the fire.

Their mother explained, "Hafgan gathered some of the men while yer father was in the forest; they've gone tae the south."

Angus looked at Niallan. "He widna!"

"He did!" his father countered. It had been learned that a group of Northmen had slaughtered a village to the south and settled in their houses for the winter. "If he werena ma' own son I'd drive him from the clan as a menace tae rational peace!" He rubbed his temples, "And if he disna finish them all, there's no tellin' what they'll do in revenge. The women are preparin' tae receive the dead, and we make ready tae defend oursel's against attack."

Toward evening of the following day commotion was heard outside at last. Aidan looked up at Niallan, who had stayed with his father to await news; mainly to keep him from going after Hafgan.

"I canna look upon him!" Aidan tugged at his red beard, growling.

"I'll go. Ye wait here," Niallan said as he headed toward the door.

Not all of the men who went out would return to see their wives and children. Hafgan was whole; he always managed to come away unscathed from his strong-willed ways, but often others who were rash enough to follow him were not as fortunate. Hafgan made a direct path to his father's roundhouse, but was intercepted by his brother.

"Unwise, brother," Niallan said.

"Which?" Hafgan grunted. "Attackin', losin', or returnin'?"

"Aye tae all... and darin' tae face Father just now."

"Do ye know how many they were?" challenged Hafgan, pride rubbed raw at the accusation in Niallan's tone.

"No."

"Well then how was I tae know, Brother?" Hafgan defended himself. "The enemy turned out tae be far more than we could've imagined; they'd spread out over a larger area than the village had been! By the time we'd realized that the other settlements werena Pictish waitin' for relief, but Northman, we'd already attacked. But when we retreated we travelled south... tae lead them away from our people. That's why we didna return yesterday."

"Why did ye rush tae attack at all?" Niallan pointed toward the south. "Only a fool would go tae such a task wi' no wits! Did ye no' even think tae study them first? Ye're a greater fool than I ever thought! Yer rashness'll be the undoing of us all!"

Hafgan's face reddened at the affront. "I may be rash, but I'm no sittin' round no' makin' *bairns*!" he growled. "Ye've a useless wife who'll bear ye no sons. I'm protecting the future of ma' *own* son."

"By jabbin' a stick into the hornet's nest!" Niallan shouted. "Ach, go in wi' ye! Stick yer head into Father's door, be ye so brave! I'll no' be there tae keep the peace atween ye!" Niallan stormed back to his own home.

The rant that Aidan burst forth against his son was heard throughout the settlement. His son was disgraced, and the men who lost their lives were mourned for their foolhardy loss. Aidan refused to see his eldest son again. Little did they know how short a rift it would be.

Early one morning in late April Iona came to Niallan's home. She greeted her son and Erlina, ignoring Caitrin (who looked far too happy and healthy for her liking). "Niallan," she looked at him directly, "yer father would speak wi' ye this morning."

"What is it?" he asked, concerned by her tone.

"He widna say, and it's got me worried. He's often spoken of ye this winter... as a good son. A good man."

Niallan took his mother by the arm, kissed Erlina on the cheek and winked, "I won't be long, love."

Erlina winked at Caitrin, who only looked away quickly with a cautious smile.

"I'm pleased fer ye," his mother squeezed his arm. "I knew she was a good match fer ye; ye look very happy."

"I coudna ha'e asked fer a better wife," he smiled.

"Far better than an Irish slave, though I'd be wantin' wee bairns soon," she added, to which he gave no reply.

They entered the roundhouse and found Aidan by the fire wrapped in a blanket about his shoulders. When he saw them he cast it off hastily. "Ach, lad! Sit," he gestured beside him. "Angus tells us ye have a peaceful home."

"Yes. I coudna wish it more so."

Aidan coughed. "I've got somethin' in ma' throat," he took a swig of ale. "Canna seem tae be rid of it." He would not mince words: "I'll announce ye as ma' tanist." Such a grand title to be used for their wee clan, and the irony was understood.

"What?" Niallan protested. "What of Hafgan? He's the eldest! And he's already got a son!"

"Ach! Hafgan's no leader! He's rash; the raid on those Northmen was just another sign of it. He's indecisive when he should take action, and too quick tae the sword when he should think!" Aidan stood and paced the floor. "He's a good shepherd, I'll give him that. But sheep dinna train chieftains! No. I've decided; ye're tae succeed me. The elders have agreed unanimously." The elders were simply two older men in their small clan, but it made the decision sanctioned, nonetheless.

"Very well. But that willna be fer many winters tae come, Father. There's no need tae decide it now."

Aidan sat down wearily. "I love life dearly, Niallan. But I'm no' afraid o' Death." He stopped to clear his throat. "I've felt it sittin' on ma' chest this winter; I've come tae think it's a house guest that willna be leavin' wi'out takin' what it came fer. I'm weary of keepin' it at bay." He winked, "I've ignored it this winter long and I think I've offended it."

"Dinna talk so!" cried Iona, jabbing her wooden spoon into the cooking pot.

"Other words willna change the fact, woman," he told her, then said to Niallan, "Somethin' sits on ma' chest at night; I can hardly breathe else I sit up. And it's tightenin' its grip," he wheezed.

"Why've ye no' said as much?" Niallan chided. "Hidin' it when we've come tae call... this is the first I've heard of it!"

"Ach, that's why – I dinna like the fuss!"

"Father, ye must rest and let Mother mend yer health. Angus and I'll see tae the work here."

"I'll be dead afore I lie back doing nought!" Aidan stood up. "I'm not gone yet, lad! And I dinna intend on going with the whimper of a dog wi' its tail atween its legs! I'd rather fall on the hunt or battlefield than hidin' behind the skirts o' a lass!" At that he had such a fit of coughing that it bent him double. Niallan led him back to his bed.

"If I'm tae be the next chieftain then ye'll give me the respect ye grant – and *I* say ye'll stay put in this bed!"

Aidan was coughing too much to argue the point; he held up his hands in surrender.

"If he leaves this bed ye're tae tell me," he said to his mother as much as his father. "Don't let bullheadedness condemn ye too soon," he added more kindly.

"Ach, aye, that'd be him," his mother glared kindly at her husband.

Back home, Caitrin and Erlina were working at the table, laughing. Caitrin had long since ceased to be a slave, and she had blossomed into a rare beauty under Erlina's tender care. They saw Niallan's expression when he entered.

"What's happened?" Caitrin went to him, taking him by the hand.

"I've ne'er seen him thus," he said. "Weak. Vulnerable. He's always been as strong as a bear." He told them all that was said and done, and they were silent. As much as they wished him well, a guilty corner of Caitrin's heart hoped for the guest to leave sooner than later. Niallan would never have acknowledged it of his own heart though that same corner lurked in him as well, a cornered happiness longing for release from its prison, though in truth they both knew that the death of Aidan would do little to change the mind of the entire clan on the point of marriage to foreigners.

The *calends* of May found Aidan feeling stronger than he'd felt all winter, and restless from idleness. One morning while Iona had gone to the stream for water, he disappeared. By afternoon Iona had searched the area near the settlement with no success, so she bridled one of the ponies and rode toward Maldor, where she was sure to find Niallan, or Angus, or both. She had the suspicion that her youngest son had fallen in love with Caitrin; she was more willing to indulge that sentiment – though never to marriage – than she had been for his elder brother as Niallan had qualities about him that should not be wasted on a poor choice of a wife. But that had all turned out for the best, and it seemed that Niallan had at last found in Maldor what he'd needed in a wife.

As she approached, she was shocked to see a solid broch on the slopes of Meall Meadhonach before her; she and Aidan had assumed the activities had had something to do with Maldor's citadel, not a separate stronghold in the hills; but she had far more important things on her mind presently. She could see smoke rising through its cone roof and she dismounted before the entrance, calling for her sons. When they emerged she told them of the clansmen already searching, and they immediately mounted their own horses tethered nearby. Niallan rode southwest, Angus northwest; Niallan ended his search when he had gone as far as a man could walk in a day, with no sign of his father. By nightfall, the clansmen had returned with no sign of Aidan.

Niallan came to his father's roundhouse with the news, where Iona was waiting with Erlina. "We'll go out again at first light," he concluded, weary from the fruitless endeavour. "Father's not wi'out his means; I'm certain he's found shelter fer the night."

Iona silently poked the fire, sending up smoky sparks. "Stubborn fool!" Hot tears streaked her cheek and she brushed them away brusquely.

Angus suggested, "Either he knows himself tae be recovered, or—"

"Or he knows his winter guest'll be leavin' soon," Niallan finished his sentence.

"He's where he wishes to be," Erlina smiled gently. "He was never one to rest."

Iona fretted, "He *did* say he'd rather perish huntin'; I just dinna think he'd be fool enough tae do it!" She wrapped her arms around herself in a sudden chill.

"We'll find him on the morrow," Niallan replied, "quite cosy in the hollow of some hole or hillock, or nestled under a tent of branches." He kissed his mother on the forehead, and then returned home with Erlina to a waiting Caitrin.

The next morning as the sun touched the horizon, the men once again fanned out from the settlement, weapons and horns at the ready. Before the sun had reached its zenith a horn sounded to the north. Aidan had, as Niallan predicted, found a hollow beneath a hillock, and had built a small shelter of branches for the night as he'd gone too far to return by nightfall; his strong will had overestimated his physical strength.

The horn called the clansmen back to the settlement, and Aidan was well enough to be cross at all the fuss raised on his account, but Iona took him immediately to task and to bed.

"Ye'll *stay* this time!" she chided him, wrapping him in blankets and giving him a bowl of hot herbed soup she'd prepared. He took the soup gladly, its warmth welcomed but inadequate.

"Do ye promise me? Ne'er again leave wi'out so much as a goodbye!" she cried, more worried than upset.

He took her hand and pulled her to him, wrapping his arms about her waist. "I promise... I'll no' go huntin' again."

She sat down beside him. "Ach, ye know I be wishin' ye many more seasons tae hunt!" she kissed his forehead, then felt it with her hand. "Ye're all afire!"

"It's the warm soup," he took her hand in his. "Ne'er ye mind, and let me rest a moment in a comfortable bed." She hesitated. "Make me yer bread?" he suggested.

At that she got up and poured out the last of the ground barley to make bread. She mixed it with water, yeast, and a splash of goat's milk. When it was ready and began to smell of roasted grains in the oven, Aidan had drifted off to sound sleep, breathing gently.

Just after the *nones* of May his guest had left, taking him on his last journey; he was placed in the clan's cairn to go the way of the earth.

Niallan was made chieftain; Hafgan sullenly accepted Niallan's authority as their father and the elders had chosen him; but Niallan was his younger brother – not his leader – and he would follow his own council. Hafgan bided his time, though he cultivated unrest within those who were loyal to him. In the first months after his father's passing Niallan had tried to reason with the elders as regards the ban on marrying slaves; but if Niallan and Caitrin had thought a marriage between them might now be acceptable they were mistaken: Aidan was not the only one in the clan with prejudice against raising the status of a slave to a spouse; Iona, their greatest opponent in the matter, would not suffer her son to go against the strict decree of his father even now.

Those times when Erlina had gone to Maldor alone, leaving Caitrin behind in the settlement to have time alone with Niallan, Iona instead saw to it that Caitrin was constantly kept busy and made miserable, cruel her with tongue and with lash if something was not done to her complete satisfaction. Caitrin was a threat to Iona's authority over her son and, by extension, the clan. Niallan could command or persuade his mother in every other aspect though in this she would not bend.

When it became clear that the marriage between the two lovers would never be condoned, Erlina could no longer abide staying with the clan; to have love so close yet denied was beyond her willing comprehension, and being a daily witness to the grief it caused, and the grievous treatment of Caitrin by Iona, was more than she could bear. That Erlina spent much of her time in Maldor had at length been accepted – after all, it was her ancestral home, and it was honourable that she was (presumably) now building a proper cairn for her deceased kin; and that she more and more frequently took her slave with her was only to be expected. Often their journeys would be so late in the day that it made sense when they did not return to the settlement the same evening; thus their increasing absence was not much noticed as they secretly began moving to the broch; foodstuffs were gradually laid up, and as the clan had begun moving the animals to fresh fields in the spring, Niallan's sheep and cattle were taken to the citadel's enclosure instead.

Angus went to Maldor as often as he could, and at times would also stay overnight at the broch, bringing wild game and fish, peat bricks and driftwood for the fire. The broch's thick walls were warm and safe, and the interior was decorated with all of the comforts of home. Angus enjoyed the company of all three at the broch; there was a peace in the atmosphere that he'd not had since Niallan had moved out of their family's roundhouse. Niallan's presence was required in the settlement for appearances; notwithstanding rumours began to spread.

Then something occurred, as is the way of nature between a man and woman: When Caitrin knew her body was responding to new life within her, she knew it could not be concealed beyond a few months. She and Erlina spoke of it together one morning while they were alone in the broch, deciding how best to let it become known as it was a delicate matter in any circumstance.

"You'll need to tell Niallan as soon as possible," Erlina said. "He will have difficult decisions to make."

"Can we truly survive here... away from the protection of the clan, do ye think?" Caitrin's voice cracked in anxiety.

"I think we can," Erlina said. "If we are attacked, there is enough food and water in the broch for a comfortable refuge even if we lose crops and animals. And I have delivered babies of your Kind before."

"Really?" Caitrin stared at her. "When would a Maldorian princess have needed that skill?"

Erlina laughed. "I have seen over a thousand springs on this earth! I've had many, many occasion to see and do countless things!"

Caitrin sat down, staring at her. She gulped, "A— a *thousand?*"

Erlina nodded.

She took a deep breath, remembering Niallan's advice not to be shocked by Erlina's *Other*ness. "Then... if *ye* think we can, we can!" She stood and paced around the fire. "We'll need tae tell Angus too – he's here too much not tae notice, and I widna wish tae shock him with findin' out on his own."

"I'll tell Angus," Erlina replied. "You tell Niallan." Just then they heard the brothers approaching, laughing about something as they tied their ponies near the broch. Erlina nodded, "Now is better than later." She whisked a net into her arms and slipped outside; Caitrin heard her say, "Ah! Angus... just in time! I could use your help collecting cockles and dulse."

Caitrin poked her head out: "Niallan... I need yer brawn fer a heavy basket."

He went into the broch, but Caitrin instead took him by the hand and set him down upon a wooden bench, one of the chests from the Northmen's ship. He looked at her curiously, wrapping his arms about her skirts and pulling her closer.

She ran her fingers through his thick red hair. "I have news, love," she watched his reaction carefully as she said, "It's destined tae change a great many things..." she took a deep breath and spoke each word slowly: "I am with child."

Instant shock flitted to excitement across his face, and at last came to rest in wonder. He reached up and gently touched her belly, smiling. The smiled faded. He stood up and began pacing around the fire. "When it becomes known..." his breath caught in his throat, an expression of deepest pain on his face. "I dare not think of what might happen tae ye! Ma' mother detests ye enough tae seek yer death, tae be sure!" He rubbed the back of his neck, thinking aloud: "I'd flee wi' ye in a heartbeat. But we canna! We canna survive the wilds on our own – especially not wi' ye in yer way, now."

"Erlina thinks we'll survive quite well here! And she can help bringin' a bairn into the world."

"She knows?"

Caitrin nodded sheepishly for not having told Niallan first. "I sought her advice. She's tellin' Angus... as we speak."

Erlina and Angus walked down toward the loch's shore. The swelling tide beckoned to them, tirelessly polishing boulders to smooth spheres, the peaty dark water tossing pebbles back and forth with a *shhh! shhh!* along the silvery stretch of the water's edge. At the shore of the loch they tossed cockles into a net to prepare for dinner, and gathered fresh dulse to wash and dry. Erlina sat down upon the pebbled shore and invited Angus to sit next to her.

"You know who I am Angus," she began. "I am not one bound to this age. And I am in love with Aradan, taken from me for the moment but who shall return one day."

"But ye married ma' brother," he replied. "Does he know ye're still in love wi' him?"

"He does; and he is happy for it."

"Ye're both a mystery tae me," he shook his head, looking at her incredulously. "Ye're married, yet there're no bairns; and I've ne'er seen a true sign of affection atween ye."

She turned to look at him, studying his face a moment. His cheeks reddened under the scrutiny as if he were a boy caught doing something he oughtn't, or a lad who should've understood something obvious and was about to have it explained to him. "Angus...

we've never been as man and wife in all the time we've been married. He knows I am in love; and I know he is in love with another. We've remained faithful to our lovers *through* our marriage."

He stared at her, unblinking. "So that's why ye've tolerated Niallan's affections toward Caitrin." He shook his head, "Aside from what I think o' the matter... ye do know it'll come tae light. Rumours already have legs."

"And what will that mean for us here?" she asked at once sincere but defiant.

He shrugged. "I canna say. But I do know what it'll mean fer ye there – in the settlement: If they learn that Niallan is still attached tae Caitrin in any way... Caitrin's life willna be safe there from ma' mother. She canna go back. E'er."

"What do you think of Caitrin," she asked, "as a woman?"

Angus picked up a stone and tossed it toward the loch, his red hair whipping in the wind and revealing blushed cheeks. "She's beautiful. Ye've done much tae improve her."

"I've done nothing but accept her for who she is, and have not treated her as a slave," she answered.

"If Niallan werena in love wi' her—" he began, but stopped. "I'm glad she was given tae ye; she suffered under ma' mother's heavy hand against her."

"I've done something else for her," Erlina added carefully, "and *that* is the true secret of her beauty." Angus looked at her warily. "I gave her to Niallan – quite some time ago – as his first true *wife*." She waited for that to settle before adding, "I tell you this now because it will become evident in a few months."

Silence was broken only by the lapping waves of incoming tide, and the sea birds' cries along the shore. At long last, Angus stood up. His expression was inscrutable as he turned without a word and returned to the broch. Erlina watched him go.

Erlina returned to the broch to find Caitrin weaving upon the loom, who saw her enter and asked, "How did he take it? He poked his head in tae see if Niallan were here, and I told him he'd gone tae check on the piglets; he looked at me in the oddest way and then left wi'out another word!"

Erlina told her of their conversation.

"I dread the confrontation dear Niallan'll have!" Caitrin said pensively, biting her lip. "And I do hope Angus returns; I'd hate tae lose his company."

Angus went off in search of Niallan in the new forest north of the broch, where he'd built a small stone pen for a pair of wild boar piglets he'd caught. On the way Angus paused near a stream as he tried to gather his thoughts before facing his brother: He'd fallen in love only twice in his short life; and both women had been given to his elder brother. Not that he felt he had a breath of a hope where Princess Erlina was concerned; he'd worshipped her from afar, knowing her vastly beyond his reach in every way. But Caitrin. He'd watched with growing consternation as his mother had humiliated and abused Caitrin at any given chance, and had watched how Caitrin used the stumbling blocks thrown in her path to climb the mountains of life and reach the top with a beautiful smile. When she'd first arrived she was a scrawny wee thing, undernourished and overworked, suspicious and short-tempered. And then he saw a look in Niallan's eyes one day as he'd watched her work in their father's roundhouse, and Angus began to look at her differently; at first out of curiosity as to what on earth could make Niallan gaze at her so, and once he'd discovered it too, could not bear to look away. But he'd respected Niallan's first claims of the heart; when he'd taken Erlina as his wife, Angus had let his hopes grow in regard to Caitrin. And now this.

"What broods so darkly on yer brow, wee brother?" Niallan asked, smacking Angus' back as he walked past him to the stream. He'd fed the piglets, and cleaned his hands in the cool water before wetting down his hair and flinging it back, the water spraying an arc across the grassy banks. When no answer came and Angus only stared at him, Niallan sat down beside his brother on the ground. "What is it?" he asked more seriously. "Ye know we can talk."

Angus had not been prepared for such an open invitation; he burst out, "How could ye? Just when I thought—" He stood and paced to the stream. "Just when I thought things were clear!"

"What're ye bletherin' about?"

"Caitrin!" he huffed, as if it were obvious.

Niallan looked at his brother steadily. "I would'a told ye today, had Erlina no' done so." He watched his brother's expression, then asked, "Are ye— are ye goin' tae tell our mother?"

Angus tossed a stone into the water. "No." He added, "I like breathin'."

"Aye, in that we agree," Niallan breathed a sigh of relief. "Ye know how long I've loved Caitrin," he went on. "We thought that once Father no longer... opposed us... that we'd be free tae our happiness. Ye know now we couldna, and perhaps I should ha'e seen that comin', but love hopes far too much fer reason sometimes."

Angus sat down beside his brother once again. "I... when ye married Erlina, I'd hoped that Caitrin and I might someday... but I knew ye loved her, so before yer marriage I didna pursue those hopes. But after... I thought—"

"Is that why yer visits grew longer and more frequent?" Niallan asked.

Angus nodded reluctantly.

"Do ye love Caitrin too?" He watched his brother carefully.

"It disna matter. Now she's ma' sister," he sighed heavily. Despite it all he was still fond of his brother, and knew he was a good man. "Tae lose her tae any other man would sting – but I know ye're worthy of her. And so I wish ye well fer I know ye love her true; may it remain a secret long enough fer yous tae enjoy life together. Yous both deserve it."

"I thank ye," Niallan sighed, "but that willna be possible much longer."

Angus looked at him. "Aye. Erlina said as much."

"Aye," Niallan smiled cautiously.

"Congratulations. And commiserations... ye know yer hand'll be forced... by Hafgan, or our mother, or the elders, or the lot. Better ye go tae them wit' yer choice, than be exiled by the sharp end o' a blade."

"At which end o' the blade will ye be standin'?"

Angus gazed out across the stream as he thought about his answer. "I imagine it depends on who's wieldin' the blade."

"Ye know we've got a place fer ye in the broch."

"Aye," he answered gravely. "When ye go tae the elders... dinna mention me. If I stay there, I'll be able tae send word tae ye if there's danger. But know this, brother," he slapped Niallan's shoulder, "if they turn against yous, I'll stand by yer side."

"I thank ye, Angus," Niallan replied sincerely.

Caitrin had been a gift to Erlina, but Iona was disappointed in the charitable treatment of the girl when she'd hoped for the spoiled nature of a princess to make Caitrin's life the harder for it; so when Erlina began taking Caitrin with her to Maldor and Niallan also became increasingly absent from the settlement, rumours began to grow. Niallan was now chieftain and no longer his own man to do as he pleased; yet he neglected his duties of leading the clan while spending far too much time in the old ruins of Maldor; far too much time in the company of his wife and her slave, whom everyone knew to have been Niallan's secret lover in the past. When the rumours grew too loud to ignore Iona knew she must act.

She called for Hafgan outside of his door one morning.

He opened, blinking in the morning light. "What d'ye want, woman? The sun's just half up!" he growled groggily, rubbing his eyes.

"Tae come in," she stepped past him into the roundhouse. Hafgan's wife and children still slept; but Iona had no intention of staying long. She turned to Hafgan just inside the door and said in a low voice, "Ye've heard the rumours no doubt... about Niallan and that slave."

"Aye," he was more awake now, and interested.

"Some o' the young lads were coming through the forest not long past... and in the distance saw Niallan in intimate embrace wi' her!" Iona's eyes nearly burst with anger. "I want ye tae go out there wi' a few o' yer men... watch... find out what's what, *really*. Nearly three winters have passed since the handfastin' and there're no bairns about. Somethin's no' right!"

"An' what's tae happen if we find the rumours true?" Hafgan pressed.

"The elders will decide. But a chieftain must lead by example in *all* things," Iona looked him squarely in the eye, after glancing pointedly toward his sleeping sons, "or leave the task tae one who will."

Hafgan grinned, "Ach, I agree. We'll set out today."

Hafgan hadn't been to Maldor since the night he'd led the raid; he was shocked to find a substantial broch on the slopes of Meall Meadhonach and more than that, to see a field of crops growing nearby and Niallan's flocks and herd scattered in the fields near the shore, a newer stone shelter for the animals built from the rocky bones of Maldor within in the enclosure of the old citadel. His men took up strategic positions around the broch and waited, but after three days of nothing the waiting had made them sour; Erlina's keen senses knew they were being watched, and all was shown as it should be outside of the broch walls, affection shown between husband and wife, slave in her proper place. They returned with disappointing news for the awaiting Iona; at least on the topic of betrayal to their law, though the news of the well-established farmstead was a surprise. As he reported what they'd seen, Angus had been present.

"I'll speak wi' the elders," Iona promised Hafgan. "Ye and yer men – return home, but make ready tae set out again at ma' biddin'."

As soon as Hafgan was gone again, Angus took up his walking staff and a cake of bread, along with his pouch containing a stone axe and knife.

"Where're ye off tae?" his mother asked suspiciously. He seemed too eager to be about his usual tasks.

"Huntin'," he held up his pouch as if it were obvious.

"Bring me back a few hares fer dinner then." She knew that would force him to truly hunt, though she suspected that his loyalty to Niallan would mean the hunting would take him toward Maldor. No matter; warned or not, change was coming.

On his way out of the settlement Angus passed by Erlina's roundhouse and gathered Niallan's weapons.

"Niallan!" Angus called as he neared the broch. Niallan was nearby, skinning a deer Erlina had brought down with her bow. "They'll soon be on their way – the elders, our mother, and Hafgan's rabble!"

"How long?"

"I don't know – Mother's speaking wi' the elders now, and she told Hafgan tae prepare."

Angus remained to protect the women in the broch, while Niallan rode out toward the settlement to either meet the clansmen on the way, or intercept them before they set out. He met them just inside the forest beyond the settlement; they stopped a safe distance from one another. At the front of the clansmen were the elders and Iona, flanked by Hafgan and his largest men, all armed with spears and swords, followed by the rest of the clansmen that could be persuaded to the urgency of the breach.

"Is there a war, kinsmen?" Niallan challenged them calmly.

The elders murmured amongst themselves; the eldest, Balfour, answered for them: "Ye're our chieftain. Yet there've been grave charges laid at yer feet concernin' the slave girl; ye know what we've decreed about that, and yet ye've been spied wi' her."

Niallan thought a moment. "It's as ye say. I'll no' deny it."

Iona stepped toward him, fists clenched at her sides, eyes ablaze. "How could ye? Yer father trusted ye! And ye spit in our face wi' that whore!"

"She's no *whore*!" Niallan shouted, making Iona flinch back instinctively. "Ye've made her so in yer own mind! But she's pure – she's only different than our kind, and that's been her only crime! She's done e'erythin' she could tae please ye, and still ye rejected her."

"And ye spit on yer place in our clan!" Hafgan stepped to his mother's side, sword clenched in one hand.

"One that ye'd gladly take up no doubt," Niallan challenged, "spat on or no'."

The elders stood tightly together conferring, while the clansmen toward the rear were thrown into confusion, whispering amongst themselves. They wanted no war; they weren't entirely certain which side they'd actually take between the two brothers.

Balfour took the only graceful way out they could, to avoid a feud; he looked up at Niallan: "Because ye've answered plainly, and we wish no kinsman's blood on our hands, we give ye a choice: Ye'll fight Hafgan fer the right as chieftain; should ye win, ye'll keep yer rights as chieftain, and Caitrin will be banished from our lands." He paused, trying to interpret the blaze in Niallan's eyes. "Or," he continued, "ye lose – or forfeit yer rights as clansman outright – and be exiled from any further contact wi' our clan."

"Then ye've made ma' choice fer me," Niallan replied coldly. "I'd ne'er banish any woman tae die in the wilds alone."

Iona took another step forward. Niallan could tell on her face that she never expected him to willingly choose exile; she'd underestimated his attachment to the slave. "But son!" she reached her hand toward him across the distance that separated them. "Ye canna mean it! Ye'd turn yer back on yer kin? Ye know what banishment means! There's no way ye can survive in the wilds, just the two of ye! There're wolves... bears... violent men abroad...! And what about me? Bereft of yer father... would ye now bereft me of ma' son?"

"I've ne'er seen ye bereft, woman!" Niallan snapped. "And ye stood against me at every turn when it came tae the woman I love – ye should ha'e known the cost! Ye're the one that drives me away," he ended coldly. "And what's more," he looked pointedly at the elders, "I've wed the Princess of Maldor, according tae our clan's customs; those lands and its forests and shores are now *ma'* claim! I'll no' cross the line tae yer lands... and I expect the same from yer clan." He glared at Hafgan. "Tae cross over means war. But," he added, "I'll respect the treaty atween Maldor and your clan if yous'll do the same: I'll come to yer aid if need be, and I expect the same of yous."

"Ye've got no army, wee brother," Hafgan challenged, twirling his short sword in a figure eight at Niallan to make the point. "What's tae stop me from takin' what's yers now?"

Niallan grinned widely, "Only a daft fool would go against the Princess of Maldor in battle! Ye've not got enough men tae make it past her arrows," he laughed derisively. "I don't need an army. I've got an *elf-wife*."

Murmurs of apprehension spread even through Hafgan's rabble. The challenge had been laid; perhaps it was too much – Niallan knew that Erlina would not willingly kill his clansmen, but it was a bluff he had to make to keep Hafgan's rash-headedness at bay, and try to keep a distance between his small, vulnerable family and those who now chose to be his enemies.

3: Now

Jon and Alexis hiked south of the digs, just off the road, with Jon's new *Ordnance Survey* map in hand. They located the same black rut he'd found earlier during his call with Alvar.

"People drive past this all the time!" Jon shook his head. "It's what...?" he looked at the map, "only ten or so metres from the road!" Okay, so it was only ten metres over ground made uneven by knolls of moor grass and bog cotton, and waist deep in heather and bracken.

At their feet was what looked like a narrow slit, but was in fact a stone stair case down into the ground, its entrance almost completely hidden by the overgrowth.

"If we hadn't seen my mother disappear down here I'd never have thought much of this hole," Alexis said, "even if it is on the map! So... now what?"

"I'll go in first," Jon suggested, as he slipped his rucksack around from back to front and pulled out his torch. "If I need help I'll flash my torch like this," he flickered the light off and on, "and if it's big enough for two down there I'll come and get you."

The top few steps were slippery with mud washed down from the last rain; it was a good possibility that the entire souterrain was nothing but a puddle. He pushed aside the overhanging bracken, and as his eyes adjusted to the dark he was surprised to see interlocking stone-lined walls, a stone pavement beneath his feet and a solid stone roof overhead, obviously made by someone who understood at least rudimentary stone masonry. The ceiling was too low for him to stand upright, and if he had just found this in passing he wouldn't have bothered to look further; it looked like any Iron Age souterrain should: A dead end, a hole in the ground for storage, hiding or defence. He could hear a faint trickle, ground water seeping into the cavern, and could hear wind teasing the fronds around the mouth of the souterrain; but everything else was filled with dark silence. A damp smell of mould and moss, peat and mud rose from the ground and dripped from the moist walls. He looked back up at Alexis, who was peering in through the narrow window of vegetation and waiting for his signal. He was about to give up and come back out, giving one more sweep of the small space with his torch light, when he caught sight of a bracken fiddlehead far back in the shelter of the walls yet gently teased by a breeze. He ducked and half-crawled, half-walked to where the fiddlehead was growing out of the damp wall and held his hand to the frond. Feeling a very slight air current from the left, he shone his light and discovered another tunnel leading off at a 7-angle from the short entrance. He went in a few steps and found that he could stand upright, with room to spare above his head. The tunnel was now perfectly smooth, almost as if someone had plastered the entire tunnel and dried it. It was even large enough for several to walk abreast.

Jon poked his head up through the bracken-draped entrance. "This is amazing!" he said before helping her down the slippery steps. When she was on solid ground again he shone the torch on his face: "This part is the souterrain, but that," he pointed behind his shoulder, "is something else entirely!"

They stepped into the longer tunnel and Jon shone his torch down the tunnel: it continued smoothly as far as the light could reach and beyond.

"This doesn't make any sense!" Alexis exclaimed. "How did this get here? And why is it not marked on the map at all? This is *not* a souterrain!"

Jon shone the light back toward what was the actual souterrain and examined the opening. He turned toward her again: "Maybe... when they surveyed for the map... that's all that *was* here... or all that they saw. So... what do you think? Should we follow it and see where it leads?"

She took his torch and shone the light around the edges of the tunnel. "It looks solid enough... *very* solid, actually. Okay – let's do this!"

The first several metres were full of that anticipation of discovery; but the farther into the dark tunnel they penetrated, the more unsure they became; if it were not solid at any point, they could be buried alive; if they were injured in any way, it would be a long trek back out; and no one knew where they were. They had no idea how far they'd walked but in the thick darkness broken only by Jon's torch it felt like miles; the last while they'd been walking up an ever-steeper incline.

"Should we continue?" he asked her, shining his torch on his face for her to see.

She looked at her watch. "Let's give ourselves a bit of a rest and then go on."

They squatted on their heels in the dark together, conserving the torch batteries just in case and taking a drink or two of water. As they stood to move on Jon shone the light on his face: "I wonder... remember my mentioning Sandy's work on the castle – the tunnel? This might be it, but from the other end... we've been climbing, so it could be leading us back to Dalmoor."

"We'll find out soon, then; at least that helps us gauge how much of a walk we have. An unknown path always seems much longer than it really is."

After some time they began to notice a faint glow ahead. But nothing could have prepared them for what they found.

Before them opened up a large cavern of stone. Two pools, one with a stream softly cascading into it from a short watercourse filtering through the wall, were situated in the centre of the cavern with an oblong stone between them that reminded Jon of a fallen standing stone, worn smooth over time; but the thing that stunned them most was the glowing stones that carpeted the entire cavern. There was no need for his torch as the luminescent blue light from the stones was enough to see by.

Jon bent down and picked one up. "Glow-in-the-dark pebbles," he said, looking up so that Alexis could see his lips. "I've seen plastic ones before, but these are glass! Very high quality." He looked around, surprised at the sheer number: The eerie glow gave the cavern a hallowed quality, reflecting dancing light onto the ceiling from stones at the bottom of each pool.

"How bright – or how long do they glow when exposed to light?" Alexis asked.

"It depends on the quality – but the ones I've seen? After about thirty minutes of light, they'll glow all day, dimming over time. These might glow a few days if exposed to light for a longer period, or maybe several hours with only a short burst of light." He turned the stone over in his hand. "Why do you ask?"

"We're below the castle, wouldn't you say?"

"There's nowhere else in the area that it *could* be, if it's connected to a surface structure."

"I know for a fact that none of this was ordered since we've moved here; I see all of the receipts, the invoices, emails and phone records." She looked around at the stones. "But someone knows this is here. Someone turned on a light in here in the last twenty-four hours, by the looks of it."

"Another puzzle piece?"

She shook her head, perplexed. "Or another puzzle altogether."

"Let's see if we can find another entrance," he suggested. "If this is the tunnel Sandy mentioned, then there should be an entrance from the castle."

They split up and began searching the walls. The most unusual thing about both the tunnel and this cavern was that they were completely solid – not concrete, but local stone strata; where one would expect layers of peat, or seeping ground water, it was as if stone had been smoothly poured to create space for just this purpose. The walls glittered purple, pink and blue, with quartz and Lewisian Pegmatite reflecting the radiance of the stones at their feet.

Alexis whispered, "Over here!"

He joined her where an old white-washed cast iron table and two chairs stood, by now not at all surprising. Against the wall stood a small dresser which turned out to contain nothing more than towels and a hairbrush. Just behind the table and completely hidden from the direction of the pools was a narrow hall curving upward toward the left; it was lit by a row of the stones along each wall. At the end of the hall they found two parallel slits in the solid rock wall. There was no door handle.

"See if we can find a key hole, or something similar," Jon whispered, but she couldn't see his lips in the dimmer light, so he pointed from his eyes to the wall and made the gesture of a key unlocking a door. They felt between the two cracks until they found a tiny screw on level with Jon's shoulders, felt with the finger though not readily visible; it held a small metal plate and Jon swung it to the side, peering through the keyhole hidden beneath it. "There must be another plate on the other side – I can't see anything," he stood up, realizing he'd said it to himself. He turned on his torch to tell her what he'd discovered.

"So... now what?" she asked.

"We'll search the castle cellar next."

They went back and sat down on the stone between the pools, trying to take it all in. Alexis seemed agitated. "What are you thinking?" Jon asked.

"If I tell you, you won't think less of me or my mother, will you?"

"Of course not," he reached over and took her hand.

She stood up and paced, wrestling within herself. "This cavern... there's something about it, aside from the very fact of its existence... there's a sense of *refuge* here, wouldn't you say? As if whatever was said here will stay here?" It was a question waiting for an answer.

He nodded. "Whatever we say or do here remains our secret."

"Okay," she sat down again. "I love the Cardinal, and Elbal... they love me; I've never lacked affection or material possessions... my mother's always given me the best of everything – education, comfort, help, love," she swept her arm out, gesturing to the cavern, "but this... they're hiding things from me! And for the first time I feel free to question why! Or feel that even though I never have, I *should*... that it's *okay* to question. It's never been forbidden... but I've just lived such a comfortable life that I never even thought to question my place in it. Having been rescued, I guess I felt grateful and therefore guilty if I questioned anything about what I'd been given. But for the first time in my life, I want *more*!" she stood, pacing around the pools. "I want answers! I want to know what's been hidden besides this cavern!" She turned toward him, studying his face with an expression akin to fear.

51

"I know you in some ways better than I know myself. But I want *that* to change too... I need to know where I come from – it's a colossal missing piece in my own personal puzzle."

"Questioning life and our purpose is part of what it means to be human," Jon replied. "I'm sure the Cardinal would welcome such ambition; she loves you, of that I'm certain."

"You're right... on all counts," she said. A glimmer of light on the water caught Alexis's attention, and she dipped her hand into the still pool; it was cool, though the other pool was heated as its cascade misted warm droplets into the air. The watercourse coming out of a cavern wall made just about as much sense as any of the rest of it. "Here we sit in a private paradise and all I can think of are problems," she shook her head, smiling. "It's a pity we haven't got our swimming costumes."

"I don't usually wear it when I go spelunking," he grinned. "Come on," he stood, holding out his hand to her, "we'd better get out of here before *whoever* returns."

They were a few metres into the tunnel when Jon heard a key turning at the far end of the cavern, echoing off the stone walls. He shone his torch onto his face and signalled Alexis to remain quiet, then turned off his torch. A beam of light shone into the cavern from the narrow hall; Jon and Alexis were already far enough into the tunnel to be in the deep shadows. Jon heard the voices of Elbal and the Cardinal speaking in a strange language, and the clank of a lid on a large pot, likely coming from the kitchen. Alexis clung to Jon, unsure of what was happening but feeling his tensed muscles frozen in silence. They positioned themselves cautiously, just until they could see what was happening yet remain hidden in the darkness of the tunnel.

The Cardinal entered alone and turned on the lights very briefly, both a chandelier on the ceiling of the cave and lights within the pools, before turning them off again; the stones on the floor shone a brighter blue, and the pools were illuminated from within in turquoise splendour. She gazed down unseeing as she unwrapped her dress to reveal a dark red bathing costume beneath (Jon breathed a silent sigh of relief). A necklace hung about her neck with a silver sphere dangling from it which looked as if it glowed from within, though it could have just been a trick of the light in the cavern. As she stepped down into the nearest pool she began to weep; fear of discovery was all that kept them from retreating, feeling as if they were intruding on a deeply private moment; they stood breathless, as still as alabaster statues.

She dipped her head back into the water, floating gently, the silence of the water filling her ears. "My beloved, where are you?" she whispered with a sob which echoed through the cavern. She grasped the sphere between her hands and brought it to her lips, kissing it.

Alexis could see her mother's distress and she longed to go to her but Jon touched her arm quietly to remind her not to reveal their hiding place. They had no choice but to silently endure.

"Have I lost your heart? Have you mistaken the absence of the orb's centrepiece to mean my own heart has been lost to you? Oh, *Eru*, let it not be so!" She rose from the water as she wept: "Have you found comfort in the arms of another? Oh, how I envy her! But no— I trust you to be faithful to me... your vows are true." She held the orb to her lips as she spoke, as if addressing it, hoping it would respond in some way. "I cannot feel your heart as I once could, try as I may... the song of *Millach var Amroré* has taunted me these past centuries! Ever loving, ever longing, never finding! I must go on trusting that you are alive, yet with no sign in which to hope!" She swam to the edge of the pool and lay her head on her arms as she cried, sobs from deep within tearing at her throat.

It took every fibre of strength in Jon and Alexis not to either flee the intrusion or run to comfort her. Jon felt involuntary tears streaming down his cheeks at the sorrow he heard in her sobs.

The tranquil waters eventually calmed her when her tears were spent. She stepped out of the water and sat upon the stone between the pools. She ran her fingers through her hair to comb it out, and as she did so she began to hum, then sing, a hauntingly beautiful melody that only Jon was witness to. The words were in an unknown tongue, but they wove a silvery tapestry too beautiful for words to express in any language on earth that he knew. When she was finished she dressed herself once again and then knelt at the pool to wash her tears away, drying her face with her long silken hair now dried. She glided silently back to the narrow hall, the door clicking shut as she left. The room lingered with the fresh glow of the stones and the gentle ring of the haunting melody.

It took a moment before Jon and Alexis realized they could again breathe normally. Moving slowly, stiffly, they stepped back into the light of the cavern to stretch and talk.

They just stared at each other.

"Wow." Jon summed it up. "Wow!"

"What happened? I could only see a small portion of what she said... something about – surely I didn't understand it correctly – it looked like she said, '*taunted me these past centuries*'!"

Jon nodded, "She did." He told her everything he could remember, though he didn't recognize some of the words she'd used.

Alexis shook her head in disbelief. "Surely that was just hyperbole."

"But – I know, and I agree – but why would she? When she thought she was all alone? She'd have no reason to exaggerate to herself..."

Alexis frowned as she thought about that. "Let's get out of here. I need to get back before she comes looking for me."

"Okay," he agreed, "but let's get away from the cavern a few dozen metres before I turn my torch back on, just in case she returns."

They held hands in the dark as they started down the tunnel. Alexis was running one hand along the wall to balance herself, when her hand ran across a gap. She stopped, jerking Jon to a stop as well.

She whispered, "Torch!"

He turned it on and shone it upon his face. "What's wrong?" he asked.

She took the torch from his hand and shone it on the wall until she found the recess she'd felt. It was roughly even with her shoulder height, and she shone the beam of light back into the dark cavity. "I can see something!" she reached in as far as she could. "It's just out of my reach!"

Jon reached in and felt around, then shone the light on his face: "This isn't a natural crevice... it's formed like these walls... it's intentional!" He felt something cloth; cloth wrapped around something solid. He felt a string of some kind and gave a tug; it was attached to the bundle so he pulled the whole thing out carefully. It wasn't that large, but heavy for its size.

Alexis held the torch as they knelt on the ground to examine their find: The cloth bundle was tied with what looked like a strip of leather made from sinew, and the cloth was a simple garment's scrap, the uneven texture of hand-spun wool. Jon opened the cloth and found a wooden box within: A puzzle box made of dark wood polished smooth by the handling, finely carved and inlaid with silver and pearl.

"A *puzzle* box? Now that's just downright ironic," he mumbled to himself.

Turning it around, pushing, pulling, sliding and twisting, they finally managed to open it. It contained flat sheets of paper, handmade and speckled with the delicate petals of heather blossoms. He carefully lifted the entire stack of papers out of the box and onto the cloth spread out on the floor of the tunnel, and held the torch as they began to leaf through the pages very carefully: They were each written with a strange script, wispy and sleek, like feathers fluttering in the breeze.

"I've never seen anything so beautiful," Alexis whispered. "It's a pity we can't read them!" She lifted one of the sheets to examine it closer, when Jon lifted his hand to stop her. "Wait! Look!" he pointed the torch to the back of the bottom sheet, holding it still to examine it. "It— it's in English!"

Nearly all of the pages had English written on the back, while the front was covered with the strange writing. They turned the entire pile over, and were surprised to find that that is exactly how it should be read: Back to front. By turning the pile upside-down, it was now English-top.

"That's almost deliberate," Jon murmured; as if to confirm that observation the first page, written in a distinctive, open handwriting, read thus:

If you have found this book, I know you have found my most sacred refuge; if you have come this far, then welcome; I know you well. Many questions you may have, dearest reader, as to the content of this coffer. I have endeavoured to meticulously translate the pages herein upon their own verso lest I be absent when this is found.

Read and be enlightened by the heart I now entrust to you.

Erlina

"Erlina!" Jon cried. The light on his face, he said, "*Erlina* is the name of Alvar's yacht! That can't be a coincidence! Alex... before we do anything else I've got to call my friend!"

"Alright," she agreed, "but I doubt you'll get reception down here." She looked at the note again. "I guess this means we can take this with us – let's head back up to my room."

He carefully laid the pages into the box; when he managed to get the puzzle box closed he tied it again into its cloth and tucked it into his rucksack.

When they neared the souterrain-end of the tunnel they found themselves splashing through shallow water; coming into the souterrain they saw why: It was pouring rain outside, and the stairs had become a waterfall.

"It looks like we're about to get very wet," Jon moaned. It took them some time climb the stairs, Jon going first and nearly pulling Alexis up through the dripping canopy at the top of the stairs. On the way back to Castle Dalmoor, Jon asked, "What do you think about what happened back there... the things your mother said?"

"What does anyone think of such things?" she shrugged. "It's unbelievable... and yet like you said, she didn't know she was being observed, did she? It might be the truth. But how could it be – it's impossible!"

"But *what* might be the truth? Frankly I'm not sure I understood much of anything, even though it was English... an orb? Lost love... you said she'd lost her love, but she spoke of it as if she'd misplaced something... or someone, not lost as in *dead*. And the song she sang... was that the taunting song she'd mentioned? And I've never heard a language like that either... I have no idea what languages it could even be related to."

When they reached Alexis's room, Jon carefully removed the box from his rucksack and spread the cloth out on the table.

"Right – I need to call Alvar," Jon said.

"Shall I leave?" she started to turn toward the door.

"No," he smiled, "I'd like to introduce you."

When Alvar came into view on Skype, he was wearing his usual blood red turtleneck. "Hello, my friend," Jon said. "You're looking... tired."

"Why, thank you," Alvar said with a mock bow.

"May I introduce someone? Alexis," Jon took her by the hand and pulled her into view. She saw that Jon's friend was handsome, and he looked kind. She smiled and nodded, and he signed a greeting to her which surprised them both.

"Hey! Since when do you know sign language?" Jon asked.

"Ainsley, I know a good many things," Alvar grinned.

Alexis waved goodbye and showed Jon a note saying that she would check in on her mother quickly in case she was needed, so that her mother wouldn't come looking for her. It didn't take her long, so she slipped back into her room during their chat and watched from a distance as she worked on opening the puzzle box again.

Once she'd left Alvar said, "Now: What news?"

"Man, oh man! Where do I start?" Jon told him about the tunnel, the surprises at the end of it, the strange behaviour of the Cardinal, and about the haunting melody she sang. "And if that weren't enough, we found a box in the wall of the tunnel, containing a whole stack of written pages – a beautiful wispy writing on one side, though it looks like most have been translated into English on their overleafs. We're going to read—" He stopped as he noticed that Alvar's breath had become laboured, his eyes gazing into nothingness.

"Hey, Alvar!... are you okay? You look like you just saw a ghost or something!" He'd never seen his friend so unnerved, and he hadn't even mentioned the name of Erlina; he looked as if he were on the edge of tears... or despair. He knew Alvar better than anyone outside of his family, but his friend had kept his emotions tightly guarded lately – since the news of this excavation had come up, as a matter of fact.

"Perhaps I have," came his shaky reply. "Into English, you say? *Modern* English?" There was a vague sense of hope tugging at his words.

"Well, I could read it, if that's what you mean. No thee or thou."

"Please – show me one of the pages!"

Jon held up one of the pages, showing both the front and the back.

Alvar seemed to stare at both with an equally hungry expression, as if he could understand both but wouldn't admit it. "Tell me more about the Cardinal's odd behaviour you mentioned."

"She was in one of the pools talking to herself: She said something about an orb... not being able to feel someone's heart?... it was all a bit confusing. And envy of someone... something to do with vows."

His friend only nodded, then muttered, "Only she would envy such vows."

"What vows? Do *not* tell me you understood any of that!"

"I did, as a matter of fact; but please," he held up his hand as Jon drew breath to ask, "don't ask me to explain it at the moment; not over the phone."

"Also, I've heard a name," he changed the subject. "Does the name *Aradan* say anything to you?"

"*Aradan!*" he whispered, eyes wide in wonder. "Where did you hear it?"

"I know this is going to sound like I've lost my cups, but... I heard the tree up on the hill say it."

"What do you mean?" Alvar asked.

"It sounded like... oh, I don't know, but I know I heard that name – when I was talking to you once... after I hung up... it was as if it was calling to someone."

"Oh, I see." That didn't seem to surprise his friend in the least.

Jon said, "Look – when are you coming?"

A talking tree didn't faze him; but *that* grabbed his attention: "Who said anything about coming?"

"You know you should," Jon replied. "I'm probably forgetting a dozen odd things; we just really need your help solving these mysteries." He could see Alvar was thinking about it. "You could come with your yacht," he persuaded, "Some time off... you look like you could use it." Alvar's yacht was a magnificent clinker-built home on the sea which he'd been sailing solo for years. "Besides, it's a good excuse to bring me some *Mysost* while you're at it."

Alvar smiled absently, trying to maintain his end of the conversation. "Are they starving you for want of good cheese?"

"The Cardinal knows how to feed her guests, but being away from home makes me miss the simple things. And don't change the subject: Are you coming? And are you going to tell me the connection? And don't give me that Viking crap – I'm not buying it and you know it. We've known each other a long time; what is it you're not telling me?"

Alvar looked away, lost in thought as if weighing a decision. Finally he sighed, pinching his nose between his fingers. "It's a long story; and not one I'm prepared to face yet. Let's just say that I have a special connection with that site..."

"Speaking of which... there are several things in the castle that you need to see for yourself."

"And what would they be?"

"Nope. You're not telling, I'm not telling," he grinned. He was thinking of the statues – one in particular that looked strikingly familiar, and the entrance hall's fireplace; he knew his friend's curiosity wouldn't let him rest after that.

"Have you found out what's in that oblong structure underground? From the scan?"

"Why is it so important?" Jon asked pointedly.

"As soon as they find any burials, let me know," Alvar sounded tired. "Especially..." he swallowed, "if any of those buried are... female."

Jon was concerned for his friend. "Are you okay? I *really* think you need to get more rest."

"Bodily rest isn't the kind I crave." Alvar rubbed his forehead, weary in heart.

"Then come... with *Erlina*."

Alvar looked up at Jon at the name of his yacht. "I only hesitate because... if the Cardinal is the Wolf, she will bolt as soon as she feels me near; if she's not the Wolf—"

Jon saw a look on his friend's face akin to fear, or desperate hope, or fear to hope; he'd never known Alvar to be anything but calm coolness and it was unsettling. "This will be the perfect time to come then; the Cardinal is going to Edinburgh for four days, the day after tomorrow. If you leave now, you'll be here before she returns. And besides, Alex and I can't put this puzzle together without your help."

"If I come, you know I'll be in a dead zone for a day or two out in the Atlantic." Satellite signals didn't always seem to be able to find a ship out on the open ocean.

"That's why I'd rather you come sooner than later."

He relented. "And if I'm bringing you *Mysost*, I'll have to take some by Fair Isle... I never sail past them without bringing them something."

"Then while you're there, trade it for a woman's jumper... small. With two matching fisherman's *keps*, if you can get them."

Alvar studied Jon a moment, then shook his head smiling, "Alright – you talked me into it. I'll make preparations and then send you a message when I'm ready to leave Bergen. I should be able to get reception once I'm near Fair Isle, and be able to gauge my arrival time better." He added with a smile, "Wish me luck in landing weather there, or you'll have more cheese than you know what to do with."

"Will do. And thank you for agreeing to come," Jon said sincerely.

After he hung up Alexis said, "You really care about him, don't you?"

"He's my best friend," he nodded. "Like a brother. And something's been eating at him; whatever the Wolf stole from him, he's desperate to get it back. But there's a *whole* lot more he hasn't told me; I don't know what or why, but I can guarantee that he won't be here twenty-four hours before I find out. How is your mother?"

"She's in her library, unpacking boxes... I think it was mainly to keep her hands and mind busy. She seemed sad, but tried to hide it." Alexis stroked the wooden box. "Shall we?"

They carried the opened box to her bed and settled in comfortably to begin reading silently together:

Anno Domini 800

Darachi lives! I tenderly replanted her roots away from the dangers of the moors, carrying her far up the slopes of Meall Meadhonach and guarding her with stone from hungry deer and wild boar. Her green shoots have grown strong; it remains to be seen whether or not her spirit has survived the trials of fire. Her sapling is now safe near the shelter of my broch where I may tend her, and perchance teach her if she awakens.

Where? Oh where are you, Lover of my Soul? Where are you, my beloved Aradan? I curse the arrow that parted the orb's centre from my necklace even as that heart protected me! In the tumult of battle I did not miss its rhythm until I was far removed from its departure, or if it fell where I first realized it, I could not find it, search though I did for a day and a night.

I must keep this journal now all the more hidden. I praise my Creator for the gift of voice, and the languages of stone and tree, for without this underground passage I would be utterly without true refuge from the harsh wilds I now find myself abandoned in. I must not give up hope. Aradan, my heart calls to you! When will you be able to answer?

"*Aradan* must be the name of her lover," Alexis pointed to the name on the page.

"That's the name I heard up by the old tree... *Aradan*," he repeated it. "Could that be this Darachi, I wonder?"

"Perhaps," Alexis said, "and her sapling... the tree in the courtyard?"

"But it says here that it's near a broch... and there's no broch around here."

They re-read it several times before moving on to the next page, and the next, and the next. There were hundreds of entries, each one more intriguing than the last.

Anno Domini 1140

Will this Man-kind never cease to strive for power? I am forced yet to further inaction by the battles raging around me! My broch must remain a mere broch to escape notice while the chieftains of Caithness and Sutherland fight King Dabid mac Mail Choluim of Rìoghachd na h-Alba, Scotland. Because brochs have at length been abandoned for more fortified structures, my home will be neither threat nor boon to them and thus ignored. These chieftains and kings cannot cease vying for power, killing or plotting; they do not know that their lives are but a breath... that it is appointed for Man to die and then face their true King to give account for their short years on this earth. But while they bicker amongst themselves it is unsafe for me to venture out to sea in search of Aradan, or fortify my home further against their increasingly violent weapons. I must wait yet again, though I may continue my work beneath the earth's surface.

In the interim I have gathered a few young children orphaned by the strife and raise them as my own. It gives me solace to know that they will grow up healthy, strong, and wise. As they grow older they will undoubtedly begin to question who I am; but for now I enjoy the innocence of their youth and solace of their presence. Some of those whom I've raised have moved away to lives of their own; but some have settled in what used to be Maldor with their families to till the land for me, for which I am grateful. I have begun a chronicle of Maldor's inhabitants, for future generations. I can watch over them from my broch, and within it they shall find the safety needed in times of attack, being able to enter safely through a long passage I've made through the earth from the south of Maldor to the roots of my broch, its entrance obscured by the bracken so dominant now.

Anno Domini 1300

This century has been yet another wearying succession of battles, crusades, and pointless death. Will this Man-Kind never learn? Vanity, all is vanity! Yet good kings have also risen, strong enough to fight but also wise enough to cease. I met such a man in 1251, King Haakon Haakonsson of Norway. I sought news of Aradan. Alas, it is impossible to find one man who is, as I am, accustomed to blending in with the current modes of dress and speech and would thus not stand out but for his giftings. I was treated with the utmost dignity while at his court; his queen Margrete is a kindly soul, tender yet passionate in her role as sovereign. She is intelligent, engaging and interesting. Sadly in 1263 Haakon fell ill while wintering in Orkney, and passed from this earth. Their son Magnus ruled and died before the century had passed.

The winter of 1250 saw great and terrible storms upon these isles. Countless lost their lives, rivers shifted course, and there grew a great chill in the air I had not felt for quite some time.

※

Anno Domini 1400

Millions passed from the earth in these generations: The Great Pestilence and famine wiped entire swaths of land clean of the Man-Kind, within twelve moons of its first onslaught in 1348. Those who survived rose up in revolts or wars, clamouring after power when they should have been investing in knowledge to avoid such folly, death and famine in future... In such times, I remain confined to my castle and environs, gaining knowledge and passing it on to those wise enough to learn, and searching for the orb's heart; I know now it is fruitless to search, but it is all I can do at such times to seek my beloved, and thus search I must, or go mad in the helpless waiting.

Anno Domini 1792

Revolution. It singes the winds as hot irons singe straw, and fans the flames of discontent. The inequality of the poor could not be greater in some parts of this world to those who plunder what little they have and live in decadence and callous indifference. The English in the south fear the sparks of Revolution in the Americas alighting on their brittle tinder of servant classes, as they have seen it spark the tinder of abused masses in France. Equality will prove a relentless opponent to oppression, just as it has done in countless generations past. Man-Kind is so very slow to learn.

I have once again returned from my travels which took me along the length of the old Norse trading routes through the Far East, under the protection of my trusted guards, children I have raised to become strong men; by names: Richard the Smaller, Richard the Elder, the brothers John and Thomas of Inverness, Henry and Robert (both of Edinburgh), and William and Edward, whom I found on the streets of London. Our route home was necessarily longer to avoid the troubled areas of the Continent. Home... that word has so many facets, but thus far for me it has always been Loch Earabol, the home of my happy youth.

More than a thousand years has it been since I last saw my beloved Aradan. A thousand years have I searched for the missing centrepiece, the beacon of our hearts. A thousand years have I hoped for, longed for his return... it becomes a taunting disappointment, until I barely dare hope; but I dare not stop, for my heart would break I fear. More than half as long have I ceased to feel his heartbeat, to see him in the visions of the night, though I know not why and it nearly broke my heart when I realized that those transportations had ceased... yet I know he lives. I know. Though I cannot explain how; perhaps it is the hope of him that keeps me alive, that keeps me from sinking into despair. I live for him. But I must lift myself from the bleak night of isolation and seek out those of this generation whom I shall raise as my own, and invest my strength and knowledge into, and my hope of life.

Addendum 1794

I have just returned from London; it is a place of news from abroad from my ships' captains, and a place to purchase those things which cannot be had in the wilds of the north. Trade has been quite profitable despite the wars, and my lands produce abundant grains to sell – my people want for nothing, and crofters often come to my lands seeking a better life than the estates under English Lords from which they have fled. The Highlands suffer as greatly as during the Great Pestilence, though this attack comes by the cruel hands of greed from landowners who care only for their own gain. I fear the Highlands of Scotland will never fully recover from this plague.

Upon our return voyage from London, we made port briefly near Edinburgh as a storm forced us to linger. As I was without occupation I went in search of the foundling hospital: Each generation bears a rare breed of individual that is intelligent and fierce in spirit; those who hunger for truth, justice and knowledge. I found such an orphan boy, born in 1785, and I have given him the name of John Fleming. As his mind is awakened by the world around him I shall train him in the natural sciences. He is adjusting well to the harsh climate of the north, though it is a paradise when compared to the soot-blackened cesspit of Town. Thus far he has been trained all his life to the discipline of the navy and to the reading of his Bible. His disposition lies rather toward the peace of the latter than the violence of the former, tenderness toward human life too profound for the butchery of war. He will do well here, of that I am confident. I foresee him either becoming a minister or a scientist, though one certainly does not exclude the other.

Anno Domini 1851

I've just returned once more from London, and the Great Exhibition. Such a gathering of knowledge! Machinery, scientific devices, wonders from countries throughout the British Empire, all on display and demonstration... I took copious notes. The building so-called the Crystal Palace was a wonder to behold in and of itself. It has given me the inspiration to add a modest version to my own home, for daylight and sun's warmth whilst being protected from the winds. I was fortunate enough to procure a meeting with Sir Joseph Paxton, who was kind enough to accept my request for such a design. He also gave me a list of Scottish craftsmen known to himself who could undertake the task with reliable success. Once the design has been procured, I shall make contact with the workmen.

Addendum 1882

The conservatory is now at last complete. It was delayed as Sir Paxton was greatly sought after in the South, and thus his presence here, long needed for adjustments to his plans due to the bedrock upon which the weight of wrought iron and glass would work against, was too long delayed; he passed from this earth in 1865. I at last managed to procure an apprentice of his, and the work was begun in 1879.

On and on the journal entries went, each one a puzzle piece, a piece of living history. Jon was so absorbed in the reading that he hadn't noticed when Alexis slid down and fell asleep beside him. Light was beginning to relume the deep blue of night as his own head at last dropped to his chest.

4: Hordaland

Once Aradan was taken away, Kjell called for his most trusted men, Sigmund and Vidarr, to come aside with him for counsel.

"You heard his challenge," Kjell began. "What say you?"

"The wager is high: Complete victory or complete defeat," said Vidarr.

"And? Your point?" Kjell said impatiently.

"There must be a catch... may it be in his throat."

Sigmund spoke up. "If he *is* from the gods, will it not be considered ungrateful to return such a gift from them? Even in sacrifice? If he is from Alfheim and we kill him, would they not seek revenge? I would advise against it; I have seen what he can do; I have felt it in my own body!"

"I was unharmed," Kjell pointed out. "Perhaps I am immune; if that's the case, it would be folly not to accept his wager."

Vidarr spoke: "He *must* be sacrificed! Would you go back on your word to me? That if I found a substitute, my son would be spared?"

"Do not question my honour!" Kjell bellowed.

"Never," Vidarr relented. "And therefore this slave will be sacrificed, to allowing my son to remain alive."

"If he dies," reasoned Kjell, "I will have defeated Alfheim." His expression darkened. "But if such beings are defeatable by man... why do we sacrifice?"

Such reasoning was lost on Vidarr, but Sigmund understood: It would defeat the very purpose of the Leirvik Nines if this slave died – *if* he was what he claimed to be. On the other hand, if he lived Kjell would have to relinquish his claims to the lands on which Oyarike stood, and whatever other demands they made.

"Alfheim is not Aasgard," Vidarr mumbled.

"What?" Kjell glared.

"Aasgard may be pleased with your sacrifice, that's all. Alfheim is not Aasgard."

"But you heard what he'd said," Sigmund reminded Vidarr of their first encounter with Aradan. "He'd been sent to make peace between Oyarike and ourselves by Alfheim *and* Aasgard. If he survives... that peace will be realized."

"Then it is right that he is sacrificed, and not my son," agreed Vidarr readily. "If he is defeated, defeat of Oyarike will be within reach before winter."

"How could such a powerful being be a slave?" asked Kjell, looking toward the door through which Aradan had left.

"Does not even Odin disguise himself among men?" Sigmund replied.

"Are you saying then, that I should not accept his wager?"

Sigmund suggested, "If Aasgard wishes peace between us, we would be unwise to ignore the wager, which requires that we hand him over for sacrifice... if he truly is from Alfheim, sent to bring peace, that is."

Vidarr added cunningly, "If he dies, he's no god and we have therefore pleased the gods with our sacrifice; if he lives, we have not killed a god, but merely tested him, and can then live in peace with Oyarike at his terms." Not that he expected anything of the sort; that went without saying.

Kjell weighed his choice.

Aradan sat next to the fire, gazing into the flames. The orb beneath his tunic beat peacefully, comforting him with Erlina's presence. He knew that she felt his heartbeat as well, and prayed that she would not be distressed by what was to come. He closed his eyes, breathing in the memory of her fragrance, walking down the tunnel in his mind's eye to the Sacred Pools: She sat between the pools upon the stone seat, humming as she twirled a young leaf between her fingers, holding it aloft for the sun to shine through it. The sound of her voice echoed as a sweet refrain in his heart, breathing strength into him. She carried the leaf high up the flanks of Meall Meadhonach, and he followed. She planted it, and it began to grow into a sapling as she sang.

Aradan was suddenly ripped back to the present when the door burst open and crashed against the wooden wall behind the door frame. Kjell strode toward him and grabbed fistfuls of tunic, dragging him to his feet.

"Whatever you are," he growled, "I accept your wager!" He released Aradan, standing toe to toe glaring at him, before turning and stalking away.

Once again alone, Aradan blinked as he realized what had just happened. But try as he might, he could not recapture the moment with Erlina again that night.

༄

As dawn broke, a large group set out from Kjellsfjorden for Leirvik, three ships laden with wives, children, provisions for the festivities, and warriors. Arriving in the area of Leirvik, Aradan looked out upon more ships than he'd ever seen assembled in one place: Sleek, dragon-headed ships of every shape and size lined the port, overflowing into the fjord and along the coast... truly an imposing force, invincible should they be called upon to serve a king united. Supplies were unloaded with most passengers before the ships were sailed to anchor somewhere up the coast. The festive mood animated the crowds jostling along the port and the road that led toward what had once been a large, verdant field of wild flowers before the horde had descended upon it; now it was not much more than a muddied patch. Along the edge of the field and spread out through the adjacent forest were makeshift shelters, tents of hide and branches or logs. A few of the tradesmen had erected tents with an oriental flare of fine cloths and sleek wooden poles. Sights and sounds were an assault on the senses: The aromas of baking bread and roasting meat mingled with horse dung, hides, mead and the travels of men.

The sounds of singing, laughing and shouting echoed through the camps, the clanks of a blacksmith plying his trade, horses neighing, children screaming with delight as they ran around between the legs of men and horses with equal confidence, talking, friends greeting and enemies agreeing to temporary truces – at least until the feast and mead flowed more freely through their veins; it was doubtful that everyone there would return home in the same vigour with which they had arrived. Skalds wandered through the crowds, some with instruments and others with only their voice, willing to compose impromptu skaldic poems for a price.

Vidarr led Aradan, hands bound behind his back, to the masters of the rituals, and handed him over as part of the contribution from Kjellsfjorden. Aradan was placed in a leather tent with the other human sacrifices, eight other men, all either slaves or exchanges like himself; apparently sacrifice to their gods was acceptable as long as it cost them nothing personally. Each man sat alone, quiet and frightened. Aradan grieved for them, but could do nothing to save them this time.

It had become known in Oyarike through their spies that Kjellsfjorden was still well guarded; the numbers left behind from the festivities were troubling, and Torsten was unwilling to leave his settlement exposed by sending a large contingency to Leirvik; so in the end it was decided that Gjurd would lead a small band of man accompanied by Runa (she was an excellent archer and shield-maiden), and

Moriel (by agreement to Aradan). Ragnar volunteered when he found out Moriel was going, and Orjan volunteered to keep his cousin in check; besides those five there were a handful of men interested in either the festivities or revenge on Kjell's men, though preferably both. The ship they took was a small, sleek craft which handled well on the sheltered interior fjords, and anchored easily close to the port between larger vessels.

Upon arriving they set up their camp as close to the forest as possible and left men to guard it. Gjurd, Ragnar and Moriel set out to find the captives' tent. As Moriel walked through the crowd one could hear the collective breath taken by the men in her wake; that she was an incomparable beauty was undeniable; but Gjurd considered her – though he would never say it out of respect for Aradan – rather a beast within the beauty. His discernment had taught him caution where she was concerned, and he'd seen her cause enough trouble between men in their own mead hall to mistrust her in such a crowd. Still, it was his duty to protect her while they were in Leirvik.

"Pull up the hood of your cloak," he growled at her for not thinking of it herself. "You'll get us all killed!"

She slipped the hood of her cloak up, its generous folds hiding enough; but her figure and her seductive saunter was still attracting too much attention; Gjurd was relieved when they reached the masters of the rituals. He asked to visit one of the captives; only after removing his weapons was he allowed to pass, Moriel close by his side, while Ragnar had been relegated to guarding the weapons under watch by the masters to ensure that they did not vanish. Once in the tent, Moriel stood just inside the entrance and allowed Gjurd to speak with Aradan alone so that he would give her the same courtesy thereafter.

"Gjurd!" Aradan called when he saw his friend enter the tent. "What are you doing here?"

"A fine greeting for your rescuer," he whispered with a grin. "Are they treating you well enough?"

"They leave us in peace, if that is what you mean. Otherwise I find the question in bad taste."

Gjurd smiled apologetically at the irony. He sat down on his haunches to talk. "As my father promised, I will take you down as soon as it is possible," he looked around to make sure no one else could hear. "If you give the word, I'll free you tonight... before it is too late."

"You cannot. I have a wager with Kjell that I do not wish to lose."

Gjurd stared at him incredulously. "How? You will be dead in a few days! Why would he wager against a dead man?"

"I'm not dead yet," Aradan grinned in mock offense. "Besides, I made him an offer he couldn't refuse."

"Does this mean we can't attack his party when they're drunk?"

"That's what it means... among other things," Aradan said sternly.

Gjurd leaned back on his haunches. "You know how to take the fun out of a festival." He looked at Aradan a moment. He lowered his voice to a breath again, knowing by experience that Aradan could easily hear him. "My father said something to me about—that you cannot die. Is that true?"

"Yes, and no. I will not die by the rope, if that is what you mean."

Gjurd looked at him to assure himself that Aradan wasn't merely trying to spare his grief. He saw sincerity in his tutor's eyes. "I don't know how... but I'm relieved to hear it. I'll not wait a breath longer than necessary to take you down!"

"Thank you, my friend."

Gjurd nodded toward Moriel, who approached. "Someone wants to speak with you. Goodbye, my friend." He stood up and left the tent to await Moriel outside.

"Moriel," Aradan nodded his greeting as she glided toward him, and then said in their tongue, "Thank you for coming."

"Of course," she bent down to caress his cheek; he could not pull away. "I would never leave you to suffer at the hands of these mortals!"

"Have you seen the place they will hang us?"

"I have... a small copse to the west of the clearing. It's obvious, as it is guarded against people setting up their camps there. I will watch tomorrow and see where it is best to position myself for your direct line of sight."

"Thank you," he said darkly.

"What is it?"

"You do realize that in so glib a description of your plans, you've spoken of the death of one of these men tomorrow?" he glanced toward them; they had been listening to the strange, lilting tongue none the wiser for it.

"And what of it? They are mortals," she shrugged; "mortals die."

"They are still unique beings of value," he looked at her, disappointed by her attitudes. "Could you not ease their pain? If you would, it would help ease my own... if it is all I – *we* – can do for them, at least it's something."

She looked from him to the line of men, some quite young, all scared but resigned to their fate. She sighed, "Oh, very well... for you." She walked along before the men to be hanged. "Heed me now," she spoke in their tongue. "When you approach the copse on your appointed day, look for my face in the crowd. Keep your eyes on mine, and you will die with ease."

"Are you... a *Valkyrie?*" one of the young men asked, mesmerized by her beauty.

She thought about that a moment, smiling at the thought. "What do you think?"

"But—" another sputtered, "we are to be *hanged*! We will not have the chance to die in battle! How could you choose from among us?" Would they be so lucky as to see Valhalla before the next moon?

At that another man kicked his leg, shaking his head as if to say *'Never look a gift horse in the mouth, especially from a Valkyrie.'*

"I shall choose one a day from among you... in honour of these festivities," she smiled sweetly. At that every man there thought himself the luckiest man at the festival. Aradan was grateful to her for that; she could be kind when she chose to be.

At that she bent down and kissed Aradan on the cheek, then winked at him as she ran from the tent at her natural speed, though to the mortal eye it had looked as if she had vanished into thin air.

They gasped, and began chattering excitedly amongst themselves, glancing at Aradan in wonder. Indeed, they wondered if they might even be sitting in the presence of Odin himself, for everyone knew that the Valkyrie did his bidding, and he had spoken with her in their strange tongue. At least it gave them hope in the face of certain death. Aradan smiled sadly to himself.

Outside of the tent Moriel went to the masters of the rituals. She smiled demurely, "You have such important tasks at these magnificent festivities." They looked into her eyes, and were to be had. "I would so wish to stand at a convenient place for the hangings... to look into their eyes as they perchance meet Odin himself! And," she gestured toward Ragnar in the distance, which pleased him to think she was speaking about him to these men, "do you see that whelp there? He will not stop following me, poor thing... I would be glad for an excuse to be separated from him." It was swiftly arranged for her to have a place of honour, wherever she chose, if one place were not convenient she could move about freely to find a place more suitable, of course, with pleasure, at your service beautiful lady, and no man would dare harass her under their watchful eyes.

As the three walked back toward their camp Gjurd whispered to Moriel, "What was that all about?"

"Just a gift for Aradan," she said simply. Ragnar had come up beside her. "Oh dear, I'm afraid I shall not be able to stand by your side at the rituals, Ragnar," she demurred. "I have been asked to take a seat of honour, and they would not extend the invitation to you no matter how I pleaded." She laughed to herself at his dejection; it really was his own fault for over-reaching his grasp. She would never accept his advances, but he was just so much pleasure to toy with that she couldn't help herself.

From the masters of rituals she learned that Aradan was to be hung on the final evening, by special request of Vidarr – no doubt to prolong Aradan's time of anxiety. She fulfilled her word to Aradan and eased the passing of the other victims each sunset; her compensation for doing so was that it was a dull affair for the crowd as those hanged barely twitched, and so feasting and wagering took more precedence than witnessing the hangings as the days wore on and the nights grew longer and louder with revelry. By the dawn of Aradan's hanging day some camps, of those either from further afield or those who wished to get a jump ahead of their rivals, had already begun to pack up, though many remained for the final throes of festivities. Kjell and his men were among those remaining, to see their wager won. King Flein Hjørson of Hordaland and Rogaland and his entourage was also present; he had another motivation than devotion or mead: He had seen Moriel.

On the evening before his own time Aradan found himself alone in the tent; the last man had been taken, and he now sat listening to the revelries beyond the tent walls. His keen ears could hear each voice distinctly; he'd had little sleep because of it. When this was all over and done, and peace had been established between Kjellsfjorden and Oyarike, he would sleep somewhere quiet... perhaps aboard one of the ships inside the boat-house. He sat down upon the grassy carpet and leaned back against a wooden chest, his hands bound in front. He closed his eyes and tried to focus his tired ears upon the heartbeat of Erlina. The sounds of the camp began to fade away, all but the crackle of a fire. He began to smell peat; he smiled as he opened his eyes and looked around the now-familiar roundhouse. Erlina sat on the ground beside a wooden chest, writing in her codex. He watched her and bathed in her tranquility. She must have sensed him, having become accustomed to that feeling of his presence. She looked up and scanned the room with her eyes.

"Aradan?" she called.

He stepped up beside her. "I love you," was all he could say.

She took the necklace in her hand and kissed the orb, as he also put the orb to his lips; he could almost feel her breath on his mouth, her sweet fragrance enveloping him. It was the closest they would come to each other for some time to come, but he was grateful for that at least.

"Do not be distressed tomorrow... I must endure a hardship, but I will survive it," he whispered to her, hoping she could understand what he spoke though he was never quite sure how much of his *transportations* were real, and how much were only the sensation of comfort from the orb to himself alone.

He heard someone coming; he slipped the orb beneath his tunic once again. It was the servant girl who brought the meals to the men each night, who had witnessed their dwindling numbers. It weighed heavily on her to see such carnage but she had no choice. When she saw only one remaining, and the most handsome of them all, she burst into tears.

"Come here," Aradan said gently, his warm voice inviting. "I will not harm you... but I can help you."

"You?" she sniffed. "Help me? How? You're a dead man!" she began crying again.

"What is your name?"

"Hilde," she replied.

He beckoned her to himself and she came, kneeling before him to give him a bowl of stew and a chunk of dark bread. But instead of taking the stew he surprised her by reaching up and cupping her face between his bound hands; they were powerful hands, but gentle. He drew her to his face, and breathed sweet peace upon her, kissing her forehead. She calmed and sniffed the last of her tears away, her eyelids suddenly feeling heavy. She placed the stew in Aradan's hands as she stood to leave. At the entrance she hesitated, then turned and dashed back to kiss him on the forehead before running from the tent.

That evening Aradan was led through the field to the copse. A chant was spoken by one of the masters of the rituals as Aradan looked around for Moriel; he found her perched regally upon a wooden platform that had been constructed for the convenience of the kings and rulers that attended. The bodies of the eight other men still hung where they had died; they would hang there until the crows had left nothing but bones, if their kinsmen did not brave the wrath of Thor to take them down. They may have been waiting for the camp to be abandoned, should they fear Thor less than the wrath of their pagan rulers.

Aradan was made to stand upon a wooden barrel beneath the branch of a tree; the noose was placed around his neck, tight, but not uncomfortably so. When the signal was given, the barrel was kicked from beneath him; he felt the weight of his body drop, and he tightened his muscles to cushion the blow to his neck. As soon as he had reached the bottom of the rope his eyes scanned for Moriel and found that she had moved from the platform to the grassy edge of the forest. She caught his gaze; he felt light-headed as the weight of his body against his neck began to drain the circulation of blood from his head; he might not die, but he would certainly pass out and have a throbbing headache for a few days. He knew from reports from the servant girl that the victims had taken the length of only four or five songs to die; he must endure it that long before appearing to die also. After that he hoped that people would soon disperse for the final feasting, for he could not appear dead and hold his head erect to gaze on Moriel.

Suddenly he felt something beneath his feet... *someone* supporting his weight. He could not look down, but he was confused: No one would dare attempt rescue of a sacrifice at such a moment! And by the reactions of the crowd, or by the lack thereof, he could tell that they saw nothing amiss in his situation. Was Moriel doing this? He saw by her expression that she was confused as well... she could sense the change in his tension; but she continued to make him forget the pain: His eyes began to lose focus; he tried to find Moriel in the mist, and when she came into focus once again her features had shifted. Her cold blue eyes became warm grey, and her button nose elongated into the perfect shape that was Erlina's. Her round, full cheeks became slender, and before him stood his love. He saw through her gaze the stars of the heavens, hearing her whisper a song of rest in their tongue. It was Erlina's voice. Or nearly. In spite of the ordeal he smiled. But whoever stood beneath him bore the brunt of his pain and weight; he realized that the crowds and revelry were farther away now than they'd been in the last nine days; it was quieter here, and not that uncomfortable now. He felt his limbs going limp in the throes of drowsiness. In the strangest possible moment he was at last able to nod off to sleep, and it even added to the pretence of dying.

"I've never seen anything like it," Gjurd shook his head in wonder, laughing. "He's asleep!" He had put his head to Aradan's chest to listen for a heartbeat after they had taken his body down and carried him inside their shelter, laying him on a bed of furs; it had been some time before they were able to get to his body to take it down, as the final day of sacrifices meant more speeches and songs.

The red marks from the coarse rope were clearly visible about Aradan's neck, but he was alive; his heart beat slow and rhythmically, as when one sleeps. Suddenly Aradan sighed contentedly, turning onto his side and shifting his arm beneath his head more comfortably. The group of men just stared at him, nonplussed.

"Let's leave him to sleep," smiled Runa. "He's had a full day."

Gjurd laughed quietly at the irony, and motioned for everyone to leave the shelter. "We'll leave him to it, then. Orjan, you stand guard over the camp first; you'll be relieved in plenty of time for revelry."

"Has anyone seen Moriel?" Ragnar asked, suddenly anxious at the thought of her unprotected in such a crowd.

They all looked around. Gjurd growled, "We split up! Orjan, you stay here. Whoever finds her, signal with two short blasts of the horn... if we can hear it above the noise, we'll meet back here; otherwise, meet back here after one circuit of the camp!"

They went off in pairs throughout the camp looking for Moriel. As soon as they were gone Orjan felt a gust of dusty breeze against his beard, but thought nothing of it.

Moriel had waited until the party split up to search for her. She had something to accomplish before they returned and while Aradan slept the deep sleep of her song. She entered the tent undetected, as fast as the wind. She watched him a moment; he was unaware of her presence. It was convenient though not as much fun.

She bent down over him and whispered in his ear in their tongue, "You would not play with me. You refused to love me in return... instead you love the very one who is the cause of all my grief! So I shall leave you... I shall find her... I shall hound her relentlessly... and make her life miserable!" She kissed him tenderly on the lips, adding, "One day you will love me as I love you! And to ensure that you seek me... I'll take *this* as a keepsake." She slipped the necklace from about his neck, slipping it around her own and tucking the orb between her breasts. When she had taken it from his neck it had seemed as light as a feather; but when it was around her own neck she began to realize how heavy it was; that such a delicate chain could hold its weight without snapping surprised her, and so she realized that the chain must have also come from Aquillis. She kissed him once more, whispering, "Goodbye," and slipped from the tent as swiftly as she had come.

Having left the Oyarike camp, she realized that she had no specific plan; that she would flee was clear; but to where? With Aradan was the only place she'd ever longed to be. And if he insisted on protecting his precious integrity he would be unwilling to pursue her; she growled at his stubbornness. If she returned to Oyarike, he would try to take back the necklace, which might prove to be diverting, and could perhaps play to her advantage in keeping him focused on her, even if it were in initial mistrust. To find Erlina she would need to get to Maldor; but travelling alone with a ship full of men would be dangerous even for her – she could not control so many at once. She could always find another *puppy*... a large one who could control men enough to do her bidding. She began to look around through the crowd contemplating her options. Suddenly she heard quick footsteps behind her. Everything went dark.

"Well, good riddance, and I think many would breathe the same," Torsten whispered as Gjurd brought news of Moriel's disappearance.

"Aradan is not taking it well; he's been quite distracted since it happened," Gjurd replied.

"If he's now decided he's ready to settle with her, he's a bit late!"

"I don't think that's it; she helped him while he was hanging, somehow... and he never had a chance to thank her. We searched the area for two days, but there was no sign of her."

"Oh. That is unfortunate. But if, as you have told me, he's made a wager with Kjell, we must move swiftly; for if Kjell thinks he's won this wager he'll be on the move to swoop down upon us before the next moon." Torsten did not at first know how to react to such good news; for so long the two islands had been at odds with each other. There had been so much sour blood spilt between them, he was not sure how lasting a peace there could truly be.

Wulf and his crew had come to the aid of his cousin; when they'd arrived and heard what had transpired they decided to stay and help Torsten secure the peace once and for all, either with or against Kjell. Aradan could barely think of anything else than finding Moriel and reclaiming his stolen necklace; but more pressing matters were now upon them.

The council was gathered and the conditions for peace were agreed upon as soon as they had learned of the wager that had been won before they even knew about it; they were deemed fair by Oyarike but it remained to be seen if Kjell would find the conditions fair enough: Kjell was to relinquish all rights to the island of Store Sotra, upon which Oyarike and its allied settlements stood; neither he nor his people could ever set foot upon the island again except in peace, coming and leaving in that same peace, as Oyarike agreed to the same terms as regards Kjellsfjorden. It was not only to be an absence of hostility, but a peaceful cooperation: Oyarike would sell them shipbuilding skills, and Kjell would sell them horses and sheep whenever they were in need; both would do so at a fair price. They were to become allies in battle, coming to the aid of one another to unite against outside enemies; to that end posts were to be established within a horn's sound of each other, stretching from Kjellsfjorden to Store Sotra. When the terms had been written, Wulf and his crew accompanied Aradan and Torgil along with a few strong men to Kjellsfjorden.

Had a Skald been present there would have been an epic skaldic poem written concerning the consternation written upon Kjell's face when the delegation was ushered into his mead hall; Vidarr would have supplied a second stanza. Kjell had assumed they'd come as those defeated by the death of a slave, and was utterly unprepared for what followed.

One of the guards at the fortress gate had come in ahead of the group to announce them (his ashen-white face should have told them *something*), and Kjell had set himself handsomely upon his fur-covered throne to receive their homage. The first face to enter, he recognized as the elder son of Torsten; not known for his prowess in battle. Just behind the young man was someone he could not yet see, and following them were men obviously sent as guard dogs. Then Aradan stepped forth from behind Torgil. Kjell and Vidarr had both watched him hang, and their eyes grew round and their faces pale as if seeing a ghost.

Vidarr pointed his finger at Aradan, shaking it. "What kind of trickery is this! He could not be the same man we saw hang! It is a foul trick!"

Murmurs went through the crowd gathered; had it been Gjurd instead of Torgil standing there, there would have been bloodshed at the provocation – which may have explained the wise choice of the delegate. Torgil stepped forward. "You dare accuse us of trickery? Do you dare question our honour when we stand before you in your mead hall in peace? We know of your wager with this man; he has come with our terms." He may not be strong in body, but Torgil was strong in spirit.

Aradan stepped forward and opened his cloak to show the rope's marks around his neck, which he had left there for that very purpose. "Is this trickery?" he asked. "Come, Kjell... examine the wound. It is *your* honour at stake, not mine."

Vidarr drew his axe and raised his arm to take aim, but Kjell held him back. "No! I have made the wager; I will examine the evidence." He came to Aradan and felt the bruising and saw the cuts from the hemp rope. "How do I know this was not made some other time?" Aradan could see the doubt in Kjell's eyes as he grasped at straws to save his kingdom from whatever terms Oyarike would surely demand.

Aradan said, "Watch." He called Sigmund to join Kjell as witness, along with Wulf and one of his largest men, and as they all watched, Aradan's wounds healed before their eyes. Kjell and Sigmund fell to their knees in abject fear... fear of the revenge to be exacted on them by the gods for having handed over one of them to be killed, and fear of this man before whom they knelt. But Aradan reached out and took their arms, pulling them to their feet; they flinched when he touched them though nothing harmed them. "We have come to make peace," he assured them. "Will you hear our terms?"

They were surprisingly receptive.

That evening the delegates feasted with Kjell and his village, as many as could fit into the mead hall. Many had come to catch a glimpse of the stranger who could not die; many of the women had heard him the most handsome among men, and had come not only to see him and perhaps catch his eye, but they had been told to do so; if Kjell could secure Aradan to himself through a marriage so much the better. Kjell's daughters were instructed to entertain Torgil; a marriage there would solidify the treaty (he would not have allowed any of his own daughters to marry a former slave, no matter who he was; it would have been an insult to their status). When mead had flowed freely and inhibition gave way to revelries, Sigmund dared approach Aradan. He swayed slightly, having built up the courage by gazing deeply into the mead barrel.

Aradan watched him a moment waiting for him to speak, but he seemed to have forgotten a speech he'd planned and was searching the rafters for it. Aradan laughed, "Sit, Sigmund... before you fall."

Men on either side of his chosen place on the bench opposite Aradan gave way as the massive brawn fell into the gap. Aradan waited for him to say what he'd come to say. "Peace?" was all he came up with.

"Peace," Aradan nodded.

The bulk of a man let out a sigh and a belch and an apology, all in one breath. "I didn't want you to hang... but Vidarr would not lose his son," he slurred. "I knew you were m-more than... m-more... you know what I mean. Thank you, by the way... for sssparing my life when we attacked Oyarike... you could have easssily killed me, I think."

"You're welcome," Aradan grinned at the drunken confession.

"When I saw your kinswoman at the festival I was convinced... you're both gods... or you should be." He thought about that a moment and grinned, "Maybe we've all died, and this is really Valhalla!" He waved his mead mug through the air in celebration, sloshing mead onto the man next to him; that man punched Sigmund in the arm for it and went back to his meal.

"How do you know she was my kinswoman? We look nothing alike."

"You *do*," he corrected, raising a finger and gradually bringing it to point at Aradan. "You're both... well, she wasss a sssight to behold and I think the women here think that abou' you," he leaned in to whisper with a waft. "But I saw her leave the prisoner's tent with Gjurd, and knew she was not of their sssettlement... so I knew she must have come with *you*."

"You are observant," Aradan smiled indulgently.

"She made a poor choiccce, though," he took a deep swig, shaking his head as he drank slowly.

"What do you mean?"

"She was not wisssse to go out unprotected. Flein had been watching her for daysss," he looked at Aradan knowingly.

"Sigmund, explain it plainly! Did this Flein take her?"

"*King* Flein Hjørson of Hordaland and Rogaland," explained Sigmund with a belch, "I saw his men following her. I heard later that your people had been searching for her... you'll probably find her at

Avaldsnes." Suddenly Sigmund found himself smiling at nothing; Aradan had vanished like the wind.

"Wulf!" Aradan caught Wulf's arm as he was dipping a beaker into the mead barrel. "Would you take me to Avaldsnes?"

"What?"

"Avaldsnes... do you know how to get there?"

"Of course I do! He's our king. But why would you want to get there? Don't you like it at Oyarike?"

Aradan explained what Sigmund had told him. "I've got to find her!"

Wulf thought about it. "I'll take you... on condition that Torsten gives his blessing to it."

Three days later Aradan was on his way to Avaldsnes. The delegation had returned to Oyarike along with Kjell and his men, Vidarr and Sigmund, and once Aradan had Torsten's consent to leave on his mission and return, it was decided that Wulf and his men would transport Aradan, Gjurd and Sigmund, together with goods to sell as to make the journey worth their while. Sigmund had been to Avaldsnes on many occasions, and knew the lay of the town well. He knew King Flein Hjørson as one of his Vikings, but knew him better by reputation; he would take the king word of their treaty with Store Sotra with Gjurd as witness, and enquire as to the missing Moriel – depending on the mood of the king. On the journey Sigmund drew a map of the settlement for Aradan, and told him where Moriel might be located, though there was no certainty of it. Aradan had been given instructions by Torsten to avoid meeting the king if at all possible: Should he attract attention in any way it may be more difficult to leave the king's court than to enter it, as he was always looking for good men for his warbands; one couldn't refuse the king and expect to leave unscathed.

The weather was fine, the breeze from the water crisp. Aradan went to stand beside Wulf at the tiller, gazing out to sea in peaceful silence.

"I am sorry to have caused you grief," Wulf blurted out. "The first time you and I stood on this ship... circumstances were much different."

Aradan nodded. "My greatest regret is that I am separated from my betrothed."

"Is she..." Wulf hesitated, "alive?"

Aradan looked at him; it was an odd question to ask a man who'd been taken captive, dragged aboard unconscious. But the look in Wulf's eyes told Aradan that he believed him to be more than a mere man, and thus the question. "Yes."

"Is she... there?" he waved toward the west, "Where we took you?"

"Nearby."

"If I could, I'd take you back. But I won't go against my cousin," he warned.

"But when I am free to leave... would you then?"

"In a heartbeat," Wulf grinned. "I owe you the life of my son."

Aradan explained the nature of his connection to Moriel and why he must find her so urgently. Wulf had heard of the trouble she'd stirred up in Oyarike, and his cousin had made it plain that they were in no great hurry to have her returned to them; he was to enquire, but not provoke the king... if the king volunteered information concerning Moriel, then so be it. If not... who were they to challenge the king of Hordaland and Rogaland?

Aradan explained briefly of Moriel's ability over men; and the burly Viking, surprisingly astute, simply replied, "Then don't look her in the eyes. Look *through* her... like when you daydream and don't look *at* someone? She might not be the wiser for it, and it might be enough to avoid her power."

He thought about it a moment. "Have you ever tried to *not* look into the eyes of someone you are angry at? To see their souls? Or not to look into the eyes of a beautiful woman? It will take every part of my concentration not to do that which is instinctual... to seek out that connection with another being. But it might just work."

They sailed into the cove on the north side of the island, though they were challenged to state their business before proceeding landward. Once in port with the goods, Aradan slipped ashore and disappeared into the forest to the east of the cove.

That first night Moriel had found herself thrown over a shoulder, dumped into a ship like a bag of wheat, and eventually dumped into a stone-and-daub room. When at last the hood had been removed from her head she saw that her jailer was not a man but an old woman; she learned that she'd been given into the watch of an old maid of King Hjørson, on the small island of Körmt. She'd also learned that this maid happened to be nearly blind; without the power of persuasion Moriel could do nothing but wait for a suitable moment. Her prison was rather a simply-furnished room; it stood alone as a small building, and nearby she could hear the clank of a blacksmith's hammer. Her hands were still bound behind her back, but she stood and walked to the nearby window, a narrow slat near the eye-level top of the outer wall. Through it she saw longhouses, a kitchen house, and stables, and near the water's edge a massive *leidang*, or boat-house, which was much larger than the one at Oyarike though similar in design.

Seven days passed; the king had come to visit her. He seemed to think he could woo her while keeping her imprisoned. But when she had come close to escaping on the third night by her giftings overpowering the king's own senses, the old maid had surprised Moriel by locking both the king and herself in the prison cell while she called for help. The king, though at first furious with the old maid, had soon realized her value; he agreed to leave Moriel's hands tied until she could be trusted. She would soon see reason and appreciate the advances he made to her. The old maid had grumbled at Moriel one day when both women were being especially stubborn, that the king had never intended to keep her prisoner in the first place when he'd had her abducted; he'd never have dreamt that Moriel would *not want* to be his mistress – no one had ever refused him before.

Finding Moriel would not be that difficult for Aradan; keen Elven hearing would serve to call and be called. Aradan stood just inside the darkness of the forest and could see several longhouses and several smaller buildings on his side of the town; between himself and the closest building were several rows of wooden stakes strung together with slender hemp rope, some hung with linen clothes drying, some others with fishing nets. He called out Moriel's name, a whisper on the wind.

Moriel sat up. Had she heard rightly? Yes – there it was again! He'd come to rescue her! "Aradan!" she whispered in return. "Here I am!"

"Hum a song, that I may find you!"

She hummed, her heart beating more alive than it had in days. Aradan was coming for her! He was coming to rescue her! He really did care! She heard him, as only she could, coming across the field from the forest to the town. As he drew nearer, the necklace began to weigh more heavily; or perhaps she only imagined it as her own anticipation swelled.

At last she heard him just outside her room; she heard him breathe sweet dreams upon the old maid sitting watch, then heard the gentle *thump* of the woman's head resting back against the wall just outside her door. A swift flick of the wooden bar that secured the door, and there he stood!

Aradan looked at Moriel and hesitated; that she would still be bound had not occurred to him. He focused on her neck rather than her face as he entered, shutting the door behind him silently. "Greetings, Moriel," he said coldly, in the distant tongue of Oyarike and not their own mother tongue. She was shocked. *Why was he here, if not for her?* The necklace. She instinctively glanced down to see that it was hidden. "Why?" There was hurt in his voice, disappointment and reproach. "How could you steal something from me? Do I mean nothing to you?" That rebuke stung deeply.

"Aradan..." she spoke softly, looking at his eyes. But his expression did not soften. That she must explain her actions to anyone had never occurred to her as it had never been necessary before. She thought quickly. "You—" she hesitated, began again: "I realized that you did not yet... love me. I felt lonely," she sighed, trying to catch his gaze. "I've been lonely for so many years, and I longed for you... and still you would not flee with me to find our happiness together in freedom! And so I decided to leave if you did not want me... but I... I wanted a keepsake of yours to remember you by."

"And so you waited until I was defenceless to steal from me that which you knew was a gift from my grandfather!" Incredulity blazed in his eyes, anger at her blatant disregard for honour. "And what is this *love* you speak of? I do not recognize it in such a selfish form!"

She began to weep at his anger toward her; but they were not tears of repentance or sorrow, but of regret at being caught, of impetuous self-pity.

"Moriel," Aradan's voice softened, but he came no nearer, "love is patient and kind; it does not seek for its own good, or grasp that which is not its own, or try to manipulate to its own goals. What you speak of is lust, not love: Lust for power, for possession, for success... for control."

Her tears ceased as she realized what he said was true, at least to him; but that understanding alone was not enough to change her heart or her desires; it simply made her purpose clearer. "Have you come to rescue me or not?" she whispered, looking intently at him. *Why was it not working? Had he learned how to undo her gifting? To heal himself of her influence?*

"Some of our party are speaking to the king on your behalf," was all he would say. That she was unwelcome in Oyarike if she were freed was left unsaid; perhaps it would be unnecessary. "But in the interim..." he stepped up to her and slipped the necklace from about her neck, slipping it back around his own. He sighed with more relief than she thought necessary for a mere trinket, even if it were an heirloom. She could do nothing to prevent it with neither freed hands nor influence over him, and she pouted.

He kissed the orb tenderly before slipping it into his tunic, then stepped away once more and turned to look through the window slot. "Gjurd is enquiring of the king about you. How were you taken?"

She told him how it had happened, and added that the king had been in to see her several times since she'd arrived.

"To see you?" he turned his head toward her slightly. "With honourable intentions?"

"He has made it plain that he wishes to win my attentions. He seems to want it voluntarily and has kidnapped me to that end," she scoffed. "He thinks he will soften my resolve through his visits. But he is no more tempting to me than a wild beast would be!"

"Have a care, Moriel," Aradan warned. "He is powerful; if you offend him it may go ill for you. Would you not wish to be queen?" he tried to soothe her anger.

She laughed bitterly at his naivety. "You still think his intentions are honourable, don't you? He has never intended to wed me! Merely to bed me!" her eyes flashed deep blue, darker than ever before. He looked away before she caught his gaze.

That grieved Aradan for her but he could not set her free; he could no longer trust her. "If he agrees to free you... where will you go?" The implication was clear: Not Oyarike.

She ignored the insinuation. "Perhaps I shall return to Maldor to see what is left... and *who*."

In his innocence he had once hoped she would; but now that he knew her character better he hoped she would not. "Or you could take the opportunity to see the world," he countered. "There is so much of it to see... you've only seen a small region of its northern sector."

"If you're so anxious to see it, why don't *you* go?" she nearly growled, but she still needed to maintain a semblance of innocence if she still wished to be freed.

"You know I cannot," he replied calmly.

"But you've served more faithfully than any mortal man could!" she pleaded one last time for reason.

"But as you're so fond of recalling... I am not a mortal man."

Yes, yes, his integrity was his to keep, blah, blah, blah. She was bored with such superiority. She said nothing.

"I must return to our ship to await news as to whether or not we can free you."

"*Waen shelaen mannan wiedar?*" she whispered plaintively.

He hesitated. "I cannot say when we shall see each other again." He turned to her, searching her face in disappointment, but still he would not look into her eyes. "I wish you well, Moriel. I hope you will learn to appreciate humanity... that you will find love with a soulmate as I have found mine." He came toward her suddenly and kissed her on the forehead. "*Govad nir Eru vaer.* Goodbye."

His whisper still lingered in her hair as the gust of wind at his parting broke upon her cheeks. Her pale blue eyes blazed dark blue with unrequited love and anger, fire and ice. "I shall reclaim your precious heirloom... then you will have no choice but to pursue me!" she seethed, "I'll not give up my hope of conquest so easily!" Tears flowed down her hot cheeks as she whispered, "I'll find you! I'll find *her*! Then I'll wait until you've found each other... and I'll make you both suffer!"

Nothing hath wrath like a woman scorned.

She smouldered at such treatment, at having her plans thwarted, at having been thrust into a damp prison with not so much as a reason. She sat on her straw-filled mattress devising punishments for the king and his men; and she would make him dance like a fool and drool mead into his own lap before the sun set.

5: Mäldor

Anno Domini 801, third calends of Quintilis

Such a strange dream I've had! Or was it a dream? I found myself, in those moments between waking and sleeping last night, in a field at the edge of a forest. Nearby the trees were hung with corpses – men, along with dogs, roosters, rams and other animals... there were eight grey faces of the Man-Kind; but the ninth, the most beautiful ever beheld in my sight, was my Beloved! I ran to him. A rope of coarse hemp dug into his perfect neck; I could not lift it from him, and so I stood bent beneath him, supporting his weight with the strength of my back. I stood that way, unable to look into his eyes... I know not how long I stood thus, but I would have done so an eternity if needed. When darkness had crept over the landscape, I saw someone come to stand before me... a young man with blonde hair and a thick beard, one of the Northmen. He took the weight of Aradan upon his shoulders and I stood aside to watch: There was a small group of men with him, and a woman with arrow drawn to bow and *standing guard; they lifted him up and slipped the rope from his neck; he fell lifeless into their arms, but I could feel the orb's heartbeat; he was merely asleep, but it was a deep, unnatural sleep – I felt something sinister about it. I awoke in that moment, my face drenched with tears. What could it mean?*

Not a moon had passed since Niallan had chosen exile, before Angus followed them to Maldor. Angus had remained with the clan to reason with his mother, to at least attempt to bring about peace between mother and son; but she was far too stubborn and bitter at what she saw as a personal defeat against herself by a slave. Not three nights after that final confrontation Hafgan had moved his family to the chieftain's longhouse; cantankerous brother, rowdy nephews and two irritable women under one roof were more than Angus could bear. He packed his belongings one morning and left without so much as a word; he knew they'd guess where he'd gone, and he didn't care. If they came after him, they risked war; but Hafgan's men were too busy watching their lands' southern borders as rumours of Northmen had reached them by a survivor from a settlement further south.

Caitrin grew strong under Erlina's care, and her belly grew fat and round. Niallan was unwilling to be away when the baby was so close to arriving, though he at times needed to leave the broch's environs for hunting or to tend their animals. But babies come when they have a mind to and not a moment sooner.

Angus had left Niallan in the forest tending their animals to fetch an axe at the broch; as he was approaching, he heard a woman scream. He rushed to the broch, sword in hand and shield at the ready; but his manly courage had never prepared him for the sight he found within, the vulnerability and carnage of birth. He'd retreated faster than he'd stormed in and overthrew his stomach as far from the entrance as possible, and ran after Niallan. When they'd returned, this time prepared for the carnage, they found a different scene before them (once they were allowed inside): Caitrin had left the birthing stool and was lying comfortably in a bed box, while Erlina held the newborn in a basin of warm water, washing him and then massaging his skin gently with sea salt that she had gathered for that very purpose. She wrapped him in a cloth, laying him in Caitrin's outstretched arms. A son had been born, strapping and healthy, with a head of bushy red hair.

Caitrin held up her hand to Niallan, and he came cautiously to her bedside, kneeling on the floor, while Angus hovered nearby.

"The most beautiful wee thing I've e'er seen," Niallan whispered, his eyes flitting in wonder from his son to his wife. "He's got his mother's looks about him."

Erlina revelled in the scene of happiness before her, and yet she marvelled: It was truly a miracle when a woman of the Man-Kind survived such an ordeal... bringing forth a life with so much pain and blood. Her own Kind had a far different experience, untainted by pain, the curse of the Fall: Their own births were serene celebrations, the babe coming forth with ease, the mother rested and refreshed by the new life.

Caitrin shifted the baby gently to Niallan's awkward arms. "What shall we call him?" she asked.

"I haven't given it any thought," he confessed, unable to take his gaze from his son.

"I'd like tae call him Alistair," she said, "...after a brother I lost."

"Alistair," he repeated, smiling. "Aye, that's a fine name."

Angus was given his turn to hold his nephew, and he was just as taken with the wee lad as if he'd been his own.

That evening the four ate a stew of rabbit, dulse, herbs and wild peas. Caitrin had brewed a fine ale earlier in the season, and they enjoyed it in the tranquillity that they had come to cherish in their new home. Angus looked at his nephew, nursing on Caitrin's lap.

"Should Mother be informed, do ye think?" Angus asked. "She is after all a grandmother once more."

"Ye *know* what she'll say," Niallan replied coldly. "She's made her choice; we've made ours. I'll not give her cause tae curse ma' wife or bairn at her leisure."

They knew he was right. They were as good as dead to Iona.

Three winters after the birth of Alistair, his sister Aina was born.

Spring was always a time of raids, as Northmen's ships sailed from their winter harbours in search of the spoils of war, treasures and slaves to sell in the east. As the years passed the raiders that had harried the Orkney Isles sought more territory further south, eventually bringing their families to stay.

One bright spring day Niallan and Angus were sitting in front of the broch cleaning freshly killed rabbits to smoke; Alistair played on the ground nearby with a wooden toy his father had carved, and Aina slept peacefully on a sheepskin. Caitrin hummed to herself as she spun wool upon a spindle whorl, while Erlina ground grain for bread in the quern. Suddenly Erlina turned her gaze toward the west, listening intently.

"What is it?" both men jumped up instantly.

Erlina raised her hand for quiet; she then turned to them. "I hear the sound of flames and cries coming from the clan's settlement. And the clash of axes."

"One of us has got to stay here," Niallan stopped Angus as he headed toward a thatched stable near the broch.

"It's too late!" Erlina told them, shaking her head. "It will do no good for you to go."

"We canna *not* go," he told her, both resigned but resolute.

"Then ye stay here and I'll go," Angus said. "Ye've got a family dependin' on ye."

"But *I've* got tae go... tae honour ma' word... tae honour the treaty."

Angus knew his brother well enough to know persuasion wouldn't change his mind on it, so he only nodded.

Niallan went to his children, taking Alistair in his arms and kissing him before handing him to Erlina. He turned to Angus: "Protect them fer me! And get that out of sight," he pointed toward their chariot resting on its shafts in the grass by the stable. Niallan mounted his horse's bare back, and Caitrin rushed to his side as he bent down to kiss her and their daughter, now in her arms. "Keep the children quiet. I'll be back as soon as I'm able, and I'll take no undo risk, I promise ye." He looked to Erlina, who nodded sombrely, knowing more clearly than any of them what awaited him.

Erlina carried Alistair into the broch, humming a sleeping tune as she took him down the stairs into the cave. Caitrin followed with Aina, while Angus hid the chariot on the far side of the hillock before returning. The horse was tethered near the broch in the grassy stable that fairly blended in with the landscape, and the broch's hearth fire was extinguished to avoid smoke giving away their position. In the cave they waited, a shaft of light coming through the smokeless chimney crawling along the floor as time passed. The children slept peacefully on sheepskins, unaware of the anxiety around them.

Erlina knew that Angus was getting restless to do something, to help, to not sit helplessly. She knew the feeling, and so she rose before he could. "Angus... guard Caitrin and the children; do not venture out of the cave until I return."

"But I *canna* stay!" he stood up to join her. "They may need ma' help – or at least I can bring news back – but this waitin'...! I'm done wi' it!"

"*I* shall go as I move far more swiftly," she said, "but I need to know that I can trust you to remain here and protect them until I return. Do I have your word?"

He looked at her, burning to go yet unwilling to disappoint her. He nodded in frustrated resignation.

"Stay hidden," she warned them all. "These are Northmen; and they intend to stay this time."

"How can ye know that?" Caitrin looked at her. She did not doubt it, but she could not believe it either.

"I could hear them speaking on the wind... they've brought their wives and children this time," she replied.

Wide-eyed in horror, Angus looked at Alistair. "If that's the case—" They'd heard enough reports to know that if it were so, there would be no elderly women or males of the clan left alive - or at least not sold into slavery abroad.

Unseen in her grey cloak, Erlina flew as swiftly as an owl toward the settlement, bow and quiver slung across her shoulder. She drew near the clan's broch just inside the forest, listening for sounds of life from within; it was silent. They had had no warning, no time to reach their stronghold. The settlement was strangely calm, and the only faces she saw were strangers to her; they were picking up fallen goods, carrying skins of water from the stream to wash away the blood from their new homes. As she wondered where the slain were, she noticed some of the blonde strangers returning from the path to the cliffs, empty and bloodied carts dragging behind. Her throat tightened as she grieved the clan's loss, but held her breath, listening for the sounds of Niallan; toward the stream she ran as swiftly as a cloud's shadow through forest and field. The strangers were further down the stream collecting water, and she slipped along the forest's edge searching the shadows of the woods until she found him. Barely alive, but breathing, Niallan had escaped to the safety of the trees after having been wounded as he'd ambushed a Northman. Erlina felt his face, cool, his eyes fluttering in sleepless pain. She lifted his tunic and saw a deep gash in his side; he had lost a lot of blood. She pulled him up gently and laid him across her back, praying silently as she carried him home.

The next days were spent in quiet waiting. That first night Erlina had called upon the earth to swallow the well-worn path between the settlement and Maldor and fill it with impassable streams and marsh; their need for it had come to an end, no more to be tread in peace or tranquillity. Caitrin cared for Niallan's wounds, too slight to kill outright yet too deep to survive. He was aware of his passing, and spent his waking moments comforting those closest to his heart. Angus would not leave his side until he could do no more. Two sunsets after the attack, they all sensed that it would be Niallan's last to look upon the earth. He asked to speak to each of them alone: To Angus he gave charge of his family, not as his brother's but as his own. He had been his brother, but more importantly his friend. He warned him to do nothing rash and to stay far away from the Northmen. Had he not charged his brother to make these vows, vengeance would have cost Angus his life before the spring gave way to summer. He told Caitrin of his love for her and their children, and asked her to take comfort in the arms of Angus if she find that she love him; he would never hold such a love against either of them, for what would give him greater pleasure than to know that his beloved wife and children were safe in the hands of such an honourable man?

To Erlina, he asked her to remember her vows to Aradan, and leave the defence of his family to Angus; he also asked her to greet Aradan for him, and tell him of their story and their friendship. He wished them well, and that they find one another soon. But he also admonished her not to waste her vast wisdom and knowledge on the barren coasts of the Scottish Highlands, to wait in her broch for Aradan's return; it was her duty to Man to guide and teach, and to live an exemplary life for others to emulate... he knew she had too much love to leave it dormant. His children were too young to remember him much beyond the summer, and so he kissed them both, giving them into the arms of Caitrin and Angus. He would be the first generation buried away from their clan's cairn; not only was it unsafe to return there, but he chose a new way of passing: He chose to be buried in the Christian fashion, facing east to await the resurrection of the dead at the end of time. They would do so by laying him at the feet of King Elgin and his sons, in a separate cist. A larger cist would be constructed around the two cists, joining them in death as they had been allies in life. He smiled and said he couldn't ask for a more honourable place of rest. He breathed his last as the nagging wind fell, and the sea reflected the billowing clouds glowing golden as the sun sank beyond Meall Meadhonach.

Anno Domini 830

The final tunnel is nearing completion. Its emergence will dictate where the outer walls of my home must eventually be built. I have allowed soil and stone to reclaim that tunnel which led from Mother's throne to the Beach of Erumara. Such memories I have of Erumara… the last place I saw my dearest mother and sister, indeed all of my kinsmen, those many years ago. Fittingly, Erumara means "Heavenward" in Aquillian, though its Gaelic name is "Tràigh Allt Chàilgeag" just as apt to my experience, meaning "the beach with streams of bereavement."

Some fragments of survivors from clans all but annihilated along the western coast have escaped to seek refuge within the stone walls of Maldor, very often children who had been out in the fields or forests when their homes had been attacked. But as seasons come and go, crops and children grow and multiply. Alistair and Aina are now grown and have found spouses in what has become the settlement of Maldor, that which has grown like new shoots from the tree stump that was once my royal home. Caitrin and Angus's other children have grown strong as well, notwithstanding the death of their beloved father following that of their dear mother last winter. I watch them thrive with both pride and sadness, knowing that I must also watch them go the way of all flesh, to age and die, all the while looking to my own, far longer future.

The Broch is now completed, towering several levels high and ready to join to the next structure when the time comes. I must bide my time, and coax stone and earth's aid but patiently. I must also remain unthreatening in size or power to hostile eyes in times of Man-Kind's upheavals. I am not ignorant to the fact that, though immortal, I am seen as a woman, a thing to be captured, owned, mated and bear children. And my undying beauty has become perilous; I must learn to vanish into each coming age. The age of

Elves has passed; I must never be known as an "Other" again.

My heart begs me to stay lest my beloved Aradan returns and finds me not. But that same heart urges me to rest not until I have sought him the width and breadth of this earth. I shall begin along the Northmen's trading routes as soon as I am able to raise a trustworthy crew, as it is probable that such a valuable prize (as Aradan is surely known to be) would be kept in kingly captivity... a gilded cage, but a cage nonetheless. I know this to be true or he would have returned to me by now.

Anno Domini 990

It has now been two hundred years upon this earth since I lost everyone I hold dearest of my own kind. And in these years I have sought the lost Hope, the orb's centrepiece. I will continue to seek it, though the chances of finding it have long overgrown and sunken into the moor. I fear I can only find it once I have reunited with Aradan and our two songs merge to call forth the harmony; but without that piece I am forced to find him by mere chance; t'would be easier finding a single golden blade of grass on the greatest mountain. The more I am forced to inaction in this age of violence and sea dragons from the north, the more restless I become. But my greatest solace is in the night watches: I have often dreamt of him, seen a dwelling where he must surely now be, and I feel his heart beating; I hear his beautiful voice calling my name, and sometimes smell his sweet aroma of fresh lemongrass, warm cloves and cinnamon; I have seen his face, and even felt his breath upon my cheek, the sweetest sensation of all! It is for that reason alone that I live; all other reasons on this earth have vanished. Perhaps he finds solace in such dreams as well, our orbs uniting our spirits; it would be a great comfort to know we share this at least.

Anno Domini 1067

At last stability has come to the kingdoms of this island, in the main at least. The seas are calmer now, the dragons having been tamed by commerce and land, marriage and children. As soon as the weather permits I shall travel to Orkney to beseech the blessing of the jarls in granting me a ship and crew to undertake my search for Aradan; I feel that he was perhaps in one of the great Norman battles further south this autumn just passed; for when news reached me of those terrible events, I realized with dismay that I had ceased to feel his heartbeat around that time. The dreams have ceased; I see him no more in the night watches, and my heart aches anew; I know he lives, though I now have no assurance but his promise. I <u>must</u> seek him out, or wither in useless waiting!

※

One season following another, passing into generations, time flit like a fleeting thought – swift, ungraspable and unstoppable. Angus and Caitrin's descendants grew and went off to seek their fortunes in the world, and eventually married, had children, lived and died, giving way for new generations to grow, live and die for their freedom in the turmoil of the Middle Ages. Erlina took Niallan's words to heart and sought to make a difference in the world beyond the Highlands, though she returned time and again to her home, hoping for the day when Aradan would find her there. She first left the Highlands in AD 1067 when the Isles of Britain began to enjoy relative stability. She sought out those children of each generation whom she sensed would have the character, intelligence and fortitude to unlock treasures in fields of knowledge such as science and culture, history and medicine. And when the time came in each generation for her to pass on her identity to the grave and assume a new one, she would return to Maldor, to tarry, to build, to dwell alone with her memories, and to hope for the return of Aradan.

Impatience is a thing of mortality arising from the inner workings that tell us that time is life drawing death ever nearer; but an immortal knows the future will arrive and may wait more patiently a thousand years than any mortal can wait a thousand breaths.

As time went on she busied her mind with the task of Aquillis: to gather knowledge, to learn and to teach. She began studying and applying techniques that would one day come to be known as archaeology. She continued to record her knowledge as she travelled the world, accumulating close companions from each generation whom she sometimes raised, but always guided and supported, only to let them go to their mortality when the time came. Losing everyone she had ever loved drove her not to guard her heart needlessly, nor to give her heart over to grief or bitterness, but to abandon her heart to the joys of love and friendship, savouring each moment she could. And when she had no choice but release a mortal to the grave she would return to Maldor, her only succour in such times of upheaval.

6: Now

After reading the mysterious journal through the night and into the morning hours, it was noon before Jon dragged himself down to the dining room. He nursed a hot tea while he tried to figure out how much of yesterday had only been a dream and how much had really happened. *The tunnel?* Yeah, he couldn't have imagined that. *The pools? The glowing stones?* There was no explanation for them either, but there they were. *The Cardinal. The journal.* The impossibility of the reality now staring him in the face... it was somehow comforting to know that Alvar was on his way; he had a way of seeing through confusion to get to the crux of a situation.

Brehani came in looking for Toshiro, but when he saw Jon he went to him directly: "We have the go-ahead to open that trench," he smiled. "Do you still want to take part?"

"Of course! When do we start?"

"Right after lunch; dress for mudlarking and meet me in the incident room at 1:30."

On his way back to his room Jon bumped into Toshiro. "I have a shopping list for you," Toshiro held up a sheet of paper. "It's more like an inventory checklist as I've already ordered it... to be picked up as a complete package at the Edinburgh airport when you drop off the Cardinal; they'll have it waiting for you."

Jon took the list and looked it over. "Wow," he whistled, "what do we need twenty metres of blue velvet for? And stretchers – do you plan on injuring people?"

"I don't know," Toshiro shrugged, "I'm just the butler – these are things the Cardinal wants."

"Like that explains a lot," Jon shook his head, reading down the very thorough list.

"And who in the world did you sucker into doing all this shopping for you?"

"Most of it? Online," he just flashed his broad grin.

"You're a pretty handy butler," Jon said sarcastically, "let me know when you're up for hire."

"Wow... hired on the basis of being able to do things a monkey could do... I'm flattered."

"Hey, don't diss monkeys... they take years of training."

Toshiro tried not to smile and nearly managed. He then frowned and said, "Hey, I know you like practical jokes... but stop scaring the women, okay? Pick on the guys if you have to. And quit rearranging our office – I have enough to do!"

"What are you talking about?"

Toshiro scoffed, "You know what I mean."

"No, really. I don't."

The butler studied his face a moment. "It's not you, seriously? Someone has been moving things around in my office, and in the storage room downstairs during the night – so I thought it must be you as you're only one of two staying here in the castle... and I know it isn't Edric as I've— I've been keeping an eye on him."

"And what was that about the women? Which women?"

"Down at the caravans; things keep going missing, showing up somewhere else entirely, clothes in the mud, dishes broken outside that had never been outside. Someone keeps dragging chains along the sides of the caravans as well, but they've never been able to catch anyone. And... well, what's really freaking them out is that they've been hearing laughter... moaning... and *screaming* out on the excavation in the *middle* of the night!"

Jon just stared at him wide-eyed.

"The electricity generator has been playing up, too; it's surged a few times, and flickers occasionally. I've checked it, and it was tampered with. I fixed it, and it happened again."

"It's not me," Jon assured him. "I would never pull stunts like that – I'm a *harmless* prankster... things like water buckets above door frames, and hidden alarm clocks."

"You call water buckets above door frames *harmless*? Don't you do that in my house and expect me to clean it up!"

Jon raised his hands in mock defence, "Of course not... I'd fill yours with confetti. Much easier to clean up." He became serious again. "But honestly, I have no idea who could be doing it. My guess is, they'll slip up at some point and get caught. Then we'll let the women decide the punishment," he grinned.

"Now I *know* it isn't you – nothing hath wrath like a woman scorned... or scared."

In the incident room Jon and Toshiro met with Amir and Brehani, all dressed for bog work; the latter pulled the scans up on the computer, overlaid to build a 3D image.

"Calculating for manoeuvring room around the anomaly," Brehani began, "the trench will be roughly three by six metres, give or take – we'll have to see just what we're dealing with once we get down there."

"How far down is *down*?" Jon asked, examining the scans: There was a strange absence of typical artefact signatures – *nothing* of significance aside from the obvious, clearly defined *blank*. It made no sense, and if the Cardinal hadn't okayed the dig Jon would have sworn it would be a massive waste of time.

"From the core samples taken, I'd say anywhere between two and three metres, not more. I've already marked off the trench with stakes where we're to dig, but we have a problem: The ground in that area is way too boggy to bring in the mechanical digger, so we'll be doing it by hand."

"That'll go quickly with everyone pitching in," Toshiro commented.

"Uh... I'm afraid not... the Cardinal has made it clear that it's not to be a general dig... we're it."

"Won't it appear suspicious to have such a small team on such a large trench? And three of us are not even mainly archaeologists..." Amir said.

It was the first time Jon had heard Amir speak; he couldn't quite identify the decidedly foreign accent, but it reminded him of an old Bedouin his father had worked with years ago.

"The main trench is yielding enough interesting discoveries right now that the students won't think much of it if I employ you on the new trench, rather than pulling them off of their own treasure hunts. And because the Cardinal's leaving tomorrow, it will throw off any suspicions that this new trench might be important to her – she wouldn't leave if that were the case. But we're not to completely expose whatever it is we find – just make it ready to open when she returns."

"What?" Toshiro said.

"When she first told me, I didn't understand why she would delay what could be the best trench here," Brehani confessed, "but then I realized: She's an archaeologist and this is on her doorstep... she's been itching at the edge of the trenches for weeks; wouldn't you want to be here for the big moment, if you were in her shoes?"

They glanced from one to another, understanding: *This* was the real treasure on this excavation, whatever it was, and the Wolf would likely be after it. Thus the weeks of delay in beginning the trench.

Jon reminded them, "She's leaving... which means I'll be playing pilot first thing in the morning; otherwise count me in."

They loaded up equipment and started the trek across the boggy ground, which seemed specifically landscaped to discourage hikers. Anything off-road in the Highlands had to be hard-won; it made the locals hardy and kept the timid to the well-worn paths. The four of them set to work clearing away the area between the stakes of *scraw*, bracken, heather and knolls of bog grass. The peat spades took some practice, but the vertical slices and extraction became easier as they worked. The peat bricks were each inspected for artefacts (of which none were found), and then set aside in stacks to dry. By the time they'd gotten a metre's worth of ground cleared between the stakes, it was already getting dark. The vague feeling in the pit of their stomachs turned out to be hunger as they'd worked through the afternoon with only the occasional tea break. They cleaned up for the night and headed back to the castle, tired but satisfied with their progress for the day.

Even though Jon was hungry, he was dirtier – so he decided to take a quick shower and then grab his share of the dinner that had been set aside for their team by Galal. He headed back to his room and stripped off his clothes. Only then did he realize how stiff the cold ground had made his back. He tossed his mud-caked clothes into the corner and stepped into the shower. As hot water streamed over his body washing mud and sweat away, his eyes suddenly popped open. Alvar. Something about his exhausted chain of thoughts started ringing bells, started flipping puzzle pieces this way and that in his mind. The connection. Erlina. The Wolf's history with them both. The whole mutual interest in Vikings, trade routes, etcetera. They couldn't be coincidences.

Jon headed back down to the cafeteria for dinner, mulling over puzzle pieces in his mind. Even though it was already quite late, the dining hall was still quite full of students. He listened as he got his dinner – the talk was mainly about the strange occurrences recently, rather than any finds in the trench.

"Ainsley," Edric greeted him as he swung his leg over a chair back to sit down at Jon's table. "How's the new trench panning out?"

"Peaty," he rubbed his neck. "I don't expect to find much down there... maybe that's why we're such a small team," he hedged.

"A Dad's Army team, more like," Edric smirked.

"So... any idea who's pulling the pranks?" Jon changed the subject.

Edric looked around. "No." Hesitation flickered across his face.

"But?" Jon looked at him.

"Oh, nothing," he shrugged. "It's just that the Scots, Duggan and George, were telling ghost stories the other night. They said a few of the local lads – they go to the *Passing Place* regularly – had told them tales of *The Maid of Dalmoor*... apparently she's been seen up here for generations, never aging, so this area might be her haunt, and the lads were asking if anyone had seen her yet."

"And you believed them?"

"Generally," he shrugged, "no – there has to be a more logical explanation. But I won't pretend that after the last few nights of chains and screams and laughter down at the caravans, the students aren't shaken by it all. What do you think?"

"Like you... there has to be a logical explanation; but the more I see here, the less sure I am of what logic has to do with this place," Jon looked around the opulent dining hall.

Clouds had rolled in and fell heavy with rain; Jon looked out the window: The trench would be waterlogged in the morning. Great; they'd need to haul over one of the water pumps and let it work before they could begin digging in the mud in the morning. On his way back to his room he peaked in to Alexis's room to see if she was in; but she was already fast asleep. Finding his way to the edge of his own bed, he sat down exhausted and slipped under the duvet; his head hit the pillow and he was gone to the world. Sometime in the early hours of the morning he turned onto his side, and breathed a familiar flowery fragrance. He pried one eye open, and then the other, and tried to focus.

"Good morning," he heard a distant voice calling somewhere in the mist. Someone shook him. "Good morning, sleepy-head." He opened his eyes; Alexis was sitting beside him on the bed.

"I brought you tea," she gestured to the mug on his bedside table. "My mother wants you to take her up in the chopper as soon as you're ready. She wants a morning survey before leaving."

He sat up, and kissed her hand. "Thank you," he took a sip, then a gulp. "This will help. Did you sleep well?" he asked.

She nodded. "I was waiting for you to get back, but fell asleep."

He told her of the dig, and at the memory of his thoughts the night before, he jumped up and grabbed his iPhone, checking his messages.

He ran his fingers through his hair, yawning as he read his messages. "Alvar's on his way... he sent a message yesterday morning and I completely forgot to look in all the commotion. He'll be arriving today at Fair Isle."

The helicopter rumbled to life. With a roar of engines and a whir of blades it took to the fresh morning sky, the Cardinal seated beside Jon but lost in a myriad of thoughts as she scoured the landscape with her eyes, as if she could see another *something*. He watched her intense gaze piercing its way through the new trench; there was a melancholic expression on her face, but she said nothing.

So he ventured: "What's down there in the new trench, I wonder."

"A cist," she murmured, not taking her eyes from the scene below.

He tried to think of a way to draw her focus away from the excavation and engage her in conversation. "It's uncomfortable, isn't it? For the living, that is, to disturb resting places of the dead?"

"Yes," she looked at him. "Someone is in there... a loved one placed them there. Whether or not that loved one lives to see the grave opened, it is a rest that should not be disturbed."

"Then why do we do it? Archaeologists in general, I mean."

"Because the need of the living to know outweighs the concerns of those who no longer live to protest," she looked down again at the site, her expression darkening. It seemed almost as if she were worried about what the skeletons might think about it.

"Then we do so with the greatest of care and respect," Jon replied.

"Exactly," she smiled at him.

As he circled back toward the helipad Jon asked, "Will it have been worth it?"

"What do you mean?" she stared at him, surprised by the question.

"This flight this morning... did you see what you'd hoped?"

"Oh that – yes! It is always helpful, thank you."

He could tell she was distracted, anxious about that *something*, but she said nothing more.

Alexis was waiting at the helipad with Elbal and their luggage when the helicopter landed. "I've packed your case with the usual things," said Alexis as she approached the Cardinal.

"Thank you dearest, and good morning," she kissed her daughter's cheek, pleased to hear her speaking in front of the pilot; it meant she really did trust him. Good.

"Good morning, Mother," she laughed at herself for jumping straight into business.

Jon loaded the luggage as Alexis helped Elbal into the helicopter, while the Cardinal looked through her emails and notes for the coming appointments.

The flight was without incident, and without much conversation. Jon was alert to the atmosphere between his three passengers, and it was perplexing: Elbal was generally unreadable, though he seemed very fond of Alexis; toward the Cardinal he was respectful, with an odd mixture of warm affection and aloof submission. The Cardinal seemed lost in her own world of thoughts, yet intensely focused on the ground that raced beneath them as if she were memorizing the landscape, or searching for something. Alexis was subdued; she occasionally took Elbal's hand beside her, and he would pat it but say nothing.

When they arrived at the Edinburgh Airport landing pad and Jon unloaded the luggage for them, the Cardinal turned to him. "I trust your time will be well used over the next few days." She glanced toward Alexis and added, "Take care of her."

"Gladly," he replied. "I'll let her see you off, if you don't mind; and I'll meet you here in four days. I've got to go and pick up Toshiro's package," he added as he looked at the list once more, and noted the location of the delivery company on a diagram of the airport; it was within walking distance.

"Not at all," she nodded. "A few moments alone with my daughter is just what I'd like."

"We'll be back soon," the Cardinal took Alexis by the arm as they walked toward the awaiting car, the driver just loading their luggage into the boot. "Amir and Galal will watch over you, but if you need anything at all, just call."

"I will," Alexis replied, "and enjoy your time in the city while you can!"

"I know that you regret not coming with me on this trip, though you have incentive to remain at home now," she glanced toward the pilot and winked at her daughter. "So, to lessen your regret at not accompanying me... I have prepared a little surprise for you," her mother smiled. "You know that I've been busy unpacking my private library boxes..."

"Yes," Alexis looked at her curiously.

"Well, I've locked the library and hidden the key! Explore your home... with Jon of course. Find the key, and you'll discover a few puzzling things. You may learn a few things about me that you don't know yet. And..." she thought a moment, as if making a decision to say something or not, "...if you should find another key, find out where it fits – for there are no keys in the castle that do not unlock something."

Alexis stopped, studying her mother's expression. "Not even the key by the tower's outer door?"

The Cardinal laughed, "I see you are observant, as always! Yes... that key opens a door. Find it, and enjoy what is revealed!" she kissed her daughter's cheek.

The Cardinal had led Alexis to Elbal, who rested his hands on Alexis's shoulders; though he could not look into her eyes he had another sense that was more penetrating than eyesight. "Be cautious," he whispered to her.

"Elbal," Alexis wrapped her arms around him. "I will miss you, but why so grave? It's only four days." She looked up at him.

"Only three days changed the course of a carpenter's followers forever," he replied. "Much can happen in so short a time."

"I'll be careful," she promised. "Jon will be with me... and your sons will be your eyes. I'll be fine. Now go! Goodbye!"

She waved to them as the car drove away and then walked back to the helicopter, where she waited for Jon; she could see him in the distance at a warehouse, talking with a man loading a baggage carrier with boxes. Jon climbed in and she watched as they drove toward her.

"They're off?" he asked as he climbed out and came toward her.

She nodded sadly.

He caressed her arms gently. "How often do you get left behind?"

"Never before. We've been nomads living out of hotels, tents and bungalows for so long that it's an odd feeling not to have a suitcase by my side... to see them off without me! To return *home*... now that's a strange concept!"

"One I hope you can get used to," he replied. "Roots are important... a place to plant yourself and grow. I've been there, done that, and I've had my fill of living out of suitcases for a while."

"That makes two of us."

Jon looked at his watch – it was only eleven in the morning. "We'll get this loaded and then we can head home."

Home," she smiled, "which reminds me: My mother has laid a scavenger hunt of sorts for *us*! It's time to explore!" She told him about the mystery of the keys.

"Sounds interesting! But first things first – I have to help at that trench; if you want to do it together it's got to wait until this evening. We can only dig so deep anyway, so we'll get done what we can and then I should have time off for good behaviour."

With her mother gone and the castle empty after the lunch break ended, Alexis decided to take the chance to read at last. She took a book from the stack on her desk, got comfortable in the conservatory and opened to the title page: *The Swan's Song*, by Alvar Thorsen. At first she merely enjoyed the story for the writing, the characters coming alive with the vivid descriptions... she could see the vibrant green of the forest, smell the misty pine and churning ocean, and even hear the crackling fire described. But the more she read, the more similarities she began to recognize with their present situation: The story took place in the Highlands; near Loch Eriboll; an ancient village near the shore; a secret tunnel, two pools with a trysting stone between them, and even a dryad that was described in the book almost exactly like the statue in the stairwell. It was as if this author – she looked at the publication date, 1901 – had been looking over their shoulders the past few days and taking notes.

After that realization she couldn't focus on reading anymore; she went back to her room and dug the mouse and keyboard out from under a pile of papers, slapping them down atop the pile with a sense of urgent curiosity. She googled, *"Alvar Thorsen, author"*; it pulled up a few Scandinavian and English websites; books from the late 1800's through 1915 on medicine and hospital practices as well as three novels, and then a gap of about twenty years; another two books in the 1930's and '40's, one about medicine, one on the history of Scandinavia (that one, she knew was in their library though it had never had a dust jacket), and one novel; another 30-year gap; another few books, this time only novels and history books; another 30-year gap; more novels. Most of the novels were set in the north... Scotland, Norway, Sweden; only one was elsewhere – set in Atlantis. Two of the titles she recognized as the books she'd purchased.

Always the same name, she thought to herself. *How can there be four authors, with such an uncommon name, within a century or two? And all writing about such similar topics?*

She switched to image search; there were images of the Alvar Thorsen whom she'd seen on Skype, but none of the older authors. "There have *got* to be images of them somewhere!" She began to look more closely at the images, and read the captions of each. That's when it hit her: They were all the same man. Jon's Alvar. His dress in some of the photos was old-fashioned; though they were only bust portraits, and men's fashions tend to change less noticeably than women's, there were clear differences: A bow tie, a cravat, a beard, changing collars and lapels, and mostly black and white images, grainy with age or faded with time before they'd been digitalized. But of the colour photos she began to notice that he wore something deep red in every single photo. A coincidence?

Probably. Not. Curious, she tried to google her mother, under "Cardinal" and archaeologist. Though she found the name mentioned numerous times in the text search, in articles and publications, there wasn't a single clear image of her. She then remembered a memo she'd dictated from Elbal to Toshiro about removing such images (he'd turned his pickpocket skills to the modern form of hacking); it was when they'd figured out that the Wolf was targeting them, and at the time it had made sense in that context. She then surfed her favourite online bookshop, the kind that prided themselves in being able to get anything, and she requested the entire list of his books minus the titles she already had... any they could get their hands on. She looked at the *Swan's Song* with new eyes. She picked it up, examining it carefully, before taking it into Jon's room to read and wait for him – she could hardly wait for him to return so she could tell him what she'd discovered.

Not long after quitting time Jon got back to his room exhausted, covered in mud and looking forward to a hot shower. He found Alexis curled up on his bed sound asleep with a book beside her; he let her sleep while he cleaned up, got dressed and checked his messages quickly: Alvar hoped to leave Fair Isle with the first low tide the morning after next, and would arrive at the afternoon's low tide at *Tràigh Allt Chàilgeag* that same day. That might be a problem: They would most likely reach their target in the trench tomorrow... how suspicious would it look if Alvar showed up just as they're getting to the goods while the Cardinal was away? They'd need to tread lightly.

He gently brushed Alexis's hair back from her face and she stirred, smiling up at him as she stretched. Her hand landed on the book beside her which reminded her of why she was there in the first place, shooting her upright in bed. She eagerly told him about the novel and what she'd discovered on the internet; he looked unconvinced.

"I've known him for years – since uni," he shook his head. "He's only managed to publish one book in all that time, and it was a history book. Besides, he's an eternal bachelor with *no* pretensions of romance in his life; how could he be the same author of novels like this?" he flipped through the *Swan's Song* sceptically.

Without a word she took his hand and led him into her room, pulling up the image search and setting him down in front of her computer. He scrolled through the images, his brow creasing as he looked. "This has to be a joke! There's no way he's that old! No way. These have got to be relations... with very strong family genes. And besides, it's not uncommon in Norway to pass on first names within a family for generations... for all I know he comes from a long line of authors."

"Okay," she sat atop the pile of papers on her desk and drew closer. "Am I speaking quietly enough?"

He nodded.

"Then there's my mother: No images of her... Toshiro's been removing them, and on Elbal's orders. And another thing: She's expert in too many things for her age; it's not just that she has a steel trap of a brain... it's that she has *intimate* knowledge... details you won't find in history books." She told him examples of what had made the Cardinal indispensible in the field of historical research. He listened, trying to take it all in. Names he'd heard occasionally from his own friend; it couldn't be a coincidence. Alexis ended with, "...and she can fluently read Old Norse and Persian, and just about any other language you can think of."

He stared at her. "Why do you mention those specifically?"

She thought about it a moment then shrugged, "They're the ones she has most to do with, I guess."

"Why that combination?" he shook his head.

"What's wrong?"

"It's just— Alvar fits this description to a T so far; he's an expert in those very language families too... for him, it has to do with the old slave routes of the Vikings – he's nearly obsessed with it, and it's got something to do with chasing down the Wolf." *Was the Cardinal the Wolf after all?* He frowned, "He knows that route like the back of his hand – almost as if..." his thoughts trailed off, and he absently rubbed the back of his stiff neck, wincing.

Alexis stood up and stepped behind him to massage his shoulders; he leaned back into her hands and she felt a moan of comfort vibrate through his neck. "Right now... no more problems, no more questions," she said softly. "What say we enjoy each other's company tonight, and give our curious minds a rest?"

He turned in the chair to face her, smiling, "In that case... I give you exactly ten minutes to stop this massage!" he turned back around and got comfortable.

"And it's been a while since we saw the stars," she suggested, pointing upward. At that she gasped. "When my mother told me about the scavenger hunt... she said the word *puzzle*! And the key... at the top of the tower!"

He turned around to face her again. "Then I think we should go and get it," he nodded seriously, but wrapped his arms around her waist and pulled her in for a kiss.

Brehani, Toshiro, Jon and Amir met the following morning at six o'clock to continue the trench, taking turns digging, and catching and stacking the peat bricks as they were tossed to the surface from the deepening pit. They sliced stairs into one of the peat walls as they went, topping each step with a heathy mat of topsoil to give them solid footing for getting in and out. Arms were just beginning to throb from heaving clumps of peat when someone's shovel hit something hard, with a *chink*. Everyone stopped, looking around to see who had hit pay dirt; it was Toshiro.

As they began clearing the promising spot Jon asked, "Hey... have you noticed that this soil is dry? That doesn't make any sense." The ubiquitous, compact soggy peat simply stopped, giving way to dry, crumbly earth. "It's like something sucked the moisture out of the peat here," Jon looked around at the strata of peat in the walls of their pit, now two metres deep, oozing oil-slicked moisture until it reached the level of the object.

"That is strange," muttered Brehani under his breath. They brushed the stone free of the dry earth and found a straight edge in one direction, then cleared along the edge to a corner and followed it around to complete a large rectangle. Corner to corner and a bit beyond each edge, the ground in contact with the object was dry. All were quiet a moment, savouring the find while Brehani bent down to examine the stone more closely: "This doesn't make *any* sense... this stone is typical Lewisian Gneiss, found all over the place up here west of the Moine Thrust," he waved his hand over his shoulder westward. "And that doesn't react to the scans the way my readings indicate for this site!"

"It could be that this is only the outer layer; maybe something inside is throwing off the readings," Amir suggested.

"Or maybe the wet soil was messing with them," added Toshiro.

Jon brushed his hands together to loosen the dirt. "Well... this is obviously a dressed stone – its edges are too well defined to be natural. It's a couple tons at least... beyond the lifting capacity of my chopper... and this boggy ground would swallow any vehicle if we tried to pull it out. How are we going to move it?"

"How did it get here in the first place?" Toshiro asked. "Did they even have the technology to move such masses in the ancient north?"

"Perhaps similar technology to that of Egypt's for the pyramids," replied Amir.

"Well," Brehani sighed, "I guess all we can do is get ourselves cleaned up as that's as far as we go until the Cardinal returns." He was itching to find out more but would never gainsay the Cardinal.

One by one the team crawled out of the trench and cleared away the tools, then cleaned off as much as possible before climbing into the golf cart. The ride back up to the castle was a subdued one; the wind was picking up but no one really noticed as they each mulled over the mystery.

Jon finally said, "Opening a grave is always emotional... it's not something I think I'll ever get used to."

Brehani turned to look at him. "How do you know it's a grave?"

"What else could it be? It looks like a cist to me," he shrugged.

"Normally, I would agree with you. But the dried soil... the sheer size of it..." Brehani looked back over his shoulder toward the trench.

Toshiro said, "Well, whatever it is, we must wait three more days to find out."

Driving, Amir said nothing; but in the eerie afternoon light streaking through distant storm clouds, it suddenly struck Jon that Amir looked ancient... like an old man projected onto a young man or vice versa. He laughed quietly at himself; he was letting his imagination run wild.

Jon cleaned up and then opened Alexis's door cautiously; she sat at the computer and when she saw him, waved him in.

"I now have time off for good behaviour," he kissed her. "Shall we do some exploring after lunch? I'm famished!"

She stood, putting on a cardigan to head to the dining hall. "Scavenger hunting on the menu after lunch," she smiled. "You've not seen her apartments yet, have you?"

"No... you blindfolded me past them the first time we went to the tower, and I haven't looked away from you since," he teased.

"Then I can't wait to show you one room in particular; I call it her *Hall of Dreams*."

"Her *what*?" he laughed.

"It's a room that you have to see to believe. There's also the library – I haven't been in there since she unpacked the last of the boxes, and that's what likely held the surprises in store for this scavenger hunt!"

"Well then, I'd say we find the keys. By the way, what were you doing at the computer? Research?"

"Yes," she said, "I was reading up on Vikings, trade routes and slavery."

"Ah," he grinned, "a bit of light reading before lunch."

As they passed her jib door on the way to the stairs Jon wondered how many other such doors there were in this castle, and would bet pounds to pence there was one somewhere in the cellar leading to the cavern.

7: Now

Edric found a quiet spot up the loch from the digs and pulled up Skype on his iPhone. The Wolf came into view, dressed in black leather. She smiled when she saw him.

"You look dazzling," he frowned. "You haven't got a date with someone else, have you?"

"Now, now... are you jealous?" she asked, honey dripping from each word.

"Yes, if you ask me directly," he said in a huff.

"You'd be my only rendezvous," she gave him a look that made him want to jump on the next ferry back to her.

"Are you teasing me?"

"Tempting," she corrected with a smile.

"When this is all over, let's leave – get away together."

"I was beginning to think you'd forgotten about me this week," the Wolf demurred, ignoring the obvious plea.

"Never," Edric replied. "Hey – are you on your yacht?" He only just looked beyond the Wolf to see the evening horizon bobbing over her shoulder.

"I'm sorry I've been so irritable when you've called lately," she eluded the question. "I'm just so...

anxious. You have no way of knowing how important this mission is to me."

"I'd like to," he hinted. "You know you can trust me."

"I trust no one," she replied, adding, "but I'm willing for that to change."

He smiled. Her body language was more flirtatious than her mere words, and it was the best mood he'd seen her in for some time. "And what would I need to do to help you change that?"

She thought about that a moment. "Die for me."

He looked at her, a hesitant smile breaking into a nervous laugh. "Well, there's not much incentive for me if you'd only trust me after I'm dead, you know."

"I mean be willing," she teased with a shrug, "but saying and doing are two different things, and how can I tell one from the other until it's too late?"

"That *is* a problem... but I'm sure we can find a better solution than one of us dying." He studied her face a moment. "If I ask you something, will you give me a straight answer... honest, and from the heart? You may not believe me or want me to say this, but I do love you – despite your scratchiness," he smiled.

"What's the question?" she frowned.

"What is it about the Cardinal that has you so obsessed? What is your connection with her?"

"She has wanted rain when I wanted sunshine," she shrugged.

"Bullocks."

"Why does it matter to you?" she snapped, her pale blue eyes briefly flashing dark.

"Because I love you," he answered calmly, "and the more I understand you, the more I can help you reach your goal," he added quickly when she drew breath to retort.

She looked down at her hands. "You shouldn't love me. You don't even know who I really am."

"I know that you're beautiful... and deeply wounded but you pretend not to be and would never admit it even to yourself... that you miss your parents, who went missing when you were younger... that you smell great in musky perfumes, look great in black, and that you have a penchant for Scotland, Norway, and all things Viking; I know that you have a weakness for a particular cocky blonde," he grinned wide enough to make her laugh. "I know enough about you to love you... the rest is just icing on the cake."

"Even if the cake is—" she stopped. She glared at him, deliberating. At last she heaved a sigh, "Fine! If you really want to know why I detest the Cardinal so much, and why I want to make her suffer... make her life miserable, inconvenienced, and unsuccessful? It is because she's ruined everything I've ever wanted in life!"

He waited. He wanted more information, and she knew it.

"Her family thwarted my parents' prosperity! My father's influence!... The plans they had to return to our home... Once I worshipped the ground she walked on – she could do no wrong, she was beloved by everyone we knew. But one day... she stole the man I love... the only man I've ever *truly* loved. I saw him first, and she stole him! She—"

"Wait a minute," Edric interrupted what was escalating into a tirade. "But she's not married... and as far as I've been able to find out, she's never even had a boyfriend! So how did she steal him? It seems to me like she lost him – and – not that it's helping my own cause any... but if she's lost him, he's fair game."

"Lost," she laughed in a whisper. "You have no idea."

"You're confusing me. Remember, I'm just a bloke... your female logic is making me dizzy."

"There is no female logic or man's logic in this situation; trust me on that," she sighed heavily. "And if this fraction of my tale confuses you, I think your brain would pop if I told you the whole story... the whole truth."

"Try me."

She looked at him a moment. "No... not yet. I need your wits about you there until the Cardinal's been thwarted and moves on to her next target."

"And then I'll have to move on with her... is that it? Are you trying to ditch me?"

"Ditch? That implies an attachment."

"You're cruel, Moriel."

"You'll just have to keep trying," she winked. "Maybe someday you'll win, and I'll lose."

"I hope you wouldn't consider gaining me as losing," he pouted.

She ignored him. "So... what news do you have for me?" He still pouted. "Please? I promise I'll make it up to you someday."

He looked at her resentfully. "Okay, fine – we'll play it your way for now," he sighed. "The Cardinal's clique has opened a new trench; word is, it's a burial."

"A burial? I wonder who?" she asked herself more than him.

"I doubt you know them, whoever they are," he laughed at her question. "I checked it out... it's exposed, but they're waiting for the Cardinal to return from Edinburgh before opening it; not sure how they'll do that as the stone's massive."

"Keep me informed, as always. Anything else? Anything out of the ordinary?"

"I'll say! The excavation itself is interesting though standard; but it's what's happening at night that has people on edge, especially those who are staying in the caravans." He told her about the strange occurrences, the noises bumping in the night.

"And what do they think it is?"

"Some of the locals think it's the Maid of Dalmoor."

"Who?" she stared at him, more amused than shocked.

"That's what they call her; apparently she's been seen up around the castle for several generations at least."

"Seen? And what does she look like?"

He thought back to the tales Duggan and George had been telling. "Long black hair, beautiful... sad. Restless – they said the local lads mentioned that she always seemed to be looking for something."

The Wolf stared at him. "Do they know what?"

"I don't think any of them have been brave enough to ask a ghost," he smirked, as if that were obvious.

She smiled to herself. "And how are the students handling the 'ghostings'?"

"The women are really freaked out; they're not sleeping much. Men are wise to keep a safe distance from them at the moment. There's only a couple more weeks before they head back to uni anyway... some of them were talking last night about leaving early, especially if anything else odd happens."

"But doesn't the success of her excavation require their work? Without the mudlarks, her project would be dead in the water."

"True," he looked at her suspiciously. "Where are you, by the way?"

"On my yacht. I'm having a few additions added, and cleaning it. Well... keep me informed. Let me know as soon as they've extracted whatever it is in the new trench that she's after."

"Will do," he replied sullenly.

"Aw, what's that matter? Still pouting?"

"Goodbye, Moriel." Edric hung up. He sat there thinking about the conversation, and about their relationship thus far, until the conclusions he approached became too uncomfortable.

Jon stopped Alexis as she began to open the Cardinal's bedroom door. "Are you sure this is okay? I mean, it's your mother's most private room."

"Of course," Alexis replied, "she told me to explore my home *with you*. I want to show you all of it, and this is included."

"Alright," Jon nodded, "lead on."

The Cardinal's bedroom was luxurious yet simplistic, with a touch of other-worldly taste: The bed was a pie-shaped corner frame, layered high with feather mattresses that begged to be sunk into; the whole was encased in a white curtain, draped back. The windows were draped with luxurious red velvet, contrasting the otherwise white decor. The rug on the floor was of the finest weave, a white design against a stone-grey backdrop; just as Jon was stepping past it he saw the pattern and froze: It was a swan, intricately patterned with endless knots, and along the neck were three circles woven in a silver thread.

He caught Alexis's attention. "This!" he pointed at the rug excitedly. "That night at the pub... Sandy drew *this* very pattern for me, from the arrow tip he'd found. I told you about our talk, remember?" He pulled out his cell phone and snapped a photo.

"There's also a pewter swan on one of the shelves in the main library I think; I put it there when I was unpacking the boxes, but I didn't think anything about it – and its design is very similar to this. And *The Swan's Song*!" she remembered the title of the book she'd begun to read.

"And the ship's figurehead on the fireplace mantel in the entrance hall," Jon added.

"I think it's safe to assume that swans are a piece of the puzzle," Alexis smiled. "We have to find the key to the library – help me look!"

They searched through the drawers, the closet, nothing. Jon then retrieved the key hanging beside the door in the tower as they'd need it later anyway for this scavenger hunt; but it was a skeleton key, and the lock on the library door was for a bladed key.

The next possibility would be in the Hall of Dreams, the most exotic room of them all: Swaths of silky gauze cloth hung like kinetic sculptures from the ceiling in every imaginable colour, and each strand was weighted with a tiny silver bell. Overhead chandeliers of silver tree branches speckled with small lights illuminated the room in a soft glow, mesmerizing ripples through translucent waves. Only those closest to the Cardinal had ever seen this room; it was something deeply personal to her that not even Alexis understood. In every place they had ever lived some form of this room had been established; but here at the castle was room enough for the Cardinal's full realisation of it, and it was grand to see.

As they wove their way through the silky cloud, hanging down nearly to their knees, a light tinkling of bell shattered the reverent silence each time they brushed one of the swaths of cloth. As he walked, Jon held out his arms to catch the gauze banners, bringing forth a high-pitched symphony of sound as they washed free in his wake. But it was for his ears alone; though Alexis seemed to enjoy his pleasure at it, it was not something he could share with her and so he lowered his arms and walked on in the fading ring. At the far end of the room they came to a pile of enormous pillows secured within a silvery frame which filled the entire end-wall. Vibrant blue velvet curtains, tied back in thick folds, framed the bed of pillows. He turned toward her: "This room is amazing! Like something out of Arabian Nights! Why?"

She flopped back onto the pillows, sighing, "Another *why* I can't answer."

"Oh, no you don't," he pulled her up by the hands. "We're on a scavenger hunt, remember?"

"Okay," she let herself be pulled back into the business at hand. "She's predictable in one area especially: She dislikes trivial delays, no matter for herself or for us, her entourage; so my bet is that she's hidden the key somewhere near that library," she pointed through the wall toward the library.

Jon instinctively followed her gesture and his eye caught a glimmer behind one of the curtains; there on a hook was a key.

"See?" she smiled. "I told you she was predictable."

"I wouldn't go quite that far, but at least we found the key," he grinned. He took it and commented, "This is an Abloy key... these are almost impossible to pick."

"And how would you know that?" Alexis looked at him curiously, akimbo.

"My sister's forever losing her keys and I had to learn the skills to keep her housed," he shrugged. "You say the Cardinal doesn't like delays, even for us," he began looking around, running his hand along the wall, "so my bet is that there's a jib door at this end of the room – otherwise she'd hang this key just inside the main door to spare us running the bell gauntlet to get to it." He felt a crack in the wall. "Voilà." The jib door was narrower than any other so far, but was near to where the key had hung. Five steps later and they were at the library door.

The key fit and the library door clicked open. Before entering Alexis whispered, "This is it! My mother said I might learn a few things about her... clues to who she is. I want to know, but... I know it might change the way I see her forever. Part of me would rather that not happen."

"But I suppose it's already too late for that now, isn't it?" Jon asked. "We've already learned a few things that want explaining... and curiosity won't let you rest until you know."

She nodded, took a deep breath and entered; Jon followed, closing the door behind them.

The walls were lined with shelves sagging under the weight of scrolls and atlases, books and bundles of newspaper clippings to do with history, archaeology and the sciences. Beneath the desk opposite the door stood a wooden chest, and around the corner of the L-shaped room was a tête-à-tête sofa in a jungle of potted trees. The floor, smooth and solid stone, was painted with what looked like an aerial view of a landscape, a bit stylized, with features painted of a forest and what looked like a town or village. The desk itself was scattered with strange objects, each one more fascinating than the last: An ornate magnifying glass mounted in a stand made of wrought iron lacework gilt in gold; an ancient vellum scroll, tied with a strand of red silk; a quill stand with assorted feather quills and an ink bottle; a large stone mortar and pestle containing some kind of resin; and a tome, bound with wooden covers of ornate design and with brass feet on each corner of the front cover.

He picked up the scroll, turning it in his hand to examine it. He caught her attention to ask, "Should we take a look at this first?"

Alexis nodded, "It's now or never."

He pulled the silk strand away and unrolled it carefully: The first thing they saw was the word *Maldor* written in a distinctive script. The document looked like some kind of plan; lines that looked like roads, or at least paths, and unusual buildings: The smaller structures reminded him of a wishbone in shape, with the roof descending in a gently rounded slope from the peak to the ground, eliminating the need for walls. They were scattered around a central, massive structure shaped like a raindrop; what caught his attention was the intersection of the larger structure's walls with a path; he framed part of the layout with his fingers, as if taking a snapshot; it was exactly like the Y-shaped intersection on one of the Geophysics scans.

"This must be the document your mother referenced for this dig." He ran his finger around what he'd remembered from the dig's scans. "Wow... if this is the actual size of that excavation down there," he pointed toward the loch, "it confirms what I've already suspected: This will take decades to explore! It makes sense, if she knows exactly what they're dealing with, to only tackle as much as we have this summer... this Y-section is more than enough to keep everyone busy until the school term begins again!"

A wispy text was written next to a large rectangle divided into two unequal parts: Within the lines of the larger box were three parallel figures, the outer ones toe-to-head with the central figure; in the smaller box also three figures, much smaller than the first three, but all shoulder-to-shoulder, and laying crosswise at the feet of the other three. Jon couldn't believe what he was seeing: From its location, it was the anomaly they had reached just that day; he took a picture of it.

"These three are east-west burials," Alexis pointed to the smaller box. "That means they were Christians. I wonder what the other burial signifies?"

Jon told her what he knew of the scans. "Why? Why would she not go for gold from the beginning of the digs?"

Alexis shook her head. "I don't know; perhaps it's a question of timing. Besides," she added, "if this is somehow related to the journal we found—"

"Then the delay is not caution... it's hesitation," he finished her thought.

She nodded. "Let's see what else is here... this book's next." Alexis ran her hand reverently over the relief of the wooden front cover, feeling the brass feet.

Jon examined the book. "I've never seen anything like this," he whispered. "The design is distinctly Celtic... but there's a touch of Norse here too. Not quite," he decided, "but something similar."

She carefully opened the front cover of the heavy book. The pages were handmade and stitch-bound.

The first few dozen pages were blank so Jon flipped it over and they began at the back of the book: Again, the strange writing. The last few pages were all the same writing; He checked the back of the pages just in case, but no English translations were there. A few pages later, to their surprise it soon changed to something a bit more discernible: Latin. His Latin was rusty, but still passively useable in a pinch.

"*Instructio encausto*," he read. "Instructions for...?" Alexis shrugged. He dusted off his mental school notes. "A recipe for ink," he decided, and looked down the recipe; one of the ingredients, Arabic gum, was easy to decipher. "That might be what this is," he tipped the heavy mortar and pestle and looked inside, "though I would think this could be bought already ground in any art shop."

"That is odd, especially for someone who doesn't like delays," Alexis commented.

"Maybe she just doesn't like modern ones; archaeology is full of delays, you know."

The book seemed to be filled with recipes and instructions, a depository of knowledge. There was a sense of elegance about it, a sense of joy in knowledge to heal, not harm. From what Jon could decipher it was more of a medicinal and household encyclopaedia than anything else. Some of the entries that he could read began to have dates attached with '*prius obtentus*' and a month... *Ianuarius*, *Iunius*, *Sextilis*; the years began as far back as *Anno Domini 795* on the pages he could read; since the book seemed to be written back to front, he could only surmise that the last pages (or first) were even older. He flipped forward through the book, and an old form of English took over from Latin; it was also passably readable to Jon as there were many words either directly Old Norse, or related remnants to it. Further on, more modern English became the standard (though erratic in spelling as it always was in such old documents). The first English entry was: *"So much knowlige heerin contaned, lost if left to teim in ye forms I'v preservd y^m, wuld serv posteritie mor fuly if transformd to y^s new tonge wich I yink destind to surveiv ye hardships of infancie."*

All of the pages, regardless of the language, were written by the same hand: A delicate one, elegant and sleek with elongated, wispy ascenders and descenders.

When Jon pointed that out Alexis had a look of terrible realization: She picked up the scroll once again, opened it and compared the writing to that of the book; it was the same. "I didn't want to say anything before I was certain, because it doesn't make any sense! The journal had made me suspicious, as it's the same writing. This is my *mother's* handwriting!"

"What? Are you sure?"

She nodded.

"Well," he shook his head, "that leaves us with two possibilities: Either she's a forger and these have been made to look antique; or they're all genuine. But that's simply an impossibility!"

She nodded reluctantly. "It doesn't make *any* sense!"

He looked through the scrolls on the book shelves nearby; over the years the weight had sagged the shelves so that the scrolls rolled together neatly in the middle. "These are all the same handwriting."

They pulled the wooden chest out from under the desk to examine it.

"How do we open it?" Alexis asked. It wasn't that it was locked; it was that it was a seamless box... another puzzle box to be precise.

"Someone's got a sense of humour," he shook his head as he studied it, trying to find an entrance point.

"Well, my mother did mention *puzzle*," she laughed, looking it over. "How heavy is it?"

He lifted it. "I'd say about fifty pounds. Whatever it contains is heavy, unless the wood is simply thick." As he set it down again he heard the distinct chink of metal against metal. "Let's see if we can't figure out how to open this thing."

By sliding individual wooden pieces of the box this way or that, up or down, they eventually opened it. Inside they found the most exquisite collection of small weaponry and armoury they'd ever seen, each one distinct in the wispy patterns, not Celtic, not comparable to any cultural influence with which either of them were familiar. Each had jewels in triple arrangements, as embedded jewels or representations engraved into the metals, or carved symbolically into the leatherwork. Atop the layers of leather arm-guards, various blades and a quiver full of arrows, was an extraordinary dagger: The hilt was shaped like an elaborate swan intertwined with gold and silver, with three jewels embedded along the neck of the swan. The blade undulated like a snake through water. Jon carefully picked it up and turned it over and around; it was priceless.

"This is the same design!" he whispered. "The same as the rug in your mother's room, and the same as Sandy described!"

She looked around, shaking her head whispering, "There was no elderly relative to inherit from, was there?"

"What?"

"What if... what if *she's* the relative she inherited from? It's just that when we moved in, though furniture was covered with dust cloths and those kinds of things you'd expect in an old castle, there were so many things missing: No family history recorded in portraits on the walls... not a single portrait – I know, because I'd looked forward to seeing who my mother had come from and I missed having those clues. No family mementos, no knick-knacks – things you always find in grand old homes. Not even darker patches on faded walls where such portraits might have hung."

Jon replied, "Well... that leaves us with two choices: Your mother is either a scam artist and all of these antiques are replicas and forgeries; or she's just really, *really* very old... and has no relatives of which to have portraits."

Alexis laughed at the thought. "Either one is unthinkable!"

"The former is certainly more plausible than the latter; though oddly the latter is also an option at this point... it would certainly explain a lot. Actually, either would explain the missing portraits, too."

"I just wish we knew," she sighed.

"We'll get to the bottom of it," he assured her, kissing her on the temple. "I think it's time for a chat with Sandy." He looked at his watch; "If Hamish is at the *Passing Place*, he can tell us where Sandy lives."

The pub was gradually emptying from lingering lunch guests. Sandy's stool at the end of the bar was empty, so Jon caught Hamish's attention and asked after Sandy.

"Ach he'll no' be bothered by company, especially one what brings a bonnie lass," Hamish winked at Alexis amiably and wiped a glass clean with a towel as he spoke. "And take this wi' ye, if ye please – he'll no' eat otherwise." He handed him a paper bag of fish and chips. "Have ye got any sticks or peat bricks about ye?"

"Uh... not usually," Jon looked at him, puzzled.

"Visitors up here make a point of bringin' sticks or peat bricks for Sandy's fire – he's no' able tae gather much himsel'," Hamish explained. "Take a few from ma' stack out back," he tossed him a plastic bag, "and bring some from yer digs next time ye come."

"I will… thank you!" Jon gathered a few peat bricks, and then they followed the directions Hamish had given them; it wouldn't be that hard to find a house that had half a row boat as the front gate.

The lone cottage was a typical Highland home, white-washed stone with a shingle roof covered in golden lichen and long pale strands of sea ivory. The overgrown garden was cluttered with the usual bits of rusting farm equipment and tangles of crab pots and fishing nets. That genuine Highland stamp was on his house, that of something made for another use and repurposed... it seemed that nothing was ever discarded. Sandy's window frames were made from old boat parts, peeling paint between weather-worn timber slats, and a boat wheel leaning against the house gave climb to a patch of sweet peas.

Jon knocked on the door. He heard a shuffle inside and the door opened.

"Ah, laddie, come in, outta the wind wi' ye." Jon introduced Alexis, and Sandy stood a wee bit taller as he welcomed them both inside; the house was dark but for the light of a lamp near a side table, and candles dotted here and there. "What brings ye out tae the wilds? I cannae imagine it's ma' charmin' company!"

Jon laughed. "We looked for you at the pub but you weren't there so we thought we'd come and find out if you were doing alright. This is from Hamish," he handed him the meal, "and here are a few peat bricks for your fire."

"Oh, aye, thank ye," he said. "Touched, but I'll get o'er it. Sit, sit," he gestured toward a sagging arm chair; it was obviously his preferred seat, so Jon took the nearby wooden chair, ensuring that Alexis could sit where she'd see their faces; the lighting was poor, and bound to be frustrating.

Sandy laid one of the peat bricks onto his fire, where drift wood had recently been added and was burning with the merriest of crackles. The tang of smoky peat began to rise and curl, reminding Jon of whiskey. Sandy then walked the short distance to his small kitchen, part of the same small room, and asked, "Tea?" as he put a kettle of water on to boil. Jon nodded, and Sandy pulled out three mismatched cups with matching chips, and tossed a couple PG Tips tea bags into an old flowery porcelain teapot, a sign that a woman had once had a hand in the purchase. The mantle was littered with family photos, each framed and fading but proudly displayed; everything had a patina of fine dust disturbed only by a lone life. Sandy saw Alexis looking at the photos.

"Ma' kinfolk," he explained. "Some in America... some in Australia, Canada.... Some survived the Clearances ho'din' on tae a scrap o' land here, but most gave up an' went abroad. But kin's kin," he smiled. He took down a gold-plated frame and handed it to Alexis; it was worn where Sandy's thumb always held it. It was the portrait of a young woman. "That's ma' Emma," he said, "a bonnie wee lass wi' fiery hair an' *ferntickles*. She left this life near thirty years past. She's right out there," he pointed through the cracked window to a grassy slope. "I might've found work on a boat out o' Inverness, but I couldnae leave her." On the slope was a stone cross, the intricate carving of an endless knot winding around its face.

Alexis turned to Jon for explanation, who repeated the gist of Sandy's information in a way she could see it. When Sandy asked, Jon told him of Alexis's difficulties in seeing his face to read his lips.

"Why did ye no' say?" Sandy chided. "Ma' Emma was as good as deaf afore she passed." He lit a few more candles to give more light. "I know what it's like… so ye tell me if the light's no' good – I'll light more candles, fer I cannae do nought about poor lamps." Alexis nodded her thanks.

"And do you have any children?" Jon returned to the subject of family.

"Two sons," Sandy replied, "But they live a long while away from here; I see them e'ery so often, but they've got busy lives o' their own tae live," he tried to sound as if it didn't matter to him. He set the tea service down on the table with milk and sugar. "Do ye tak' a wee tait o' milk or sugar?" He began spooning it into his own cup.

Jon and Alexis both helped themselves to milk and sugar, and sat on the wooden chairs once again.

"Now," Sandy settled down into his sagging chair and then took his hot tea to his chest. "What can I do fer yous?"

"You told me you'd tell me more stories next time we met, and we wanted to take you up on the offer," Jon began. "We wanted to hear stories about Dalmoor, if you know any."

He grinned secretively, "Oh, aye… I know a few."

"We'd really like to hear whatever you can tell us about the place; we have a mystery to solve."

"Ach, if it's mystery ye're after, ye'll find yer fill there no doubt. As far as the castle itself, it's been there as far back as generations can recall."

"How do you know that?"

"The map lichen," he said simply. "I've been up there many a time o'er the years, and along the walls ye can see map lichen larger than this chair. That means it's been there, exposed as it is, fer a very, very long time."

Jon shook his head. "I didn't even think of that. Of course! And speaking of *long time* – could you tell us anything about the woman at Castle Dalmoor?"

"The Maid o' Dalmoor," Sandy said wistfully.

"No – I didn't mean that one... I meant the Cardinal... the archaeologist living there now."

"Aye? And who'd ye think I meant?"

Jon blinked. "The ghost? That's what the lads at the pub had called the ghost – the Maid of Dalmoor."

"Ach, they're daft! There's no ghost up there – The Maid o' Dalmoor is yer Cardinal, if that's what she calls hersel' now. An' she's a sight tae behold fer sure an' certain, though she's ne'er here long."

"What do you mean, 'never here long'? I thought they just moved in." Jon glanced at Alexis, who was watching intently. He didn't want to mention the fact that Alexis was her daughter just yet.

Sandy just eyed them over the rim of his tea cup as he drank, waiting for the penny to drop.

"So... no one was living in that castle before the Cardinal arrived?" Jon ventured. "No old maid, old dowager relative?"

Sandy shook his head, "No' a sign o' life. No smoke, no light, no nothin'. An' I can see the castle very well, if ye please, out ma' parlour window." He stood up slowly, getting his limbs moving before picking up his tea cup again. "Bring yer teas – come wi' me."

Sandy led them past the entryway, past a bedroom and to the room at the far end of the old longhouse, flipping on a light switch, then lighting a candle nearby for good measure. The room was indicative of the Scottish penchant for holding on to things of the past: Stacks of boxes and old newspapers were piled everywhere, a bookshelf filled with ornaments stood along the back wall, and a dusty pedalled sewing machine table stood beneath the light of the window.

"The *whigmaleeries* an' sewing machine are Emma's. I left them as she did," he waved his hand toward them as he went to the back corner and pulled out a large piece of cardboard folded in half. "It may not look it, but I'm right organized! I've got time... and someone's got tae guard the memories o' the past," he added sadly. He opened the folder, stuffed with paintings and sketches. "Ma' family's always been fond o' this; winters are long up here, though longer in my youth than now, mind ye."

He began flipping through the papers in the folder, all ranging in size from A5 to A2. He pulled out an A3-sized pencil sketch: "This was done by ma' father's father when he were a lad," he looked up at the ceiling to calculate, "1880 give or take." He brought it to the light of the window: It was clearly Castle Dalmoor, but with the glass conservatory under construction, half-complete. "Ma' granddad used tae say he drew it as a reminder o' his first love. Ma' gran' understood, an' always said she felt honoured tae be in such fine company."

"Did he know the people who lived there then? Who were they?"

"Well," Sandy scratched his chin stubble, "Ye'd read it easier yersel' – ma' eyes arenae so good as they were." He pulled out an old wooden crate labelled *Smoked Mackerel*, rummaged through it and set aside a leather-bound bundle of letters and odd papers. From below that bundle he pulled out a plain brown notebook bound by hand-sewn stitches. He flipped through the yellowed pages until he found what he was looking for: On one side of the page was a very rough sketch of what might be a woman and on the other, a date and journal entry.

"Read it out fer us?" Sandy asked Jon.

"It's in English?" Jon asked, surprised.

"Ach, aye. We had tae learn tae write it, though we spoke Gaelic at home right enough. But English was the written word, an' Gaelic that o' the heart an' hearth."

Jon took it in hand and read:

" '21 June 1881: I saw her again today. She's as a wee wildcat, only seen with stealth and patience. Dressed in her vibrant red...' Jon looked at Alex, wide-eyed, and Sandy, who only smiled with a nod to continue, '...as red as just-overripe strawberries. This time she had her thick black hair tied back, plaited as my gran used to plait her own. She's always looking for something. She's *a wee haunted sprite, haunting the glens and lochans, haunted by something. She wears a grey cloak, though <u>grey</u> does it no justice. If she knows she's been seen, she'll pull that cloak about her and fairly disappear.'* "

Jon handed the book back to Sandy, commenting a bit nervously, "It must run in her family... that penchant for red... hunting for lost treasure." The more obvious connection just didn't want to make sense in his mind. He reached out to touch Alexis's hand, making certain she was alright.

Sandy flipped to another page, handing it back to Jon with a nod. "Read us," he said.

" *'I came across the glen today and found myself face to face with her, the lass in red, the bonnie Maid of Dalmoor. My heart jumped to my throat I was that surprised! She spoke, songs as sweet as honeysuckle. Her grey eyes, like the sea under a stormy sky, pierced my heart. Lost am I! As far above me as the stars, yet she spoke to me. In my life I'll marry and love another, but this day will live vivid in my memory ever more.'* "

Jon finished reading and fell silent.

"Odd, isn't it?" Sandy broke the silence. "Red... thick black hair... grey eyes." He watched Jon and Alexis's faces. "If ye care tae know more, I'll tell yous."

"Go on," Jon looked at him, holding his breath.

He leaned toward them. "I may be old, but that's just it – I *am*! An' I remember her beautiful face, an' the face o' her dark, large companion. From ma' youth I remember them! Back when I didnae need spectacles tae see! That much I know I know!" his eyes gleamed at the memories. "Ach, aye, they've been here afore. I hold naught fer the rumours o' her inheritin' the place; it's been Dalmoor o' the bonnie maid's many a generation. She didnae come back until after the Second World War, an' then disappeared when I was just gettin' tae that age tae think o' taking a wife – though I'd never've had the pluck tae ask the likes o' her. She returned again this year, but once a man's been struck by that beauty, he ne'er forgets," he nodded knowingly. "E'ery time she returns, the weather saddens. When she laughs, the sun bursts forth; when she weeps, the sky weeps wi' her. Mark her moods, an' mark ma' word, an' decide the matter yersel'."

Jon looked at Alexis: "Remember the rainstorm we faced when we came out of the souterrain the first time?"

Her eyes widened, and she nodded.

Sandy sat down on a box, as if that might make what he were saying easier to understand, before continuing: "She's been known as the Maid o' Dalmoor since ma' great gran's gran were a wee lass. It's the same woman in all the tales," he waved his hand dismissively, "sagas an' stories that go back further than writin'. I know. Because as a young lad, like I said, I was in young love wi' that *same* woman." He watched how they were taking this information so far, and then added, "When I first told ye o' that tunnel lad, I didnae tell ye all; the owner was no' o' the green welly brigade... no Englishman from the south; it was *her*, the one ye call the Cardinal, an' she was there all the while."

The evidence was stacking up in Jon's mind against common sense, and all he could do was shake his head, not in disbelief but incredulity. He looked at Alexis. She was bursting with questions, but was hesitant to speak in front of someone she'd just met. Jon nodded, encouraging her to speak.

"Sandy... I think Alexis has a few questions, if you don't mind," he said.

"Aye! Of course, lassie!" he answered, hands on his knees as he sat down atop a stack of magazines to face her.

She fought to overcome her fear of speaking in front of someone new.

"I dinnae bite, lassie," he smiled with a wink.

That made her laugh, and relax. She asked, "How old is my mother?"

"Yer *mother*!" Sandy exclaimed. "Now *that* I didnae know! Why'd ye no' stop me?" Sandy reproached Jon.

"We wanted to know," Jon apologized, "and didn't want a biased tale. And Alexis is the adopted daughter of the Cardinal."

"Well..." Sandy looked from one to the other. "All that we say stays in this wee room, aye? Agreed?" They readily agreed. "I've no way of knowin' how old the lass is; but she doesnae age... she could be fifty, a hundred and fifty... or a thousand years old."

"You said she's been here before," Alexis continued, "and that Elbal – the large, dark companion of hers – was with her. How old was he then? Has he aged? And were his sons with him then too?"

"Sons... those that are with them now?"

She nodded.

"They were lads last I saw them; but that's ferlie...strange," he translated for Alexis whose confused look said she didn't recognize the Scottish word, "fer that would ha'e been in the year..." he thought a moment, "I'll admit tae comin' intae this world in 1929; I must ha'e been nineteen when they returned tae Dalmoor... so t'was 1948. His sons looked tae ha'e been about ten at the time and the father, in his forties – though I've learned that time disnae pass there," he waved toward Dalmoor, "as anywhere else. Aye, the men ha'e aged slowly, but she hasnae." Sandy then picked up the journal, flipping to a page and holding it up. "I found ma' granddad's journals after his passin', an' it struck me: His description brought only her tae mind. An' the sketch... he wasnae a brilliant artist, but—" he stood up and walked a few steps away, "look at it from a distance; it's as he worshipped her... from afar." It was as if the thing unclear close up suddenly came into focus; it was an ingenious sketch meant to be drawn and viewed at a distance of several feet.

Jon jumped up as if bitten. "It's *her*!"

Alexis just stared at the sketch, blinking in disbelief. Sandy just smiled.

Jon took the sketch, holding it at arm's length, then closer, then propped it up on a box and stepped back. "Amazing," he whispered. "But how? How can it be?"

"How open are yous?" asked Sandy, studying their faces.

"At this point, we'll hear any theory you've got!" Alexis answered.

※

Jon and Alexis had talked on the way home until nothing more could be said, no more sense could be made of what they'd learned until they found out more.

"When is Alvar arriving?" Alexis asked.

"He'll be anchoring his yacht somewhere near Trài— that beach we went to," he gave up trying to remember the Gaelic name as he re-read the SMS. "It just says here that he'll meet me on the beach at 14:00 tomorrow."

"And have you thought about what we'll say? The staff will want to know why we suddenly have an unannounced guest."

"The truth," Jon said. "He's my history professor who was in the area, so he came by for a visit... in a way, it's true."

"In a way," she grinned. "Alright, then we'll give him the grand tour. Where's he going to sleep?"

"Uh... I hadn't really thought of that; he usually sleeps on his yacht, but since he's reluctant to anchor closer—"

"Leave it to me." Just then Alexis's stomach growled. "I guess tea and biscuits weren't enough..."

"We'll be back in time for dinner," Jon looked at his watch, "and then after that... let's go in search of the cavern's hidden entrance – as soon as the volunteer crew are done in the kitchen, that is."

"Then let's go prepared this time," Alexis smiled; "let's put on our swimming costumes beneath our clothes, just in case we find it!"

In the dining hall there was one topic of discussion that overshadowed everything else: That morning one of the students, Hamish, had been injured when he came out of his caravan; someone had put a trip-wire across the door, and he'd sprained his shoulder in the fall; on the ground he had met a carpet of nails sprinkled along the worn path to his door, and injured his face and hands on impact as well. When his roommate investigated he found the same traps set before each caravan and everyone was warned not to come out until it had all been cleared away. Moods were sour, suspicious, and jumpy: The injury could have been much worse, and in people's minds it was.

One of the women, Martha, stood up and called for everyone's attention: "I don't know about the rest of you... but I'm tired! I haven't slept for several nights in a row because of all the screaming and moaning and chains and noise at the site! Who's doing it?" she demanded, glaring down each one in turn. There were no guilty expressions in the lot. "Well... there's only a fortnight before the new term begins so... I don't know about the rest of you, but

I'm leaving! I'd leave tonight if I could, but as it is... I'll leave first thing in the morning. If someone could give me a lift to Durness to catch the morning Postbus, I'd be grateful."

Once the floodgates had been opened, the entire caravan population took the chance to escape; one by one the other women stood up to join her, their nerves raw, and then one by one the male students stood as well.

Toshiro stood up: "You'd leave, just like that? While the Cardinal's away? Will you not at least wait until she returns in two days, to say goodbye properly? And what about Brehani? Will you just leave him to wrap up the excavation site for the autumn by himself?" He looked from one student to the next, his disappointed look chiding them as well as any mother's guilt trip could have.

One by one they sat down reluctantly. George, one of the Scottish students, said, "It wouldnae be fair tae leave so, ye're right; but after this," he pointed to Hamish, whose left arm was strapped to his chest in a sling and his face and hands speckled with puncture wounds and bruises, "What choice do we have? We've got tae leave soon anyway... and I suspect we'd all like tae leave whole."

A murmur of agreement spread through the dining hall; Jon heard the 'Maid of Dalmoor' and the 'ghost of Dalmoor' in the whispers. Fear was mushrooming. No matter what was going on, or who was doing it, serious injury had been intended with the trip-wires and nails. Whatever misunderstanding there was on just who the Maid of Dalmoor was, there was no denying that whatever was happening was real.

"I'll make a deal with you," Brehani stood up; everyone turned to look at him. "If some of you will stay and help me wrap up for the autumn... clean the equipment, preserve the digs for the winter break, and finish written reports... Jon will fly five of you to Inverness, where you can catch a train south. Just three or four days, and if all of you help, we can secure the site for the season." He looked to Jon for approval of that plan, and Jon nodded. It wasn't as if such a flight were gratis, but the Cardinal was a generous employer so he could afford a charitable flight.

Edric was the first to stand. "I'll stay on – I'm not afraid of bumps in the night," he grinned.

"Easy for you to say! You're staying in the castle!" Martha quipped.

George answered for himself and Hamish: "I'll stay tae help while Hamish recovers, as we're here together with ma' mum's car; but only on the condition that *we* can stay here in the castle as well – we'll sleep on the floor if need be, but we'll no' stay down there another night," he pointed toward the loch.

"It won't be necessary to sleep on the floor – we'll bring the beds up from the caravans," Toshiro assured him.

Two of the women volunteered to stay on under the same conditions, though the rest could only be persuaded to stay in the castle until the Cardinal returned in two days' time; the rich finds of the dig were not enough to entice them to stay when compared to the danger and unrest they'd been having. The conference room became a camp room for the men while the women were given the library. Once the decisions had been made the students returned to the caravans to pack up, clean, and move to safety. They'd finish the work with considerable more ease of mind, gladly putting in one last, guilty burst of hard work; it was put to use in preparing the site to weather the Highland winter.

Once the dinner crew had cleaned up and left the kitchen, Alexis and Jon began searching the cellar's storage room; the only other room in the cellar, the kitchen, was lined wall-to-wall with a refrigerator, counters, sinks, ovens and stoves.

"That's odd," Alexis pointed to a box on the top shelf labelled *Sewing Threads/Twine*. Every other box on the shelf was labelled *Archives*. "Either that box has been misplaced, or it wants to be found." She pulled the nearby ladder into place and climbed to the top, handing the box down to Jon. It felt empty, but inside they found a grey cloak.

"This must be what my mother was wearing when we saw her enter the souterrain," Alexis touched the cloak.

"Sandy's journals mentioned her in a grey cloak as well," Jon stared at it in awe. "Do you realize... we're not just looking at a piece of history; this thing *is* history... living, breathing history happening right under our very noses."

At first touch they knew the cloak's material was unique: It felt like they were putting their hand into a box of cloud and trying to grasp it. Not even sure he had hold of it, Jon took it from the box and held it up: It was floor length and with a generous hood; the volume of material should have weighed at least five kilograms, yet it had the weight of a feather. Alexis put it on; it dragged the floor on her smaller frame, but she immediately said that it felt refreshing; warm, but not hot; cool but not cold. Jon tried it on and understood what she meant, though neither could explain it. They laid it out carefully on the table, spreading its folds out to examine it closer.

"What could it be made of?" Alexis asked.

"I'm no cloth expert... but I've never seen a smoother weave. The strands of material... if you could call them that... are finer than human hairs!"

"Yet it weighs almost nothing," Alexis held it in her arms. "Not that I'm a cloth expert either, but I do know a thing or two about shopping, in markets from here to Singapore – and I've never come across anything like it."

"Well, let's put it back and keep looking for that entrance." When Alexis folded the cloak to fit it back into the box a note fluttered to the floor; it read:

Dear Alexis

If you've found this cloak, it's a piece to your puzzle of who I am. When you find the door unlocked by the key from the heights of the tower, please return this cloak to its usual place upon a hook a few Steps beyond that door.

Love

The woman privileged to be called your mother

Alexis smiled when she read the note. "Do you see this? She capitalized *Steps* – it might be a clue!"

She hung the cloak on a hook behind the storage room door for the time being and they returned the box to the shelf. As they headed toward the stairwell however, Jon stopped Alexis and pointed toward the stairs – he could hear footsteps and he motioned for her to keep silent. Galal and Amir were talking as they came within sight of Alexis and Jon though they had not yet noticed their presence. Galal was very similar to his brother in appearance, both bronze-skinned with olive-black eyes. They wore their usual apparel, black side-buttoned Mandarin shirts and black jeans.

Amir was saying, "...but I examined the scene, and all I could find were slender footprints... not shoes, but bare feet, and those of a woman, no mistake."

Alexis read their lips easily, and as the penny dropped she exclaimed, "It's the Wolf!"

Amir looked up at her in shock. "You... you speak in front of him?" he pointed toward Jon. "Does he know of your...?" he gestured toward his mouth.

"I do," Jon smiled at Alexis, squeezing her hand.

Galal replied, "And besides, it can't be the Wolf; Amir said the footprints belonged to a *woman*."

"Exactly," said Jon.

Before he had time to react Jon was flat on his back with Galal straddling him, a snaking Kris at his throat.

"Stop!" shouted Alexis. "Don't hurt him!"

"Galal!" Amir tried to reason with his brother. "You're overreacting."

"I'm on your side!" Jon held up his hands in surrender.

The blade didn't budge. "What do you know about the Wolf?" Galal hissed into Jon's face.

"I'm after the Wolf too!"

At that the blade eased slightly. "Explain!"

"It's known that the Wolf chooses targets and then hounds them – and the Cardinal is the favoured target right now. But the Cardinal's not the only one who's had things stolen... a friend of mine had something valuable taken and he wants it back. If we can catch her here we might be able to get back what is his."

Galal stared at him. "And why do you think the Wolf is a woman?"

Jon glanced at Alexis. "My friend knew her years ago, before she became known as *the Wolf*. Though from what I've been told her agents are usually men, so you've been half-right."

Galal replied, "Well, it makes no great difference to me whether he's a he or a she's a she; either way we'll catch them." He stood up and held out his hand to help Jon to his feet; but as Jon rose Galal clasped his arm at the elbow and jerked him closer, hissing in his face, "If you deceive us, my blade will find its mark wherever you may hide."

"Then your blade will hang useless at your side," Jon held his gaze as the air crackled.

Galal looked at Alexis, weighing a decision. Suddenly he laughed and sheathed his Kris, the tension evaporating like mist in sunshine.

"You must forgive my younger brother," Amir said to Jon while casting a reproachful glare at Galal. "He's impetuous, and these strange events have made him more than a bit irritable and suspicious."

"Of course I forgive him... he's got the knife," Jon laughed nervously, straightening out his rumpled shirt.

Alexis checked Jon's throat, but it was unmarked; she cast a scathing glare at Galal. "But back to our point, before we were so *rudely* interrupted... the Wolf's sabotaged our work before, but never in this way... each time has been different so I didn't recognize the pattern until just now... but this would make sense! She's playing with local tales of ghosts and folklore, don't you see? Hindering work, disrupting plans, making the accomplishment of the Cardinal's goals difficult... she's done it all before!"

"Really?" Jon asked. "Then what's her point? I mean, if her real goal were to get what the Cardinal is after from an archaeological viewpoint, then she would do nothing to keep the Cardinal from reaching that object. So if she has a habit of hindering...?"

"Maybe she just likes to be annoying," Galal huffed.

"But she's never directly injured anyone before now; annoyance and injury are two different things," Alexis pointed out.

"If she *is* the ghost, she's obviously somewhere nearby this time," Amir replied. "Now what?"

"The strange occurrences... the screaming, the chains... they're theatrical," Jon ran his fingers through his hair, thinking. "I think she likes an audience. And if her audience has now moved to the castle... my hunch is that she won't be far behind." Jon's mental list of things to tell Alvar was getting almost too long to remember it all; he felt like he was cramming for an exam.

Amir sighed, "If news spreads of this shift of focus from the caravans to the castle, we'll have no students left by tonight – but Brehani needs their help to winterize the site. Whatever course of action we would take now, we must wait for the sake of the excavation."

"In that case," Alexis pulled out the skeleton key from her pocket, "Jon and I have a scavenger hunt to continue. Have either of you seen an invisible door around here?" she asked.

Galal grinned, "If it's invisible, we cannot see it! But no – we have been told by Gra— by the Cardinal to give you no clues. You must find it yourself."

Between the third and fourth steps up from the cellar floor they found the secret entrance at last, the stones of the wall camouflaging the keyhole cover flawlessly and the skeleton key a perfect match. Alexis retrieved the cloak from the storage room and they went through, closing the door behind them with a quiet *click*. The door was perfectly hung and well oiled; it was effortlessly opened with a slight push from the stair-side, while from the cavern it merely needed a pull with the key turned, the key acting as a portable door handle.

The luminescent stones had lost their glow; Jon pulled out his torch and they found the light switch, which turned out to be the same dimmer dial as the one in the Hall of Dreams. A few steps from the door they found a hook and returned the cloak to its place.

"It's been a very long day," Alexis sat down on the stone between the pools. "So much to take in... so much to unravel, so much more than we began the day with!"

"There *is* a lot to take in," Jon replied. "But I have the feeling that the puzzle pieces, as bizarre as they seem right now, will make a full picture once we know what we're looking at. The trick is seeing the big picture." He looked around. "Well, we have our suits on," he patted his hip. "If the stones have soaked in enough light for you to read my lips, what say we douse the lights for a swim and get our minds off of things for a while?"

They did just that, tossing their clothes over the table and chairs near the door and gliding into the heated cascade pool, the blue stones illuminating their bodies underwater in silhouette as dancing waves of light reflected on the roof of the cavern.

8: Now

It was two o'clock. Alexis checked her watch again as she waited with Jon at the bottom of the sandy steps that led from the car park down to Tràigh Allt Chàilgeag beach. There was a man and his dog at the far end of the beach near the water's edge, so far away at the ebbing tide that they were mere specks; otherwise they were alone.

"What's Alvar like?" Alexis asked nervously. She was anxious to meet this friend whom Jon had spoken so highly of... he sounded so perfect... she hoped he'd approve of her.

"Quiet," he looked at her, "typical historian... studious, melancholic... and I guess you could say *emotionally guarded*. And I know he'll love you," he kissed her forehead.

"I wonder what he'll be able to help us figure out? Or are we putting too much hope in his coming in that respect? I mean, how can he help solve the riddle of someone he's never met?"

"There *has* to be a connection; at least in areas of expertise and the Wolf; in all our puzzling I think we've lost sight of the fact that the Wolf has a spy here; that the spy has left a note and a dagger; and that your mother, whoever she is, is a target as Alvar once was. More than that I think we'll have to leave to fate."

"Do you believe in fate?" she asked.

He shook his head slowly. "Not fate so much as a plan laid out; our little choices determine the direction of our lives as much as a little rudder guides an entire ship to its destination. You could say in that context that a captain knows the rudder will do its job and how to guide it, but passengers have to take it on *faith*."

As he spoke he watched the waves crashing along the rocky cliffs to the east of the bay. Suddenly he smiled and pointed. Alexis saw something in the water.

"Is it a seal?" she looked back at him.

"No," Jon shook his head laughing, "it's Alvar! He's insane!" Alvar had never been afraid of anything that he knew of; drowning in a riptide on an unknown strand didn't appear to mean anything to him. He was effortlessly swimming against the ebbing tide – a tide too cold for any sane person to voluntarily subject themselves to. When he reached levels shallow enough to stand, he waved to them in the distance and headed straight for them.

Alexis noticed that he was wearing a rucksack, and as he got closer she saw his blonde hair; even from a distance she could see that he had a Viking physique, well presented in a maroon drysuit.

When he reached them Jon pulled him into a bear hug and slapped his rucksack. "Great to see you!" he smiled. "Did you have a good trip?"

"Getting away from Fair Isle was difficult, but after that it was fair sailing." He turned to Alexis, and as Jon introduced them Alvar began to sign his name to her.

She let him finish and smiled, but now had the confidence to speak. "It's nice to meet you, sir. I've heard so much about you." Aside from the fact that she'd seen him on Skype and Google, she recognized his face from elsewhere though she couldn't place it.

"And I you," he said in return. "Thank you for allowing me to come."

"Where is your yacht anchored, if I may ask? Didn't you want to anchor it closer – in the loch? There are many suitable places there," she suggested.

"Perhaps later," he replied. "I know of a discreet anchorage just around the rocks there," he pointed, "that is safe from the battering of the ocean and prying eyes."

"Really?" she was surprised. "I didn't think there was anything in that direction until Rispond."

"I did say *discreet*," he smiled.

Before they left the beach he stepped into a deep crevice in the vertical stone cliff and changed out of his drysuit. He came out dressed in a dark red Merino shirt and casual black slacks. He brushed the sand from his feet and slipped on comfortable shoes, then snapped the water from the drysuit with a flick, rolled it up and strapped it to the rucksack. Alexis thought to herself that he'd probably look flawless, even in a potato sack. The rucksack, a Lowepro, was completely waterproof; he pulled out a dry cardigan and slipped it on. He and Jon chatted about the crossing as they walked up to the car park, and Alvar handed him a package before stowing his gear in the luggage rack at the back of the golf cart.

"Cheese," Jon smiled at Alexis, and thanked Alvar as they climbed in. He drove and let the other two become acquainted in the back seat.

"How long are you here for?" Alexis asked.

"It depends... I have a few things I'd like to do while I'm in the area. But I wouldn't want to be an inconvenience to you; I can get a Bed and Breakfast."

"Nonsense," she said, "I've arranged a guest room for you."

"Thank you, that is very kind," he bowed slightly in gratitude.

They talked, each more than willing to find the other pleasant, and by the time they reached Dalmoor they were firm friends. Alexis felt secure in his presence, almost like a father though he wasn't old enough to be her father; but if she had ever had one (or had a choice of one) he would be just like Alvar.

They parked the golf cart in the garage just outside the portico and led Alvar in through the courtyard. As they passed the tree Alexis stopped to examine it.

"This must be where that dagger hit," she ran her finger over the gash.

Alvar stepped up beside her and caressed the gash, whispering something that Jon couldn't quite make out; it wasn't English but could have been Norwegian. As they reached the entry hall door, a low rumble rattled the nearby window panes.

"What was that?" Alexis exclaimed, feeling the vibrations.

Jon said, "Probably a military exercise out at Cape Wrath." He glanced at Alvar to see him looking back at the tree and smiling.

As they reached the top of the entry hall steps Alvar saw the fireplace and froze, his gaze riveted to the mantelpiece. He stepped cautiously forward, staring from one symbol to the next while tracing them with his fingers. Weariness settled on his shoulders.

It seemed to Jon as if his friend's emotional guard of calm sovereignty had just been ripped aside somehow, like a thick curtain being pulled aside to reveal a turbulent storm outside.

His friend breathed, "She was here!"

"Who was here?" Alexis asked; the name had been spoken without moving the lips.

"She," Jon shrugged, facing her but keeping his eyes on his friend.

Their voices tore Alvar from his reveries and he gently caressed the nearest figure, that of a ship's prow. "Someone I once knew," he explained. His expression became unreadable again behind his emotional shield. "She went missing many years ago."

"I'm sorry," Alexis whispered, "I didn't mean to pry."

Alvar looked at her kindly, touching her arm. "You could not have known."

"But she was *here*?" Jon asked. "How can that be?"

"This fireplace... the symbols," he explained. "They could have been made by no other. But it was many, many years ago..."

"You understand these symbols?" Jon stared at him.

"What do they mean?" Alexis touched the mantelpiece.

"Jon told me that you two found a map with the word *Maldor*... that is the story told here," he looked from one to the other.

They were about to ask more but the front door opened; Edric came striding up the entrance hall stairs.

"Oh, hello," he shook Alvar's hand, "I'm Edric. Are you here for a visit?"

"Yes, just a few days," Alvar replied.

"Oh? Visiting a friend?"

"He's my history professor, just in the area on business," Jon replied for him.

"You studied history? For your pilot license?"

"Being a pilot just pays the bills," Jon replied casually, but made it clear he wasn't in the mood for a chat. "What are you doing up here at this time of the day?"

"Storage room – Brehani needs more bags to tag artefacts," he shrugged with a grin, "so I volunteered to warm up my toes."

Alexis stepped between them, smiling politely at Edric and pulling Alvar's and Jon's arms as if to follow her.

"She can't talk but she sure can be bossy," Edric scrunched his nose at Alexis and she returned the gesture but had her way. Edric watched them leave, glanced at the fireplace curiously, and continued on his way.

At the first landing along the stairwell Alvar approached the statue as if it were an old friend. "It's... it's Darachi! A dryad... the dryad of these forests!" he smiled, gazing at her and shaking his head incredulously as if it were a true reunion.

Alexis came close to whisper in case Edric were nearby still. "Forests? What story is that?"

Alvar laughed, "Oh... a fantastical one... I wrote about her in one of my novels, that's all."

Jon knew that tone: Alvar was a terrible liar. But he admitted to writing novels, plural; interesting.

Alvar looked back at the statue, an expression of admiration but of great sadness too. "This is exactly as I... imagined her." He touched his heart and bowed his head in parting farewell and they climbed the first flight of stairs.

Jon watched this exchange carefully. He was beginning to read between the lines of his friend's replies, the puzzle pieces flipping in his mind. A picture was beginning to form.

Upon reaching the landing of the first floor Alvar saw the statue in the alcove of the spiral stairs. "This... this cannot be!"

"What?" Alexis exclaimed. "How do you seem to know so much more about this castle than I do? Have you been here before?"

He took her by the shoulders. "Who is this Cardinal? Tell me!" He looked at them both, his eyes pleading them to answer.

"She... she is my adoptive mother!" Alexis replied, confused.

"What does she look like? Exactly?"

"Raven black hair," she stammered, a bit unsettled at the hungry look in his eyes. "beautiful eyes... porcelain skin." Alexis began to understand. "Do you know her?"

"I— I daren't hope again," he said at last, releasing her shoulders, touching his heart and bowing sadly to the statue. That description could have been either... and it reminded him to be cautious.

"Hope *what*, Alvar?" Jon asked pointedly. "And why do you pay such respect to these statues? It's not like you," Jon shook his head. "You'd better start explaining!"

Alvar thought a moment, looking around. "Not here," he whispered. "Somewhere private."

At the third landing it no longer shocked Alvar to see a statue, lifelike and familiar to him. He turned to them, pointing down the stairs: "The second statue was that of Queen Amanis of Maldor; this is her husband, King Elgin." He again touched his hand to his heart and bowed.

"Come," Alexis said, "We'll go by your room; you can leave your bag there and then to my room for some tea."

"And explanation," added Jon.

In the guest room Alvar hung his dry suit behind the door and slid his rucksack under the bed; when he stood up and turned around Alexis gasped, staring at him wide-eyed. "I know why you looked so familiar to me! That expression you just had on your face... in the cellar," she lowered her voice to a whisper, "there's a statue that looks exactly like you, with that very expression!"

"And... is there a statue of your mother anywhere?" he asked.

"No, I'm afraid not. But there is another statue of a woman at the landing to the tower," she replied.

The heaviness returned to Alvar's expression. Moriel's detest for the Gatekeeper's family might drive her to keep their likenesses, to gloat over. He wanted to know for certain, but was afraid of being forced to look upon his beloved's countenance of stone; for if it were Erlina's statue it could only mean that the mother of Alexis was truly none other than Moriel, and all his worst fears would be realized.

"We'll finish the tour later," Jon studied his friend's face with concern. "Right now I think we need to talk."

In Alexis's room they sat at the table with freshly brewed tea. The air was electric with anticipation as Alvar gathered his thoughts. At last he looked up from his tea: "I don't really know where to begin... but you've both discovered recently that, shall we say, life is not as *elementary* as most people think; your friend Sandy told you his theories about the existence, or possibility, of other life forms," he looked at Jon, "... *Elves* as some have called them – though that is merely a general term for a variety of immortal species." He paused, looking at both of them, weighing how much he should tell them... how much they could handle. "What I'm about to tell you stays between us; agreed? No one is to know until I deem it so." They both nodded their agreement readily. He took a deep breath: "These particular immortals you've recently heard of are not elves as you understand the term; they are in fact what you might call... aliens... from an Earth-like planet beyond the Shaft of Aquila, near the star Altair. They are peaceful travellers; they live where they find a pleasing environment, learn all they can – they are avid collectors of knowledge and wisdom, as well as teachers; and when either the situation or environment becomes hostile, or they have simply learned all they can from that region, they move on; but they never forget anything... you might say they have minds like steel traps. When they tire of travelling they return home to their mother planet, *Aquillis*, taking their knowledge with them and adding it to the collective understanding of their Kind." He studied their expressions a moment before continuing: "Universal expanse being what it is, the Aquillian developed a way of travelling great distances in the blink of an eye: Their planet's core is made of self-replenishing *Mithrian* diamond, a substance far superior to earthly diamonds; such types of planets are known even to your astronomers. This substance, converted into particles as fine as dust, acts as a key between worlds; portals can be opened by those trained in the art, and they are known as Gatekeepers;

each travelling pod has at least one." Here he stopped to let the information sink in.

Jon looked at him suspiciously. "How do you know all of that? Or are you having us on? I mean, I've heard of a diamond planet they're supposed to have found – *55 Cancri e*. But this?" he shook his head in disbelief. "You've got to be joking."

"I will tell you plainly," he looked at his friend earnestly. "*I* am an Aquillian Gatekeeper. My true name is not Alvar... but Aradan."

Jon knew that look on his friend's face – only when Alvar was being dead serious about something; those kinds of moments that, in the past, meant Jon could take what Alvar had told him at face-value, as truth. But this time...?

Alexis didn't know what to think; she looked at him as if she wanted to reach out and assure herself he was real; he reached over and took her hand with a smile.

"Wait, wait, wait!" Jon shook his head trying to find reason. "You're telling us... you're an alien? As in E.T.?"

"No... I'm an alien, as in a real extraterrestrial humanoid from another planet." he grinned at Jon. "Did you really think Earth was the only populated planet in the universe? I mean think about it: There are a hundred billion stars, average, per galaxy; at the present knowledge of man there are an estimated hundred billion galaxies in your known universe. If only one percent of those stars has populated planets, we're still talking about a billion populated planets in *one* galaxy alone. Yet the nearest star to your sun is in the Alpha Centauri system, over four light years away, or over forty trillion kilometres away... that's a long flight. And that's still within your own thin outer spiral branch of the Milky Way Galaxy."

Alexis, her expression a mixture of shock and revelation and understanding, said, "They never forget anything?"

"Not once we've learned something," Aradan nodded.

"That would explain a great deal about my mother," she exclaimed. "About her success as an archaeologist!"

Jon stared at her. "You believe this?" he waved toward Alvar. "And why would you—" it suddenly hit him... all the stories Sandy had told them, all the puzzle pieces tumbling into place. *Immortal.* "You're right," he nodded numbly. Jon stared at his friend as if he were a stranger seen for the first time, and in a way it was true. *Aradan.*

"I realize that I've given you a lot to take in," Aradan eyed his friend cautiously.

"I'll say!" Jon nearly shouted. "Why didn't you give me any warning in our calls lately that you were part of this whole tale?"

"You knew that I'd been after the Wolf for *some time*... I just didn't tell you how long. And you knew that I'd lost someone I loved—"

"Yes," Jon interrupted, "but you let me assume that *lost* meant dead, not *lost* as in a misplaced glove!"

"You don't know how often I was close to telling you; but things tend to get awkward after someone finds out. I wanted to tell you face-to-face... I didn't want to risk our friendship any sooner than I had to. You wouldn't have believed me if I had told you over the phone."

"Yes I wou— yeah, you're right," Jon sat back. After quite some sinking-in time he chuckled, "So... that haunting suspicion I've always had that you had some kind of past you'd prefer to keep hidden... I wasn't that far off was I?"

"No," Aradan smiled, "though I doubt you would have allowed for such a fantastical explanation."

"No, but it explains a lot... I've always said you were from another planet – though I was never serious! And... that means you haven't forgotten any those practical jokes I pulled on you at uni, have you?"

"Not one," Aradan shook his head as he laughed. Visibly relieved, he sat back with a sigh. "I'm glad you know now... that you've been able to accept it, whether or not you believe me yet."

"Can I ask something?" Alexis asked, and he nodded. "You said your planet's name is Aquillis? Beyond the Shaft of Aquila? But what do *you* call it? I mean, I assume Aquillis is the name related to the shaft from our perspective, though I doubt you'd associate the planet with the shaft from your own planetary vantage point."

Intelligent woman. Jon smiled smugly at Aradan, crossing his arms.

Aradan looked at her, smiling, "Haven't you ever wondered how your astronomical objects got some of their names? Or even how your proto-languages came into being?"

Her eyes widened at the suggestion. She then said, "If my mother is one of your kind, it would explain a great many odd things that we've discovered lately."

"I'm certain she is," Aradan replied. "But there's more I must explain: The one you know as the Wolf is called Moriel," he said to Alexis, "and she is Aquillian; she was taken captive the same day I was, in a battle at this very site in AD 789. She gradually turned *Morquillian*, or 'dark'. Her giftings are treacherous; I watched time and again as she instigated battles just because she could. And, for me most perfidious, on more than one occasion she made me believe that she was *Erlina*," he looked at Jon. "Erlina is the eldest daughter of the king and queen whose statues stand guard in the stairwells of this castle. She was my betrothed."

"Your *lost love*? And what do you mean *was*?" Jon looked at him wide-eyed. He'd known the fact of Alvar – now Aradan's – lost love almost as long as he'd known Aradan; but he thought it was a typical break-up-with-a-girlfriend-that-he-never-got-over kind of lost love, not death of an alien.

"Moriel became covetous of my love for Erlina," he explained. "She tried everything she could to dissuade me, to win my heart... when it failed, she began to use deceit; she made me see things that were not, as though they were. But my love for Erlina alerted me in time, again and again. When at last she knew she would never defeat my love, she drew me in again to a half-dream she wove, stole my betrothal necklace, and vowed to find Erlina and lead her to her death."

"Wait! You said that your kind are immortal, so how could Erlina be dead?" Jon asked.

He explained the laws of immortality to them in the simplest of terms: Immortals defending a mortal life risked death by sacrificing themselves.

"But what about the statues... the fireplace? If only Erlina could have made those, then the Cardinal has to be her!"

"Depending on when they were made, and what transpired between then and now," Aradan reasoned. "The statues are no proof; it could well be that Moriel gloats by keeping such things as belonged to Erlina..." he paused, distraught. "I would give anything to believe you; but I've been deceived by Moriel so many times in the past... my heart dare not believe again until I am absolutely certain."

"A psychotic wannabe girlfriend with a treacherous power? Wonderful. And I thought *my* relationship decisions were bad. Present company excepted, naturally," he smiled at Alexis.

Her expression told him that he'd be spilling the beans on that score soon enough. "But I'm confused... how could you mistake your betrothed for such a woman?" Alexis asked.

"Moriel was powerful in her gifting, and she'd grown more potent," he began: "She stole my necklace once, long, long ago but I was able to reclaim in within the year. Shortly after I'd retrieved it I heard that she had deeply offended the king in whose custody she was held captive. He ensured that she was sold through Constantinople to scrupulous traders, but knowing her she most likely manipulated her way into a better situation than he'd planned for her. After that our ways parted for nearly a century; in that time, because I had the necklace I could sense Erlina... and I know that she could sense me. Visions of the night were my solace as I visited her in my dreams... or perhaps even transportations – they were so vivid that I could smell the aromas of peat fires in Scotland even as I lay in a tar-scented longhouse in Norway," he told them, a far-off gaze of wonder in his eyes as he recalled those days. "I was pledged by my honour to serve my captor, who became my friend, and from there in successive generations I was called upon by dying kings to pledge my support and counsel to their fledgling sons who took their places upon the thrones of their fathers. In 1066 I at last found a way to return to the British Isles, as counsel to my king who was called upon to serve his high king by joining his ships to the forces of Harald Hardrada, a distant relative. I would neither fight nor defend, but was personal physician and counsellor to my king, Magnus Rødskjegg, Redbeard. Between the infamous battles of Fulford and Stamford Bridge, our ships sailed by day and we camped on land by night.

"One night as I lie in my tent asleep, I heard my Aquillian name called. It was more vivid than my visions of the night, and it awakened me immediately. At the tent entrance, lit by campfire light from behind, I thought I saw the form and heard the voice of Erlina. She behaved in such a way as to convince me it was her; when I looked into her eyes I was certain I was looking into the eyes of Erlina. She told me how she had searched for me since the time we had been parted, and when she heard of this great army's victory, she was certain I would be one of their number. She said she had enquired of the men from the North about a man renowned for his healing touch and had been thus directed to my tent. Because I had looked into her eyes, against my knowledge Moriel had drawn me in to her web of deceit, a false vision. I allowed her to draw near to me; but suddenly I felt my limbs grow heavy with sleep... I could not move, though I tried, and I realized my grave error too late. As she slipped the betrothal necklace from about my neck, she vowed to find Erlina within the century and lure her to her death. Her exact words were, 'The princess is too loving to stand by and watch the innocent suffer. With such a weakness for mortals she shall be all too easy to defeat'." He paused, a pained expression etched on his features as he gazed into the nothingness of distant memories. He looked at them and concluded with, "Shortly thereafter I ceased to feel Erlina's heartbeat... to see visions of her... to sense her presence. There can only be one conclusion."

Alexis and Jon listened with rapt attention, not daring to stir a muscle during the whole of the tale.

"Betrothal necklace!" Alexis suddenly remembered: "We saw a necklace around my mother's neck... when we saw her in the pools."

"She wears it?" he breathed. "If I could but get close enough... I could retrieve it! Only then will I know whether or not Erlina lives, or whether Moriel succeeded in deceiving her where she failed with me!"

"But... my mother is not dark, or deceptive. What if she is your Erlina?"

"If I am her true target, Moriel could lie undetected in wait in the guise of an innocuous occupation of her time – such as archaeology. She can be kind when she tries." He thought a moment, hope warring with caution. Finally he shook his head, "I dare not trust my eyes; I must meet this Cardinal and judge by what transpires. Tell me: Where may I confront her alone, with assurance of no interruptions?"

Alexis shivered, "How do I know that I can trust *you*? What if you are in fact the Wolf in disguise, as you just described? Or the Wolf is truly a man as we've always thought? If I tell you where to meet my mother privately, you might fulfil the plan you claim is another's!"

"You are wise to question," Aradan said. "I can only think of one way to prove to you what I have said: Take me to Darachi... the old gnarled tree you spoke of."

"What will that prove?" Jon asked.

"She cannot be deceived as she sees beneath the surface to the roots of any being. She will testify as to who I am."

Jon stood up, rubbing his temples. "Wait, this is getting a bit too weird, even for me! Now you're telling me there's *really* such a thing as dryads?"

"You yourself told me what Sandy mentioned," Aradan reminded him, "and you said you heard the tree speak my name."

"Yeah, but – but it was just creaking in the— oh, never mind! What have we got to lose?" His reasoning had gone south and he knew it.

They dressed for a hike and headed up the slopes of Meall Meadhonach. On the way Aradan explained the origin of dryads and other such creatures that had fallen into myths, legends and Hollywood back lots; many were alien species transplanted or stranded for one reason or another; some remained into the era of man's dominion on the earth, though most had left with only traces of themselves to hint of their existence. Some men, more clever than others, had discovered those traces and given life to the myths through their writings, though Aradan warned them not to become so fixated on such things so as to neglect the reality of their own present lives; such things were to be admired for their variety and uniqueness at best, but not worshipped as some higher life form. They were simply Other, created by the same Creator of all, no more or less.

When they reached the level dip in the slope where the gnarled tree stood, Jon was surprised by the appearance of the tree. "The last time I saw this tree it looked like it was starting to recover from a long illness; it was just showing buds and newly sprouted leaves; but now! How do you explain that?" The tree was bursting with green, verdant as if it were a young tree. He couldn't be sure, but it even looked as if the trunk were straighter than it had been.

"She is awakening," Aradan whispered in awe. He knelt beside the tree as the other two stood further back and watched to see what would happen. Aradan called, "Darachi? Are you awake?" There was no response, but he knew she lived, and knew that she had spoken (at least in her sleep)... had perhaps even recognized his voice when he'd spoken with Jon on Skype. He touched the bark, and a shiver shook the leaves of the crown. "Darachi! Awaken!" he called again.

The tree rustled and began to sway slowly back and forth, as if a strong wind tugged at the trunk; it was windy, but by now Jon knew that didn't mean anything where this tree was concerned. The trunk gradually straightened. The earth rumbled deep within and pheasants in a nearby clump of bracken suddenly took flight. Jon described to Alexis what happened next: The sound of autumn leaves, needles, shredded bark and twigs colliding, as if swirling in a strong breeze, and then a rumble, a brown timbre (if he could use colour to describe a sound) grew steadily louder, as if roots were stretching.

Aradan stood and stepped back. He turned to them with a smile. "She is coming. Don't be alarmed – she will not harm you."

A swirl of debris picked up speed from the ground up, like a dust devil in the desert sands that Jon was familiar with; but this dust devil was made of shredded bark, petals, seeds, rich brown twigs, leaves and green mosses, pulled up from the surrounding landscape. The swirl grew, gradually taking on the form of a woman. The statue come to life.

"Greetings, Darachi," Aradan bowed, "matron of a noble race. It is a very great pleasure to see you once again!"

"Aradan," she spoke (though Jon couldn't explain the sound to Alexis, or even how it was possible. He quit trying to figure it out and just admitted he was awed). "You have returned to awaken me at last."

"I?" he was surprised. "Have you slept all this time?"

"What time has passed since we last met?" she asked.

"Over one thousand, two hundred earth-years, my lady," he replied.

Jon realized that Aradan's accent was gradually shifting from his usual Norwegian to something subtly different; the more he spoke with Darachi, the more it changed.

There was a whistle in the wind, and she bowed her head in sadness. "Does Princess Erlina still live? I have not met with her..." she thought a moment, "since the earth-year of 1069. I fell into sorrowful sleep at the destruction of my Kind further south in that infamous harrying by the king rightly called *The Bastard*."

He stared at her. "Erlina was here that recently?"

Darachi gestured toward the castle, her arm a fluid motion of debris rustling gently. "Yes. Her home was but a broch then. And my child, Baccata, was growing in the shade of her walls."

"Baccata is there still," he replied. "She is stirring within the courtyard, in the throes of sleep; you must teach her to awaken." He then said, "Noble Darachi,

I am in need of your advice: How would I recognize Princess Erlina, if a *Morquillian* had taken her form?"

"*Morquillian!*" a gasp of cold wind rattled dead leaves. She shook her head, roots growling below, then calming once again as if the answer had come to her. "Only the daughter of Queen Amanis may call forth the eternal light of *Glânöir*."

He shut his eyes and bowed his head in relief, "Then I pray she has retained it." He thought of the first time he'd seen the blue light of Erlina's ring as it lit the tunnel of escape she strove to complete before the terrible battle.

"And one more thing," Darachi continued: "*Morquillian* have a dusty stench," she shuddered as she growled, "the reeking of mould and decay upon their souls."

"Of course!" he brightened, "I have smelt that which you describe, and it is true!"

"Princess Erlina's fragrance... do you remember it?" Darachi asked. "I cannot... please... remind me," she yawned, roots creaking deep within the bowels of the hill, the trunk of the tree stretching upward even as the swirling form of the woman stretched her arms.

He smiled, closing his eyes and taking a slow breath as he drew the memory from deep within: "She is the subtle breath of the Immortelle... and a touch of spring almond blossoms mingled with spicy vanilla."

"Yes," Darachi smiled. "That is the true distinction between the Princess and the imposter."

The two of them spoke for some time, as good friends and yet with a regal bearing in their conduct, as

Alexis could imagine two nobles of old tales speaking with each other, an elegant dance of motion in their manners. When the conversation was concluded, the form of the woman waved farewell to them all, turned back toward the tree and, arching upward as if diving into it, dissipated.

The walk back to Dalmoor was a thoughtful one, and slow for it. Jon asked only one question: "What is the eternal light the dryad mentioned?"

"It is a ring, simply put. It contains a drop of our planet's closest star... though I know that is impossible to the human mind and technology, it is perfectly logical to an Aquillian," Aradan smiled at Jon's sceptical glance. He told them about its glow and the first time he'd seen it. "If she has this ring still, it would prove to me whether or not it is truly Erlina – though her fragrance should be enough for me to know. If it is Moriel in the guise of my betrothed, she'll not know how to wield the ring's power; indeed, may know nothing about the ring itself. Alexis," he turned to her, "Does your mother wear a beautiful blue ring?"

Alexis shook her head. "She wears no jewellery at all. Except the necklace, which I'd never even seen before. She kept it well hidden for me never to have noticed it all these years." There was a touch of disappointment in her voice.

"Maybe she usually keeps it somewhere safe," Jon suggested.

Aradan nodded in response, but stopped and turned to look at Alexis, taking her gently by the shoulders. "Take heart: Whoever your mother proves to be, remember that you are dealing with someone who has had over a thousand years to learn the necessity and art of camouflage... learned to hide her true self in a new identity each generation, whether before peasants or kings. It is an armour that few penetrate; believe me, I know," he looked at Jon, "and why even I needed the advice of Darachi to discern wisely."

Alexis's mind raced with questions. She asked, "But if, like her, you choose new identities each generation, then why have you kept the same name for so many generations? I mean, I assume all the books I found online are yours. Didn't you run a huge risk of people becoming suspicious about you living several lifetimes? Where is the camouflage in such a tactic?"

He smiled, "Do you know the story of Hansel and Gretel? They left a trail of bread crumbs to follow. I was hoping that if Erlina lived, she would read my books and follow the trail of crumbs. I admit it was a long shot. And in Norway it was not so much of a risk as in other cultures," he explained, "as there's a tradition of handing down family names."

Alexis so wished for a trail of crumbs in her own life, answers to those questions which had been plaguing her more and more lately: *Who am I? Who are my real mother, my father? Where do I come from?* She needed to know.

Aradan continued, "I must now set about finding out just who this Cardinal is."

Alexis replied, "You have her assistant and daughter to help."

He took her hand in his and gave it a gently squeeze. "For that I'm truly grateful."

"Hey, hey," Jon teased, "quit trying to muscle in on my girl, you Casanova."

"Very funny," Aradan laughed. "Me, who you've accused of being an eternal bachelor?"

"Well, now we know better, don't we? Eternal yes, but eternally engaged."

Aradan only nodded, a weary smile tugging at his mouth.

"Sorry." Jon looked at Alexis, his mind churning. "Alv— Aradan... you mentioned that you have a healing touch. What exactly do you mean by that?"

"Did I mention that?"

"Just in passing... when Moriel went looking for you in 1066." Jon couldn't believe he'd just said that so calmly.

"My gifting is touch; Erlina's is that of her voice; Moriel's is that of her gaze. All Aquillian gifts have to do with the senses." He held out his hands to both of them. "Please, give me your hands."

They each placed a hand in his, and immediately there flowed through them something akin to an electrical shock, only pleasing; if they could describe it they would be tempted to use colours. He released their hands, though the sensation lingered.

"Wow," Jon looked at him. "But how could you have kept that a secret for so long? I mean, we've shaken hands before – even a good man slap on the back! I've *never* felt that... I would remember!"

"I can choose to release my power or not," he said simply. "I can heal or kill by mere touch."

"Then I'm glad you can control it! But what kind of gifting is that? It's a good party trick, I'll grant you, but what else can you do?"

"I can do much more," Aradan grinned at Jon. Suddenly he was standing, casually, half a mile away.

"Aw, now, that's just creepy," Jon commented loud enough to be heard.

Before they could blink he was back at their side.

"But... if I could move that fast – I mean, why would you even bother to walk anywhere?" Jon asked. "Or travel by boat for that matter? That fast... I'd think you could run across water without sinking, like those lizards in South America."

"I could, but where's the pleasure of enjoying the moment in that? And besides, it's harder to explain if caught doing it. But there's more... Alexis," he turned to her, "how did you lose your hearing, and your tongue?" She told him briefly. "If I restore you... I would need to do so gradually; it would be too overwhelming for you all at once – and I think we have too much to do in the next few days... it takes much time and energy to adjust fully."

She looked at him, afraid to trust her lip-reading. "You... you could restore it? But hasn't it been damaged far too long? What about scar tissue? Brain re-wiring, and all that?"

"That is why I would do it gradually – you will hear and comprehend more as time passes; and yes... I can do this for you... if you wish me to. If I do, it will bring tremendous change to your life, and you must be aware of that before you decide."

She looked at Jon, pleading with her eyes, desire fighting fear.

"Whatever you decide Alexis... it will change nothing about how I feel about you... as long as you don't ask me to sing," he grinned. He longed to be able to share other things with her – sounds that he enjoyed, but he wouldn't sway her own decision; it was hers alone to make. He loved her no matter what might happen.

She laughed, tears of relief. She nodded at Aradan, "What should I do?"

"Trust me," was all he said. He stepped close and cupped her face in his hands, gently pressing his palms over her ears, gazing into her eyes. She then felt him place a finger in each ear, as far in as he could reach without hurting her. A warmth spread over her whole body, an electric vibration pulsing between his hands. She gasped as it intensified, her eyes wide with terrified excitement. His lips were moving, and he spoke a language she was not unfamiliar with – that of her mother's private language with Elbal and his sons. She felt tired. Completely relaxed. When he pulled away she was disappointed... his warm hands had been so comforting. "Alexis," he said quietly.

She burst into tears and hysterical sobs, and Jon pulled her to himself. "What did you do to her?" he asked.

"Ask her yourself," Aradan smiled.

"Oh... Jon!" she cried, "I can hear!" she laughed. "My – my voice sounds so... so strange!"

He looked into her eyes. "W— what?" he stammered. "What's that supposed to mean?" Jon looked from Alexis to Aradan, anxious to know what had happened.

"I can hear you," she laughed, shaking her head. "Say something... anything!"

"I love you!" That was the most important thing he wanted her to hear.

"I love you too," she replied. He brushed her cheek with his fingers and kissed her tenderly, laughing with her.

"Alexis, you're hearing our words as you read our lips, but your brain must learn to interpret speech once again," Aradan explained, then showed her his hands and added, "but your mind will adapt at an accelerated rate."

Alexis threw her arms around his neck, thanking him with a kiss on the cheek.

Aradan laughed and said that he would have done it sooner had he known he'd get such a thanks. "But... it would be best to keep this our secret for now; you'll need to act as if nothing has changed," he warned, "until I know whether or not your mother is Erlina or Moriel; if Moriel is at hand she would bolt like a wild horse if she knew me nearby – a healing would be unmistakeable." He also told them that she would probably feel tired as the brain adjusted to the new stimulation, and not long after they arrived at Dalmoor she went to her room and lay down for a nap. The men withdrew quietly after Jon looked in on her to assure himself that she was okay.

"How did you do that?" Jon asked after they'd returned to Aradan's room and closed the door.

"It is not something explainable in human terms," Aradan replied.

"Is it...? Was Jesus...?"

"One of us? No. He truly was the Creator embodied on earth... in the form of a man, much like this vessel I am in now, like the one you are in. He came to Aquillis as well, but we responded very differently than Man-Kind. My giftings are merely evidence of God's infinite character just as you and your giftings are. Intelligence, creativity, talents or giftings... they are all expressions of his being... the supernatural fingerprints of our Designer, if you will, just as a potter leaves his fingerprints in the clay of a vessel he forms."

"So... you don't look like this," Jon gestured from head to toe, "on your planet?"

"We have no need of this vessel there... it would be incompatible with our environment. But we do not look all that different; it is as if this human vessel is an outer layer, a suit, with the perfect form of who we truly are just beneath the surface. It will be the same for you once you've passed through the veil of mortality to immortality... when this vessel," he pinched Jon's arm lightly, "is shed, releasing your essence – your spirit – to journey to your chosen destination."

"You mean heaven... or hell?"

"Precisely."

"So... you believe they exist?"

Aradan laughed. "You humans... you're so fixated on this temporal journey called Life that you fail to realize... this is just laying the foundations for reality beyond this material existence! The choices you make while in this mortal time frame determine your destination and home beyond it. And yes, they both exist: Just as time is one dimension and space another, so heaven and hell both exist; other dimensions altogether, perceivable only once you've left your mortal frame behind. But come," he pulled out the desk chair for Jon to sit on as he sat down on his bed, "such discussions must wait. Right now we need to discuss the Wolf."

"Wait – just one more question: What do swans have to do with all this..." he waved his hand vaguely, meaning 'everything'.

"Swans? They are part of the royal coat of arms of Erlina's family." They weren't earthly swans, but he let it pass.

"That would explain why they're everywhere, I guess." Jon sat down. "Okay, the Wolf: I know this may sound like an obvious observation, but how could the Cardinal be the Wolf? There's obviously two of them, so one has to be Erlina."

"Let me ask you this: Has Alexis told you what the Wolf has done to her mother in the past?"

"From what I've gathered so far, only empty threats... taunts... anonymous notes, phone calls in the middle of the night, harassments, something like what's been happening here lately – ghostings, and threatening messages that never came to anything but unsettledness – and she told me how, after each such contact, it's never been long before the Cardinal packed them all up and moved on somewhere else. That, and the Wolf has stolen artefacts any chance she gets, through her agents she plants on the teams or buys within."

He nodded, "It sounds like her... hit and run taunts, dangling the bait and then gloating. She takes most pleasure in unsettling others' peace."

"Others," repeated Jon. "Which brings us back to the premise that there are in fact two, not one. And besides, empty threats aren't exactly leading Erlina to her death," Jon pointed out.

"But if the Cardinal is Erlina," Aradan said more to himself than to Jon, "it would make sense that she moves on... she would try to avoid any circumstance in which she might need to defend a mortal. If on the other hand she is really Moriel, she would simply use the ploy to unsettle those around her... constantly on the move to deprive mortals of rest."

"Maybe Moriel's lost the motivation to carry out her threat after all these years," Jon suggested.

"But if not..." Aradan tapped a finger to his lips in thought, "then she's waited, watching Erlina, waiting for me to finally find her... to strike at our reunion. Perhaps she's been waiting for an audience... me," his brow creased. "If so, the Wolf won't be far behind once she knows I'm here. Which means that if I find Erlina I can never let her out of my sight until Moriel is caught."

Just then a knock came at the door; Alexis had slept well though briefly, and looked refreshed...

glowing. She joined them in their discussion – mainly just listening, absorbing the new sound of voices to her ears. Slowly she tuned in to their rhythms, tones and acoustic punctuations. She sat down on Jon's lap, and he wrapped his arms around her waist as they continued.

Aradan said, "First I must determine who the Cardinal truly is... meet her somewhere secluded."

Jon replied, "She returns tomorrow; her first priority will be that new trench; but otherwise you'll most probably find her in the cavern, if you have the patience. Alex and I figured out that that must be where she's disappeared to so often when she's been found later in the cellar."

"This trench... have you found out what's in it?" he looked at Jon. "I... fear what will be found, if Moriel indeed succeeded in her plans."

Jon pulled out his iPhone, and showed him the photo he'd taken of the map in the library. "It looks like it will be a cist, and there seem to be six figures in there; three Christian, three unknown."

Aradan studied it. "If these proportions are correct... the three largest will be Erlina's father and her two brothers. The other three... perhaps from Aidan's clan, though no," he shook his head, "it wouldn't make sense – they had their own burial cairn across the range, toward Durness," he pointed west, absently. "Niallan told me about it once..." this he said more to himself and offered no explanation. He studied the image in close detail.

"The anomaly is giving Brehani a challenge with the readings; it absorbs everything that's thrown at it."

Aradan had a subtle flurry of expressions that passed over his features, but he said nothing. He thought a moment, then asked Alexis, "Is there any circumstance in which your mother would wear jewellery?"

Alexis thought a moment. "Perhaps state dinners, or solemn occasions. But I see where you're going... I'll see if I can remind her of the ring without letting her know that I know of it."

"Perhaps you've *dreamt* of it," suggested Jon.

She grinned. "Oh, yes... how does it go?... 'I dreamt of a ring that glowed with blue light in a dark tunnel'? Hey!" she cried, "the glowing blue stones in the cavern! Maybe that's why she chose that colour!"

They spent the evening speaking of everything that had transpired over the past weeks, and of Aradan's long, eventful life; many of the stories he had written into his novels, fantastical-sounding adventures that had taken him along the rivers and routes of the Vikings, and had seen the changes of the Norse cultures from a blood-thirsty religion to Christianity, though the original expression of the church as an entity was rather a political weapon than a divine gift or true faith. Aradan's vast knowledge about the Viking trade routes, Norse history and focus of his studies made perfect sense in the light of his past. Again they tried to reason that perhaps the Cardinal had also become an expert in those areas in her attempts at searching for him; but he countered with the fact that Moriel had become acquainted with them as a slave herself; he had studied them in trying to trace where Moriel might have ended up, and had searched for her the length and breadth of the Norse expanse. He'd learned that she'd eventually risen in rank to become wife of wives to a powerful man, and borne him sons; beyond that he had lost track of her. Aradan would not dwell on the possibility that the Cardinal was Erlina; until he had the chance of seeing her, of discerning just who she was, he could afford no hope... it had been dashed too many times in the past.

For the first time Jon and Alexis also began to see the Viking raids on Great Britain in a different light: Not merely as aggressive hunger for gold and slaves (though that was certainly no negligible factor), but as revenge on the symbols of the religious institution that had been forced upon them by Charlemagne, often at the point of a sword; the close association of the militant form of religious power with his own political power were always made clear to the Saxons and Norse. Bitter battles had been waged between the kings who misused Christianity as a weapon and those who fought for their freedom of land and hearts. The expulsion of the bloody ways of Aasgard were welcome to Aradan, but the way it had been done was not acceptable to him; he had sympathy for both sides in the misguided history of religious power. Not until the spread of Saint Francis of Assisi's influence did Aradan feel genuine warmth for the ways of the Church.

Aradan was shown the tower and the cavern; he knew from Jon and Alexis that the Cardinal knew of the cavern yet he held his heart in check. But the more he saw, the more difficult it was becoming not to allow hope to rise from the ashes of shattering disappointments. The female statue on the uppermost floor turned out to be that of the Princess Eris, and Aradan was indeed relieved (as it had been unrecognised by Alexis) that it was not Erlina.

Before sunrise the next morning Jon and Toshiro took off for Edinburgh, leaving Alexis to spend time with Aradan. They had just over an hour in the air to chat, and Jon found himself thinking of Sandy. "I was talking with an old local at the pub one night," he said. "He told me a few local fairy tales... do you have such stories where you grew up?"

"I think every culture has them," Toshiro replied.

"Do you have any... about immortals?"

He thought a moment. "There's a story I knew as a boy that always fascinated me; it' called, *'The story of the man who did not wish to die'*... not a very creative title, perhaps, but it is the name of the story. It's about a lazy, wealthy man named Sentaro, who did not wish to die; he went off in search of the elixir of life so that he could drink it and live forever... instead he was taken to the land of Perpetual Life, where no death comes. He thought he would be happy but the citizens there grew tired of living – for them death was something desirable to obtain, because they had heard of Paradise that could only be reached by dying. At first he couldn't understand their wish, but after three hundred years he began to grow weary of living, and wished to return to his home. He was able to return, and was given a book to teach him right precepts to live by; he learned to live a good and useful life, eventually growing old and dying."

"Long life... hundreds of years... would you want such a thing?"

"I think it would grow very lonely," Toshiro mused. "Everyone you ever knew would grow old and die... you'd be forced into solitude, or into perpetual rebuilding of your life; either one would be wearying. I think I'd become a hardened cynic... it would become difficult to enjoy life. No," he concluded, "I would never wish such a thing."

"And what do you think... of the *Cardinal*?" Jon asked pointedly.

Toshiro looked at him.

Jon said, "There's no point in beating around the bush; I think you and I both know that she's at least older than she seems. The question is, how *much* older."

Toshiro nodded, confessing, "Since you brought it up... I've been in the service of the Cardinal for over three decades and I've come no closer to answers myself; but I can live with that. I just remind myself that one should never look a gift horse in the mouth... if it weren't for the Cardinal I probably would have been killed in a street fight before I reached fifteen."

"And how old do you think she was when you first met her?"

"As she is now; she hasn't changed," he admitted.

"And Elbal was with her?"

"Yes, but I have watched him age, though very slowly. If they're related he is only half her own kind."

"What *kind* would that be?" Jon looked at him pointedly.

Toshiro shrugged. "Like I said, I've come no closer to the answers, so I've just learned not to ask."

"And you're satisfied with that?" Jon looked at him curiously.

"It is what it is; satisfaction or not won't change anything. Sometimes ignorance is bliss, but," he laughed, "I will admit to seriously wondering if they'd found that elixir that Sentaro had set out to find."

Jon left it at that as they were approaching the airport and he needed to talk with the tower. They approached the helipad and Jon grinned, "Show time," as he glided to a stop and killed the engine. "This conversation stays between us, agreed?"

Toshiro grinned, "I wouldn't know what to do with it if I tried anyway."

9: Now

When they met the Cardinal and Elbal in the waiting lounge, the Cardinal was surprised that Alexis had not come to meet them.

"Well, actually she's not here because of me – or I should say, a friend of mine," Jon explained. "My history professor was in the area and dropped by unexpectedly, and Alexis is hosting him while I'm away."

"Ah," she smiled, "I'm glad to see you feel at home enough to invite friends around. And Alexis will make a good hostess, I'm certain."

Jon thought the first comment was a bit odd given that his job there was nearly done for the season; he'd been thinking about what that meant, and what would come next; he didn't want to lose Alexis. The second comment, he heartily agreed with.

"I'd like to meet this professor of yours," the Cardinal interrupted his thoughts.

"I'm not exactly sure of his plans," he hedged, "but I'll ask him if he has time before he leaves." They'd meet soon enough, but in Aradan's way.

As they flew back to Dalmoor Jon focused on flying, though his brain still had plenty of space to think about recent events and trying to wrap his head around the fact that he was flying with someone over a thousand years old who didn't look a day over 30. Elbal was easier to understand – at least he *looked* older.

Once back at Dalmoor, Toshiro put their luggage into the golf cart and drove the Cardinal and Elbal the rest of the way home, leaving Jon to go through his post-flight checklist.

"I trust you have news," the Cardinal said once they were out of sight of the pilot.

"They've been exploring," Toshiro grinned. "They found the entrance to the cavern."

She nodded, "Excellent! And have they been into my library?"

"Yes; they found the key quite easily... you were right to hide it where you did; I was wrong when I said it would be too difficult for them to find."

"Don't underestimate my daughter," she smiled with pride.

"Do we trust this pilot?" Elbal spoke. "You take a great risk in simply allowing him to look through your private library and who knows where else."

"Alexis trusts him, and that is enough for me," she replied.

"Trusting the pilot is the least of our concerns," Toshiro said. "There has been a mutiny due to strange occurrences on site –the students have been convinced by locals that there's a ghost at the castle... they call it the *Maid of Dalmoor*, but I was speaking to Amir... Alexis seemed to think the pattern of harassments and inconveniences indicates the Wolf. The students are so spooked that they were going to leave yesterday, but we convinced them to at least stay to say goodbye to you properly. They all slept in the castle the past two nights, and are probably packing up to leave first thing in the morning. Hamish was badly injured, though nothing broken, thank goodness." He told them about the trip-wire incident that was the catalyst for the mutiny.

"The *Maid of Dalmoor* is no ghost," Elbal scowled. "She is flesh and blood!"

Toshiro was surprised by such a declaration, but said nothing.

The Cardinal reached back and patted his knee. "Don't take it personally," she soothed, though her worried tone betrayed her concern. "Do you really think it's the Wolf? If so, who is it? Who is his agent?"

"I do," Toshiro replied, "Who else could it be? And we haven't been able to clearly identify the agent. Their role seems to be quite different here than any other time we've had the aggravation of their company... it's as if this agent is laying low... perhaps waiting for an opportunity, or perhaps waiting for the Wolf to act. And another thing Amir told me: The Wolf, according to our pilot who has some mutual connection, is not a he, but a *she*!"

"A *she*!" the Cardinal exclaimed. "A she," she closed her eyes and sighed in what Toshiro thought sounded like deep relief. "If the Wolf truly is a woman, it would explain a great *many* things," she glanced toward Elbal, whose brow creased – she knew he'd understood her insinuation.

"No matter who it is," Elbal growled, "if they succeed in driving away our workers, they will frustrate our plans yet again... with the students leaving, that's the end of the dig for this season."

"Brehani is gutted... he's been itching to open the anomaly in the newest trench... he'd hoped to do so before winding up for the season and returning to Ethiopia," Toshiro said.

"Oh, we will open that together – students or not," the Cardinal assured him. "But... I realize that a few things must be clarified before we proceed with that."

"Clarified?" Toshiro asked.

"There are particular things I must... *explain*... before we open the cist."

"So Jon was right," Toshiro commented, "it *is* a cist."

As the three of them entered the courtyard they were met by Alexis, running through the entrance and waving. "Hello! You're back! I've missed you!" she hugged Elbal first, and then her mother. Toshiro took the luggage inside and went in search of Galal to let him know they'd returned.

The Cardinal looked at her curiously. "Your voice... it's much clearer.... And I've missed you too!" she held out her hand to take her daughter by the arm.

Alexis nearly burst into tears at hearing her mother's beautiful voice for the first time. She held on tightly and looked straight ahead trying to compose herself as they slowly walked arm in arm across the courtyard.

"What is it, dearest?" her mother stopped to look her daughter in the eyes.

Alexis was bursting to tell her. Instead she only said, "I'm just so glad you're back!" before embracing her again. Alexis tried to compose herself as she shifted the focus from herself to business; she asked, "How was your time in Edinburgh? Productive?" She tried to change the way she sounded to match *before* – though she could only go by how it felt in her throat.

"Yes," the Cardinal replied as they walked on, "I was able to help clarify, enlighten, la, da, da... it's quite tedious at times, but the chance to delve into the libraries there makes it worth my while."

"Well, can you blame them for calling on you? You only need to look at an artefact, even the most obscure, to tell them what its use was... almost as if you had been there." Alexis watched her mother carefully, who only smiled slightly.

"And what did you find on your scavenger hunt? Was it successful?" her mother changed the subject.

Alexis mentioned the book on the library desk, and finding the cavern entrance; she advanced cautiously, unsure where the reality of the scavenger hunt ended and the flood of information and revelation of the past few days began. Beyond that there wasn't much to tell – or not much she *could* tell; she could mention a few emails but honestly had slightly more important things on her mind.

"And how is Jon?" her mother asked. "He seemed quite preoccupied on the flight home."

"Oh... he's fine."

"Is there anything I should know about between you two?" she asked pointedly.

"Not yet, at least not beyond what you've already surmised," was all she said.

"But you hope? He's a good man... I like him."

"He *is* a good man," Alexis confessed, "I love him."

"I see," her mother smiled. "Does he feel the same?"

Alexis nodded, her smile telling more than any words could.

"I'm so pleased!" the Cardinal reached up and stroked Alexis's hair.

Alexis remembered her mission to stir up the sentiment of the ring within her mother somehow. "Mother, may I ask you something?"

"Anything."

"I had a strange dream last night... very vivid! I saw you in a long, dark tunnel... you were singing – it was very odd because I seemed to *hear* you in the dream – and you were wearing a ring that glowed blue! I know it sounds strange, but it seemed so real!" she hesitated innocently. "Do... do you have a blue ring? I've never seen you with jewellery, have I?"

Her mother looked at her distractedly. "No... I don't believe you have."

"Does it make any sense to you?" she probed. Alexis could tell it had struck a chord within her mother.

The Cardinal kissed her on the cheek before releasing Alexis's arm and wandering off absently, Elbal at her side. She stopped and turned back to

Alexis with a half-smile, half-confused expression: "It was just a dream, I'm sure. Are you coming?"

"I'd like to wait for Jon if you don't mind," Alexis answered.

"And where is this friend of his he mentioned? The professor?"

That surprised Alexis, but she hedged, "I think he went on a long walk."

"Very well." She turned toward the entryway again and followed Elbal inside.

Alexis's question had unsettled her... *a blue ring in a tunnel?* Alexis had found the cavern, and likely the tunnel, and perhaps the journal; but had she ever wrote of *Glânöir* thus?... described it? She would have had no need to, because she would never leave such a precious gift for another generation; her recorded knowledge was her gift to share. The course of thoughts naturally led her to think of Aradan, and she lingered as long as possible in such bittersweet memories, lost in thought as she came to the entry hall's fireplace. Something called her name from deep within her heart. It was a fragrance... a subtle trace lingering about the mantelpiece.

"Elbal!" she grasped his arm in realisation and shock.

"What is it?" he moved to take hold of her, to protect her from any unseen threat.

"No," she soothed, and he relaxed. "But do you smell something unusual here... near the fireplace?"

He breathed deeply. "I do not," he confessed. "What is it you smell?"

"Cinnamon," she breathed in long and slow, conjuring up the memories vivid with the fragrance, "a pure, warm cinnamon unlike the common spice. And fresh lemongrass... and the tangy aroma of living cloves! I have not smelled anything so lovely for over a thousand years!" she cried, laughed and breathed in the fragrance, all in successive gasps, overwhelmed by the surprise of joy at the sensation. "I— I dare not hope after so long! Perhaps... it's that I long for it so greatly that I have conjured up this fragrance from desire."

"Is that the fragrance of Aradan?" Elbal asked quietly.

"Yes," she breathed.

Dalmoor was quiet. Elbal called out for his sons. No reply. The Cardinal reminded him that Amir was most likely at the dig site on duty, though the absence of Galal unsettled them. But as they started up the stairs to the Cardinal's storey they met Toshiro running toward them, wiping his hands on a bloody towel.

"Quickly," he whispered, "I do not want to cause a panic but – follow me!"

They found Galal crumpled in an unconscious heap on the floor of the Cardinal's hall, a stain of red seeping out from beneath his head. Toshiro said, "I've checked him though I did not wish to move him. He lives, and aside from the blow to the back of his head there appears to be no other injuries."

Just as Elbal moved to kneel beside his son, Galal stirred with a moan. He winced and held his head as he sat up, dazed. "How long...?" he looked toward the library and tried to stand up, but tottered back.

"Oh no you don't," Toshiro scraped him up off the floor. "You're coming with me so that I can patch up your head!"

"Hold still," Elbal whispered as he felt his son's head. "It is not cracked – with this much blood, I'd say you are very fortunate," he sighed in relief, as the Cardinal placed a clean towel in his hands to clean them on.

"And thick-skulled," murmured Toshiro, looking at the blood-slickened floor as he helped Galal stand.

"Do you know what happened?" the Cardinal asked. The library door was ajar, and there was a musty reek in the air.

"There have been strange things happening at the excavation; the students have all left, except for one," Galal began. "Last night the men sleeping in the conference room were awakened by the chairs being flipped over in the dark, and sinister laughter... a woman's – they nearly packed up and left right then and there, except they were afraid to leave the room. This morning, after you and Jon left," he said to Toshiro, "we found a few things in the castle in disarray... the dining hall's tables and chairs were all shoved to the far end, and on the windows was written just one word in dark red lipstick: *Leave*. That was all it took – they all left together, apologizes and goodbyes hastily given. The only one left is Edric, because he said he gets too carsick to have gone with them, and would be glad to catch a ride any time Jon flies next." Galal swayed slightly as he looked back toward the library once more, shaking his head to clear it and remember what happened next: "I heard someone in the library... when I went to investigate, I saw very briefly a woman in black from head to toe; she flashed a snaking blade at me – it looked like the one you'd found in the courtyard," he said to the Cardinal, "then laughed and just disappeared! I heard her laughing again on the stairs and ran down the hall to try and catch her... and the next thing I knew... you were here."

"You are whole; that is all that matters," she responded. "Elbal and I will take care of the library... go with Toshiro and let him tend to your wound."

The library door stood ajar and, after listening within, they cautiously entered.

The Cardinal cried in distress, "It has been ransacked!" Scrolls from the shelves were scattered about the room and the desk's contents were thrown in disarray. The book from her desk was spread open upon the floor, but she was relieved by its safety. As she lifted it back to its proper place a slip of paper fell out from beneath it:

It had been well over a thousand years since she had seen Aquillian writing other than her own. She had long suspected that the Wolf was Aquillian simply by the span of time their lives had become entangled;

but why would one of her own Kind become a Morquillian? And who was it? It was not Aradan's script. For centuries after the great battle she had assumed that only she and Aradan had been marooned on earth; and when the visions ceased and his heartbeat within the orb fell silent, she had secretly feared that Aradan's love for her had ceased, and that he might have found solace in the arms of a human... for it was clear that Elbal was more than merely human; he had been with her nearly two centuries, and did not even know his age then. His direct progenitors had died, his father countless lifetimes older than his appearance at death; the implications were obvious. But now that it was certain there was a third she was somehow greatly comforted.

"Mother?" Elbal touched her shoulder. "What is it? Why the silence?"

"The Wolf is Aquillian," she stared at the note, still in shock. She read the note to Elbal: *"When your treasure is discovered, I will be on the prowl. Watch your back. The Wolf."* The subtleties of the long, wispy letters were indicative of someone who had learned the proper script from the hand of another Aquillian; but the dialect was strange to her. She had been taught to recognize the dark aspect of the tongue, but had never known anyone to use it in polite society; it was low and guttural, grating on the ear and tongue, where the common language of Maldor and Aquillis floated on the tongue of the speaker and caressed the ear of the hearer.

"But how can that be? From what you've told me of Aquillis... that *cannot* be!"

"It can be and it is," she replied. "It is the dark tongue of a Morquillian. Who else would know the writing of Aquillis yet leave such a message?" She watched Elbal carefully as she added, "And you know what Toshiro told us... the Wolf is a woman. You have always wondered who your *urfather* was..." he stiffened, "...who gave you the long life you have both suffered under and thrived with. But what if it was never an ur*father*? What if—"

"*You* are my mother," he stopped her from finishing her thought.

"But you are not of my making. And only she can tell you where you truly come from."

"You may not have brought my ancestor into this world but in every other sense of the word you have made me who I am today," he bowed in respect.

She placed her hands on his shoulders gently. "And I have been honoured to do so. But only your *urmother* knows your heritage... only she can answer those questions that have long hounded you and your children... whom do you come from, and why did they abandon your forefather with no explanation as to who they were?"

"I know that I have a portion of the blood of your Kind flowing through my veins; that is enough for me, truly... all that I need learn I have learned from you."

"Very well." She knew it was not enough, but she let it go for the moment.

The chest below the desk had been dragged out and bore the scars of several thwarted attempts to open it. One wooden piece of the chest was still slightly askew. She knelt beside it, quickly manipulating the lock mechanisms to open it.

Frustration, resignation, anger and grief churned within her as she exclaimed, "Several pieces of my Maldorian armour are missing! *The Wolf*!" The last words were nearly a growl as the afternoon sky blackened, roiling with dark clouds, and a sudden blast of cold Atlantic wind rattled the windowpane.

"Mother," Elbal knelt beside her, reaching out his hand to calm her with a touch, "We will find a way to rid ourselves of this burdensome nuisance. Though that term does no justice to your loss!"

"We *must*... it is exasperating to be relentlessly pursued! I cannot defend those mortals closest to me should a threat become real... and so I must move on," she sighed. "If this threat grows any more... I haven't got the heart to tell Alexis we must leave again."

"Two people have already been injured," Elbal agreed. "I will tell her. But we must prepare to move on; I'll not see you risk yourself in the spur of a moment – that's my job," he reminded her gently, "and my sons' jobs... though we cannot be everywhere at once."

"I would not have you endangered any more than you would wish it for me. Thank you," she whispered, "for all you do for me."

"Nonsense," Elbal chided respectfully.

She looked around at the mess. "Well... let us find out what else is missing."

As she began picking up the scrolls that had fallen to the floor, the Cardinal saw the painted map she'd walked over so often lately, mindful of the images emblazoned there of past and present. It had been nearly a lifetime since she last lived at this castle, and it pained her to think that they must move on again so soon. She stood over the map, that scene of the last battle in which so much held dear had been lost. "Maldor," she whispered wearily, "as it is etched in my long memory. As it once and last was." The forest was long gone, and the landscape and features had changed since she had painted the map.

Elbal asked quietly, "What is it, Mother?"

Rain began to fall outside, splashing the windows in heavy drops; her tone when she replied betrayed the heaviness she felt in her heart: "I've survived solely because of my promise to Aradan; visions of the night once kept him close to me, but long ago the orb fell silent and those visions ceased. I learned to live with a broken heart... though I could rejoice with others for their own happiness, I resigned myself to such separation as no other creature has ever had to bear! A lifetime comes to an end, the body falls to dust and the spirit of Man is freed from the confines of time and space to its true home... yet I have never known such relief as that. One day even you, who have been my solace for centuries, will succumb to the dust of the earth, leaving me alone once more."

His only solace for her was his silence, for he could give her no comfort knowing her words were true.

The dark clouds slowly began to dissipate, the sounds of the rain gradually fading away. "Perhaps we need not leave," she reasoned more sanguinely. "If the Wolf has now accomplished her purpose – that of thwarting my excavation – perhaps things will calm once more." She hesitated. "Elbal... you know that we must move on soon anyway; I would prefer to leave Alexis with a home."

His expression showed that he understood her meaning. "Not yet," he answered, his voice uneven.

"Elbal, you must let Alexis go – I know you see her as a daughter, but she is not like us. We have been in this generation long enough to raise suspicions. Those closest to us have known for quite some time we are not aging in the usual manner. It will soon be time to relinquish the joys of this life and move on. We are from a race of travellers, after all."

"Just a few more years, Mother," he pleaded. "I cannot leave Alexis without knowing her future is secure without us."

She relented the pursuit for the moment; she understood more than anyone else how he felt... it was never easy, but she also knew it was easier than continually watching those you love grow old and die, generation after generation. She only said, "Very well... we shall see. But in the meantime, I have a few surprises in store for the companions we shall leave behind. Please have Brehani come to me here... it is time."

Elbal bowed and withdrew, closing the door gently.

As she waited she paced while reading the note again and again. Should she, could she, hope that Aradan was still alive somewhere in the world despite the silence of the orb? That he still loved her? That he had been faithful to her alone? A surge of relief swept over her to suddenly realize that there could indeed be a third Aquillian at large on the planet, trapped in this world of mortality. She then thought of the cist; Brehani was on his way: It was for the very reason of the cist and all it represented that she had undertaken this elaborate excavation and most especially flown her oldest companions to her home for the purpose. Did she not risk losing the loved ones she longed to see if the Wolf thought that was her prime goal, and as so often in the past snatched her treasure away from her? Losing trinkets was one thing; losing corpses was quite a different matter.

When Brehani arrived the Cardinal saw his look of anticipation; Toshiro had clearly already given him the good news that the cist was to be opened, so she wasted no time with preliminaries: "Now that I am back... how soon can we open the anomaly?"

He said, "It depends on how long it will take us to make a lever... to get the heavier stones out of the way."

She could see the worry on his face. "Leave the heavier stones to me," she said simply. "Can you be ready in two days' time?"

"Of course... we could be ready by tomorrow morning, if you'd like."

"No... there are a few things I need to explain before we open the cist."

Edric walked along the shore of the loch, kicking in the occasional stone until he thought of the scene from Lord of the Rings, when two of the hobbits provoked the Watcher in the Water; he doubted Loch Ness would pop up in Loch Eriboll, but he stopped all the same. A chill ran down his spine as he thought of that monster from the film and a split second later, as if one feeling reminded him of another, he thought of Moriel. He brushed that feeling aside as ridiculous. But once he'd thought of her he couldn't *not* think of her: After leading him on over the course of several Skype conversations, she'd finally admitted to being the ghost of Dalmoor. She'd made a fool of him by not telling him, and then laughed in his face at his annoyance. He was irritated with himself for not having recognized her characteristic tactics. Not only had she not let him in on it from the beginning, but she had been in the area for some time and never told him or attempted to see him – he'd always had to call her. She'd never even told him where she was based for those hit-and-runs, but during their last conversation he'd recognized Sango Bay at Durness in the background. It's as if she didn't need him anymore, and he was being humiliated and tossed aside. That thought made him furious, and jealous. But he only seemed to be capable of being angry with her when they were apart... when he didn't look into her lovely pale eyes – as soon as he did that he was a goner, and he'd do anything for her. The things one does for love. He'd do anything for her and she knew it. She used him. And he let her. He pulled out his phone and Skyped her.

"Moriel," he nodded a curt greeting when she came into view.

"Awww," she pouted her lips, "are you still upset with me?"

Her large, pale blue eyes shot through him like adrenalin to the heart, and his started pounding in his chest. That look – she *knew* he could never resist it. He tried to withstand it, but he could feel his anger with her, however justified it had seemed a few minutes ago, melting away. Why did he let her torture him like this? Oh yes. He loved her. "I am..." he managed to say, sounding like a git.

"It's not very handsome of you... holding a little fun against me. I'd prefer you held something else against me."

He said nothing, but he was listening.

She didn't elaborate. "How is she?" she asked suddenly.

"What do you mean?"

"I mean, does the Cardinal seem content? Or lonely? Depressed?" At the blank look on his face she rolled her eyes with a tsk, "Oh, never mind! Neanderthal."

"Well what do you expect? I'd have to get close to her... and she's guarded... like you," he added, his male pride wearing thin. "One complicated woman in my life is enough, thank you."

She cooed, "Oh, that's right... you're in love with me!"

"As if you'd forget. You're brutal, Moriel, you know that?"

She smiled. "Oh, very well," she soothed. "I'm flattered, truly." It wasn't enough. "I promise... I'll kiss you when I see you next. How's that?"

"Then when are you coming? You're not that far away," he smiled seductively. He might have a love-loathe relationship with her on the best of days, but they both knew how to turn on charm like water from a tap.

He really could be irresistible when he wished and it was dangerous; entangling herself with him was not in her plans. "Perhaps once she's moved on, you and I can spend some time together," she hedged, just enough sincerity to appease him. "Any other news to cheer me in the meantime?"

" 'Word is, they're going to open the contents of the anomaly's trench in a couple days. I don't know how they can – the sheet of a stone that's covering it is massive, and there's no way they can get the digger in there to shift it."

"Let me know when you find out what's in there. And I hope you can finish soon... I miss you." Her eyes drew him in. "If you were here," she whispered, "I'd kiss you now."

"You're a tease, Moriel. But I'll hold it against you when I see you next. Oh," he remembered, "you told me to let you know if there were any newcomers; the history professor of the pilot showed up yesterday. I think he's just passing through."

"Old... or young?"

"Young. For a professor."

"Blonde?" she sounded alarmed.

"Yeah... do you know him?"

"Is he Norwegian?"

"He did have an accent... I met him up at the castle."

"Did you catch a name?"

"Alvar, I think he said."

Her brow creased. "Meet me on the shore-end of Loch Sian's beach in two nights' time; there's a lane that runs along the shore there." She could come earlier; but if the professor was who she thought he was, she'd give them a day or two to think they were secure before smashing their little reunion.

"You're coming?" he lit up at the thought. "Why wait two days? You could come now, you're so close," he added accusingly.

She ignored the insinuation. "My yacht engine needs repairing, which takes time, and for that I must return to Orkney to my trusted shipwright. Once it's repaired and I stock supplies, it should take about six hours to reach Durness from there," she calculated. "Once I clear Hoy I can speed along nicely. I'll call you now when I'm ready to leave."

"I'll hold you to that kiss," he smiled, eyebrow cocked.

She blew him a kiss as she reached forward and terminated the connection.

He sighed, lingering a moment. The way she teased him was maddening, slapping him one minute and caressing him the next; he loved it, he loathed it. He loved her. He never knew where he stood with her and that was frustrating, but it also aroused his pride of conquest. He felt sometimes as if there were another man he should be jealous of, but he knew of none closer to her than himself. The thought of sharing her affections with anyone else made him jealous and spurred him on to win her heart; he'd do anything to secure her love for himself.

※

Aradan found the entrance of the tunnel through the souterrain, though it was very well hidden. When he came into the tunnel proper he needed no light for his keen eyes, and could see that the walls of the tunnel were Erlina's handiwork, as smooth and solid as poured stone. Haltingly, he reached out and touched the wall which had been spoken into existence by the voice he'd longed a thousand times to hear again. A spark of hope that Erlina still lived burst into flame, and he sped to the mouth of the cave unwilling to delay another moment. Coming to the crevice that Jon had told him about, he retrieved the journal they'd returned, and then stepped into the cavern: The stones had lost their glow but for a lingering shimmer at their cores, each one a faint star on the firmament of the floor. When he saw the pools with the stone between them – the very stone they had sat upon together so long ago – he wept, fanning that flame somewhere deep within his heart for the first time in centuries. He began to recall every detail of what Jon had told him of their discoveries in the past weeks, and the more he thought of them, the more the flame of hope consumed the kindling of doubts, fears, hopelessness, resignation and even the years of loneliness. He remembered every detail of their ancient trysts, and even Erlina's fragrance came flooding to his memory at the sight of the stone, as if her scent lingered there. He sat down upon it, tracing his fingers across its ancient contours, then closed his eyes: His heart recalled the glistening of moonlight upon the watery deep through the canopy of leaves overhead; the distant song of nightingales; the gentle slap of waterfall on one of the pools; the perfume- and oaken-scented breeze that rustled through the forest. "*Kianaer*," he whispered the name of that place, long buried in the mists of time.

He opened the journal still in his hand: The first page was at the back, as was customary with their writings, and her unmistakeable script startled him... he ran his fingers gently across the lettering... it was as if she spoke to him; she was there through her writing... she had touched those very pages. Hungrily he read one page after the other, reading her fluid, feathery, exquisite words in the tongue of their heart.

He read on and on until he heard voices just outside the door. He swiftly collected the journal and retreated into the darkness of the tunnel, far enough back to be unseen even by Elven eyes. His keen ears attuned to the slightest sound, focusing on the area around the pool.

The voices stopped; he heard a skeleton key turning an ancient lock well greased. Five soft footsteps. A hand turning the dimmer switch, flooding the cavern with brilliant light only a few minutes before turning the lights off and allowing the stones' soft glow to suffice for the keen of sight.

More soft footsteps, the swish of soft material. Shoes slipping from feet. Someone sat upon the stone between the pools. He could bear it no longer and moved closer to see who it was: A woman lay upon the stone bench, one knee bent with a bare foot resting on the stone, her long raven hair flowing down as a curtain of satin. A teardrop fell into her hair and she sighed deeply. Was she a vision born out of a desperate heart? He was cautious. Her sigh reached his ears and he sighed too at the beauty of that one sound.

She rose in a flash and faced the darkness of the tunnel. "Who's there?" she whispered. At that moment the breath of his sigh carried his distinct fragrance to her, that of warm cinnamon, fresh lemongrass and the aromatic scent of cloves.

Hesitatingly, he stepped into the light, holding his breath against disappointment at this illusion. He stared at her wide-eyed, as if seeing an apparition. She wore the crimson colour of bereavement, as did he. "Erlina?" he whispered, avoiding her gaze.

She gasped at the sound of her name as she stared back at him. Unsure as to whether it was truly him or her heart had at last conjured his likeness for her again, she took a step toward him. He watched her approach. A tear moistened her cheek. "Is this – is this another haunting of my dreams?" she wept in weariness of hope thwarted too many times. "How long have I desired the return of these visions! But are they only a taunt now? Do they mock me?"

"Can it truly be?" he asked himself in a whisper. "If you be real and not a vision... touch me!"

"This vision truly speaks!" she gasped, wide-eyed.

"Do you taunt me?" he asked pleadingly. Or are you truly the one I—"

Erlina took another step toward him and cautiously reached out, slowly stepping ever nearer, afraid to awaken from this delicious dream, afraid he would vanish like smoke on a breeze as so often in the ancient past.

As her breath reached him, her unmistakeable fragrance, of spicy vanilla mingled with spring almond blossoms and Immortelle, enveloped him. He breathed her in as a drowning man coming up from the depths of the ocean gasps for that first breath. He closed his eyes and crumpled to his knees in relief.

"Are you a waking dream... or are you truly solid form?" she whispered through her tears. She touched his hair , first tentatively with the tips of her fingers, then ever surer, she ran her fingers through his hair.

His skin tingled at her touch, and he opened his eyes. He laughed through his tears, "You're... you're barefoot!"

Erlina, knowing it was no longer just a delicious dream, wept through tears of joy, "As when we first met!"

He looked up into her eyes, running his hand lightly along the folds of her dress as he rose. "Erlina! Is it really you?" he caressed her cheek, she pressing into his hand with a gentle sigh.

"Aradan! You are *not* a dream... you truly *are* here!" she caressed his face, his jaw, his neck, not daring to remove her hands from his solid form.

Ever more assured it was not merely an illusion which would evaporate, they held each other in a tearful embrace, never willing to let go again. Erlina's orb throbbed wildly between them.

"Aradan! Oh, how long has it been since I allowed my heart to dwell on your name! How often I have longed to call you – *Aradan*! To hear my own name called!"

"Then I shall say it evermore – *Erlina*!" he kissed her, lingering in the sweet fragrance of her essence blooming forth. His touch electrified her entire being as he imbibed deeply, kissing her neck.

"It *is* you!" she cried with laughter. "How I have missed you – such banal words for so deep an ache! Those deep watches of the night when you would come to visit, or when I floated in a dreamy mist through your longhouse... oh, *why* did those *visitations* stop, my love?"

"My part of the orb has been taken," he told her briefly of Moriel and their history. "In one of her deceptions she took on your form... my eyes were blinded by your appearance; only later did I realize with deepest regret that my sense of smell had warned me... it was not *your* essence, but I only realized too late to prevent the theft. *That* is why we stopped sensing each other... and why it has taken me this long to find you at last," he kissed her temple.

She closed her eyes in relief. "All this time... I thought... I hoped you were still alive, but feared that perhaps your heart no longer... that you no longer—"

"Oh Erlina! I have *never* stopped loving you! You were my only reason for living! I could never— to abandon my love for you would be to abandon life itself!"

"We are together again... that is all that matters," she kissed his hand.

He drew her lips to his own, caressing her soul with tender passion. She sank into his strong embrace, unwilling ever to part again. How long they lingered thus mattered not.

Hours later they still sat upon the stone bench talking: "How did you find me at last?" Erlina asked, resting in Aradan's arms upon the stone bench, tracing his face tenderly with her finger.

"Your pilot... my spy, and my friend."

"So," she laughed. "Jon was your spy! And to think – I hired him for numerous reasons, not the least of which was for Alexis. She has longed for a soulmate, but my lifestyle had not allowed for contact with anyone that might suit her; I decided to return here and settle for her sake, using the excavation as an impetus. I interviewed dozens of pilots, but more than any of the others I felt that he not only had the skills needed in this climate, but a good heart and a strong mind, and might be good for Alexis, if love should bloom between them. I was right. Now it pleases me to no end that he comes with such a treasured friend attached," she kissed his hand.

"If I had known it was truly you here, I would have stopped at nothing to come," his voice was pained at the thought of the time lost which he could have been with Erlina. "And speaking of Alexis... I have restored her hearing, and intend to restore her tongue as well."

Erlina sighed the happiest of relief, reaching up to kiss him in deepest gratitude. "I thought I heard a change in her voice – one that betrayed the ability to hear oneself; it must have been so difficult for her to keep her secret when she and I met upon my return!"

"I did not know if you were truly my beloved or my nemesis," he replied, "and so I bade her keep her secret until I was certain." He breathed in her essence with a sigh. "When the dreams and visions faded shortly after my orb was stolen, I had feared the worst – that Moriel had succeeded in—" he left it unsaid. "After centuries of fruitless searching I had given up hope of finding you alive; but when I began hearing rumours of the Cardinal, and those spanned more than a natural lifetime, I was convinced *she* was in fact the Wolf; for each time I came near, the castle had been abandoned shortly before, which convinced me all the more... she was running from me. This time, I sent Jon to find out for me."

She sat up and looked at him in shock. "You've been here before?"

"I've come here many, many times over the centuries, searching for you."

She sighed, sinking onto his lap once more. "I had the same urge! I searched for you the length and breadth of the Spice Route, the Norse slave trade routes... time and again my restless heart urged me away to search, and I searched, always in vain. In the past century, I moved often for another reason too: I promised you I would never defend a mortal, and to that end, each time the Wolf's threats have grown dangerous to those I've loved, I have simply moved on to protect them. If I had known you came here... I would have rooted myself to this place beside Darachi!"

"We think too much alike, it would seem," he smiled down upon her as he caressed her hair. "I'm so grateful that this time you tarried."

"I did so for Alexis. Moreover, once I had decided to excavate I could not leave it for long."

"Why did you initiate this excavation? Why now, and not earlier?"

"As I said, partly as an excuse to settle for Alexis's sake; also, this generation of friends includes archaeologists whom I know will respect the rarity of Maldor and all it represents, and I wanted to give them the honour of the find of a lifetime. And speaking of which," she sat up, holding her hand out to him, "Come... I want to introduce you to everyone! We must eventually leave our sanctuary here and return to the mortal world to celebrate!"

"Wait," he pulled her back to himself. "I would wish for nothing more, but first we must turn our minds to Moriel... the Wolf."

"I'd hoped for nearly two centuries that there was a third Aquillian on the earth," Erlina replied, "for my bodyguard, Elbal, has been with me that long... and since I knew that I was not his biological mother; I had hoped that you were not... had not—"

"Never," he assured her again as he kissed her hand.

"—and so there had to be a third. But I still thought in terms of *urfather*... perhaps someone taken with you in that battle... never suspecting—" she stopped, her mind flooding with events in her past to do with the Wolf.

"She has tried for over a thousand years to seduce me," he told her, "through deceptions, illusions, coercion, bribery... the most devious use of her giftings, and those things I detest the most!"

"What is her gifting?"

"Her gaze," he replied, "she can make you see anything she conjures. Never look into her eyes! It drives men to maddening love, to war, to violence, to whatever she deems of value to herself at the time. I know there must be a good soul beneath her *Mor*ways, but it has been buried deeply for so long."

She smiled at him, "And I am in the business of *un*burying, remember? I have to believe we can bring her back to good."

"You will undoubtedly have your chance, and soon. If I know her at all, she will not be far behind now that I have found you at last. In fact, I think she's already in the area."

"The ghostings," she nodded sombrely. "Yet now that I know she is Aquillian, no matter how dark, the thought of the Wolf has lost its pull of anxiety... anonymity was a powerful weapon of fear."

"But do not underestimate her... you are surrounded by men here, and they are her primary weapons – even those closest to you can be manipulated."

"Then we must prepare them," she responded simply. "Come, my love," she stood, holding out her hand to him.

He took her hand and rose from the bench. He reached up and touched her orb, examining it. "How was the centrepiece lost?"

"As it deflected an arrow in that fateful battle. I have searched in vain for it all this time."

"Oh, Erlina! You have truly searched in vain, beloved! For my grandfather once explained that if it should ever become separated it falls into *mists* – as invisible to the physical world as a single drop of water in a churning ocean – and only when both halves of the necklace are worn by the lovers united can it be called forth. Erlina," he said gently, "we must find her; we must risk everything to retrieve my half of the orb. For without it we cannot find the orb's heart; and without that, we can never return home."

"*Home?*" Erlina blinked.

He shook his head, "I never had the chance to tell you everything concerning the orb," he began. "The orb, when once we have been joined, becomes both a beacon and a key."

"Can this be true?" she asked excitedly. "We have a chance to return to Aquillis?"

"I was sent home as a young boy to learn the ways of the Gates," he explained. "That is when my grandfather gave me the orb, both as dowry and as key."

"And my mother left me a small vial of *Mithrian* dust!"

He paced, running his fingers through his hair as he thought. "*That* is why no one has ever returned for us! Our mothers knew that between us we would have everything to open the Gate! They could not return for us because of it!"

"Our mothers!" Erlina repeated. "I have thought of my mother much, especially lately... you have heard, no doubt, of my plans to open the cist?"

"I have seen a photo of your map," he nodded. "Who are the six buried there?"

"The three smaller ones are Angus, Caitrin... and Niallan."

"Niallan..." he repeated. "In one of the earlier visions of the night, I saw you in a roundhouse with him and another woman... Caitrin?" She nodded. "I'm grateful that he watched over you in my absence."

"And he bid me give you his love, his friendship, and his brotherhood when next we should meet," she smiled at the memories.

"And I assume the larger three in the cist are your father and brothers?"

"Yes... I do not look forward to the moment of seeing them again thus, but I wanted to give the honour of such a moment to companions who would respect the sacred nature of a tomb and those interred."

Aradan nodded, "We must devise a way of transporting your father and brothers with us to the Gate."

"Why?" Erlina was confused. "They are gone. Even if we can get back... I would not wish to confront my mother with the decayed shell of my father and brothers... I could not do such a thing! It will be torment enough to see them myself."

Aradan took her by the shoulders. "You do not know! Of course – how could you?" he was incredulous. "All this time you thought—! Erlina, my love... they are not *dead*!" He told her about their final moments, and that he had released their essence before their earth-bound shells breathed their last.

"What?" she cried. "They live! But how?" she shook her head in disbelief. "They have been locked within stone and earth for centuries! Oh, what have I done!"

"No, no, my love," he laughed, "They themselves linger in the *Breath of Aquillis*... they only need to reunite with their Aquillian forms to return to their loved ones! Their forms lie suspended – asleep as it were – and freed from the dust of the earthen vessels that have decayed from around them... that which is now in the earth need only be retrieved for our departure!"

"Then it is clear," Erlina trembled, "we must retrieve your necklace from Moriel so that we can depart and return all to life! And if Moriel can be turned again..."

Aradan kissed her, laughing in pure joy. "Oh, Erlina! You are truly a creature of purest love! So many wrongs Moriel has done to us and yet your first thoughts are of her redemption!"

"Now... come!" she took his hands in hers and pulled him toward the door. "I want to introduce you to the world! I must tell Galal and Toshiro to organize a celebration dinner for this evening... there isn't much time!"

"And speaking of celebration," Aradan rang his fingers along her silken dress, "this colour of mourning no longer suits us, I think."

10: Now

Toshiro was in the butler's pantry putting away groceries that he'd stocked up on in Durness. He heard someone approaching and turned to see the Cardinal, glowing with a smile that came from deep within, and his heart skipped a beat - it had been a long, *long* time since he'd seen her smile like that. Well actually, never quite like that; she was more radiant than ever before, if that were possible.

She handed him a piece of paper. "I'd like Galal to prepare this dinner tonight; do we have the supplies?"

He looked it over, nodding, "It's a good thing I keep a good stock. I'll get Galal on it right away – and send him reinforcements if I can."

She handed him a second paper. "I'd like these to attend this evening... in the room Alexis refers to as my *Hall of Dreams*. Amir shall stand guard there."

He took the list, reading through the names and nodding. It was everyone in the castle except for Edric and Jon's guest. Edric could be kept busy in the cellar kitchen under Galal's watchful eye – at least until Galal was serving. He looked curiously at her: "What's this all about, if I might ask?"

"I have wonderful news tonight!" Her smile would have melted ice; she danced out the door.

He laughed and shook his head in wonder, heart bursting with joy for her... whatever had happened since their flight home from Edinburgh, he was relieved to see her so happy.

Unwilling to be parted from each other, Aradan had waited outside the pantry. She took him by the hand and led him to her bedchamber.

"I have something to show you... I never *truly* gave up hope." She led him to her wardrobe and opened the doors: Amidst a row of red dresses was one of pale emerald green; she touched it lovingly. "I've always made sure I had one dress... just in case..."

He kissed her tenderly. "You amaze me. I am very sorry, but I have nothing on hand... I really did not expect to find you this time."

"Well, there are quite a few men here... I'm certain we can find you something suitable," she smiled.

The Hall of Dreams' banners raised to an elegant canopy, their bells dangling aloft, ringing high and clear in the slightest breeze stirred by movement. The long oaken dining table had been positioned down the centre of the room, laden with the trappings of a feast, and overhead the chandeliers of silver tree branches illuminated the room with their soft glow, scattering the delicate shadows of banners. Seated at the table were Naeem, Brehani, Toshiro, Jon and Alexis; and the foot of the table sat Elbal, with not one but two empty seats at the head of the table. The room was electric with curiosity of what this momentous occasion could signify, though only Jon and Alexis could guess as to what was about to happen. Everyone else whispered in quiet conversation until after the wine had been poured.

As Elbal rose, a hush rippled down the table. "The Cardinal has invited you here tonight as her valued company of companions. From this night forward," his base voice rumbled, "your lives and perspectives will forever be altered. Are you prepared?" he waited. "Do you solemnly swear to guard the sacred history that shall this night be entrusted to you?"

He heard them all consent, and with one word he picked up a silver bell and rang it: "Rise."

The door opened and everyone rose as they turned to watch: A woman entered, robed in a whispery gown the colour of green sea glass that shimmered iridescent in the soft light. She wore a shining blue ring upon her right ring finger, and the orb necklace. Behind her close at hand followed a man of radiant splendour, dressed in anthracite trousers and a side-buttoned shirt in a darker iridescent emerald than the woman's dress. That this man was Jon's guest was clear and though they recognized him as such, it was if they were seeing him for the first time. The two figures were resplendent, mesmerizing... otherworldly. The Cardinal had never looked so radiant, unapproachable and regal, and the mortal men needed to look away yet could not... it was exquisite torture. She floated majestically, silently past each guest and took her place at the head of the table with the man beside her.

"Welcome, my companions!" her voice sang with barely-contained joy. She motioned for them to be seated while she remained standing, holding Aradan's hand as he sat down beside her. "No doubt you are all curious as to the purpose of this evening, and as to the identity of this man beside me," she gazed at him lovingly. She weighed her words carefully and then continued: "I have called you all here for manifold reasons. I must ask you all to keep an open mind, and to trust me that what I tell you is nothing but the solemn truth. Do I have your trust?"

There was a moment of silence as they all looked from one to the other. Naeem, the oldest of the group of companions, rose with a respectful bow: "My lady, I believe I may speak for all present: You have never given us reason to doubt you. You shall always have it." They all murmured their agreement as he sat down again.

"Very well." True to her custom, she did not begin where they thought she would; she left the gentleman at her side an enigma for the present. She glided slowly around the length of the table as she spoke, the mysterious man's eyes never leaving her: "Do you remember our dinner together the first evening here, and the story I told you of Maldor?" With the exception of Jon all had been present, but he was by now far more informed than anyone else. "I would like to tell you the rest of the story: I told you that the people of the kingdom of Maldor were renowned as immortals... *elves*, as some have called them. But they are not elves in the literary sense of the definition – that is simply a generic term. They are far more... The

Maldorians were... *are*... part of a race from another world; a planet to be precise, called *Aquillis*, which lies near the star *Altair* beyond the *Shaft of Aquila* – as seen from Earth. They arrived on earth long before the mainland of Great Britain became an island, and one group, or *pod*, eventually settled in the north of what would become Scotland. In the year AD 788, there was a battle on the very site of our excavation between attacking Norsemen and the local Pictish tribe together with their allied Maldorians. In that battle stood the king of Maldor and his two royal sons; unbeknownst to him his eldest daughter also fought in the battle while the rest of the women and children had taken refuge on their ships near the beach of Tràigh Allt Chàilgeag to the north. When the battle turned against the king, he and his sons fell defending the mortals and the ships took flight. But in the chaos of the battle the daughter, Princess Erlina, was victorious though wounded, and while her form healed in unconsciousness, two of her Kind were taken captive: Her betrothed, called Aradan, and a woman called Moriel." She stopped for some time, overcome with emotion. The room was absolutely silent, suspense building to a painful pitch as she returned to the head of the table and took Aradan's hand in her own before speaking again: "The Cardinal, as you have known me, is no more. *I* am in fact this fabled Princess Erlina of Maldor. And this," she looked at Aradan lovingly, "is my betrothed, Aradan." He raised her hand to his lips and kissed it tenderly.

Toshiro stared at Jon – he hadn't taken the conversation in the helicopter entirely serious.

Jon just grinned back at him with a, *'See, I told you so'* look on his face.

Brehani stared at his glass of wine, a blank look tweaked occasionally by an incredulous shake of the head, a blink, a frown, a grin, a half-choked chuckle.

Naeem saw the exchange between Toshiro and Jon; he looked at Brehani and saw the same reactions he felt bubbling up within himself, though his were delayed. He thought of the first time he'd met the Cardinal; he was a young man working in the largest library in Cairo. He had been buried in the study of a text when something red caught his attention from the corner of his eye and he'd looked up: His heart leapt as he saw the most beautiful woman he'd ever beheld. He remembered the very moment he'd first heard her laugh, the sound of wind chimes and crystal. It was at that moment that he had fallen in love with the Lady and never fully recovered, though he had since married and loved his wife.

As the shock began to settle, low whispers of incredulous surprise swelled. It's not that they did not believe the Ca— Erlina; it's that what she told them was simply unbelievable. They'd suspected something when age had crept upon their own bones while leaving her untouched by the passing decades; but they had never supposed anything so fantastic.

Erlina said with a playful smile, "I know women are generally to be reticent about their age... but by your earth reckoning I am two thousand, two hundred and seventy years old, and Aradan is three hundred years older still." She looked at each of them. "I know you have many questions; let them come, and do not be shy." At the hesitant silence she asked, "Naeem, have you never wondered how I knew so much of the past that was unrecorded? And Toshiro, have you never wondered, in all the years you've known me, why I have not grown older? And you, Brehani – have you never wondered about the maps in my possession? About my uncanny ability to draw you a map of any of our previous excavation sites, from Egypt to Asia to Africa, that laid out things exactly as they would prove?" She paused. "It is because I was *there*. I had walked those streets, seen the towns and markets... and knew the merchants by name... and I *never* forget a detail. If I had not been there myself I'd at least heard the stories, told so vividly by my father and mother, that I knew them intimately as well."

Toshiro finally found a voice. "Were you... or your parents... there at the birth of Christ?"

"No... it was not known at the time that such a significant event of human history would unfold in such an insignificant place," she admitted.

As the news began to sink in, a trickle and then a flood of questions came pouring out. Erlina revelled in it, at last able to share her secret with her friends... to reveal her true self.

Brehani asked, "You said that your people are immortal, and yet you mentioned that your father and brothers fell in battle... I assume that means *died* – yet how is that possible?"

She explained to them the laws that governed their conduct as immortals among mortals, and that by defending a mortal they risked their immortal lives. "However," she smiled at Aradan, "among our people, within each travelling pod, or group, are those trained in the art of opening the Gate – the portal through time and space with which we travel. These *Gatekeepers* also have the ability to rescue those who have risked their immortality by laying down their temporal frames... if they can reach them in time. It is a bit much to explain further; but you will soon see the effects of that which I speak."

"How so?" Naeem asked.

"Opening the anomaly," she nodded toward Brehani.

"You know what's in there?" Brehani asked, incredulous.

"More to the point... *who*. The reason I invited you all to this excavation is that you are my favoured companions of this generation, and I wanted to give you the honour of being part of the greatest archaeological discovery this world shall ever know!" She told them of Aradan's role in the lives of King Elgin, Ealdun and Sidhendion. "I am uncertain what we shall find as regards these three; I have never seen my Kind fallen, and Brehani's instruments have been unable to penetrate or decipher the contents or even the composition of the stone that shelters them. As to the latter three, which are human burials," Aradan handed her a vellum scroll and she held it up for them to see, "I have recorded their lives here for posterity; their ancestry, descendents, feats and accomplishments. Such detailed records of commoners are unprecedented in this region of the world, and I can guarantee their antiquity... I wrote them myself, beginning in AD 810. You will know more about the people who once lived down there," she gestured toward the excavation site, "than you do about your own neighbours."

Naeem shook his head trying to comprehend it all. "Nothing has been found in the histories of the greatest libraries of such a civilisation as you've described! I would have come across something of it, had it been so... would I not?"

"Our race passed into legend; our people into myth," Erlina replied quietly. "Our own records passed beyond the ken of Man when our ships left. Many written human accounts were destroyed by fires... the monasteries, libraries... or lost to man's barbarisms during what became known as the Viking Age. Some stories only survived in fragments... others became bards' tales of mermaids, others of lost cities swallowed by the sea or buried by volcanoes," she glanced at Aradan. "The remaining fragments of truth are dismissed by many learned man as stories for children, or folklore, or fable. But I can assure you," she smiled, "we are no myth; and many of the stories that have been relegated to fairy tales have a grain of truth behind them."

Brehani, whose thoughts hovered around the anomaly and what it could be, asked, "Why, after all this time, have you decided to unearth the cist *now*? You've known about it for... well, always."

"I have," Erlina admitted, "though for a long time I was unwilling to face my grief... to see my loved ones so close and yet so far. And I was never here long, as time and again I was driven to search for my beloved," she looked at Aradan as he caressed her hand. "But I'd made a decision before we moved back here to Castle Dalmoor: It was to be an end of my existence as far as this generation was concerned," she glanced at Elbal, whose expression was resigned. "I was preparing to disappear again, to re-emerge later in another guise, another lifetime, as I have done for centuries... this excavation was to be my parting gift to you all." She looked at Alexis, who stared at her mother in shock. "Dearest, my disappearance would have also guaranteed your safety from further harassment by the Wolf. I tried to ensure – and hoped I'd chosen wisely – to provide you with a secure future before I departed... a home and loved ones," she glanced briefly at Jon, then to Elbal and his sons.

"I won't let you go!" Alexis ran to her mother and threw her arms around her.

Erlina held her tenderly. "Dear one, I must eventually go."

"But not for many years! I love you!" she wept.

"And I love you!" Erlina kissed her temple. "Now that Aradan and I are united... perhaps we'll stay here," she comforted.

That Alexis spoke had shocked the companions; when it became known that Aradan had restored her hearing, shouts of joy and thanks nearly made Alexis cover her ears at the din, with so much smiling beginning to tire her face. She was passed from person to person with embraces of congratulations.

Night had fallen, and still no one could bring themselves to retire. Questions were asked of and answered by both Erlina and Aradan: Where they'd come from, about Maldor, the Vikings, the Wolf, the whys and the wherefores of a hundred subjects, each one fascinating enough to fill an entire book (and many did just that as Erlina had recorded it for them in her private library). Aradan also explained the history of Moriel and his own wanderings in greater detail, including the tale of the stolen necklace and their need to retrieve it. That Moriel had succeeded in her usual aim of disrupting Erlina's plans was obvious, but did that mean that she was now gone, or still lurking nearby, as Aradan seemed to think?

When it was suggested that Edric was the agent of the Wolf, Aradan cautioned them against judging him too harshly: "If he is her agent, understand that Moriel is only using him, whatever his role is, however willing or unwilling he is... she likes toying with puppies, and to that end will lead him on as long as he is useful; but any expectations he may have will be dashed – that is her way... her entertainment, if you will." He warned them about her gifting, and that to safeguard both themselves and Erlina they were to avoid eye contact with both Moriel and Erlina. "Though," he warned, "that might be easier said than done... her giftings are likely far more formidable than when I last encountered her. But I know her greatest weakness: *Me*. In her warped perception, anything that stands in her way of having me is considered fair game... intense jealousy is the reason Erlina has been her target, though Moriel's plan of eliminating her competition was frustrated... most likely because Erlina is so well guarded," he bowed in gratitude to Galal and Amir, and looked toward Elbal who, though he could not see the gesture, was included in Aradan's thanks. "Precisely because Erlina and I have now been reunited, Moriel will show herself soon."

As dawn began to relume the eastern sky, Erlina and Aradan at last withdrew. Jon and Alexis were far too exhilarated by it all to sleep, so they went to the tower to enjoy the sunrise, turning the Capsule to face the rising sun.

"How are you?" Jon asked. "You've had a lot to take in the past few days... and that's the understatement of the century!"

Alexis looked at him, brushing her fingers along his chin in wonder. "You have a beautiful voice," she said.

"Well," he laughed, "if I'm interesting enough to hold your attention after all we heard tonight... last night... this morning... whatever – then I must be riveting!"

"You are," she winked, adding more seriously, "it's just that every sound is beautiful... you can't imagine what it means to hear your voice, or to hear something as simple as the wind. I never knew it had sound!"

"And this morning it's so still," he shook his head, "but wind can whistle, howl, groan..."

"I look forward to hearing it all, but most of all I like the sound of your voice."

He pulled her into his arms and gently placed her ear to his chest. "Can you hear that?" she listened to the rhythm of his heart. "Every beat is for you," he whispered, his heart thumping faster. And faster.

She looked up at him. "What is it?"

"I want to make you happy..."

"But you do!" she smiled.

He struggled. "Do you remember my first words to you when you could hear?" He really hoped she did as he couldn't think straight at that moment, he was so nervous.

"You mean... about loving me?" she blushed, smiling.

"I do love you," he nodded, "more each passing day. But it's gotten to the point that it's painful."

"Painful?" she looked at him, hurt and confusion in her frown.

"It's painful because the more I love you, the more I dread ever being parted from you," he took her hands. "It's a pain that has only one remedy."

She studied his expression, still confused.

"I want to spend the rest of my life with you... will you marry me?"

Instead of the response he'd hoped for she was silent, glancing at him before looking down at their hands. He didn't know what to think; it was some time before she replied, and all he could do was wait helplessly.

"But... why *me*?" she asked.

He took her gently by the shoulders and she looked up. "I love your spirit, your intelligence, your humour, the way you make me feel. I love the way you walk, the way you get that mischievous look in your eyes. I love your courage, your strength. You make me want to be a better man... want to provide, protect... I love *you*," he shrugged helplessly. "I want to be everything for you... to give you a family – my parents, my siblings... and," he swallowed, "maybe someday..." He took a deep breath and held it, hoping she would end the suspense.

"But my question still remains," she pulled away, more determined. "Why *me*? I don't even know where I come from, or who *I* really am!" She looked into his eyes, a wave of conflicting emotions pulling her apart. She stood and began pacing: "*You* know who you are... you have parents, siblings, and a past. I have an assumed name – I don't even know what my maiden name is supposed to be! You have no idea what a hole that leaves inside of me! I've lived a double life in many ways: On the outside I've been the confident – even sassy – daughter of the Cardinal, her assistant, flexible traveller, organizer; but on the inside, I've been confused... lost! I live with constant questions. I've been able to ignore them for years... even silence them and get on with life. But since you and I began discovering things about Erlina – my adoptive, *alien* mother – those questions have grown louder and impossible to silence. Until I know the answers to those questions – who I am, and where I come from," she slumped down onto the seat in defeat, "I... I can't commit to our relationship without knowing myself."

Jon saw his hopes unravelling. "What am I supposed to say to that?" he shrugged helplessly. "I can understand your reasoning to a certain extent... but—" he shook his head as he rose. "I'm tired, and you're probably tired after such a long and eventful day. Goodnight." He turned and walked to the tower stairs.

He returned to his room, Alexis's words playing over and over in his mind. He was angry at being placed second to a woman who'd abandoned a baby; that a woman who'd vanished so many years ago would ruin his chances for happiness. He couldn't let that happen. He heard Alexis's door close quietly, and he threw open his door and ran to hers, entering and closing her door before she'd have a chance to turn him away.

"Look – before you say anything, please hear me out," he raised his hand as she was about to speak.

She looked at him expectantly, though beyond that he couldn't tell what she was thinking.

"Okay – so you can't commit yet. Then let me help you find out the answers to those questions that are holding you back." His breath caught in his throat at the thought of what it might mean if they couldn't trace her mother.

"How can you?" she shook her head. "It was twenty-five years ago; I don't even know what she studied. The Cardinal told me that the nuns mentioned my mother had a decidedly English accent, and that's it."

"Well that's good... that narrows it down considerably," Jon encouraged.

"Not enough," she sighed in resignation.

"Don't give up," he pleaded; he started to reach for her hand but stopped short of touching her. "For your sake; for my sake. For our sakes!"

She looked at him hopelessly, but nodded. "In the meantime... can't we just keep things as they are? Is that possible now?" she sighed.

"We can try," he shrugged. "Though I won't pretend not to be disappointed... and as long as it's not a *no*...." He held out his hand to her. "Friends?" he asked.

She hesitated at the word, but took his hand and held it in hers. "Friends. And it's not a *no*... I just can't say *yes* yet."

"Then I can live with that for now if you can."

Later that day Jon found Aradan with Erlina in her library. Lately that was the only place to find them when they were findable; they were constantly writing. "Do you both have a minute?" he asked.

"Of course," Aradan looked at him curiously.

Jon came in and closed the door. He stood before the desk, his hands stuffed deep into his pockets; Aradan recognized that posture in his friend when he was unsure or frustrated, so he gave Jon time to gather his thoughts. "I wanted to talk to you about Alexis," he began.

Erlina heard his distraught tone and looked up from the sentence she'd been writing. "What is it? What's happened?"

"I proposed," Jon shook his head, "but she refused."

"On what grounds?" she gasped.

He told them about their conversation. "If she can't find out... she won't marry me." He ran his fingers through his hair in helpless frustration.

"What do you know about her past?" Aradan asked Erlina.

She told them the scant information that Jon already knew adding, "Alexis's records were lost in the orphanage fire when she was five. I searched through university records in Cairo, with no results... there were no English women enrolled there the year Alexis was born, so I concluded that her mother must have been a tourist from England. I had friends in the airline industry check records for passengers that might fit the profile, but again, nothing conclusive. I even contacted a few of those potential passengers, but to no avail – if she flew it wasn't a direct path with England; she could have been going to or coming from anywhere. Alexis is the name that woman, whoever she was, gave her daughter... that's the only connection we've got."

Aradan shook his head, "There *must* be a way to find her! Someone knows where she's at... we just need to find that someone." He thought a moment. "Do you have a good, recent photo of Alexis, as well as one from her childhood?"

"Yes," Erlina said. "Why?"

"I have a friend who works in London, in police forensics... I'll contact him," Aradan replied. "And I'll need a blood sample for DNA... I know someone who works in genetics... they might be able to help narrow down the search geographically, assuming her mother was English and not European with a learned English pronunciation."

"I want it desperately," Jon stuffed his hands deep into his pockets again, "but it's a delicate matter... what if that woman's current situation won't allow for a missing daughter showing up out of the blue? Maybe she doesn't want to be reminded of her past... or maybe she's not worthy of Alexis... I don't want her getting hurt by rejection again."

"We would never subject her to that," Erlina assured him.

"I know you wouldn't – I'm sorry," he apologized.

"If we find her I'll contact her directly myself and assess the situation," Erlina decided.

"Do you think you can find her?" Jon frowned. "Because if you do, we've got to convince her to contact Alexis or allow contact... otherwise I'll never—" his voice broke.

"No promises," Aradan replied quietly. "But if we do, I'm certain we can arrange discrete contact. And remember," he added with slight smile, "I found Erlina after over a thousand years, so I think we can find her."

"*I* found Erlina. And I haven't got that much patience," Jon managed to grin.

Erlina stood at the edge of the trench gazing down at the sealed cist. Aradan stood nearby speaking with Elbal, Alexis and Jon, though his eyes wandered to Erlina often. Brehani and Naeem arrived as the sun edged toward the western horizon; Toshiro was on distraction duty, getting dart lessons from Edric at the pub.

Amir spoke to Erlina in Aquillian: "How are you?"

"How am I?" she repeated, wistfulness in her voice. "For the first time in over a thousand years I have been reunited with my beloved, and now will once again look upon the faces of my father and brothers. I shall see them but it will be no reunion as they'll not see me; for that we must wait... must keep them safe until we can leave with them. Part of me wants to leave them safely in the ground as they have been for over a millennia, though part of me cannot bear to leave them in the cold earth a moment longer! I am torn with longing and trepidation."

He touched her arm. "Grandmother... there are risks with this action; the Wolf will not be far behind but you are by no means alone. We have knowledge this time about her and the situation that can only be an advantage for us. And you *do* have a safe place: Your castle is well guarded."

"Yes," she smiled at that, but touched his cheek: "You call me grandmother Amir, which I bear with great honour. But that honour in fact belongs to the Wolf, though I doubt she is yet aware of this connection."

"The Wolf? She is my enemy," he growled, "for she has robbed you time and again of your joy!"

She took his hand. "I shall always be your grandmother, but I am only so in spirit. I've had nothing to do with your siring. And perhaps you may turn your *urmother* once again to the good in her. That would be worth every joy robbed, every trinket lost."

He looked at her admiringly. "Your grace knows no bounds. You stand on the brink of your last remaining source of sorrow," he motioned to the trench, "and yet you speak of redemption for another."

"Nothing else truly matters." She kissed him on the cheek.

The massive stone of Lewisian Gneiss still lay where it had remained since the day it had gone from a palace paving stone to a capstone for its king. The entourage stood at the edge of the trench and grew silent as they turned their attention to Erlina.

"This stone you see exposed," Erlina looked at those gathered, "is a secondary capstone which conceals two chambers, and below this stone are two primary capstones: The smaller section contains a woman between two men," she looked at Aradan; he would see the mortal remains of his friend Niallan, whom he'd last seen alive. "The larger is that which contains my father and brothers. The latter will most certainly seem strange to all of us who are used to human exhumation, though neither Aradan nor I know exactly what to expect," she hesitated. "We've never seen our Kind thus before."

She stepped forward as the group watched; she'd never looked more vulnerable or more radiant. She began to whisper an otherworldly song, nearly inaudible though the earth heard her. The ground began to vibrate, the dry dust of debris bouncing along the top of the slab. The stone then gradually began to slide off to one side, a grating moan, as if a massive grinding stone were being turned. She sang stronger and it slowly tipped upon its side. The song was so beautiful; it was as if it echoed back from the sky and reverberated through every blade of grass at their feet, though it was still, quiet. Every colour became crisper, every other sound hushed; even passing clouds seemed to slow, clearing a view for the sinking sun, as if time itself were pausing to listen. Aradan's tears flowed freely as he listened not only with the comprehension of the voice's beauty, but of the words: She was singing of purest love for her father and brothers, and thanking the earth for having guarded them so deeply and safely until she came for them; the words were sweetest melancholy, the lightest whispers of clouds intertwined with the rich browns of earth. The stone slipped down the side of the cist and landed with a reverberating thunder; there was an audible gasp not just at the miracle before their eyes of the two-ton stone simply tipping aside, as if it were a book instead of an enormous block of Gneiss, but at the sight of the stone beneath: The anomaly.

The smaller chamber looked like a typical stone cist, but solid and well-built; the other was unlike anything they'd ever seen or heard of: It had the rainbowed, iridescent structure of polished spectrolite yet was akin to translucent crystal. It appeared completely sealed, as if grown together into a smooth, oblong capsule, yet that it had a lid was apparent as there was a distinct line encircling the top section. Erlina and Aradan stepped down the heathy steps into the trench and she brushed her hand gently along the crystal cist. As she leaned over the cist she felt the tug of her necklace toward the unusual stone; she slipped it from beneath her tunic and saw that it seemed to be attracted toward the obelisk as if it were drawn to a very powerful magnet, though no other metals seemed to be affected by it in that way. She looked at Aradan in wonder.

Through the crystal one could see the shapes of three men, in life strong and tall, laying peacefully, their clothing, swords, and bodies unaffected by time; it was as if they had just lain down to rest before battle. The faces of the three were beautiful, if one could use that word for such manly features that put any human face to shame. Their eyes were closed, but Alexis imagined that they would be piercingly beautiful like her mother's. It was clear that they were perfect; decay had left them untouched; not only that – even the bouquets of wildflowers Erlina had lain atop their chests were still as fresh as the day she'd picked them, sealed with them in that strange capsule.

Before those gathered could awaken from their stupor long enough to consider how to move the obelisk, or what the implications of opening the sealed cist might be, it began to rise beneath the hands of Aradan on one side and Erlina on the other. Before one could have imagined it the entire cist was at ground-level and floating, quite as if it were a helium balloon, about half a metre above the ground. The humans felt as if they were intruding on a sacred moment, and stood frozen as these mesmerizing creatures slowly, majestically proceeded up the path toward the road and to the castle, less of a funerary procession than a homecoming. All the while Erlina sang a melody of haunting beauty.

Only once they were nearly half-way to the castle did the others stir. At first they could only stare at each other.

"We *did* all just see that... didn't we?" Brehani asked. They nodded. He looked back at the other cist, quite forgotten in that moment of awe. "They'll wait; I don't know if I can take any more surprises today."

As the procession had moved from the burial site toward the castle and crossed the quiet road, along that road, hidden in the night shadows of a hawthorn bush, was an old man. He stood as quiet as a mouse, leaning on a branch he'd fashioned into a walking stick. Though Sandy was old, his eyes shone at the sight as if he were a wee lad again and gazing at purest beauty for the very first time, at the myths and legends of the Highlands come to life. He became aware of the sensation that he was standing there on behalf of all his forefathers who'd rightly loved the Bonnie Maid of Dalmoor, and he sighed with a sense of completion.

Edric paced along the dark shore between clumps of heather and bracken. He had a lot on his mind: *Why was Moriel coming this time, when she'd never bothered to come before?* It was true that, where this target was concerned, "before" would have meant flying to the Middle East (and he knew she had an aversion to the entire region) or further afield... and this time it was nearly on her doorstep. But it still didn't sit right with him somehow; it was this obsession of hers with the Cardinal that nettled him... there was something she wasn't telling him and he resented it. He wanted the truth this time. He saw a boat light in the distance. Or did he? Then he remembered with a groan: *Why did she insist on coming under the cover of darkness? And travelling without lights on her yacht – did she have a death wish?* Still... darkness might be to his advantage this time; people tended to be more relaxed, bolder in the dark. Maybe it would keep him from getting so infuriatingly tongue-tied in her presence, and help him say what he was planning... an ultimatum of sorts.

The distant, gentle hum of a well-tuned motor came floating over the waves. There was definitely a small ship on the loch, but the land spit jutting out blocked his view toward the mouth of the loch. Gradually a dark blotch approached, blocking out the reflection of the moon on the water's surface as it came closer. He hurried down to the beach closest to where she had stopped and was tossing out the anchor; she looked up and saw him – that much was clear in the dark – but didn't greet him; he couldn't tell what mood she was in as she silently hoisted a dinghy to the water with a winch. He watched her start its motor with a muted whirr and come toward him.

"Get in," was all she said. They rode back to the yacht and climbed aboard in silence.

Edric nearly forgot what he needed to say when to his surprise the Wolf took the hand he'd offered to help her out of the dinghy; not only that, she didn't release it.

"We have some unfinished business, I think," she purred, running her hands up his arms and along his chest to his neck. Her velvety black cat-suit left nothing to the imagination... not that he was complaining. That look in her eyes was a hungry one; just the kind of look he'd always wanted to see there. Before he could say a word she stroked his cheek with the back of her fingers and bent his head to kiss her. His lips were hungry... and found her surprisingly responsive. That blew it – he had no idea what he'd thought was so urgent. He tangled his fingers in her hair as he pulled her closer with a moan. But long before he'd gotten started she suddenly pulled away. Dangling the bait. Again.

"Aargh! Why do you do that to me, Moriel?" he shouted, running his fingers through his tousled hair.

"Ooh," she cooed, "don't you like my kisses?"

"That's not what I mean and you *know* it!" *It's too late to brush my teeth; why does my mouth taste dusty?*

She laughed, "If I made it easy you'd get bored." she reached up and tangled her fingers in his hair, then ran her hands down his chest, stopping at his waist. "You're armed?" she asked.

"As always," he smiled, reaching for his belt buckle. "If I get bored, I practice; you never know when it will come in handy."

"Show me," she ran her hands down his arms, sending shivers through him.

He turned what looked like a button in the centre of his belt buckle, and out sprang a small stack of throwing stars, four thin blades. "Stainless steel with a titanium oxide finish," he showed her one, turning it over in his hand.

"How many do you carry?" she was suddenly very interested.

"Just these four. Why do you ask?" he was suspicious.

"Oh, no reason... I just like to know I'm in the arms of a man capable of defending a damsel in distress."

He arched an eyebrow and laughed at the irony of those words coming out of her mouth. "I'd never dare use that term when it comes to describing *you*!"

"I'm not as strong as most people think," she wrapped her arms around his neck and whispered in his ear, and felt him shiver again. "So... have you found out anything interesting?"

"Yes," he murmured into her neck as he kissed it. "I overheard something about finding a key," he whispered as he worked his way up her throat. He felt her freeze in his embrace and he looked up. "What is it?"

"Is that what she's after... in that trench?" she asked.

"No one seems to know what's down there," he shrugged. "It could be, though I doubt it's anything that small... from the size of the hole they've dug I'd say it's more like something a key would open. They were all down there this evening when I ditched Toshiro at the pub to meet you here."

"If they brought up something valuable, do you know where they might take it?"

"You're not thinking of going in there, are you?" he stepped back to look at her. "They'll be on high alert for the Wolf!"

"Please," she scoffed, "I'm not exactly a defenceless damsel, remember?" she stepped toward him and pulled his arms around her waist again.

He kissed her, "If you were ever that damsel, I'd be your knight in shining armour."

"Really," she returned his kiss. "How? What would you do to prove your love? To gain my trust?"

"Anything you want," he looked down at her with a grin.

"Anything? Promise?"

"Short of murder? I promise... anything."

"I'll hold you to that," she cooed, kissing him passionately.

He was a goner.

He was so predictable. "If it's any consolation," she whispered into his lips, "you don't make it easy for me to resist, you know."

"Why would you want to?" Something in her tone was unsure and it gave him a spark of hope.

"Because... my course of action was set long ago," she played with a lock of his tousled hair, but her eyes were far off; she wasn't with *him*, in *his* arms. "The Cardinal's going to—"

He pulled away, staggering as he turned his back on her. He felt his limbs growing heavy, and felt a bit dizzy. "What *is* it with you and the Cardinal?" he slurred. "This obsession?" The silence gave him hope that she might actually be contemplating an answer.

Finally she said, "On the merit of her title she's earned the... *love*... of someone she doesn't deserve. I'm going to remedy the situation... set things right." She slid up behind him, wrapping her arms around him. "You don't make it easy to stay on course with that goal... that's why I have to resist you. Do you forgive me?" she whispered, her voice tinged with just enough sincerity to get his attention.

He felt sleepy, as if he'd had too much to drink. "That depends," he muttered.

"On?" she prompted.

He freed himself from her arms and walked a few paces away, keeping his back to her. "Moriel," he took a deep breath trying to clear his head, "Where do we stand? And don't say, 'on a ship on Loch Eriboll' – you *know* what I mean. Why are you here... really? No coy answers."

She countered, "Let me ask you this first: Why do you love me?... *really?* No coy answers."

It was a serious question and it was his one chance to get it right before her walls went up again. He'd thought a lot about what he'd say if she'd just ask. He turned toward her: "I love you, because despite your bravado you really have no idea how wonderful you are... or at least you *could* be if you weren't so unpredictably bitchy sometimes."

She shot a quick glare at him, but had to smile... she knew he was right, but at the same time she was angry at herself for letting him get to her like that. "You have no idea what I've been through in my life," she replied coldly, "and you wouldn't believe me even if I told you."

"Try me." He felt her walls beginning to go up again. He cautiously pulled her into his arms, though he felt like he was fighting a big dose of morphine; her body stiffened and her breathing quickened, but she let him pull her to him. "You could be loving, and learn to accept love – which you're not very good at," he glanced down at her with a sleepy grin. "I get the impression sometimes that you feel compelled toward a target that you know you'll miss... like fate's drawing you in... a moth to the flames. I may not be the most sensitive guy on the planet," he swayed, "but as a knife-thrower... I recognize that feeling of missing the mark. I know you've been rejected – maybe not a lot, but it hurt you when it happened. I'd like to make that up to you." There. He'd said it, and she hadn't—

She pulled back suddenly. "Why should I let you be the one to *make it up to* me? Who are you to me... *really*?"

He staggered back as if she'd just stabbed him. *Why am I so dizzy?*

When he didn't answer she should have felt regret but she didn't. "You think that just because you love me, you're somehow entitled to know me better... to have some special place in my heart! Do you think you're the only man in my life? Honestly?"

"Who is he?" he growled.

"There have been thousands," she shrugged, "but only one has ever come close – and it's *not* you," she laughed disdainfully.

"Right," he snorted in disbelief.

She was exasperated now; this puppy was so persistent! It had been an endearing quality when it suited her but now it was just getting annoying; she would have dumped him overboard right then and there, but she might still have use for him. "Alright," she answered, "if you really want to know who it is... I think my next lover will be the history professor," she pointed toward Castle Dalmoor.

Edric stared at her, mouth agape. "You can't be serious! You don't even know him!"

"That shows how little you actually know me," she tsked condescendingly.

He stared at her. "*He's* the love the Cardinal doesn't deserve? So *that's* why you asked all those questions – if he were from Norway... young...! You've set your sites on him!"

"Bravo," she clapped slowly.

This time she *had* stabbed him. He fought the increasing urge to sleep and stumbled into the waiting dinghy, started it up and drove it out several meters from the yacht before he turned. "To get to your date you're going to have to swim," he jeered. "Be sure to bring a change of clothes with you."

"Edric," she pleaded sweetly. "Don't be like that... you know I love you. Please come back."

How could she sound so infuriatingly convincing? Before he knew why or how, he was back and standing on the deck.

She wrapped her arms around him tightly and put her head to his chest. "I'm sorry."

I must be a glutton for punishment. "If you do that again... you'll regret it."

"Really?" she brightened. "How would you make me regret it?" she asked as if he'd just offered her a diamond necklace.

"You forget..." he swayed – *Have I been drinking and just didn't remember?* "...I know your weaknesses."

"Plural?" she smiled, "Oh, do tell."

"The Cardinal," he listed on his fingers, though he seemed to be having difficulty focusing, "and *her* professor."

At that she blanched. He had her.

The next thing he knew he was looking up at the stars; the moon was gone and he was laying flat on the yacht deck. He sat up, his head pounding as he tried to make sense of it: She'd said she was sorry; was she sorry for what she had done... or what she was going to do? He jumped up quickly – the dinghy was gone and the Wolf was nowhere in sight. She'd set him adrift.

11: Now

Stillness had settled over the castle. Darkness too, except for one light on the upper level. Moriel slid like a silent shadow up the path toward the courtyard entrance where she paused – there was something out of place about the courtyard tree: She looked around cautiously before getting closer, to see that it was bursting with scarlet yew arils, revealing not only maturity but vitality, though the last time she'd passed it, it had been far less verdant. A warm breeze rustled the tree branches and swirled about it before evaporating; odd that it had been warm, when the Highland night was rather chilly. Her keen ears heard a woman's quiet laugh, the unmistakeable crystalline quality of her Kind: Erlina. A man's quiet but rich tone followed with his own laughter and her stomach tightened: Aradan. She'd not seen him in centuries; he'd been searching for her along the old slave routes, but she'd always outrun him.

She was now torn between the instinct to flee again and her compulsion to eliminate her rival. Yet now that she was approaching that confrontation she hesitated; Edric's remark replayed in her mind – that she'd felt compelled toward a target that she'd miss... like a moth to the flames. She growled at her own weakness in letting the mere words of a mortal hit her heart, and shook her head violently as if to shake away the thoughts. She had never even met Erlina per se, true; she'd seen her from afar when they were both girls, one from the village and the other from the palace; one couldn't help but admire her... be drawn to her. But upon her own coming of age Moriel had been formally presented to the king by her father, Vilnin, even in the midst of preparation for the battles that would change the course of her life forever; Erlina hadn't even bothered to show up for that momentous occasion – she consequently knew the princess to be arrogant and conceited. Aradan deserved so much better than that! She could give him what he needed... she only had to make him realize that somehow. A lump rose in her throat as she knew she could not flee now; it was time to end it.

Her eyes darted around before gliding silently to the entrance door. It was unlocked as the other times she had haunted the castle recently; why would it not be, out here in the middle of nowhere? She chuckled softly in contempt of their naivety. Once through the door she moved more cautiously than ever, flitting from one dark corner to the next. She knew from her previous visits that Erlina's quarters were on that uppermost floor, though she wasn't familiar with any of the rooms except the library, which she had ransacked. In the blink of an eye she had reached the uppermost level, and saw that the light she had seen from outside shone under the door to the right of the stairs. Cautiously she slipped into the room to the left of the stairs.

Inside the room was still and dark, but her Elven eyes could see clearly. She gasped as she smelled Aradan's essence, lingering in the air... he had been in that room not long ago, and a sense of panic warred with longing in her. She stepped into the room, and what met her eyes was not altogether new to her, but wholly unexpected: It was a replica of the Maldorian royal banquet hall's decorations that night she first saw Aradan. The queen had hung whispered silky banners weighted with silver bells from the high ceiling... the same bells hanging there now. She reached out and touched the closest banner, and her eyes welled with tears as every detail came flooding back:

It was a grand feast; Moriel had been sitting next to her mother and talking with a friend when the clear silver trumpet called their attention. Regally, overwhelmingly beautiful even for their own Kind, the royal family entered. Until that night Moriel had admired Erlina from afar; almost worshipped her; this was the first royal banquet in many years, and she revelled in the splendour of the occasion. But as she watched the royal family walk up the aisle to take their place at the head table, she had seen *him*. He stood across the aisle, leaning to speak with his younger sister standing at his side. She'd tip-toed up to whisper something in his ear and he smiled with a gentle laugh, and Moriel's heart melted. From that moment on she had watched his every move, listened to every breath he drew, longing to be the air if only for one instant. Time seemed to slow to a complete stop when he spoke. He never even noticed Moriel, but she didn't care; she was in the same room with him. His father spoke to him and gestured toward the king's table; she watched him walk up the aisle, as beautiful as the dawn. Then something happened she would never forget: He glanced her way; he might have even looked at her. But then her nightmare began: He was presented to the royal family and though it was a brief encounter, when he turned back toward his own table something had altered in his expression; there was a deeper rhythm of life, something inexpressible in his eyes that made him blind to everyone else in the banquet hall. Moriel's world and the life she had already begun to imagine unravelled before her eyes, and Erlina hadn't even noticed him! The rest of that night he never took his eyes from the eldest princess for long; by her giftings she had bewitched him – Moriel was convinced of that – what else would captivate him so thoroughly? In that instant she began to loathe the princess though she was bound to her in a perverse way, for where Erlina was Aradan was sure to be; if she wanted the one she had to endure the other. In another way she was also indebted to the princess: The thought of a gifting becoming so powerful as to control a man's every waking moment was intoxicating, and had impelled Moriel to develop her own giftings.

At that moment, standing now in the darkened replica of the banquet hall, she realized what she had always truly wanted: It wasn't to destroy Erlina – but to *best* her! To steal Aradan's heart in direct competition with Erlina, and leave the princess bereft of love forever... to dwell in utter despair. Aradan had not seen Moriel in centuries as she honed her skills on mortal men; with pride she thought of the wars she had started... she was the epitome of *femme fatale*, at least for mortal men. They were so predictable that way. But not Aradan, and therein laid the challenge. Moriel had developed her giftings to a formidable pitch; surely now she could win Aradan's heart. And if not? She'd need Edric. As that fresh sense of purpose washed over her, she looked around the room with a newfound appreciation; Erlina no longer presented a threat but a challenge. Moriel could be magnanimous with the princess, perhaps even pity her in a perverse way.

She crept further into the moonlit room, senses alert. She looked beyond the banners and stared in disbelief. *It can't be!* At the far end of the room nearly hidden beyond the banners lay King Elgin with his sons on either side of him, on three beds draped with blue velvet. She approached slowly, reverently. The king, she remembered well, had been kind and generous; no matter how she felt about his daughter she could wish him no harm, and it nearly grieved her to see him lying so still. His hands clasped the hilt of his sword to his chest; his crown had been returned to his royal head, and his sons were adorned in similar fashion. The clothes they wore were unmistakeably Maldorian; the very clothes they had worn in battle so long, long ago. Had so much time really passed? Had it all been a dream? How was this even possible? How could she be seeing what was before her very eyes? Yet the three figures were undeniable; they looked as if they merely rested, floating in a dreamless sleep. She reached out and carefully touched the king's hand but pulled back abruptly – he was too cool to be alive, yet not deathly cold. She touched him again: He *was* cool, but there was some source of warmth beneath his skin, deep within; then she noticed that his skin was unlike her own: He had no pores, no scars, no signs of life on this earth or indeed of over a thousand years of death-like rest... his skin was perfectly smooth, as if an outer, human layer had fallen away. *So this was the treasure Erlina unearthed! What is her intention? Does one of them have the key with which to return to Aquillis? If so, how can I use it to my own advantage?* She looked more closely at the two princes, both most handsome in life, and they were the same perfection as their father. The eldest looked most like his sister Erlina, with raven hair, perfect full lips and the high cheekbones of their queenly mother. At the thought of the princess however, her reverence vanished; distracted by the myriad of memories chasing through her mind, too late did she hear quick footsteps behind her. Before she could react someone had pinned her arms firmly behind her back and slipped a cloth sack over her head.

She heard an unfamiliar man's voice whisper in Aquillian to someone standing nearby, "I believe we have caught both a ghost and a wolf in one."

There was no point in struggling. Whoever had bound her hands held her strong and secure; her eyes were covered, her gifting useless. She felt herself being led out of the room and down a hall; heard a door open; several sets of feet took position in a circle around her. Strange... she smelled a vaguely familiar fragrance mingled with an unknown scent, and that multiplied three times – to her back, left and right. She tried to place the familiar essence; it reminded her of her mother. The unknown aroma was not quite that of the Man-Kind. She stretched out her senses beyond those, and smelled *him* – the unmistakeable aroma of his essence. She scowled in anger at being presented before him thus. The other essence must be Erlina – a sweet, pure scent alive with the spices of... joy? Yes, yes, there was the mingling of fragrances she remembered all too well, but somehow they were joyful, and nearly overwhelming in their intensity because of it. It made her feel sick to be so close to it. The only malice Moriel detected came from the three bi-form essences, and oddly that helped to counter the sickening purity of the she-elf. She blanched when she felt an anger equalled by contempt radiating from Aradan's direction. All of this she sensed in an instant, before she'd even been brought to a complete standstill.

"Should we?" Moriel heard someone ask. There was no reply, but she could feel the apprehension in the atmosphere as it sharpened the senses of those around her. There must have been a reluctant agreement, as the next thing she felt was a hand grasping the hood over her head and pulling it free.

A moment passed before anyone spoke... they at last looked upon the Wolf, her face familiar to only one in the room. She looked at each face in turn:

Aradan's (the first she sought) was a mixture of fury, disappointment, triumph and disgust. She could see how he battled to rein his emotions in, and none of it was the affection she had hoped for, had imagined for so long. He probably had much to say and she suddenly had no desire to hear it. He saw her appraisal, and when he knew she was looking glanced down with a sparkle of triumph in his eyes: He was holding Erlina's hand. They were in the library she had ransacked, though it was now in perfect order once again with no sign of her vandalism. Behind Aradan and the she-elf was a large desk below a window that was opened slightly, the pale grey of pre-dawn glowing outside. She appraised the three bi-forms next: Bronze-skinned, jet-black hair and piercingly pale blue eyes. *Her* eyes stared back at her curiously from three sides. That is to say *two* stared back; the one holding her firmly was blind, his eyes netted over with an intricate web of white lace, though he seemed to be observing her all the same. It was probably by Aradan's design that a blind man held her captive. She turned her attention last of all to Erlina: It was an encounter she had imagined a thousand times if one; had planned how she would behave, how she would wound, how she would put the princess in her place, rightfully below herself. But now face to face with her unwitting nemesis – the one she felt undeserving of either Aradan's love or a royal title – she felt her resolve unravelling, melting away like wax before a flame. *'How is she <u>doing</u> that?'* She sighed in frustrated anger, abruptly reminded of the fact that she wasn't the only one in the room with a gifting, as she'd been accustomed to for centuries. Erlina's eyes gazed back at her, tears brimming over... with joy, *not* triumph. Purest joy was written across the genuine smile Moriel saw radiating at her, and she was confused. Undone. But only momentarily. Erlina's presence was infectious but Moriel would not succumb to it *ever* again.

Erlina took a step toward Moriel. "Please... forgive my guards for their reception of you – I think you know partly why they react thus," she looked at Amir, the guard to Moriel's left, with an indulgent chide. She then looked back at Moriel. "We are not your enemies; if I may have your solemn word to be at peace here, I may be able to persuade them to release you." Her tone was gracious, kind, and genuinely delighted.

Galal growled quietly. Moriel instinctively growled back. Erlina sighed; it wasn't a frustrated one, though perhaps disappointed; it was a patient sigh.

Erlina said, "I'm *so* glad you came at last," and she meant it. "I'm simply overjoyed to at last meet another of my own Kind once again! But I do so wish—" she hesitated sadly, "I wish you had not viewed me as your enemy... that you had not eluded me for so long. We could have been a comfort to one another all this time... sisters." Then she brightened, and the sun's rays began to glow on the eastern horizon. "But enough! You are here now – that is all that matters!" Erlina suddenly stepped forward and warmly embraced Moriel.

Aradan cringed automatically at his beloved coming so close to a Morquillian.

Moriel stiffened. She had yet to speak a word and the she-elf had already assumed peace between them. The arrogance! Had she also assumed victory where Aradan was concerned? At that thought Moriel took a step back – she couldn't push Erlina away as her arms were still bound.

Erlina withdrew, blinking in surprise. Moriel's essence was not unlike Elbal and his sons, yet it was mingled with the stench of rotting forest compost, that musty, dusty reek of a dark forest's floor where mould, moss and fungi grow best.

For the first time since Moriel had entered the room Aradan stirred: He stepped to Erlina's side and slipped his arm around her waist protectively as he drew her back to a safer distance. He glared at Moriel, though not looking directly into her eyes, staring as it were through her, focusing on infinity. "Why have you come?" he challenged. A wave of hostility rolled off of him toward her.

"To make peace," she whispered. It was the first time she had spoken, and the atmosphere in the room began to tranquillize. She looked at the guard to her left. She caught his eye and smiled. "What is your name?" she asked innocently.

"Amir," he answered numbly. His mouth felt dusty.

"Ah," she smiled, holding his gaze, "*prince*! This Aramaic name suits you well. And you?" she turned to Galal. He told her his name and she cooed, "*Majestic... splendour.* How appropriate your name! But how do you decide which of you is preeminent when one is majestic and the other, prince? Who is the commander between you?"

"Our commander," replied Elbal for his sons, "is Princess Erlina. We are all equals here, sons and father alike though we be."

Moriel tried to turn toward him, but his grip tightened. Exasperated she pleaded, "Is this treatment really necessary? I mean you no harm now."

"Elbal," Erlina said gently, "release Moriel's arms."

"But leave her hands bound and hold her binds tightly," added Aradan firmly. Erlina did not challenge his wisdom. Elbal released his firm grip on Moriel's arms, but held the end of the cord tied at her wrists.

※

What had happened? One minute Edric had felt like he was finally making progress with Moriel, and the next he was flat on his back on a drifting yacht. Fortunately it had been on an incoming tide and he'd been flushed up the loch rather than pulled out to sea. He anchored quickly to keep from running aground while he gathered his bearings. A quick look in the cabin told him that someone had changed in haste – he opened the small port window to air it out... it always smelled like mildew in there, which was strange out on the briny sea. He checked a trunk of his own he'd once put on the yacht for contingencies on one of Moriel's indulgent days; at least that was there, and still had his things in it. He looked through the log book and saw all of Moriel's information there – address in Orkney, berth numbers for port docking in both Stromness and Kirkwall, as well as a few other ports like Scrabster and Inverness. He saw a list of items she'd recently repaired or replaced on the yacht – an engine filter replaced several months ago; a small welding repair on the winged keel recently, along with light bulbs for the main cabin and how much the full tank of petrol had cost. He knew all of that – that wasn't what he was interested in; it was the missing information that told him what he'd been looking for: She'd not had the engine repaired, and there wasn't much purchased in the way of supplies. In other words... why had she delayed by two days to come? And what had happened on the deck before he fell unconscious? He hadn't had anything to eat or drink, so it couldn't have been poisoning, but he'd most definitely been knocked out. It couldn't have been her lipstick that was poisoned... she wouldn't. Yes... she just might. He knew she played cat and mouse with him, but that was no reason to mistrust her... because despite it all he still worshipped the ground she walked on. At that thought, he looked toward the castle – Moriel might be in trouble by now... he knew she was headed there and knew that they were alert to the impending arrival of the Wolf. She was too headstrong for her own good sometimes; it looked like he'd need to be the knight in shining armour after all. Dawn was an hour or two old, which meant she'd had plenty of time to get into trouble.

He hoisted the anchor and turned on the motor – it hadn't been tuned but then it hadn't needed it as she'd claimed. Something didn't sit right with him...

either she was contradicting herself, or *she* was the contradiction that didn't fit into the equation forming in his mind. And what was it about her life that she felt he wouldn't understand? He steered the yacht toward the main digs; not that far west along the shore from there was an old abandoned cottage that had an access road and would save him from hacking through the boggy bush to reach the main road. He'd have to get his trousers wet for that short wade to shore from where he was able to anchor; he packed a dry pair with extra shoes over his head as he waded, and changed on shore. Taking longer than he wanted but probably faster than it seemed, he'd reached the digs. Someone was in the finds office – probably Brehani, tagging artefacts... he was the only early riser from the castle; he wouldn't mind walking if the golf cart got borrowed.

Up at the castle nothing much was stirring yet. Edric slipped into the courtyard and past the fountain, into the main entrance. Someone was in the kitchen... it sounded like Toshiro, singing. Edric slipped out of his shoes in the guard room and headed quietly up the stairs: If they were anywhere, they'd probably be somewhere in the Cardinal's apartments. At the top of the stairs he stopped: There was a light on in the room at the end of the corridor. Listening a moment to make sure it was clear he crept, as quietly as humanly possible, around the back hall toward the hinge-side of that door. He heard Moriel's distinct voice saying, "Who is the commander between you?" Edric stood silently to hear how many were inside the room and assess the situation before he formed a plan of rescue. The voices were quiet, but he could hear them well enough in the quiet of the morning hours. But wait – who was Princess Erlina? He listened intently to find out more.

※

"How do you come by such loyal servants when you are without kingdom or title, *princess*?" Moriel asked Erlina, thinly-veiled contempt in her voice.

"Love and compassion need no kingdom, and they command the highest honour," Galal retorted, a warning glance from Aradan reminding him to avoid eye contact with Moriel.

Amir added, "And she 'comes by' us by *you*, actually." His smile toward Erlina changed abruptly to a guarded scowl toward Moriel, though he'd answered her question honestly.

That news surprised her. She looked more closely at their faces and the connection began to dawn on her – the fragrance reminiscent of her mother's yet mingled with Man-Kind's, and her own pale blue eyes in their faces. She laughed acerbically. "How did you find each other?" she looked from Erlina to the three men in genuine wonder.

"I have a gift of foresight," Elbal replied, "and she has great compassion. We were drawn to each other... she took me in as a young man and raised me as her own. But where *our* connection lies is more of a mystery," it was more of a question than a statement.

She debated a moment within herself: Anything they told her might be used to her advantage. Her best ploy in the present situation was to feign cooperation until her lot could improve; not escape, but conquest. She decided to play nice... to give, perhaps to get back in her turn.

"I will tell you of the connection," she began: "I was sold into slavery after being abandoned by my own," she glared at Aradan, then shrugged smugly, "I was able to *persuade* my way into position as wife of a *tourmarchē* of the *Thracesian Theme*. My only other choice was a far worse lot. I gave him many sons... all of which but one died young in headstrong battles. I can only assume that the one who survived is your forefather."

"Where was this?" Amir asked. "What are the tourmarché, or Thracesian Themes?"

"Thema were regions of power in the Byzantine Empire. The Theme of the Thracesians was in Asia Minor, what is now modern Turkey," she replied. "The turma, or tourma, were commanders of a division of each Theme's armies, and rulers of their regions."

"And what year was that son born?" Elbal asked.

"By modern reckoning... 1015."

Galal spoke, disdain in his voice. "And why did you not remain with him? Teach your son of his heritage, so that he could in turn teach his children?"

"He was a grown man when I at last found my way of escape," she gazed back through time, remembering her conquest with satisfaction. "In 1038 there was a Varangian guard wintering nearby. I slipped out of my home disguised as a countrywoman to seek news from them of—" her eyes flickered toward Aradan, "—of someone; but one of the men tried to violate me. I managed to kill him, then persuaded his very friends and fellow guards to laud my conduct; they gave me his possessions as compensation for his treatment of me – I must say, his was no unusual behaviour for Vikings but I did not try to dissuade them – and they treated their friend as if he were a coward having committed suicide. They stripped him and left his body to rot," she gloated. "They took me under their protection, and I persuaded them to return me safely to Norway. I began to search—" again she looked toward Aradan impulsively, "—and there ends my tale."

"And there begins my tale," Aradan said sharply. "She found me... in 1066, in Britain. There she *persuaded* me," he threw her innocent word for such manipulations back in her face, "and stole a most valued possession... which I want back." His tone made it clear that she wouldn't be leaving until she'd returned it to him.

She whispered through false tears, "To say it thus makes my efforts sound so selfish."

"Were they not?" Aradan accused. "You knew exactly what you were doing; you had stolen that necklace once before and failed!"

"But I searched for you because... I wanted to make sure you were well... and I only wanted something to remember you by," she pleaded against his growing anger; he still denied her his direct gaze.

"It was never yours to take, Moriel!" he growled, his eyes sparking in fiery anger. Erlina reached out her hand and took his again, which calmed him.

None of them looked her directly in her eyes, and she now realized that: They stood encircling her, though none connected with her eyes – the windows to her soul and theirs. Her way of holding sway over them. If Aradan would not look into her eyes, one or the other of them would. She would have them. She sensed out the other men – her descendants. The one called Amir seemed less hostile than his brother, and she already had some idea of how easy he was to persuade. She turned to him:

"I am sorry I was unable to see you grow up. You've become a fine young man." She looked back at Elbal, who stood firmly between herself and the only exit. "How long have you been blind, my son?"

Elbal bristled at the intimate address. "Nearly twenty years," he replied coolly.

" 'Tis a pity *you* were also unable to see him grown up." Her voice smacked of both pity and mockery.

"On the contrary," he replied calmly, "he is by now nearly one hundred."

That surprised her not a little, but then she had no experience with such bi-forms. He didn't look much older than mid-twenties. "And how old are you?" she asked Elbal.

"I do not know exactly... time was not calculated but in moons where I was born. I am over two hundred and fifty."

She was momentarily fascinated. But she returned to her tactic and turned toward Amir again: "It is cruel to leave your father thus, don't you think? There is one in the room who could easily cure his blindness, after all."

"What?" he forgot his instructions and looked into her eyes; that dusty taste in his mouth returned.

She held his gaze. He felt her genuine concern, her motherly care for his father; he felt it would only be right to welcome her back into their family with open arms... to integrate her. "But of course!" she purred. "Aradan could have healed your father with a touch. Why does he withhold such a blessing? Who does he really care about?"

Galal growled at her.

Unable to look away, Amir said to his brother, "Enough, Galal! Where is your courtesy to our *urmother*?"

"She may be our *urmother*, but she is deserving of no courtesy!"

"She is a *woman*," Amir reprimanded him. "All women deserve at least your silence, if not respect."

Moriel smiled to herself; disunity was beginning to take root. "Your brother may have his opinion, if he will. He can remain in ignorance of my heart... if he chooses."

"Enough!" shouted Aradan. "Release him!"

She looked toward Aradan but he was looking at Amir. Still... the words had been spoken... disunity begun. Next she turned to Elbal. "And have you no desire to see?" she asked him.

"Of course I do. It is a human desire."

"But *you* are not entirely human, are you? And what of your wife? Their mother? You have had to abandon her to the decay of mortals."

"I never abandoned her," even the calm Elbal nearly growled at that affront. "But she was not of my Kind."

"And what *Kind* is that?" she challenged. "You and your sons are hybrids... *half-breeds*. Your place is neither here on earth nor on Aquillis."

At that, the brothers glanced at each other in confusion, and it did not go unnoticed by Moriel.

"Don't tell me you have never heard of it!" she laughed. "How long have you been with the princess and yet she has not even told you of that part of your heritage?"

"She has told us – that is not why we—" Galal stopped.

"We merely see ourselves as only earthly mortals, for that is what we are," explained Amir more gently. "If one is half mortal, one is only mortal."

"And yet here you stand," she cooed, "One hundred, as vigorous as any youth. You will be hard-pressed to find a wife of your equal here," she commiserated.

"And whose fault is that?" Galal spat back.

"Should I not have given birth to sons? Should I have suffered as a slave in ancient times?" She at last caught his eye with that. She held his gaze with a grin as he felt a fine, musty powder settle over his eyes, yet it wasn't one he could blink away. Other sounds in the room, voices that sounded urgent, were fading into a pleasant white noise in the background. He heard her speaking in his mind: *"Rather you should blame the only one in this room that is to blame; the one you know least... the one I know best. Had he not refused me...*

abandoned me to that fate... you would be Aquillian! You would be immortal, capable of returning to our true home when they return for us."

That made no biological sense, but he was falling down the proverbial rabbit hole. Galal felt his detest for her melting away... He found himself thinking, *'It is truly unfounded... after all, I've never even given her a chance to prove herself to me, to declare her intentions, to explain the actions of a thousand years past; and what had she truly done to Erlina after all, except inconvenience occasionally for a few trinkets of passing value?'* Suddenly he saw before his eyes an Arabian slave market: He could hear the calls of the merchants, smell the mixture of spices and camels and man, and even feel the dry desert wind upon his face. His eyes were directed toward a ravishingly beautiful woman, pale blue eyes, cowering in fear in a corner; she was dressed oddly... out of place for that market, in something for a warmer climate and not the desert heat. The rope about her neck became taut and she was dragged out for viewing. Bartered and bargained over, not unlike the poultry in the next stall, a price was finally agreed upon: The man who had purchased her was another slave trader, and wealthy by the size of his girth – he ate well and wore his wealth for all to see. He was from Constantinople; he would have taken her as a woman had it not been for her gifting. She could make a man impotent with a single wilting glance, and Galal understood that it had protected her many times. From Baghdad she was shipped past the southern tip of the Arabian peninsula and back to Constantinople, where she was eventually bought for the man she would persuade to marry her, the tourmarchē she had mentioned earlier. He was much older looking, wealthy in girth, and had many concubines. But through her powers of persuasion she convinced him that she was magical, perhaps a genie of old, and he gave her anything she wanted, including pre-eminence above all concubines as wife of wives. But as the scenes unfolded before Galal's eyes he could see that through it all Moriel was unhappy and homesick; she was not with the one she truly desired.

The others in the room could not see what Galal was seeing; they only saw him transfixed, looking around as if he were seeing something specific yet far away. As involuntary tears escaped his eyes and ran down his cheek, Elbal sensed his son's distress and finally slipped the hood over Moriel's head. She only laughed quietly. So predictable; a hood wouldn't stop her giftings once she was inside of that person, but she let them think so for now.

"Wh— what did you do that for?" Galal asked, bewildered at the sudden ending of the visions. "It was fascinating! I saw her story... her husband – our ancestor!"

"I am sorry," Elbal said, "we had no way of knowing what she was showing you, and whether what she showed you was true or not."

"Tell them," Moriel whispered to Galal, a new understanding between them.

He told them what he had seen and felt, and Amir wished to see it too; Elbal could neither be drawn into her visions nor would he have trusted her version. He cautioned his son, but Amir removed the hood from Moriel's head and looked into her eyes.

Instead of the same scenes, she showed Amir her son, their ancestor: He was a self-indulgent man; his girth was so large that no litter could hold his weight and thus he was bound to his house; but he had married young, and had wives. Moriel showed him one particular wife: A dark-skinned beauty, a minor princess sold into marriage for the price of a peace treaty and a secured trade route for her father. She had a pale-blue-eyed boy upon her lap. He was playing with an intricate necklace, a chain as fine as a hair, and upon it hung half of an orb. Suddenly the vision stopped.

When Amir told them of the vision, Aradan's eyes narrowed upon Moriel. She had him.

"Would you like to see it?" she whispered.

He could not take his eyes away; he nodded numbly. Now that she had him, she had no intention of letting him go. The sounds in the room began to fade, his eyesight becoming dusty and dreamy, but he clung to Erlina's hand and she to his, his only anchor to reality now. To Aradan she showed an image of misery, loneliness and dejection. She showed him tears, homesickness, a love so intense for him that it banished all rational conduct. She showed him that he was the only one whom she had ever cared for. He felt himself thinking, *'She cannot be blamed for anything she's undertaken as it was out of love for me, and love is a pure motive. I now realize – I've known all along – that I'm the only one for her... and she is the only one for me. The other one* (she would not allow the princess to intrude upon her visions) *was merely a matter of prestige, my father's choice for his heir but not my own choice... how much better I understand Moriel; after all, we spent so much time together... my heart beats only for her. I'll never be satisfied by any lesser being than her. She will make me happier than I've ever been, and my love will fulfil her perfectly.'* He saw Moriel, a vision of perfect beauty, in a light green dress, waiting for him, arms open, beckoning him to her. He took a step toward her.

Somewhere in the twisted vision a song began to intrude; a beautiful crystalline melody, the throbbing of a heartbeat as its continuo. Moriel's ears hurt at the sound... to her ears it was a raw shriek, too pure for her senses. It distracted and confused her... made her lose her concentration. Aradan began to feel the warm hand of Erlina in his own once again, where it had been all along; with her free hand Erlina had pulled the orb from its hiding place beneath her dress and it called him out of his stupor, joining with her own song.

When Moriel realized that she'd lost her hold over him she looked up, dazed in surprise. Then she saw Erlina's orb. "Where did you get that?" Moriel snapped, her pale eyes darkening to midnight blue.

Erlina replied, "I—" but she stopped as she felt Aradan squeeze her hand. "It was a gift," was all she would say.

Suddenly Moriel understood: That's why it had been so important to Aradan... his was the other half!

A rage rose deep within her. She had been a fool... a fool to think that cooperating would gain her time to win him! That she had ever thought she could win his affections had been foolish. All of this vying to gain the allies of her own kinsmen here... to divide them from their loyalties to Erlina... and the visions she had shown them... was all for naught, if Erlina's gifting could undo it all with song! In one desperate attempt she pleaded: "But *I* am the one you should love, Aradan! Since the first moment I saw you in the king's banquet so long ago – I knew you would be mine! *You're* the reason I stayed behind... became trapped here... *I* love you." Being forced to make such a confession stung her pride, but perhaps feminine vulnerability would be his undoing.

Aradan began to form an angry retort but Erlina gently squeezed his hand, calming him immediately.

"Beloved," Erlina whispered, though it was well within the hearing of everyone in the room, "I can only praise her good taste in this... it is no fault of hers to have loved the most worthy of men! On the contrary... I should find fault in her, had she not. Her only fault is in her expression of that love... but it arose out of desperation and therefore, again, I cannot fault her in that. Yes, she took something from you of great value. But I am sure she now understands the futility of such a course of action where you are concerned." In all of that she addressed Aradan, and Aradan alone. In all of that Aradan did not take his eyes from Erlina's gaze.

Moriel stared at Erlina, willing her to look her in the eye; her fury knew no bounds, and as soon as she had the princess within her power she would make her feel pain as she had never felt before.

Suddenly the princess looked into Moriel's dark eyes as she felt the longing for that connection from Moriel. Just as suddenly everything went wrong, and Moriel reeled in confusion: Erlina's eyes were as pure as diamonds behind their exterior grey colour, a prism of colours danced there, and hurt Moriel's eyes with their purity – but she could not look away so fascinated was she, and yet so determined to destroy. She shot forth thoughts of sharp pain, misery... of watching Aradan walk away from Erlina and choosing the other. But Moriel winced in excruciating pain as those perfect eyes reflected those images back into her own mind! She crumpled to the floor as the pain backlashed. Erlina was too pure, too powerful to be penetrated by such attempts. No matter what Moriel tried, she could not penetrate the barrier of goodness. Erlina still radiated pure compassion, pure love toward Moriel, and it undid every attempt of assault; the greatest insult was that Erlina did not even seem to notice the attempts at all.

"Moriel! Are you well? Is something wrong?" Erlina asked sweetly, genuinely concerned at the look of pain and consternation on Moriel's face.

It was like pouring acid into an open wound. In that moment it was as if time slowed for Moriel: She understood that no man, not even Aradan, could resist the pure love of Erlina; the princess commanded every man in her presence; her skills and scheming were far beyond Moriel's, no matter how much she'd honed them over the past centuries. She realized that her attempts to seduce Aradan to love *her* had turned any affection he might have had to a loathing too deep for even her to overcome. She realized she had no chance of defeating true love between soulmates; Aradan had been lost to her from the moment he had met Princess Erlina. What was there now to do? What options were left to her? What options would her pride tolerate?

Aradan saw the confusion and dawning of realization upon Moriel's expression. He saw the hardening of her heart as clearly as if he'd watched water instantaneously freeze. The window of opportunity of her cooperation was closing rapidly; he must act swiftly. "Moriel," he called her out of her brooding, "the orb that you see is part of a key. If we could reunite the parts, we— we might be able to go home."

She looked at him. "What is that hesitation in your voice?" she demanded.

He looked at her earnestly, yet not daring to look her in the eye again. "Moriel... you have broken many Aquillian laws – this you know?" he asked for confirmation.

"I've done little more than survive on an alien planet!" she rose to her full height, her dark eyes flashing black with indignation at the accusation.

"You have started wars here!" he shouted. "You have killed mortals for your own pleasure! You have interfered with earth's history in dire ways! You have turned Morquillian, and you know it!"

"Then," she glared at him darkly, "why on *earth* would I want to go to Aquillis? I've never known any home but this one. And returning to face judgment is no great incentive," she pointed out sardonically.

He looked at her, disappointment etched across his features. "Have you no remorse? No desire to make amends? To right wrongs? To see your parents once again? Your friends?"

"If they were truly friends, or loving parents, they would have at length come for us!" she spat.

"You know they cannot, no matter how greatly they desire it," Erlina replied gently. "They are forbidden by Aquillian law, so long as both key and Mithrian dust are known to be present in a realm. The Gatekeepers know what they left behind... they cannot come for us – we must go to them or here be forever trapped."

At that last word, Moriel realized she had but three choices: The first, to return to Aquillis for judgment... to an alien society she knew very little about or about its laws or the punishment meted out to Morquillians; in all, she was quite ignorant of that unknown planet and its ways, and besides – it was no desirable option for someone as free-spirited as herself. The second: If, by some miracle Aradan and his she-elf found a way to return to their precious Aquillis, she would have no desire to go with them and would thus be stranded on earth alone; free to do as she chose, but also doomed to watch generations come and go... caring for anyone would hurt too much after a time, and not caring would only make her harder; not that she minded any of that really; what she did mind was being trapped with the knowledge of her failure – that she had failed to make Aradan love her and remain with her. She could not have withstood the mockery of each new dawn. There was a third option, and the more she thought about it the more appealing it was becoming. Only she knew the hidden location of Aradan's half-orb. If she could somehow find a way to accomplish that last option, she could take that information with her, trapping Aradan and the princess here on earth, dooming Erlina to eternally look upon the lifeless forms of her father and brothers knowing they would be forever separated from their essences.

As Moriel glared at Aradan and Erlina deciding her course of action, a breeze gusted in through the window's narrow opening; it was that same, oddly warm wind she had felt earlier in the courtyard. Through the window began streaming twigs and leaves, bark chips, heather needles and flowers. The whirlwind split into two distinct whorls, each taking shape either side of Aradan and Erlina. The shapes became two dryads.

The guards were unprepared for such apparitions and drew their blades in defence. That did not go unnoticed by Moriel.

"Peace," Erlina lifted a hand to stop them. "These are our allies and friends." She bowed in respect to the larger dryad. "Welcome, Darachi. It is good to see you as always."

The swirl of leaves, bark and heather sprigs seemed to bow – if one could say that – the rustling of leaves swaying as she did so. "Princess Erlina, I am honoured. I present my offspring, Baccata, now awakened and released from her yew."

The second figure, made of greener debris, bowed an awkward greeting. She undulated above the floor in a more restless and impatient fashion than Darachi.

"My Baccata has a grievance with your prisoner."

"Not her," Baccata's green leaves whistled and fluttered angrily, echoes of thunder rumbling deeply. She dived toward the floor and glided to a form at the wall beside the door, pointing at the wall. "With *him*!"

Aradan understood. He signalled for Amir and Galal to investigate: They stood with swords drawn, and threw the door open. Amir flew down the main hall to block off the exit toward the stairs, as Galal chased the eavesdropper around the back hall toward his waiting brother. It was an easy catch between the two armed guards, and they took Edric by the arms back to the library to join the party; he was brought to a standstill and Galal bound his wrists. Amir stood guard beside him in the back corner of the room to Moriel's right. She turned and, catching his eye, let him know how glad she was to see him; let him make his own assumptions as to why – it didn't matter to her. Galal returned to take his position between Erlina and Moriel.

Edric's face grew ashen white when he saw the dryads; in all the strange things he'd overheard, he couldn't place their voices and now he saw why... they shouldn't even *have* voices!

Baccata swirled into a fury toward Edric. "Him! It is he who stabbed me! No just cause!" she howled, a cold winter's wind sending shivers down Edric's spine.

"I'm sorry!" he cowered at her rage. "I didn't know – how was I supposed to know a tree cared?"

Darachi evaporated into a swirl of autumn foliage, coiling around her daughter and drawing her back with a windy "Shhh!"

"They always care," Erlina gently replied, "they simply cannot always communicate it in a way you would perceive."

"Did I not heal you without your bidding?" Aradan asked Baccata. "You can surely forgive his ignorance... I doubt he would dare it a second time," he looked at Edric, who he wasn't entirely sure wouldn't faint from fright.

Edric managed to shake his head in confirmation of Aradan's words.

"Very well," Baccata replied, returning to her undulating form beside Erlina, calmer once again. As Darachi returned to her place beside Aradan she passed Moriel, a deep rumble of roots groaning broke forth from her, brown earth grinding. "Morquillian!" she hissed. "Rot and mould, decay and slime! Only weed follows such seed!"

Darachi turned to Aradan and Erlina, speaking with them in the common tongue of Aquillis, giving and taking council together. In the distraction provided by the dryads, Moriel realized that her best option was quickly becoming a possibility.

12: Now

Edric's eyes were wide with disbelief. Had he really just seen debris talking? What was going on here? And what was all that he'd overheard outside? Could Elbal really be as old as he'd said? And his sons? That made sense – they'd always creeped him out. And Moriel? Was *that* her secret he'd never believe? She might have been right about that before, but now... he was a lot more open to weird. So she was older... *lots* older. It did creep him out that she had children hundreds of years older than himself. But all in all? He could deal with it if she loved him. He was flexible that way.

The dryads were still speaking with Erlina and Aradan. Moriel turned to Edric, and in his mind (how was she doing *that*?) he heard her voice: *'My love. Thank you for coming.'*

"Your *love*?" he whispered.

'Of course,' she thought, winking at him, then continued, *'Do you remember our conversation once... about your dying to gain my trust? You said perhaps we could find another solution.'*

He nodded toward her to let her know he was listening – as if he could have done anything but.

'I know the solution.' She began to show him scenes, what he assumed were memories, of Erlina and Moriel

in another place and time: A banquet hall; a royal family with crowns upon their heads; a grassy meadow; along a loch's shore; on a forest's path... through each scene he saw time and again how the Cardinal – now he was hearing Erlina as her name – ridiculed Moriel, lorded it over her, gloated at the beauty's misery, revelled in brow-beating her. In his vision Moriel began to cry; he could see her wounded soul, and it made him ache with helpless anger, a growing rage at the callous actions of the royal class toward the commoner. He saw Moriel cowering in dark corners, driven to isolation to escape the bullying, all the while her heart crying out for a champion, her knight in shining armour, her rescuer... someone to prove his love and trustworthiness to her.

"I will," he heard himself whispering.

'Are you still wearing your throwing stars?'

He looked at her puzzled, but nodded.

'You promised. Anything.'

"What do you want?" he asked, barely audible.

'To escape. Distract them – throw a star at her – my nemesis!'

"I won't kill anyone!" he mouthed at her carefully, so as not to attract attention.

'Not kill,' she whispered into his mind, *'provoke! Distract the guards, who will move to protect her, so that I can flee! Throw them all, rapid fire – that should give me enough time.'*

Edric looked around: The dryads were talking about something to do with leaving. After facing an angry dryad he'd rather wait till they'd left the room. But while everyone was distracted with the leaf-ladies, he slipped one of the blades from his belt buckle and began slicing through the binds at his wrists, bound in front of him. He sliced it just enough so they wouldn't fall off, but one swift pull and they'd snap free. Then he held the blade between his clasped hands and waited.

At last the dryads took their leave: Darachi arched up, looking at her daughter briefly and then dived out through the window, a wave of autumn debris mingling with the greenery of Baccata as she followed her mother from the room. A tangible satisfaction breathed in the room, that kind of feeling you get after a great conversation with an old friend long overdue.

Edric's senses became alert, as they always did in target practice: He zoned in his concentration on where everyone stood, on trajectories, on where his aim would plant the blade – he would never aim to kill, especially an unarmed woman; he might be a cad sometimes, but he was a sometimes-gentleman cad. He would aim for the wooden chest just visible between Erlina and the professor (Aradan was the name Moriel had shown him). He mentally took aim, then chose his next target.

He'd been so focused that he hadn't notice Moriel shift her gaze to one of the guards, Galal. By his alarmed expression, she was showing him dangers; tragic scenes.

Edric made his first throw, sinking the star into the wooden chest. A gasp went forth at the shock as he pulled out his second star, sinking it into the window frame between the shoulders of Erlina and Aradan before the guards even had time to react. Elbal jumped to take up a position of defense in front of Erlina. *Why wasn't Moriel running?* Edric pulled out the third star.

But then everything went horribly wrong; it was like a bad dream: Moriel still hadn't run. As Edric lifted his arm to throw the third star Galal's hand flashed to his side and he threw his Kris toward him, intending to incapacitate him... but it never reached his intended target. In the slow motion of a bad dream you try desperately to awaken from but can't, when you want to shut your eyes but can't for horror, Edric watched as Moriel threw herself between himself and the approaching Kris. He heard himself shout her name at the same moment he heard the sickening crunch of the blade through her chest, at that precise gap between ribs. She sank to the ground. The room froze in shock.

Edric was the first to move. "Moriel!" he cried, and fell to his knees at her side; but he was pulled away and held back by Amir.

Aradan knelt over Moriel. "Why did you do that? You know what this could mean!" He began to open her blouse to examine the wound, but she pulled his hands away, gasping for breath through a punctured lung; there was the sickening rasp of air leaking out between breaths, air being drawn into the lungs only to escape.

"I know," she grimaced. "I wanted this. Don't—don't heal." She shook her head.

"Moriel," Aradan said tenderly, "why? You have so much to live for! To learn!"

"You were all I had to live for. I've learned that I can't have you. So I'm done," she gasped.

"No," he shook his head. But before he could continue, she spoke again.

"Edric... please!" she was getting weaker. Her mouth was slowly filling with blood.

Aradan looked at Amir and nodded. He released Edric who fell to her side, taking one of her hands in his. "What is it, my love?"

"Thank you for... being my rescue."

"Moriel! I won't let you die! I can't... I don't want to live without you!"

She looked into his eyes a moment. "I know," she smiled weakly. "You won't have to." Before anyone knew what was happening she'd drawn the Kris from her chest and plunged it into Edric's stomach.

Edric fell backward, dazed and confused. Searing pain seeped through his body, but the worst pain was the turn of events... realizing that all that time she had just been using him. She'd never intended to leave the room alive. Somewhere in the mist of his thoughts he heard voices frantically calling his name, felt his numb body being tugged at, cool morning air hitting his bare, moist chest. Gradually he became aware of the Cardinal leaning over him, singing a magnificent song... was she really an angel? She wasn't in red, so she must be, except she seemed to be calling him back from somewhere far more comfortable, and he didn't like that but somehow knew he should follow her voice. He heard Aradan speaking to Moriel. He was speaking in a strange language; Erlina quickly handed a necklace to Aradan and he clasped it in his hand as he spoke over Moriel. Whatever he was saying, Moriel didn't like it; she struggled against him, shaking her head in protest, but he wouldn't stop. Suddenly her eyes widened in horror, and she fell silent, her breath escaping her body one last time.

Edric, flat on his back with tears rolling into his ears and hair, reached out to take Moriel's hand in his. But she was gone.

Aradan turned his attention toward Edric, whose shirt had been ripped open; Aradan lay his hands on the wound, speaking that strange language again. Edric felt a heat growing inside where the numbness had begun. It was as if Aradan had laid a hot, cauterizing coal in Edric's gut, but it didn't burn uncomfortably – it was like a heating pad on a cold shoulder, soothing, relaxing, relieving. The leaking feeling began to subside; then he began to notice a different sensation, as if something were sucking inside... sucking the haemorrhaged blood back into his veins. He felt as if he were awake for a major surgery on himself with the alert detachment of a bystander. The pain was gone. The flesh around his wound began to tingle, then itch. Before he even realized it, he'd reached up to scratch – and there *was* no wound.

He sat up, bewildered. "Wait! I should be dying!" he looked at Aradan in shock and confusion. "Shouldn't I?"

Aradan offered him his hand to stand up. "Easy. How do you feel?"

"How do I feel?" he repeated incredulously. "I just got stabbed!" he looked at his stomach. "Didn't I?" The only evidence was his bloody, shredded shirt.

"Physically, you'll be fine," Aradan replied, glancing toward Moriel.

Edric followed his eyes, and fell to his knees beside Moriel's body. "Why?" he murmured to her. "Why did you do it?"

"It was her attempt to escape," Aradan answered the rhetorical question.

Edric stared at him. "Some escape. And she tried to take me with her!"

Erlina knelt beside him and put her hand gently on his shoulder to comfort him.

"I'm so sorry," Edric shook his head, "I never intended to hurt you! She only wanted me to distract you all so that she could escape!" He looked from one to the other, hoping they would believe him. "Really – I never miss!" he exclaimed.

At that Galal scoffed, looking at the damaged chest and window frame. "Right."

"I can prove it," Edric offered. "Please – let me!"

"It *is* his only defense," Amir nodded to his brother. "Let him show us."

"If you attempt anything otherwise," Galal growled, "your wound will be permanent next time!"

Aradan pulled Erlina away from Edric and stood between them.

Amir chose a target – the vertical support of one of the bookshelves at the far end of the room – and Edric threw his third star with little time to aim, hitting it perfectly centre.

Erlina smiled. "I believe you."

"So why did she not attempt escape when we were all distracted?" Elbal asked the group.

Aradan looked at Moriel. "She did escape – the only way she knew how... by sacrificing her life in defense of a mortal."

"*Mortal?*" Edric repeated. "So what I overheard... was the *truth*?" his eyes widened at the thought.

Erlina nodded.

"But what Moriel did *not* know," Aradan said, "was that I had the means to thwart her attempt."

"Thwart," Edric looked at Moriel. "I hate to point out the obvious, but it looks like she succeeded. Nearly – I'm still here. Aren't I?" He patted his chest and pinched his hand just to make sure he wasn't hallucinating it all.

"Her earthly vessel has expired, it's true," Aradan nodded, "but I was able to release her essence before her mortal breath ended. She fought it because she didn't want to face judgement on Aquillis; but they will now be able to reach a verdict for her Morquillian crimes." He looked at Erlina sadly: "One thing she would not divulge, however... she was only too happy to deprive us of... she took the secret location of the orb necklace with her. I tried to reason... I told her that it's our only way back to Aquillis. But she refused. She wanted neither our 'pity, help or piety, and certainly not our happiness'."

"Huh?" Edric blinked. "You lost me."

"It's a long story," Aradan smiled wearily. "Perhaps Jon can explain it to you someday."

"At last the threats, harassments, and the constant unease with which we have lived these past decades are over," Galal remarked as he cleaned his Kris.

Elbal sighed with relief, "We can settle... come to rest... and remain here together."

"By one thing I am comforted at least," Erlina knelt beside Moriel's body to brush back a strand of hair from her blood-splattered face, "that she will have a second chance to change... an opportunity to repent."

"The question is, will she? If she refuses, what will become of her?" Elbal asked everyone and no one.

"That is for the high king to decide," Aradan responded, before kneeling beside Erlina. "My greatest joy is my greatest comfort," he took her hand in his, "that we have found each other at last. Whatever we face now shall be either a shared burden halved or a shared joy multiplied."

"We face the future together, never to be parted again," Erlina brought his hand to her lips and kissed it tenderly.

Amir shook his head, "Toshiro will not be happy about this mess to clean up," he waved his hand toward the blood-stained floor, "and your beautiful hand-painted map has been ruined, Grandmother."

"No matter," Erlina waved her hand dismissively toward the floor. "But you are right – we cannot leave Moriel thus. Galal – would you please prepare a fourth bed for her? At the feet of my father."

"Of course," he looked down at Moriel. "What should I use for her drape?"

"You may use the red velvet drape from my own bedchamber," Erlina replied, "for she passed in grief, and will yet bring grief to those on Aquillis."

Galal bowed and left the room to prepare Moriel's final resting place.

"How can she still cause grief?" Edric looked at her.

"Her family must face the loss of the daughter they once knew, and see her face judgment."

Edric shook his head, his eyes cast down, "I cannot tell you how sorry I am for my part in all of this. I was blind! I saw it sometimes, but couldn't pull myself away from her... she was like an addiction to me."

"Edric," Aradan spoke, "Do not think you are the first in her history to experience the same sensations. Her giftings were formidable – many a man fell prey to her persuasion."

"Thank you; that's comforting in a small way, I suppose, though it doesn't lessen my own guilt. I'll do everything I can to make it up to you," he looked at Erlina pleadingly.

"I see your heart," Erlina assured him, "and I know that what you've said is true. I accept your remorse as apology enough."

"I do apologize... and I can't tell you how much remorse I feel. But I also know that it's irritating for someone to keep apologizing... so I'll try to prove it by my actions from this moment on, and not just words." Edric looked at Moriel's still form. "She had such a tragic end... everything she attempted – to get you," he looked at Aradan, "to kill me, to ruin Erlina – failed.

She felt herself a victim, trapped, all her life." He remembered the scenes she'd shown him of her abject misery; now with a clear head he'd realized that the Cardinal – Erlina – would never have treated anyone with the contempt Moriel had tried to persuade him of.

"You're right," Aradan nodded. "But now she will be at peace."

"How can she find peace in judgement?" Amir asked.

"Aquillian punishments are unlike those of earth."

"What will they do to her?" Edric asked.

Aradan replied: "I cannot say exactly. Such a situation arises rarely there, by what I've learned. My grandfather showed me the history of such a Morquillian, long ago. They had been sent to live among a civilisation far more advanced than our own, to learn humility and compassion for lesser beings – of which the convicted had become by virtue of their inferiority or primitiveness compared to their hosts. If they repented of their dark hearts, they would then be allowed to return to Aquillis to reintegrate into society. But what they do now, and in her particular case, I cannot say; her crime was repeatedly interfering intentionally and detrimentally with human history."

"But isn't the very fact that your Kind come to another planet running that risk?" Elbal countered. "My sons and I, and our forefathers and all their accomplishments should by all rights not be here. We would never have affected our histories, had it not been for her presence here; what does that make us?"

"I said *detrimental*," Aradan replied. "Organic changes, organic improvements within the context of a life within its own age, are within the bounds of our mission. Which brings me to you," he touched Elbal's shoulder. "Organic improvement," he smiled. "I apologize for waiting, for allowing Moriel to use your blindness as a divisive ploy; it was simply safer to have one in the room who could withstand her giftings, should it be necessary."

"Wait," Amir said, "are you going to—" he gestured toward his father's eyes.

Aradan nodded, smiling.

"Galal!" shouted Amir down the hall, to where his brother had gone to retrieve Erlina's drape. "Come! Quickly!"

His call of urgency brought not only Galal, but also Jon and Alexis. They arrived to the surreal scene of an unknown woman's body on the blood-stained floor, Edric – with a shredded, bloody shirt – sitting beside her, and the others serenely oblivious to it all. But all attention was on Aradan, as he turned Elbal's powerful frame to face him. He placed his thumbs gently on Elbal's closed eyelids.

"*Eli ichthale thondral Eru*," Aradan breathed warmly upon Elbal's face. A long moment passed in motionless suspense, as Aradan repeated the Aquillian phrase calmly. Before releasing Elbal's eyes he said, "Open your eyes very slowly; take your time."

When Elbal's eyes were opened at last, clear, pale blue eyes shone. He looked from face to face in bewilderment and awe; the one most altered, and whose eyes shone with tears, was Alexis. He held his arms out to her and she ran into his warm embrace. A cry of joyful cheer broke out in the room.

"Thank you," Elbal wept, looking at Aradan in wonder. "To see my loved ones' faces again... and the prospect of a long future once again sighted – I cannot thank you enough!" Elbal released Alexis and wrapped his powerful arms around Aradan, pulling him into a bear-hug.

Aradan laughed, embracing Elbal in return. He stepped back, saying, "It is I who have you to thank – you rendered your service of thanks long before you ever met me, in that you cared for and protected my beloved."

Erlina stood before Elbal, both crying tears of joy as he gazed on her with seeing eyes once again. She embraced him, kissing his temple.

Erlina returned to Aradan's side, where he wrapped his arm around her waist and she snuggled into his arms, tears of joy flowing unabashedly down her cheeks. He kissed them away.

Galal and Amir hugged their father tightly, laughing.

"Thank you!" they both cried out to Aradan at the same moment. "These words will never be enough," Amir added.

"Your faces express your joy fully," Aradan smiled. "But while we're on the subject... Jon," Aradan looked at his friend abruptly, "may I, as your best friend, have permission to kiss your girlfriend?"

"Uh... yeah." Jon was still stunned by the whole scene before him. "Who's she?" he pointed to the body on the floor. "And why are you—" he pointed to Edric's bloody shirt.

" 'Long story," Edric answered dryly.

Aradan took Alexis gently by the shoulders, grinning, "I prefer to kiss you, as the alternative would be for me to stick my hand into your mouth. May I?"

She nodded uncertainly, before realization dawned on her face and she nodded with a wide, disbelieving smile.

Then he kissed her, with parted lips and longer than either Jon or Alexis had expected. Alexis was shocked at first but for some reason didn't pull away – her eyes just got rounder and rounder, and she even grasped Aradan's elbows and clung to him tightly.

"Hey! Hey, Casanova," Jon objected. "You said *kiss*, not steal!"

But when Aradan stepped back with a wide grin, he only said to his friend, "Let *her* object if she wants to!"

Alexis was crying, with her mouth opening and closing as if she had hot coals in her mouth and wanted to spit them out and swallow them at the same time. "Jon!" Alexis called his name, pure and clear. The *n* was as clear as the sounds that had required no tongue to form.

He stared at her, shocked. "What the—"

She laughed, and stuck her tongue out at him. A full, perfect, pink tongue.

Jon laughed, sweeping her up and spinning her around in his arms. He set her down and asked Aradan, "How did you do that? No – don't answer that," he held up his hand, "it won't make sense anyway," he shook his head in wonder. "Don't look a gift horse... and all that."

"That's the first time I've been called a horse," Aradan teased, light-hearted.

"There's a first time for everything," Jon grinned.

"Or was he calling *me* the horse?" Alexis winked at Jon, standing akimbo.

Jon kissed Alexis, smiling through their tears of laughter, then grabbed Aradan and pulled him into his arms for a big man-slap of a hug, thanking him again and again for everything.

The grief of the night melted away into the joy of the morning, and the room couldn't contain the joy, laughter, and relief, as it spilled out of the hall and flooded down the stairs. Toshiro, Brehani and Naeem heard the celebration in the upper hallway as the group gradually began to disperse, and marvelled at the wonders that met their eyes as they came up to join in: A sighted Elbal, and a chattering Alexis. Questions flew at them faster than they could answer, but joy overrode amazement despite their curious, intellectual minds.

Galal and Amir took Moriel's body to clean her wound and lay her upon the bed prepared at the feet of King Elgin, dressed in one of Erlina's own Cardinal red dresses. The Hall of Dreams became the Hall of Rest: With one of those resting in grief, the swaths of cloths with their silver bells were taken down, being too reminiscent of happier times for the purpose the room now bore. Edric had gone to his room to shower and change, while Elbal invited Alexis and

Jon, along with Brehani, Naeem and Toshiro into the dining hall, where he told them the story of the events as they had unfolded. Aradan and Erlina were alone once again.

Aradan gazed at Erlina a moment, trying to comprehend all that had taken place in the course of one night. He looked down at the blood-stained floor and thought of Moriel. "We must come to terms with our sojourn here being a permanent one," Aradan said gently as he took Erlina's hands in his.

"*You* must," she replied, "for until you arrived I never knew any other choice had been open to us."

"Then what shall we do with the time now granted to us?"

"I think our joining is at last on the horizon," she smiled, "and a honeymoon... that should occupy a decade or so," she pressed her lips tenderly to his.

Just then someone cleared their throat at the door. It was Edric. "I'm sorry to interrupt... may I speak with you please?"

"Of course. Come in," Erlina said graciously.

Aradan stood alert to danger, more out of habit than of mistrust now.

Edric said, "I would be grateful – I mean I would really be relieved – if I could stay on here... work for you... in some way repay you for your kindness to me. I want to make up for my own..." he searched for the word he'd heard, "*Mor-ways.*"

She walked over to him. "You are more than welcome. Brehani has decided to remain here and lead the excavation for the foreseeable future. He will need reliable help over the winter, bagging and logging the artefacts already found; Naeem will return to his family in Cairo next week, and the students will not be back until next year."

"You mean you're still going to excavate? I mean – I thought it was only to find that cist."

"I initiated this excavation for the sake of my companions," she explained. "It will be the find of the century when it is all revealed: A city of advanced technology, building skills, an island of knowledge in an age of stone and bronze, axe and iron. It will be like finding an iPad in the Middle Ages. Layer upon layer of lives lived, each one known by me, and documented for posterity. I could not give them a better gift, nor could I find better people to share this history with."

"Then... with your permission, I'd like to return to Orkney and set things in order there... sell the house, get my things, and all that. I could be back within the month, whether I get the house sold or not."

"Then go with my blessings. Your room will be here waiting."

"Before you go," Aradan still held Erlina's necklace, "if you are truly sincere in your penance, I would ask that while you are at Moriel's haunts, search with all your might for the matching piece to this." He showed him the orb and its necklace.

Edric examined it carefully, then looked at them both: "You have my word – I'll look for it, and bring it to you if I find it. If I can't find it, I'll bring all of her journals, records... anything I can find that might help in the search."

"You would have our greatest thanks," Aradan smiled.

As Edric was packing his things to leave, he heard Jon return to his room so he went to his door and knocked.

"Good morning," Jon opened cautiously on seeing Edric; that was usually safest where he was concerned.

"I'd like to apologize," Edric began.

"For which infraction this time?" Jon asked sarcastically.

"For everything. Can I come in a minute?" Jon stepped aside and Edric walked in. He told him the whole story, and that he'd realized too late the influence Moriel had become in his life. "It's no excuse – but just to say that from now on, things will be different. I was a fool; feel free to remind me of that as often as needed."

"Oh, don't worry," Jon grinned. "I'm good at that. But I am sorry for what happened," he added more seriously. "It can't be easy losing the one you love... especially like that."

"There's probably never been a *like that* in history before."

"So how are you getting to Orkney?" Jon asked. "Do you need a lift?"

"No, thanks. I've got Moriel's yacht. I guess I've just inherited it."

"So how will that work? I mean, I assume an immortal didn't think about writing a will or naming an executor of her estate."

"I was Moriel's administrator – she hated dealing with technicalities or paperwork, so it shouldn't be overly complicated as my name was used as her front," he shrugged. "My name is officially on her deeds – it made it easier to get things done." He stepped back toward the door. "I should be back in a few weeks – it looks like you'll be stuck with me for a long time; that is, if you stay on here. And I'm really sorry I was such a cad."

"*Fool* is the word, I think," he grinned. "And thanks. I haven't decided yet whether I'll be staying here or not. Now that Erlina won't be moving around anymore, I might take Alexis to meet my family in Norway."

"But you'll be here when I get back, right?"

"You haven't even left, and you already miss me," Jon grinned.

"You're growing on me."

"Like a fungus," Jon laughed.

"See you then?" Edric thumped Jon on the arm.

"Later," he thumped him back, harder.

"Ow!" Edric complained.

"I had two brothers to practice on... so don't start anything you can't finish."

※

Now that the excavation was closed up for the season and there was no longer a need to guard against the Wolf, the artefacts were brought to the castle and the conference room converted to the finds office as the house staff spent their time with Brehani in cataloguing the artefacts that had been found in the main trench – pottery fragments, midden contents, coins, tools, weapons and the fine specimens of jewellery, belt buckles and sword hilts.

Alexis knew where to find Jon in the mornings, if she was quick enough: He always woke up with a tea with cream and one sugar – she knew how he liked it. She went into the dining hall and sat down to wait, but not long.

He came in and started to fix his tea.

"Good morning," she said, as she got up and walked over to him.

"Good morning." He kept his eyes on his mug.

"We've missed you in the finds office... everyone is pitching in," she hinted.

"I've been busy," he hedged, "making contacts with the locals; I thought maybe I could start up a helicopter tour company."

"Jon," she touched his arm, "are you... avoiding me?"

He stirred cream into his tea a bit too long not to be noticed, and didn't answer. It was answer enough.

"I'm sorry," tears began to well in her throat, and he could hear it.

He sighed and turned toward her. "It's just awkward for me... working together with you. The limbo is uncomfortable; I mean our relationship – our future – hangs by the thin thread of finding a stranger who's been impossible to find for twenty-five years! I'm just supposed to accept that fact and get on with life with you as a friend?" he shrugged. "I can't... not when I want more."

She backed off, nodding. There was nothing she could say though she wanted to say so much.

"Look – I'm trying to understand; but you've never even known this woman who gave birth to you, and yet she has precedence in your life over me, who wants to give you a mother and a father, siblings, husband, family..." he shook his head in exasperation. He waited, but she gave no answer; he could see the conflict in her and he felt like a cad for causing it. "I'd better get going," he murmured as he turned toward the door with his steaming mug in hand. "Aradan needs me."

"Have a good day," she called to his back as he walked through the door, and he paused in his step, but didn't turn.

"I got your note – good morning," Jon called to Aradan as he stuck his head in Erlina's library door.

Aradan looked up from his laptop, Erlina by his side writing in her large book. "Good morning. How are you doing?" he asked.

Jon shrugged, glad for the tea mug in his hand.

"That's what I thought. You need something to do: How long would it take to fly to Oxford?"

"Oxford," Jon thought a moment. "That would be about three hours from here."

"I'll make the reservations," Erlina said; "One helicopter parking and two hotel rooms for... five days?" she looked to Aradan for confirmation.

"That should be enough," he agreed.

"What is this all about?" Jon asked.

"You'll see," Aradan grinned.

Five days later they'd returned, Jon still none the wiser as to what they'd been up to as they wouldn't tell him; they remained cryptic as they invited him to a private dinner in the conservatory on the evening of their return.

When Jon arrived at the conservatory, he saw a table set for four; it would be one of those awkward dinners, then.

Alexis arrived next, at first confused when she saw him, then resigned; her mother was obviously trying to reconcile the young couple. "Hello," she said tentatively, not looking him in the eye. "I see we're to have dinner together." Her voice was flat.

When Aradan and Erlina arrived, they greeted the two, but gave no hint as to their purpose until after Galal had served their dinner and withdrawn.

As they ate and discussed their banal days, Alexis couldn't bear the suspense any longer. "What is it?" she challenged.

Aradan asked, "Do you remember the blood sample you gave us?"

She nodded. "My mother said it was to find out my blood type."

"That wasn't exactly true," Erlina admitted, "but I didn't want to get your expectations up in case we couldn't succeed."

"Succeed at what? It shouldn't be that hard to find out a blood type," she pointed out.

"I contacted a friend," Aradan said; "he works in genetics, and has personal contacts with scientists involved in what is essentially the *Doomsday Book* of genetics for the British Isles. The project is being conducted by a team at Oxford under Professor Sir Walter Bodmer. Naturally they began their research near home... collecting DNA samples from the faculty, students, and the general population who fit their criteria – those having lived in the same area as all four of their grandparents. He pulled some strings and had your autosomal DNA tested, and ran a comparison check through their growing databanks."

"Autosomal DNA can be traced to either parent, whether the child is male or female," Erlina explained.

What they were saying began to dawn on her gradually. "Do you mean... were they able to find out where I come from?" Alexis looked from her mother's gentle, cautious expression to Aradan, who was smiling at Jon knowingly.

"You— you've *found* her?" Jon stuttered, eyes wide.

"My birth-mother?" Alexis gasped.

"We have!" her mother reached out and touched her daughter's hand, laughing at the overjoyed confusion in her expression. "And Alexis," she smiled, "she's been searching for you for years!"

"She— she's been searching for *me*?" Alexis blinked as deep throbbing sobs of relief rushed to the surface and burst forth.

Jon closed his eyes and bowed his head with an exhale of relief.

"I— how is that possible?" she gulped for air through her tears. "I never thought—"

"There was a clear match in the databanks," Aradan told them. "My friend couldn't give me that information as it's highly confidential. But Erlina has, shall we say, a persuasive presence, and that's why we went to Oxford," he smiled at Erlina. "When we met him casually for lunch he unwittingly let enough information slip that we were able to track them down."

"*Them?*" her eyes widened, incredulous.

"Alexis," Aradan grinned, "we've not only found your mother... but we actually found her *through* your father! Or more precisely, his autosomal DNA... he's faculty at Oxford and had taken part in their studies. We spoke with him of this delicate matter, and he knew where your mother was... because they are married!"

Erlina told her, "Your mother said that they had been in contact with the Mercy Orphanage in Cairo periodically throughout the years, hoping for any sign of life from their lost daughter."

"But then why did they abandon me?" Alexis choked out in shock and disbelief.

"Your mother was single at the time... a young archaeology student travelling around the Middle East on holiday – I realize it sounds like a convenient coincidence, but the fact is that Cairo is a destination for many in our field, and thus it is that I found you there," Erlina explained. "She didn't feel able to care for a child, still feeling too much like a child herself. Her boyfriend, who hadn't even known she was pregnant or struggling with such a decision, eventually married her. They now have a happy marriage, with a son and a daughter now in their late teens, and their one greatest regret was never knowing what had happened to their first daughter... it has haunted them far longer than it has haunted you."

Alexis stood, shakily. "I— I need to be alone!" She ran from the room.

Erlina, Aradan and Jon sat in silence for some time.

Finally Jon spoke. "I can't believe it. You found her!" he shook his head, smiling, uncertain, torn between elation and concern for Alexis. "Did we do the right thing?"

"Yes," Erlina replied. "She'll need some time to adjust. But it's what she needs to feel whole within herself... before she can complete you as your soulmate... a partner in life."

"She'll come around," Aradan patted Jon on the shoulder. "Give her an hour or two, and then check in on her. Take this with you when you go," Aradan placed a buff folder on the table.

"I'm not sure... I don't know if she wants me to be the one by her side or not," he confessed.

Erlina stood and walked over to Jon, touching his arm as she knelt beside his chair. "I know my daughter," she smiled, "and I know she loves you. This identity crisis of hers had nothing to do with you, yet everything to do with you: You are her future; but she needs to know her past to make sense of the present... to make sense of her own heart and desires."

"Give her time, and then go to her," Aradan encouraged.

Jon nodded as he picked up the folder and thumbed through it: It was the record of their search, and the contact information for Alexis's family was clipped to the inside of the front cover. He read, "*Residence: Oxford. Place of Family Origin: York.*" He stared at the names: *William and Emma Thorpe*. "Thank you," he said to them both sincerely.

Two hours later Jon knocked quietly on Alexis's door. No reply. He cautiously stuck his head in to find her asleep atop her bed covers, curled up on her side and surrounded by used tissues; evidently she'd cried herself to sleep. He sat down beside her on her bed and the movement awakened her.

"How are you doing?" he whispered.

She nodded, gazing into his eyes remorsefully.

"I..." he didn't really know where to begin. "I want to apologize. I let my disappointment taint our friendship, and that was wrong of me. A friend is a friend... if you can't give me more than friendship then—"

She stopped him, holding her fingers to his lips. "No – it was my fault! I shouldn't have gotten our hearts so entangled before I really knew who I was. It's my fault that I hurt you by pulling away, and for that I'm sorry. But now," she looked up toward the library, "that's behind us."

Shocked, he stood up. "Oh... right. If that's how you want it, I'll go."

"What?" she jumped up and caught his hand. "No! I meant that the *suspense* is behind us!"

He pinched his eyes closed and breathed a sigh of relief. He felt her slip her arms around his waist, laying her head to his chest. He put his arms around her; it felt right. He rested his head gently against her hair, breathing deeply. "I've missed you."

"I've missed you – so much!" she looked up, and he bent down to kiss her.

"So," he whispered into her lips, "are you ready to contact them?"

She took a deep breath and held onto it as she nodded, "I'm ready."

He smiled, picking up the buff folder from her bed, waving it.

She took it, trembling. "Do... do you think they'll be at home?"

"Aradan told your parents they'd be telling you today... so they'll most likely be waiting for your call."

"Then it's time – they've waited long enough."

"So have you," he stroked her hair. "I'll be right here until you tell me to leave."

"No! I mean I won't tell you that!" She sat at the computer. She took a few deep breaths, then put on a new headset with microphone and took her time adjusting it. She took another deep breath, then dialled the number into the SkypeOut interface. The phone rang.

"Oxford 865." It was a man's voice. Deep, and warm.

"Uh... hello. This is Alexis." Her voice trembled, and she clung to Jon's hand.

There was a momentary silence on the other end that had her immediately worried. But then a voice brimming with emotion replied, "Hello, Alexis. Thank you for calling."

Where does one begin with a lifetime to catch up, and on something as impersonal as a phone? They talked and talked, first her father, and then her mother; the siblings were out. They made plans for her parents to travel to Scotland as soon as could be arranged, as their younger children, fifteen and sixteen, were in school and they couldn't wait until Christmas holidays to meet her at last. Besides, they wanted time with their daughter alone first. Jon would pick them up at the Inverness Airport in two days.

When at last Alexis ended the call, she slumped back in her chair with a happy sigh. Before she knew it, Jon was on his knee beside her chair.

"Will you be able to say *yes* now?" he asked, holding out a small ring box. He looked so adorable when he was vulnerable.

She laughed and nodded through tears, and he opened the box; inside was a beautiful white gold ring, undulating waves outlining a river of blue enamel.

"I chose blue as a reminder of Erlina's ring. And waves... well, it's Scotland. So... do you like it?"

"No," she shook her head, "I love it. I love you!"

"In that case you can have both," he teased. He slipped the ring onto her finger, and then put his left hand into his pocket and pulled it out wearing a matching ring, his slightly wider with two waves of enamel.

"You have one too!"

"I want people to know we belong together," he smiled.

"We do... we always will." She knew at that moment that she would love no other as she loved him. She was at *home*. She wrapped her arms around his neck, kissing him tenderly. His lips pressed hungrily to her own, breath and heartbeats mingling.

"We have some catching up to do," he smiled into her lips.

The reunion was everything Alexis had hoped for, and far more: She'd always imagined finding her mother, and that perhaps after a few awkward contacts she would gradually accept the fact that her past was now closed and she would be able to move on with her life; but in fact she discovered both a loving mother and father, and felt very much as if she were their daughter. She had the eyes of her father, the complexion and hair of her mother, and (apparently) shared a similar personality to her sister. For a week they barely did anything else but talk, Galal gently intruding long enough to keep them nourished. Alexis was thrilled to know that the mother who raised her was adored by her birth-mother, Emma, and that Erlina embraced her parents as if she'd known them all their lives. Jon and Aradan were adored equally by her parents, and in a rare breath of a moment when William was separated from the bevy of women, Jon asked his permission to marry his daughter. To gain a daughter and a son within a week was nearly overwhelming for him, but his joy was all the more boundless. At the end of the week, when they needed to return to the teens they had left behind to fend for themselves, it was decided that the entire family would return for the Christmas holidays.

Five weeks after Edric had left, he finally returned. Having taken care of the logistics of Moriel's estate, he had spent nearly a fortnight combing through every possession of Moriel's for the lost necklace, finding nothing. As promised, he packed every document he could find, including her laptop, and returned to Dalmoor. Erlina and Aradan, Edric, Alexis and Jon spread the boxes out in the main library and systematically worked through the material. Five days, and all to no avail.

"It's *got* to be here somewhere!" Aradan ran his fingers through his hair, frustrated. "We've got to be missing a clue!"

"If it was as valuable to her as Aradan has said," reasoned Alexis, "she wouldn't have had it very far from her person; I'm surprised she wasn't wearing it."

"You went through everything of hers?" Jon asked. "Deposit boxes, any hidden drawers in desks?"

"I even used a Minelab CTX – a metal detector – to go over the property around her house," he nodded. "Unless it's made of something that won't show up as metal, I can't imagine it's there. I've also checked her car and yacht from top to bottom. Nothing."

"Her yacht?" Aradan looked at him. "Is that how she got here?"

"Yes. But as I said, I've checked it... even turned her pillows inside out," he shook his head. "I'm sorry – I wish I could help."

"Perhaps you have," Erlina spoke. "Your comment about it not showing up as metal is perhaps not that far from the truth; it is metal, but may not disrupt any frequencies calibrated for earth's metals – we could easily test it on my own necklace."

Aradan looked at her. "You're right! And it must be somewhere within her possessions – she would not be careless with the one thing that assured her of my pursuing her."

"Maybe it would help to have several sets of eyes looking through her house, or haunts... see something you missed," Alexis suggested to Edric.

"Well then, there's nothing for it: Let's go hunting in Orkney," Aradan stood.

Edric and Aradan planned their route before setting out: Once they'd checked the weather forecast, the wind speeds and visibility the following morning and all was a go, the five of them packed their bags and headed down to the shore. Aradan's clinker yacht was anchored much closer than Edric's, so while Erlina and Aradan prepared his ship to follow Edric's, Jon, Alexis and Edric took the dinghy out and prepared to cast off. Sailing was smooth until they hit the Sea of Orcs, otherwise known as the Pentland Firth. The waves slashed against them from all sides, a confusion of currents ricocheting off of islands, sea stacks and the northern coast of the mainland and whipped up by the Atlantic winds.

Once they'd given Stroma and Swona a wide berth to the west and made their way into Scapa Flow, the waters calmed considerably. Edric docked in his private berth at the Stromness marina, while Aradan went to a public berth, and they met up at the marina office. A cab later, they were on their way to Moriel's house on the outskirts of Stromness.

Inside her house smelled like forest compost, rotting dust. They threw open the windows and let the Atlantic breeze clear it out while they sat down for a council together. They made a searching plan and carried it out meticulously; all for naught. They spent a week going over everything with a fine-tooth comb. Nothing. Disappointed and frustrated, they sailed back to Loch Eriboll, anchoring together nearest the access road from the abandoned cottage along the shore.

Anchoring a mere stone's throw away from Edric's yacht, Erlina suddenly gasped.

"What is it?" Aradan ran to her.

She stared wide-eyed at her chest where the necklace hung. "It's... it's throbbing! Barely perceptible, but yet—" She scooped it gently into her hand, looking intently at it. A faint pulse vibrated on her hand. "It's the first sign of life it's given me in well over a thousand years!" she laughed.

Edric was just lowering the dinghy over the side with the winch. "Edric!" Aradan called. "Stay there! We're coming aboard!"

Once aboard Moriel's yacht the pulse became stronger and Erlina knew it must be close. They all began searching the ship from top to bottom: They unscrewed light bulbs, tapped wall panelling to listen for anomalies, pulled the couch apart and put it back together checking every cushion, and overturned any and every object on the yacht.

"Nothing," cried Aradan, "but it's so maddeningly close!" He fell back onto the couch, running his fingers through his hair in frustration.

"How do you know? We've searched for weeks now," Jon countered; "assuming she didn't just dump it overboard somewhere between here and Orkney, I don't think we're going to find it without a miracle."

Without a word Erlina took Jon's hand and turned it palm-up, placing the orb in his hand, which still hung on the chain around her neck. He felt it faintly pulsating and jumped back in surprise.

"It's close!" she smiled, gesturing to the orb.

He stared at her, wide-eyed. "Well, I guess *that's* our miracle," he nodded toward the orb.

Aradan noticed the captain's log; curious, he began reading through the entries while the others continued searching; they checked the masts, decks, railings, and window frames; every bolt and screw was examined. Aradan looked over the entries Moriel had made just before departing Orkney for what would become her last voyage on earth: An engine filter replaced, a small welding repair on the keel, light bulbs in the main cabin, and how much the full tank of petrol had cost. He read it again. He jumped up and ran to search the desk.

"What is it?" asked Alexis.

"Have you found something?" Erlina sounded hopeful.

"I'm not sure... just a hunch." He pulled out a manila envelope wedged between two ledgers and labelled *receipts*. Inside he finally found what he was looking for: The receipt for the welding repair. It wasn't specific, but that was the point: It only had written upon it the amount, which was negligible, and one word: *Addition*. Without a word Aradan rushed up the steps and to the railing, jumping overboard with barely a splash into the deep water, bringing a wave of people to the jump-side of the deck and rocking the boat.

"What is he doing?" Edric asked.

Jon looked at the paper Aradan had been staring at, and couldn't figure out what the excitement was about. Erlina looked at it; it was perhaps the size of the repair that had made him suspicious.

"He's been down there a long time," Alexis pointed out after a few minutes, worried.

They all watched, looking for a sign of him. Nothing.

"I'm going in," Jon started taking off his shoes.

"No," Erlina called. "He's fine," she assured them. "We cannot drown... he's obviously found something worth seeing."

Jon shook his head laughing, "No wonder he's fearless of rip currents! But doesn't he need goggles?"

"Our eyes see perfectly," she laughed at his surprise, "and adapt to our environment."

Far longer than possible, there was not a bubble on the surface. At last Aradan resurfaced.

"You nearly gave us heart attacks," Jon chided him. "*We're* mortal, you know!"

"I'm sorry," Aradan grinned. "I need an underwater blowtorch."

"What did you find?" Erlina whispered, breathless at the thought of their treasure.

"The small welding repair... but it's not a repair. It's an *addition*; at the T-joint at the back of the winged keel... a metal box," he explained as he climbed back onto the deck and accepted a towel from Edric. "It obviously had the lid welded in place recently, as the other seams are of a different quality."

"Okay, hold on... I've got a blowtorch on me somewhere," Jon said sarcastically, feeling his pockets.

Aradan laughed, incredibly light-hearted all things considered. "If we haven't got one here," he looked to Erlina, who shook her head, "then we'll fly to Inverness – one more day in eternity will not dampen my hopes," he smiled.

"That might not be necessary," Jon said. He pulled out his cell phone and called Sandy – though he wasn't a fisherman himself any longer, Sandy knew everyone in the area, and a suitable blowtorch was soon borrowed from a friend of his who used copper alloy netting around his fishery and made his own repairs. In an hour they were back on the yacht.

Aradan disappeared beneath the yacht once more with the blow torch. Erlina sat upon a cushioned deck bench and waited quietly, while the others hovered near the spot Aradan had gone down; she could scarcely believe that only metres beneath her feet lay the end of all their pursuit. A pursuit that had taken more than a millennium. Yet she couldn't deny that the orb around her neck pulsed steadily, if faintly. Wherever it was, it was nearby. *What would that mean? How would the two parts aid them in finding the missing centrepiece?* It was all so unprecedented in her experience. All she had experienced of the orb were those vivid, delicious waking dreams so long ago... impulses, shadowy glimpses of an existence foreign to her own history. She remembered the deep, gut-wrenching anguish in 1066 the moment she'd realized that those transportations had come to an end. The doubt that had plagued her mind for a century, then the limbo of waiting that followed after that; hoping, unable to move forward, unwilling to accept the loss. But now she and Aradan were reunited, never to be parted again. *What would finding the orb mean?* Everything she had ever known or come to accept in this world was about to change.

Suddenly Erlina felt a pulsing sensation as the orb came to life, beating powerfully with the rhythm of their hearts, a melody cascading from within the orb. A flood of emotion swept over her, like a breaking wave upon a delicate sandy shore. He'd found it! His part of the orb rested against his heart once more.

Alexis shouted, "I see him! He's coming up!"

Aradan broke the surface without gasping for air, as if he'd just bobbed under momentarily. Without a word he handed the torch up to Jon and then climbed aboard. In his hand was the metal box, warped from the blow torch and prying it free. Around his neck hung a silvery chain as slender as a hair, the orb as polished as if it had just come from a jeweller's. The wide smile on his face was blinding joy tinged with relief. He looked at Erlina, and knew she felt it too – the orb was pulsing strongly now, throbbing out his excited heartbeat even as he felt her fearful one. She looked up at last, trepidation in her eyes.

He fell to his knees before her and took her hands in his. "What is it, my love? Why this fear?"

"Oh, Aradan!" she cried. "What shall we do now? I have never known any other existence... I've never had the hope, as you've had, of the prospect of ever leaving this realm! And now the possibility is upon us! I... I do not know what to think, how to feel! I am elated, relieved, apprehensive, and – dare I say it? – even saddened, for I shall leave everyone that I have come to love behind!" She looked up at Alexis, whose face showed the same sadness.

He gently kissed her cheek. "My fairest love, we shall only leave when we both feel ready."

She looked at Alexis once more. "We cannot leave until after their wedding," she said to Aradan.

"Of course not," he smiled at her. "And remember... we do not return alone. He brushed his fingers along the chain about her neck, down to the orb, sending a tremble of peace through her. "Now we just need to find the centrepiece,"

"*Just*," she managed to smile. "Just find a thing smaller than a ring, lost more than a thousand years, that I had searched in vain for because it is invisible? Just!" she laughed.

"Since when have you become a cynic?" he teased. "You, who move earth and sky, have no reason for doubt." He looked up as he said *sky*, and realized that the last light of the day was quickly fading to the west. "We shall begin our search in the morning."

That night Erlina lay in Aradan's arms. He stroked her hair, breathing in her sweet perfume. "Just think... we'll soon be reunited with our families!"

"Do you think they'll be there?" she whispered. "We are Travellers, after all."

"They would never travel without us a second time, of that I think we can be certain," he smiled ruefully.

"My sister... she is now older than I was the first time you and I met!"

"She is perhaps a mother... you and I doubly aunt and uncle to my brother's and your sister's children," he thought of his younger brother Megildur, and the flowering love that had begun before the terrible battle. "Their joy will be made complete when we return home."

"Home," she repeated, looking into his eyes. "What is it like? I have never been there, even though I know it is my true home."

He leaned up on one elbow beside her, caressing her forearm with the back of his fingers. "Even though I have only been there once, and that only a century for my training, it is still fresh in my mind," he began: "The colours! Far more than the atmosphere of this planet allows, and far more vivid, subtle, and diverse... the prismatic division of blue alone has a thousand shades. Gravity is different there too," he looked at her smiling. "We move as the wind here... but there we can easily fly! And what we know as ground level here simply does not exist there... there are floating islands upon which is built to weigh them down; the sky hangs with them at varying levels, like raindrops suspended in their fall. The architecture... slender, gentle spires rising heavenward. It is vast, yet never the sense of feeling crowded, or isolated. And there are waterfalls of purest water cascading everywhere," he looked far off in his thoughts.

"And are there seasons?" she asked.

"Mild ones," he nodded, "and the day cycle is far longer than that of this planet, with roughly thirty-five earth-hours. The night is pure, with stars, galaxies, nebula, moons and planets from horizon to horizon! My grandfather once took me with him on one of his night watches, and we sat on a small island high up in the atmosphere, observing the passage of the night's splendour."

She sighed. "I am grateful you were there... it will not seem so *foreign* to me now."

"Once we are home, our lives can truly begin. We will celebrate our joining the Aquillian way with our families, and settle into our home – I'm sure our mothers have at length prepared it for us."

She looked at him. "Why would they?"

He grinned, "Because they are both Gatekeepers... they know we will be coming... that we will find our way home. And they are mothers – they will never give up that hope." He whisked a strand of hair back from her cheek, and caressed her neck with his lips. "Enough talk of travelling and reunions," he murmured. "Where were we?" He ran his hand along her arm and down her leg, sending electric waves of energy pulsating along her skin.

"Yes," she gasped, "where were we?"

※

Jon woke up to a bright day; there were unusually many recently... it would be the talk of the pub. When Jon had gone to borrow the blowtorch the evening before, Sandy had nudged Jon about the weather and reminded him of the notion that weather followed the Maid of Dalmoor's moods. To Jon at least, it didn't sound all that far-fetched now.

Alexis met him in the dining hall for breakfast, but otherwise it was a quiet place; without the cafeteria-style tables filling it, the long dining table was back in place and the occupants could all sit together. Edric was still too cheery in the mornings, and Brehani had already come and gone to the incident room.

"Erlina and Aradan left early this morning," Alexis told Jon as they sat down to breakfast.

"Searching," he nodded. "I hope they can find it – that it hasn't... I don't know, gotten buried too deep over time, or washed into the Loch. I mean, it's been a thousand years," he shook his head laughing, "I can't believe I just said that so calmly."

"Erlina told me that Aradan thinks it won't matter, now that they have the two other pieces together; something about them calling to it," she replied.

"Well, let's hurry – I don't want to miss anything" he gulped down his tea.

Alexis and Jon found the Aquillians walking along the road; there was never enough traffic to be bothersome; they were walking along slowly, holding hands.

"What's that sound?" Alexis asked.

Jon said, "It sounds like crickets. But where's it coming from?"

Aradan heard him ask as they approached. "It's coming from these," he pointed to the orb. "Odd that you would hear it like that... to us, mine emits a faint, high melody and from Erlina's there is a lower, base melody throbbing forth." Her heart beat in his, his in hers. "You might be perceiving only its higher frequency."

"But how is that even possible – I mean that it plays music?" Jon looked more closely at the orb as Aradan held his out for him to see. The jewels sparkled in the sunshine, all except one; it seemed to be indifferent to the weaker light of earth's star as it shone with otherworldly iridescence. It was most definitely emitting a sound, but Jon could only perceive it as the fast frequency of (extremely talented) crickets.

"How does my ring contain a drop of our star?" Erlina held up her hand to show them the ring, in answer to his question. The silvery band of the ring was intricately laced, interwoven strands ending in flared prongs that secured the unfaceted oval cabochon. But it was the stone itself that outshone the beautiful setting, literally. At casual glance the ring might just be seen as reflecting ambient light; but the longer one gazed at the stone, the more mesmerizing it became: The source of blue light, dancing at its core with pearlescent rainbows, was alive and far deeper within the ring than was physically possible; it was like looking through a window into the universe.

Jon shook his head, looking from the ring to the Aquillians. "Amazing," he looked back at the ring. "How— never mind! But I feel as if – if I stared at this ring long enough – I could be transported through it. If that makes sense."

"It does," Aradan smiled. "I don't know of this ring having that capability... but I'd be careful, if I were you," he warned.

Jon looked up at him quickly, and saw the flash of a smile buried beneath the poker face. His eyes narrowed on his friend. "Beam me up, Scotty."

Aradan laughed, and the orb burst forth in joyful song.

Alexis could barely take her eyes off of the ring. "What makes it shine so? I know you said it's a drop of your star... but it looks alive!"

"It is," Erlina smiled, "and responds to my bidding." She put the ring to her lips as if she would kiss it, then whispered, "*Glânöir... glawaer glom firach!*"

The ring began to glow brighter and brighter, and even in earth's sunlight its light looked purer, brighter and younger.

"Touch it," Erlina encourage Alexis.

She reached out her fingers and gently caressed the ring. It was warm to the touch. "Incredible!"

"So... where are you going to look for the missing piece? Can we help?" Jon asked.

"Your company is always welcome," Aradan shook his head, "but no one can locate the orb except us. We've been looking where she last had it... in the final battle of Maldor, AD 788."

Jon commented, "That's probably going to be under a *lot* of dirt."

"Not necessarily," Erlina replied. "It's not uncommon to find things buried a millennia in the top few inches of soil."

"Then why was the anomaly buried so deeply?" Alexis wondered.

"Because I wished it so... to protect it, to hide it."

"Wait... *wished it so?*" Jon repeated. "How does a wish bury something?"

"As Aradan's gifting is touch, so mine is the gift of voice. I requested the soil to take Maldor's fallen deep enough to hide until I desired it to be found. That's what happened," Erlina said simply.

"That's what happened," Jon smiled, shaking his head, "I hope I don't need medication when all this is said and done."

Aradan laughed, "You're too healthy and intelligent for that – believe me, I wouldn't have brought you into all this if I didn't know you could handle whatever came your way."

"That's comforting," Jon slapped Aradan on the shoulder as they walked on. Alien or not, he was still his best friend and he'd treat him as such... as long as he still had the chance.

The four of them wandered along the road, the Aquillians listening to the music of their hearts and for the missing harmony of the centrepiece.

"Where was the battlefield originally?" asked Jon, looking along the modern road and noting that there were most likely missing landscape features.

"It ranged from the shore – that original shore is beneath the waves of the loch," Aradan pointed toward the water, "into the citadel, the settlement, and up into the forested hills," he swept his hand along as he spoke, from the excavation site toward Castle Dalmoor.

"*My* battle was fought mainly in the forest and on the bracken-strewn lower flanks of Meall Meadhonach," Erlina frowned at the memory, "against a smaller party who were likely attempting to swing around and attack from behind, though they never made it. We begin our search here much lower as it may have washed down with time."

They had at length passed the excavations walking toward Durness; they were nearly between Loch Duail and Loch Sian when a faint harmony began to resonate. Erlina and Aradan heard it though the others could not.

"This way!" they both cried out at the same moment. They crossed the road toward the west.

The Scottish Highlands made themselves known immediately.

"How are we going to walk through that?" Jon asked the obvious. A nearly impenetrable tangle of bracken, heather, moss, peat bog, bog cotton and grasses lay before them.

"One step at a time," Erlina smiled, and headed into the fray. The bracken and heather clumps stood waist-high, clinging and grabbing at their clothes, and the boggy ground was a treacherous unknown invisible beneath the carpet of fronds. They trailed, single-file, behind Erlina. It was slow progress. A nearby nye of pheasants took flight at their approach.

"Were we planning to make it there by nightfall?" Jon asked sarcastically.

Aradan plucked a twig of heather and threw it back at him.

Gradually the harmony became stronger; the louder it became, the more perceptible it was to Jon and Alexis too. They moved on in silence, awed by the song: It was light and yet heady; it was difficult to say exactly what made the song seem otherworldly, but it most definitely was. The melody alternated between uplifting and melancholic, and the harmonies shifted from major to minor and something subtle between the two. All their concentration focused on the ground, on the song; they stepped quietly, unwilling to disturb the beautiful refrain. At last Erlina and Aradan both stopped; they had inadvertently headed back closer to the flank of the hill between the castle and the excavation site as they'd followed the sounds. Aradan looked at Erlina, a spark of anticipation in his eyes.

"Now what?" Jon asked. "Should I go get a few shovels?"

"That won't be necessary," Erlina smiled politely. "But whatever happens, don't be frightened."

Alexis took Jon's hand just in case.

Erlina knelt down. From somewhere deep within, very similar to that impossible depth of the ring she wore, Aradan could hear a song forming, though the others could not yet perceive it. It rose in her throat, a breathtakingly melodic whisper, colours woven with emotion, shades intertwining through melody and harmony. Alexis grabbed hold of Jon's arm to steady herself as the ground began to shake; they all stepped back. It wasn't moving as if being ploughed or broken up with a shovel or machine of any kind; it was *shifting*, the bracken and the heather, their roots, fronds and stems all sliding aside. The bare patch of oily peat now cleared began to bubble as if it were a mud geyser, though it was no different texturally than it had been a moment before. As one bubble would pop and the next began rising into the burst centre, the outer debris would churn back beneath the surface, as if someone were folding it from underground like so much kneaded bread dough.

At last, in the centre of a bubble emerged a hardened clump of clay. Erlina stopped singing, and reached out to take the clump from the liquefaction. As she stepped back, the bracken and heather slid back into place leaving no trace of what had just taken place. They all stood staring at the muddied disc: It was hard to believe that so much grief, uncertainty, searching, and hopes hinged on so small an object. Erlina, with hands atremble with excitement, washed it clean with a small flask of water she'd brought. When it was rinsed and dried it shone as if it had just been polished – not a sign of centuries in the ground, neither a speck or a dent out of place nor erosion or decay of any degree. The design was as intricate as the interwoven lace engraved on the outer two parts of the orb, and each part held one of the three sacred stones of Aquillis, and this centrepiece's stone was the largest of the three, representing hope. Erlina looked to Aradan, and he nodded encouragingly. She held her breath in anticipation, and reattached the centrepiece to her orb's half. It latched into place with a firm snap, as if it were strongly magnetic, and immediately the strength of the song increased, perceptible now by all four of them.

"We cannot join the orb into a whole just yet," Aradan warned. "I don't know what will happen, and we must first be prepared for our journey... be ready to leave."

Alexis and Jon suddenly realized what he meant: They would be leaving... forever.

※

In the autumn Erlina and Aradan travelled to Norway with Jon and Alexis to enjoy a family reunion as Jon's parents had returned from Cairo for a sabbatical. Jon's family were elated not only to finally see Jon happy, but also his friend, the eternal bachelor, at last having met the love of his life — beyond that they never need know.

Alexis's parents and siblings arrived at Castle Dalmoor for Christmas. Her younger brother and sister were elated to have an older sister, and her parents could not express their joy of having found their lost daughter after so many years of searching, hoping and praying. Alexis revelled in not only having true family at last, but also of them all having the chance to meet the woman who had raised her as her own. It was the best Christmas Alexis could ever have dreamt of, having all of her loved ones in one place together; she would cherish that moment in time forever.

In the spring, the walls of Castle Dalmoor were witness to a wedding: Jon and Alexis were married in a simple ceremony with family, close friends and Aquillians alike. Their families stayed on at Castle Dalmoor a fortnight in the company of Aradan and Erlina, as Jon and Alexis travelled to the Scilly Isles for their honeymoon, enjoying the white sands and beautiful weather of the islands. When they returned to a quiet house with only the entourage in residence, their growing sense of melancholy became tangible; through all of the celebrations they'd experienced together with Erlina and Aradan, Jon and Alexis had felt as if they were saying goodbye. Each encounter with friends, each meeting of family, each meal together... they were all savoured as final moments. When Naeem returned from Cairo at the request of Erlina, they knew that the departure of their friends was eminent.

How do you prepare for a journey for which you can take nothing with you but knowledge and memories? In many ways, for the mortals left behind it was as if they were on the verge of losing loved ones and yet it was a confusing sense of grief and guilt as they felt they had no right to grieve: Aradan and

Erlina would return home, reunite with their loved ones, and go on with their true lives; the only bereavement would be the loss of fellowship, of friendship, of mutual experiences in life.

The company of companions were each given a small box of unusual gemstones, which Erlina had sung into shape from the mysterious stone cist in which her father and brothers had been interred: The Mithrian stone had been formed in the first few months after they had been buried, during the process in which the Aquillians' outer, earthly vessels had fallen to dust and their inner, true selves shone forth. It formed as a protection, but also as an ample supply of Mithrian should any Aquillians be in need of it; it was their way home. What had not been turned to gemstones and given away, or needed for the return of the six Aquillians, was taken by Erlina and Aradan in the dead of night and buried deep within the loch. If there was ever need of it in the future, the Aquillians' long memories would know where to find it.

The companions were also given treasures from Erlina's collection of antiquities: Maps to Brehani; books to Naeem; and a Maldorian dagger each to Edric and Toshiro; Elbal and his sons were rewarded more than generously for their service not only with gemstones, but antiquities that had personal meaning to them and their family. They were free to go, but they chose rather to remain in the service of Alexis and Jon; their futures would be long, though none knew how long. Toshiro would stay on as butler and all-rounder, while Edric would finish his degree in archaeology and return to continue the excavation with Brehani. To Alexis and Jon the Aquillians not only gave numerous Mithrian gemstones, but made them their sole heirs, and guardians of the secrets of Maldor and Aquillis.

As Erlina and Aradan prepared for departure and the final goodbyes of the company of companions, there was only one other farewell that Erlina wished to make: They called on Sandy.

When Sandy opened his door, at first he saw only Jon and Alexis. "Well!" Sandy smiled, "Come in, outta the wind wi' yous!"

"Wait," Jon held up his hand, "There's someone I'd like to introduce you to."

Sandy poked his head through the doorframe to see where Jon gestured, and there stood the Bonnie Maid of Dalmoor in the flesh; a man as blindingly beautiful as she stood beside her, holding her hand. Sandy's knees nearly buckled at the shock and Aradan reached out to steady him with his touch; suddenly Sandy's chronically ailing heart felt much better; younger, even. But he was not at all willing that such magnificent guests should grace his hovel with their presence; he was embarrassed of everything he had to offer, though he'd offer it all to her if she only asked.

"Jon has told us of what a help you were to him in understanding the enigmas of certain *aspects* of local history," Erlina smiled at Sandy, and he nearly fainted for pure joy. "I would like to invite you to dinner this evening at Castle Dalmoor to show our gratitude."

His protests were in vain as he was far outnumbered by goodwill and undermined by his own desires and curiosity; he was also aware of what an immense honour it was, a rare glimpse into that mysterious world that his forefathers since time immemorial would gladly have shared.

Jon picked Sandy up that evening with a golf cart, and dinner and the company was enjoyed by all. Sandy soon felt comfortable in Erlina's presence, and felt only too pleased for her that she'd at last seemed to find what – or who – she'd been searching for. He knew that if his old heart gave out that night he'd die a happy and satisfied man, though his heart felt stronger now just being in her presence (so it seemed to him); he felt himself growing younger by the minute. As a parting gesture Erlina alone drove him home and saw him to his door.

"It was an honour to meet you," she reached out and embraced him, and he nearly swooned. "Before we part... I have something for you," she handed him a small jewellery box.

He opened the dark blue velvet box: Inside rested a silvery arrow tip, identical to the one he'd found and lost so many years ago. Beneath the arrow tip was a dozen small gemstones. "What are these?" he couldn't take his eyes from the pearlescent stones; they seemed to dance with light deep within.

"They are a little something I made... extremely valuable," was all she would say. "When you sell them, you are to take them to this jeweller's in Edinburgh," she showed him the business card in the base of the box. "Jon will fly you there whenever you have need. This jeweller will know that they are from me, and is charged to give you an honourable price for them; and Jon is informed of their value, to ensure that honour. This will make your last years pleasant ones; they will provide for all your wants and needs."

"Ach! Bonnie lass – I cannae accept them!" he snapped the box closed and tried to get her to take it back. "Fer the arrow tip I thank ye – 'tis touchin' indeed... but as fer the stones – I cannae – it's too much!"

"Sandy," she smiled sweetly, "I wish to give you this – surely you would not deny me the joy of giving you something I value?"

He shook his head in protest at the very idea of denying anything to her.

"Then do not disappoint me by your refusal. The arrowhead is something to remember me by, and the gemstones are my way of caring for you in the twilight of your life. With these tokens I thank you and your forefathers for having guarded my secret for generations... until the time was right to relinquish them."

"Then if it pleases ye, I accept," he glanced up at her blushing, "but gift or no', I widnae e'er ferget ye, lass."

She kissed his forehead. "That pleases me deeply."

As he watched her leave he sighed... life was grand, and could be no grander.

When at last the time came for Erlina and Aradan to take their leave in the summer, long farewells were made at the castle, and then Jon and Alexis accompanied them to Aradan's yacht, moored at a newly-built pier on the loch near the excavation site.

It was stocked as if for a two-week honeymoon voyage, with food, clothing, books and wine, even wedding cake. And four bodies.

"Remember," Aradan recited to them, "In eight days' time you are to contact the coastguard and report us as missing – we should have called by then. And no matter what you hear... remember – we cannot drown or die," he grinned.

"I will," Jon nodded. He knew it was to remove any suspicions of foul play after their wills had been so recently drawn up, but it was still difficult for him to see his closest friend leave, never to see or hear from him again. He wished they'd had more time... that his friend could be there for more milestones in their lives: Children, if they were blessed that way; all of those insignificant experiences and shared memories that make a friendship unique; and growing old together. Then he realized how often Aradan must have had to endure just that – watching his friends age and die, leaving him behind. Suddenly it was easier for Jon to let him go.

Aradan knew his friend well enough to guess where his thoughts had led, and knew there were no words that would remove the sting of separation. He only said, "Perhaps we shall see each other again one day. We are Travellers, after all. But I think it will not be for many years to come – our families have been without us for over a thousand years, so I doubt they will part again so readily with us..."

"You belong in your world," Jon nodded. "Please give my greetings to your family, and tell them that I am grateful to have known you."

"Gladly," Aradan smiled. "They will come to know you through my stories... including your propensity for practical jokes."

Jon laughed, "Don't make any enemies for me on an alien planet, if you please! And besides... I've mellowed on that score since university anyway, and especially now that it's my house, and my butler that will skin me alive if I pull an ice bucket prank."

Aradan laughed a bittersweet laugh. "I'll miss you... but I don't think you'll ever be in want of good friends," he glanced toward the castle, and Alexis. "Tell your children all about us... in case we return one day."

Jon nodded, a lump in his throat at the thought.

Erlina and Alexis spoke in hushed tones together, Erlina stroking Alexis's hair, brushing tears from her cheeks. Goodbyes were never easy; permanent goodbyes were the hardest of all.

"I leave you now with family of your own," Erlina soothed. "Your family are wonderful, and they look so forward to having you in their lives at last. I'm glad I was able to meet them; it will make my departure the more comforting for it."

"But I don't want you to leave!" Alexis clung to Erlina, sobbing.

Erlina wrapped her arms around her. "Dearest... how often have I had to watch helplessly as my children grew old and died? I am so grateful that I will not be forced to endure such torment with *you*."

Alexis sniffed her tears back, nodding; she understood, but it did not make her own loss any less painful.

"Do you remember finding the key in the tower, and seeking its lock the first time?"

Alexis nodded, confused at the sudden change of topic.

"The key was a clue left for you to follow; a bread crumb if you will. I wanted you to ask, I wanted to tell you everything, but you were not yet ready; first you needed to discover some things on your own. My hope was always that you would at last find love, find someone to awaken that hunger for discovery, for *more*. You have Jon now," her mother smiled as she glanced toward him, "for which I shall ever be grateful! And Elbal, Galal, Amir, and Toshiro will remain with you. I doubt you will ever be able to rid yourself of Elbal," she laughed quietly. "He loves you too much like a daughter to ever willingly part from you. I fear he must endure what I am no longer willing to, for he will likely outlive even your grandchildren," she whispered. "Live long... and prosper. Be blessed, satisfied with good health and loving relationships all the days of your life, and always remember the Creator of us both. Apart from those three things, there is nothing greater to be desired."

Aradan embraced Alexis. "I am glad to have met you... to know that I leave Jon in very good hands."

"Thank you... for everything!" Alexis hugged him tightly. "For my tongue... my hearing... for Elbal's eyesight... giving me time with my mother... and sending me my best friend and husband... I owe you more than words can say!"

"Then do not try," Aradan kissed her forehead. "Live long, happy lives together... that will be thanks enough."

Erlina said to both Jon and Alexis: "The journals and scrolls in my library will explain the history of our people to you... the histories of the statues, carvings... it's all there, recorded over time. It should answer any questions you might have. Guard the secrets of our truth well."

Aradan laughed, "Personally, I would recommend using it as inspiration for novels as I doubt anyone would believe it as truth anyway!" He then added more earnestly, "Remember to record your own lives for future generations."

Erlina kissed Alexis goodbye, and Jon and Aradan embraced each other as parting brothers. Erlina and Aradan lighted onto the yacht and cast off, waving as they faded away into the distance toward the mouth of Loch Eriboll.

Epilogue

In the years that followed, Jon and Alexis always had room enough for both of their families at Castle Dalmoor, and it became the meeting point for holidays and celebrations. They were blessed with children, and their family grew under the protective eyes of Elbal, his sons, and Toshiro. Brehani eventually returned to his home, and Elbal and his sons organized the excavations along with Edric and Jon's father, his parents having taken a house nearby. Jon ran a helicopter tour business throughout the Highlands and islands once a week, devoting the rest of his time to his family and their growing excavation enterprise. The site became one of the greatest archaeological finds of the century, with vast quantities of quality artefacts, building structures and burials so minutely detailed in the ancient documents of Erlina's private libraries that they could use the information as a site map, thus making tremendous advances in understanding the daily lives of the Picts and peoples that followed them.

A fortnight after Erlina and Aradan had said farewell, their yacht was at last found adrift northeast of Iceland near the Jan Mayen Fracture Zone, reported by a Norwegian meteorologist stationed on that eponymous volcanic island; they had evidently been lost at sea as the ship's log had recorded rough seas and unusually high waves. The last ship's log entry also recorded an unusual display of Aurora Borealis, which had been confirmed as far away as Hudson Bay to the west and Tromsø to the east: Rather than a typical green curtain, this display was more like a vertical shaft of rainbow.

The Aquillians' homecoming was more splendid, fulfilling, glorious, colourful, and celebrated than a mortal mind can fathom. The bodies that had accompanied Erlina and Aradan were immediately taken to the High Temple, an elegantly spired edifice floating on one of the highest islands. There, those gifted with life-reviving skills reunited the essences of King Elgin, Prince Ealdun, and Prince Sidhendion with their Aquillian forms. The reunions with their loved ones were beyond the capability of mere human words to convey the glory, comfort and the boundless joy experienced by all.

Moriel's revival was one of bittersweet relief, for when she found herself returned to her Aquillian form, she knew her hopes and dreams to be like that of the mortal dust of her earthly form – lost to her forever, and worthless in her new life. Her family was reunited with her only long enough to say farewell as she was sentenced to a season of restoration. Moriel was sent to a civilisation far more advanced than Aquillis, beings who would teach her compassion, humility and charity. There she learned the ways of peace, of releasing claims to either possessions or relationships, for in truth we can never claim either as our own; we are granted them for a time, yet they are ever a privilege, never a right. When she returned to Aquillis in the high season of travellers returning, she was reunited with her family at last, and then presented at the royal banquet in celebration of returns. There, when she was welcomed by Princess Erlina and Prince Aradan, this time she accepted their affectionate greeting with the freedom of genuine joy for the happy outcome of them all. At that very ceremony, Moriel caught the attention of one who would love her, and she found her own happiness at long last.

The royal joining celebration of Erlina and Aradan was a glorious and lavish occasion enjoyed by all of Aquillis: Erlina's father, of the royal Aquillian line, was the first to congratulate them, followed by his overjoyed wife and queen. Aradan's parents, Talis and Atisse, followed Queen Amanis, and then one by one their beloved siblings.

Her family once more whole and united, Erlina revelled in every moment spent in their presence, and Aradan was the full complement to her boundless joy. Her sister Eris had given them nieces and nephews in her union with Megildur; Ealdun and Sidhendion travelled on to new worlds, met their wives as travellers, and occasionally returned to Aquillis.

Eventually Aradan and Erlina, together with their children, travelled to distant realms, their lives rich, fulfilled, joyous and eternal. As with every journey, there were adventures along the way; perhaps one day we'll find out more.

Glossary, Alphabetical

Bairn (Scottish): *Baby or small child*

Calends: Roman Calendar reference: First day of the month.

Eejit (Scottish): *Idiot*

Eli ichthale thondral Eru (Aquillian): *Receive the wholeness (healing) of God.*

Erumara (Aquillian): *Heavenward.* The modern name of this beach is **Tràigh Allt Chàilgeag**, *The beach with streams of bereavement*; it lies along the northern coast, east of Durness.

Ferntickles (Scottish): *Freckles*

Glânöir (Aquillian): *Jewel of Light* Erlina's ring with the blue light of the Star of Aquillis.

Glawaer glom firach (Aquillian): *Grant me your starlight (by which to see).*

Govad nir Eru vaer (Aquillian): *May God's blessings go with you*

Ianuarius (Latin): *January*

Iunius (Latin): *June*

Kianaer (Aquillian): *Sacred Pools* [**kia** (*sacred*) + **naer** (*pools*)]

Millach var Amroré (Aquillian): *Orb of Love's Song*

Mysost (Norwegian): A ubiquitous brown goat cheese very popular in Scandinavia, with a peanut-buttery flavour.

Nones: Roman Calendar reference: Ninth day before the **Ides** of a month.

Prius obtentus (Latin): *obtained in the past*

Scraw (Scottish): A sod of grass-grown turf from the surface of a bog or from a field.

Sextilis (Latin): *August*

Waen shelaen mannan wiedar? (Aquillian): *When will we see each other again?*

Whigmaleeries (Scottish): *little ornaments, knick-knacks.*

Cast of Characters

Maldor

Amanis: Queen of Maldor
Aradan: Eldest son of Talis, Gatekeeper
Ealdun: Crown Prince of Maldor
Elgin: King of Maldor
Eris: Younger princess of Maldor
Erlina: Elder princess of Maldor
Jarnae: Elder daughter of Talis
Lothiriel: Younger daughter of Talis
Megildur: Second son of Talis
Sidhendion: Younger prince of Maldor
Talis: Ruler of Talisant, Councillor to Elgin

Clan

Aidan: Leader of the Pictish clan, ally of King Elgin
Angus: youngest son of Aidan and Iona
Caitrin: Irish slave
Hafgan: Eldest son of Aidan and Iona
Iona: Wife of Aidan
Niallan: Middle son of Aidan and Iona

Oyarike, Norway

Bard: Adopted son of Torsten and Dagmar
Dagmar: Wife of Torsten

Gjurd: Younger son of Torsten and Dagmar
Hedda: Daughter of Torsten and Dagmar
Kjell: Jarl of enemy settlement along Kjellsfjorden
Moriel: Maldorian taken captive with Aradan
Runa: Adopted daughter of Torsten and Dagmar
Sigmund: Counsellor of Kjell
Torgil: Eldest son of Torsten and Dagmar
Torsten: Jarl of Oyarike, on Store Sotra
Vidarr: Right-hand man of Kjell
Wulf: Cousin of Torsten, Viking

Present

Alexis: Adopted daughter of the Cardinal
Alvar Thorsen: History professor, friend of Jon's.
Amir: Son of Elbal. Guard.
Brehani Abaynesh: Ethiopian. Geophysicist/IT.
Cardinal, The (Raneli Lamdor): Archaeologist, museum liaison, consultant. Adoptive mother of Alexis.
Edric Bronwen: British. Older archaeological student on the excavation team.
Elbal: Devout Coptic. Blind. Personal guard to the Cardinal. Father of Galal and Amir.
Galal: Son of Elbal. Guard, head chef.
Jon Ainsley: Helicopter pilot.
Naeem Nahas: Egyptian. Researcher.
Sandy Campbell: Local elderly man who knows a thing or two about Castle Dalmoor.
Toshiro Nagasuru: Japanese. Butler, all-rounder.
Wolf, the: Nemesis.

Author's Note

As the acknowledgements indicate, a lot of historical research went into the writing of this tale. For the most part, any historical figures that appear in the book were real characters from the pages of history; for example: John Fleming, though not an orphan, was born in 1785 and was both a natural scientist and a theologian. Moriel's account of her encounter with the Varangians is taken from the *Skylitzes Chronicle*, which covers the reigns of the Byzantine emperors from 811 to 1057, and is a direct use of a woman's tale told therein from 1038. Sir Joseph Paxton (1803-1865) was the designer of the Crystal Palace, which was built for the Great Exhibition of 1851; it was destroyed by fire in 1936, but remains a symbol of the Victorian Age. Sentaro and the story of the man who did not wish to die is a Japanese fairytale. Countless minute details in the book are authentic, sprinkled throughout to give depth, realism and a sense of time and place, whether Norwegian kings, the vegetation of a region, the daily activities of a people group, their housing, clothing, or – as far as my abilities reach and was suitable for a modern readership – their mentalities and language.

For images & extras associated with this book, please see The Cardinal's page at :

<u>www.stephaniehuesler.com</u>

About the Author

Hi! I'm Stephanie Huesler, from Zurich, Switzerland, and I'm an eclectic Indie writer in genres ranging from historical literary fiction to science fiction, contemporary fiction and fantasy (more on the way!). Communication has always been important to me in every expression; to date I've sung vocals on four albums and have published book articles, and I love writing novels and five weekly blogs. My first novel, *The Price of Freedom*, launched me into the new-found passion of story-telling in all its facets. I began writing the kinds of books I love to read – intelligent, witty, touching relationships that inspire, and in an expression of language and level of research that pulls me into another world. There are more stories brewing!

If you enjoyed this book, please take a moment to let me know! If you would recommend it to your friends, and write a review for Amazon, that would be wonderful – every single one is important to me, and the more, the better! Great reviews encourage me to live up to those expectations and to keep writing!

I'd love to hear from you! Online, you can find me at www.stephaniehuesler.com, as well as any of the other blogs I write: History Undusted, Candle & Quill, and Cuppanatter. Sign up to follow my blogs via e-mail so that you won't miss a thing! Keep an eye on my website for other release dates and information!

Acknowledgements

The hours of research poured into this novel would have been extended into the next life had it not been for the aid of others who were both knowledgeable and willing. Grateful thanks go to the museum curators and volunteers, who were enthusiastic and willing to provide answers and expertise to a stranger full of odd questions. Nothing replaces the value of physical emersion into those environments, and I was privileged to go, and meet people face to face who helped me immensely. Among those I would like to thank are: In Norway, the Nordvegen History Centre near Avaldsnes on Karmøy, as well as the nearby Viking Farm on Bukkøy – Thank you to their dedicated and informed staff! Also, the various Stave churches in the Telemark and Jotunheim regions of Norway for their great help and expertise (in particular the Eidsborg Stavskyrkje and cemetery), and to the Visitor Centre in Durness, Scotland. Many thanks go to the countless authors of history from which I was able to glean. Some documents that I drew on for inspiration, information, details and insights into the ancient customs and mentalities portrayed in these books are as follows: The Anglo Saxon Chronicle, The Poetic Edda (The Prose Edda), The Heimskringla (The chronicles of the kings of Norway), and the Orkneyinga Saga.

And finally, thanks goes to my wonderful husband Stefan for his support, his intelligence, his encouragement, and his enabling me to spend so much time in the craft I love. He is my hero, my best friend.

The Price of Freedom

A CHANCE ENCOUNTER

Adriana Northing, daughter of a fisherman, and James Westford, son of a wealthy merchant, forged a secret friendship in childhood against all social mores. But her family holds more secrets than even she could guess.

SOCIETY

Coming of age, Adriana is propelled as a companion into the society of Georgian London with all its intoxicating splendour and intrigue. This taste of the wider world bears consequences of which she could never have dreamt. Will friendship survive, or will loyalty, trust and love be smashed on the cold rocks of society?

The Price of Freedom is the first book in the Northing Trilogy, by Stephanie Huesler.
Available in Kindle and Paperback.

'...but his death at such a ripe old age could not conveniently be avoided I suppose...' - "A great snippet of dialogue. It's exactly this kind of sly humour, that Jane Austen did so well, that earns for Regency fiction the tag, 'comedy of manners'."
– Sue Moorcroft, Author

REDEMPTION

ONE WOMAN

Mary Northing, young, beautiful and naive, embarks on adventure into the society of Bath. Revolution is brewing in France, making military officers a romantic and intoxicating topic for every warm-blooded young woman looking to her future.

TWO LOVERS

One, the heir of a miser, and the other, the third son of a nobleman. Only one man loves her truly, though both declare that love to be theirs. Which will she choose? How can she know what the future holds for either of these men? Will she allow herself to be guided by vanity and the lust for position and consequence? Or will she listen to her heart? The dust of the wrong path still clings to the garments of a penitent traveller.

REDEMPTION is the second book in the Northing Trilogy, by Stephanie Huesler.
Available in Kindle and Paperback.

ASUNDER, book three in the Northing Trilogy, coming soon!

The Cardinal, Part 1

8TH CENTURY AD

Maldor, the mysterious and peaceful kingdom of mist and whispers in the ancient forests of Scotland's northern Highlands, succumbs to the onslaughts of longships, axes and violence at the birth of what would become known as the Viking Age. Its inhabitants are scattered and must find their way home or be stranded and separated forever. Most Maldorians escaped, while some were laid to rest in stone cists of the north. The Maldorian princess is left to ally herself to the ways and mores of a neighbouring Pictish clan if she is to survive the age of violence; others must learn to survive as Norse slaves until they can find their way to freedom.

NOW

More than a thousand years later, archaeologists have begun uncovering the legacies left by Maldor even as inexplicable occurrences threaten to unravel their resolve. With every fresh discovery, they are increasingly faced with believing the unbelievable.

The Cardinal is a two-part Science Fiction/Fantasy novel.

Made in the USA
Charleston, SC
20 November 2014